THE SUSSEX POND MURDER

RICHARD SORAPURE

Copyright© Richard Sorapure 2023

The right of Richard Sorapure to be identified as the Author of the Work has been asserted by him in accordance with the Copyright, Designs and Patents Act 1988. No part of this book may be used or reproduced without written permission of the author except in the case of brief quotations embodied in critical articles and reviews. All characters and events in this publication, other than those clearly in the public domain, are fictitious and any resemblance to real persons, living or dead, is purely coincidental.

www.ricsorapure.wordpress.com

Chapter 1

I used to complain about the predictability of St Wilfrid's prep school for boys, where fate had placed me as the English teacher. But the day they fished the body of Michelle Gagneux out of the school pond changed all that.

Michelle was our school French teacher and my friend. The groundsman discovered her early one morning in January as he walked along the pathway through the woods that lead to our school. It had been a wind-charged night when heavy rain tore across the bleak Sussex Downs and ripped through the fabric of thick overcoats to numb fingers and toes. She was wearing a mini-trench coat, jeans, and a scarf when he found her floating on her back on his morning rounds—arms outstretched on the pond surface; her sightless eyes gazed up at the sky. It was a shallow pond. She was at the side, buoyed up by a rockery, which stuck out to form a narrow shelf where the boys liked to catch tadpoles.

When I arrived at school at 8 a.m. the drive was busy with police, ambulance and a hushed crowd of shocked staff stood watching. As I crossed the quadrangle, two police officers stopped me. As I was last to arrive, it was easy for them to identify me.

'Mr Michael Fletcher is it?' said the senior officer, referring to a clipboard.

'Yes, that's right. What's happened?'

'I am Inspector Bishop, and this is my colleague Police Constable Jimmy James. We are from the Pulborough police station. Did you know the deceased?'

'Someone has died?' I asked, alarmed.

'Who is it? I have only just arrived.'

'Of course, sir, we are not suspecting you, but we have to question all her colleagues. She was a young woman, so we must look for any associations. Did you know Miss Gagneux well or ever take her out socially?'

'Miss Gagneux, you say. Oh, not our French teacher—a beautiful lady. What happened to her?'

'Well, we can't say until we get the pathologist's report, but it is an unexplained death. Perhaps she slipped in by accident. Maybe a suicide? Or was there foul play? One of the staff found her. But on the balance of probabilities and considering the unusual setting, a forced drowning by a person or person's unknown is the best explanation. And what was your answer to my question?'

'Sorry, you have lost me. What question was that?'

'You said she was a beautiful lady in answer to my question of whether you ever went out with her. I believe you were both single, so it is possible you did.'

'Were we a couple? No, not really. We attended the usual school functions, along with other members of staff. But she wasn't my girlfriend.'

Jones, the Latin teacher, interrupted us. Although sarcastic and cynical from teaching Latin to non-receptive boys for ten years, he was also honest and a good friend.

'Awful business, Michael. It's a great shock.'

'I can't understand it. Who could have killed her?'

'The local police suspect it's an inside job. Many of the staff live in or close by. I think we can rule out the boys.'

'Now, Mr Jones,' said the inspector. 'We haven't quite finished with Mr Fletcher, so if you could give us a minute.' Jones wandered off to look at the covered corpse, laid out in the ambulance, before PC James moved him back to join the other teachers.

'Michael, when did you last see Miss Gagneux?' probed the inspector.

'I passed her outside the changing rooms on Saturday afternoon when I was heading for the showers after supervising one of the rugby games. She said she might see me later at the pub.'

'Would that be the Three Horseshoes?'

'Yes, that's right. The younger teachers like to meet there on Saturday nights. I went there later for a few drinks with Jones. She was in the public bar with a man I didn't recognise. It was the last time I saw her.'

'Thank you, Michael. You are one of the last people to have seen her alive.'

'Hold on a minute. This was Saturday night, and she was only found on Monday morning? Surely someone saw her alive over the weekend. She was staying in staff quarters at our school. I suggest you speak to the staff.'

'As you say, we know she had lodgings at the school. Sadly, no one has come forward to say they saw her. They assumed she was away for the weekend. I am sure you have nothing to worry about, Mr Fletcher. The pathologist will work out an accurate TOD when he performs the autopsy.'

'TOD?' I looked puzzled.

'Time of Death, Mr Fletcher. And Mr Fletcher, can you tell us your movements after you left the pub on Saturday night?'

'Sure, I had a couple of drinks with Jones and left around ten and drove straight home. It's just a country road with hardly any traffic so I would have been home by ten-thirty. I remember it was a bitterly frosty night.'

Inspector Bishop took down Michael's address, looking thoughtful.

'The Old Rectory—is that *your* address?'

'No,' I admitted. 'It's my parents' house.'

Bishop looked up from his notebook. I could see him wondering how to pigeonhole me. Obviously, I was a young lad in his early to mid-twenties, still living at home with his parents. Therefore, per se likely to be single or maybe divorced.

'Hmm, so that was about a thirty-minute drive. And no doubt your parents can vouch for you?' Michael looked uncomfortable.

'No, I didn't see them to speak to. In winter, they do not stay up late. Once the log fire dies down, they go to bed early, sip Horlicks and read for a bit. They don't wait up for me and I keep silent if I get back late so as not to wake them. But it was early, so I expect they heard my car drive up.'

'They sound like an elderly couple. Your parents.'

'Not really. My father is Major Fletcher. He retired from the army last year. He is 61 and my mother is ten years younger than him.'

Inspector Bishop noted it for reference. It was useful to have the background of suspects.

'It's not a very convincing alibi, is it, Michael? Why do you think Miss Gagneux was still alive at the weekend? Is it not possible someone could have killed her on Saturday night after you saw her at the pub with another man? A man you could not recognise?'

Michael looked uncomfortable.

'Of course, that's possible. I don't have a clue who he was. I have never seen him, but he is obviously a prime suspect.'

Higgins, the arrogant sports master—a bully and unpopular with the boys—joined us. He was easy to dislike, and the feelings were mutual, but today he looked shattered.

'Terrible thing to happen, Michael, a shocking case. I doubt if she had an enemy in the world. Jones tells me you were one of her friends, so I wonder if you have any idea who could have done this. My view is that someone from outside is to blame. There is no security here.'

The police had finished their questioning, and the ambulance was drawing away, taking Michelle to a cold resting place in the morgue. Feeling hollowed-out and deflated, I headed for the staff tearoom. Miss Cresswell, the History teacher, greeted me as I entered the smoke-filled room.

'Mr Fletcher, we have cancelled classes for today in deference to the deceased. She was such a trooper. She would have wanted us to carry on as normal, but I do not think any of us can face that. And the poor boys are aghast, but we must not tell them any details. Just say we found her drowned—most likely an unfortunate accident.'

'Of course, Miss Cresswell. History will have to wait another day.'

'History teaches us that a day lost can sometimes be a day gained. I will take Trueman for a walk and go home early. But first I must comfort poor Father Roderick, who is absolutely distraught.'

I permitted myself a wry smile. Miss Cresswell was never parted from her annoying little dog, a terrier called Trueman. She got on best with the most puzzling member of the staff, Father Roderick, young and good-looking from a certain perspective, but a rigid conformist with strict ideas. Roderick inculcated religious education with a humourless intensity and belief that all the boys in his care had a mental age of ten.

I grabbed a cup of tea and went to sit down between matron and our Science and Mathematics teacher, Nigel Caldwell-Brown. Just a few years older than me. He seemed quite normal, in fact, boringly so.

'It's a turn-up for the books,' said Nigel.

'You can just see the headlines in the press—French Teacher found murdered in Pond at Sussex Prep School.'

This shocked matron. 'You can't say things like that. Besides, they don't run headlines that long.'

'I'm just stating the facts,' said Nigel.

'Well, don't,' said matron. 'Michelle was far more than just a French teacher. Before she came here, she was a PhD student working in a university in research chemistry.' Both Nigel and I looked surprised.

'She never discussed her past with me. *That* is a surprise,' I said. 'Why switch to teaching and come to St Wilfrid's, of all places? I find it hard to understand.'

'My thoughts exactly,' said matron.

'She came here to be closer to her elder brother and her father, who run a laboratory somewhere near Southampton. I think her brother's name is Mark, but with a different surname. Michelle's father is English, and her parents divorced when she was very young. This job was a chance to establish her own identity. She still had a great interest in chemical research.'

There was a stunned silence while we digested this information. Michelle was suddenly a far more complicated and interesting person. Sadly, I was discovering this too late.

'And where is our headmaster during this crisis?' asked Nigel, switching the subject. 'Shouldn't he be providing some leadership?'

Both Nigel and I disliked the head and his obsessive love of discipline and obedience, supported by the school secretary, Mona. The headmaster was having a hard time trying to contact Miss Gagneux's family in France. When he got through, a flustered woman did not understand. The headmaster could only manage basic French. A man came on the line—Michelle's grandfather—and he spoke good English. Devastated, he said the family would come over as soon as possible. Mona was already planning a memorial service at school and the only issue was when the police would release her body for burial. Of course, the family might wish to make their own arrangements.

Although they had cancelled classes, it annoyed me that sports were going ahead. My unenviable duty was to supervise the games period that afternoon. The rugby pitch was on open high ground looming above the school complex, a Siberian gulag populated by shivering prisoners. Students and teachers alike were subject to a harsh education regime with compulsory sports.

The clock in the common room inched towards 3 p.m. I had five more minutes before I must change into my kit in the frigid changing rooms. I must shift or I would be late. Not a good idea. The field was within sight of the headmaster's study. That pedantic sadist would check up on me, even on a day like this. Rising from the comfort of a worn leather chair in the common room, I noticed the *Times Educational Supplement* on the coffee table. My eyes focused on an advertisement highlighting 'Academic vacancies in Singapore.'

'Strongly motivated, enthusiastic, and experienced geology teacher required for Dunearn Academy, an independent school in Singapore. The ideal candidate should possess excellent communication skills and a passion for teaching following the GCE curriculum of "A" levels and to assist with sports training. The position is for commencement in August 1983. Preference is for a degree qualified candidate, but recent graduates with some teaching experience may also apply. Dunearn Academy offers a generous salary for the right candidate, including free single status accommodation at the school. Please send your curriculum vitae with a cover letter and two references addressed to the attention of the Bursar to arrive by 31st January 1983.'

Grabbing the paper, I rushed off to get changed. I would apply for the job. At St Wilfrid's my brief was to teach English, but also geography. Geology also concerned the land and resources, so it should be easy to adapt to teach that to gullible students. After three years' experience, it would be a speculative shot, as I was sure there would be loads of better-qualified candidates than I.

Back home, after such a dreadful day, I relaxed by the log fire as my parents watched the BBC News. My news from school was much more devastating, but I held off mentioning it just yet. Since leaving the army, my father spent most evenings slumped in an old leather-backed chair, a customary whisky and soda nestling in his hand with a folded-up newspaper as he scowled at the television. Today, he sported an eccentric look with purple trousers topped by a hand-knitted woollen pullover over an open-necked check shirt. His hair was short and grey tinged with some remnants of its former black, but it still had energy above a face, which was full and florid with burst blood vessels, deep lines, and a large nose with dense nasal hairs offset by heavy eyebrows and bloodshot eyes. Viewed alongside Nelson, our old black Labrador, the dog was ageing the better of the two.

My mother sipped at a gin and tonic as she concentrated on solving a crossword puzzle. She was quite neat with good legs, trim figure and lean as a whippet. Her auburn hair was still her best feature and much admired by the women of the local WI group. She seemed subdued in her husband's company with no strong opinions, although I knew this was a bit of a facade. She held independent views and spirit. Like many married couples, they showed no overt signs of love or affection. I could recall nothing deep to this union, which drifted on by habit and convention. The strain of having him around the house all day doing nothing was showing.

Nelson lay in a stupor at my feet. The dog and my parents seemed to merge into some sort of harmonious mass which excluded me—an intruder just passing through their lives—someone who should move on and leave this rural backwater.

'How was your day, Michael?' my mother asked out-of-habit. The news was as dull as ever and she did not approve of families staring, like tired cattle, at the TV screen for hours on end.

'Oh, the French teacher, Michelle Gagneux, has met with an unfortunate accident. They found her drowned in the school pond,' I said offhand. I was not being callous. However, there was no good way to break the bad news.

'What? How did this happen?'

'The police suspect foul play. They will know more after the autopsy. I expect it will be in all the papers tomorrow.'

'When was this?'

'The groundsman discovered her body flat out in the pond this morning. The police suspect someone killed her. They think it happened sometime between late Saturday night and today, but we will have to wait for the autopsy results.'

'How dreadful!'

'I glimpsed her in the pub on Saturday evening after school when I met up with Jones. Unusually, she was in the public bar with a man I didn't recognise. I didn't join them because I had a bad feeling about him. He stared at me before Miss Gagneux pulled him away.'

'How odd.' She called my father over, but he had overheard and was already approaching.

'As a governor of St Wilfrid's, the headmaster should have contacted me. This is a serious development. I'll phone him straight away.' He shuffled off to the phone in the hallway and soon we heard some harsh words. For once, I felt sorry for our headmaster.

My mother recalled that I had once brought Michelle over for tea. 'She was such a nice girl. I remember she loved your photos of seabirds. Didn't you go on a bird spotting trip together?'

'Yes, we went to Brighton last November. She was a keen photographer. We had a pleasant day out. Who could have done this?'

'The lamb stew is ready,' said my mother as she opened the Aga door to retrieve the overcooked baked potatoes, some of which had exploded, splattering the oven, and releasing an acrid smell. 'But after that sad news, we may not have the appetite to eat it.'

'I've just got the peas to cook.' She slit open a frozen packet without enthusiasm, spilling many on the floor. We ate in silence to the sound of the TV in the drawing room and loud snores from Nelson prone in front of the fire. To change the subject on all our minds, my mother made some small talk.

'Your news is awful,' she gave up the effort of eating abandoning the half-eaten stew. Immediately, I followed suit and left the table to pour myself a large shot of whisky with a dash of water. Not something I ever did. My father looked at me inquisitively but remained silent. What an awful day. The murder of my friend had rocked the school to its foundations. More reason to leave this area. I hoped my job application would succeed. At last, a first step towards independence—anything to get away from here. Until this life-changing decision, I had planned no major change, living for the moment, devoid of ambition. I even bored myself.

Singapore was a big career move. I knew the island was near the equator, a centre of tourism and a modern business hub with a successful economy, prosperity and harmony and an interesting colonial history. I had enjoyed reading the novel *'Tanamera'* by Noel Barber. This story of a forbidden love between John Dexter and Julie Soong, set in Malaya and Singapore from the 1930s through to the 1950s, had been the subconscious trigger, which made me apply for the job—a job I was most unlikely to get.

Chapter 2

Awake and restless on another dark cold winter morning, I can hear my mother in the kitchen boiling the kettle and telling Nelson to wait for his food. She talks more to that dog than to my father or I. The clock moves on and with a sigh I fold back the blankets and eiderdown to be hit by a wall of Arctic ice, which is the normal winter temperature of our house. I drag myself from my warm bed and head for the bathroom.

I look at myself in the mirror as if, through someone's critical eye: taller than average at six feet three inches, light brown hair, blue eyes, slim, athletic, and fit, but less fit than I used to be. All the usual vices of smoking and drinking too much must take their toll, judging by my nicotine-stained fingers and the sour taste in my mouth. I am brushing my teeth when my mother calls that breakfast is ready. This morning I feel wretched from my confused mind and lack of sleep. After the gruesome discovery of Michelle's body in the pond, I had trouble sleeping, my over-active mind dwelling on the crime and its incongruous setting.

'I expect your school will be the centre of attention today with the death of that poor girl, so try to look smarter! Put on a clean shirt, tie, and a blazer. I imagine the press will be at the gate.'

My mother placed a full English breakfast in front of me with a bang on the table to wake me up.

'You are late again this morning. They notice when you slip in last at the morning assembly.'

'Who told you that?'

'It doesn't matter, dear. But it wasn't the headmaster, although of course, he sees these things. Just attempt to be on time. Your school values punctuality. As a teacher, you must set a good example. You do not seem so well motivated these days. You were never late last year.'

'Yes, mother. I wish people would talk *to* me instead of going behind my back.'

'Of course, dear, we all wish that. You were always off on nature trails with your camera last year. You even won a prize in some competition from the Sussex Wildlife Trust, didn't you?'

'It was nothing special—just a picture of a barn owl in flight. A lucky shot. Once the weather improves, I will visit new wetlands or the local woods. With a keen eye, it's amazing what you can discover.'

On arrival at the chapel for morning assembly, the press hounds were scrutinising every car and only letting those with parents and children pass through unopposed. They were looking for sole occupants, likely to be staff—whether cooks, groundsmen, or teachers. Anyone who had known Miss Gagneux was a target. I kept my windows shut, and the doors locked. Driving an old Morris Minor ensured they ignored me, so I penetrated the media scrum with ease and sat down in time for morning assembly between Jones and Miss Cresswell.

The headmaster coughed to gain everyone's attention as he marched up to the dais on the stage. The usual form was for school announcements from the head, followed by a brief morning prayer from Father Roderick and a rousing hymn.

'I just wanted to say all our thoughts and prayers are with Miss Gagneux's family after the dreadful discovery in the pond yesterday. Police officers will be at the school today, continuing to interview staff and anyone who knew the deceased, so I ask everyone to cooperate with their enquiry. Thank you all for your patience and please if you could all refrain from talking to members of the press or television. Certain members of the media are already letting their imagination run riot and proposing many ridiculous theories without evidence, so, until proved otherwise, we believe this was an unfortunate accident. Life must go on. I have some announcements: Saturday was a day of mixed fortunes for our rugby teams. The Under 13s played Midhurst, a strong team. We lost but were not outclassed.'

The headmaster paused for dramatic effect before resuming.

'The Under 12s had a cracking win over Arundel.' There was a polite ripple of applause. 'And Mr Fletcher's training has had an impact. Well done, Mr Fletcher.'

The school clapped again, forcing me to rise from my seat, blushing, to acknowledge the adulation.

'Ah, that's why you are on time today,' remarked Jones. Miss Cresswell looked puzzled. She had never known me to be singled out for praise before.

Father Roderick oozed a few words of unctuous platitudes featuring 'My dear children—amid life there is death. Do not take anything for granted, but always be prepared.' How could you prepare to be a sudden murder statistic? He had the embarrassing habit of asking idiotic questions and staring out at the serried rows of boys to elicit a response. Usually, he directed his question to some poor victim who had not been listening and ended up answering his own question. Even the staff grew impatient for him to finish.

'Ghastly, wasn't it?' said Jones. We were walking to the classrooms. Higgins overtook us, as always, in a hurry.

'The success of Under 12s is nothing to do with you,' said Higgins.

'Rugby is not my game—I far prefer cricket. You are a better coach than me.' I flattered him with false praise. After all, he was the senior sports master, and I was just an amateur. 'But it's a pity your team took such a hammering.'

'Midhurst are dirty cheats. They had some over-age players.'

The banter was an escape from the grim reality, but there was no escaping the police presence. I was heading off to teach my first class of the day, the Under 12s, when Mona told me there was an officer wishing to interview me in the library. The library was one of my favourite places. I liked to spend my free time there to read or prepare my lessons. It was a calm hideaway, free of interruptions, with a high roof stacked with bookshelves to fill every space with a vast collection of antiquarian Victorian and Edwardian books in science, medicine, engineering, and valuable volumes of Punch magazine from 1841 to 1890. The treasure trove housed many priceless books.

When I entered the room, I saw a new face alongside Inspector Bishop from the Pulborough force. The new man introduced himself as Detective Inspector Preston from the Brighton police, the Senior Investigation Officer, or the 'SIO' as he liked to be called, newly assigned to solve the bewildering *'Case of the Sussex Pond Murder'* as this morning's *Daily Mail* was calling our incident.

'Michael,' Preston motioned for me to sit down. He was a young man of about thirty, black hair, brown eyes, tall, thin, and well dressed in a dark suit. He exuded quiet energy. 'You don't mind if I put on the tape recorder, do you? It saves taking notes. Inspector Bishop has given me a full update and I want to follow up on the brief interview you had with him yesterday, okay?'

'Fine, anything I can do to help,' I said; aware of those searching eyes studying me.

'We are trying to establish all we can about Michelle Gagneux, and one task is to make a timeline of her last known movements. According to Inspector Bishop, you met her in the Three Horseshoes on Saturday night.'

'It wasn't like that,' I said. 'After classes are over on Saturday, the teachers often visit the pub. It's a tradition to unwind after a stressful week. She asked me if I was going. I said yes. But it wasn't like a date. I had a drink with Jones in the lounge bar, where we normally meet and noticed she was with a friend I didn't know in the public bar.'

'I see—so you never spoke to her in the pub?'

'Well, I waved and said "Hi" to acknowledge her. I stayed for a couple of drinks and left early to head home. I already told your colleague this yesterday.'

'Early to bed,' said Inspector Bishop, as if this were significant.

'And your parents will confirm you were back early on Saturday night?' said Preston.

'No, I didn't see them. They don't stay up late at their age. Maybe they heard my car come back. You would have to ask them.' The police officers exchanged glances. I sensed this was not going well.

'Bishop says your parents are quite elderly. Are you still living at home to help care for them?' asked Preston.

I laughed with embarrassment. 'No, they are just middle-aged. My father retired from the army last year. He is ten years older than my mother. Somehow, I think of them as old, but they are both quite fit still.'

'So, you are guilty of the usual youthful perception that everyone over 40 is over the hill, washed out and decrepit,' said Bishop, who had just turned 40 and was feeling sensitive about his accelerating hair loss. Michael dared to smile, which enraged Bishop more. Preston stared across at Bishop—a stare intended to stop the Pulborough man interfering with time-wasting distractions.

'Michael, we have heard from some of your colleagues that you and Michelle were a bit more than casual friends—in fact, best friends. Could you enlighten us on your relationship?' Preston went for the jugular.

'We were colleagues. Friends, yes, I don't deny it. Our school is very formal, you see. We call each other Mr this or Miss that. We never use Christian names. Once I took her home for tea to meet my parents so she could see how a typical English family live. She found it fascinating having hot buttered crumpets and Earl Grey tea. Oh yes, scones and cream as well—she loved a cream tea with strawberry jam. It was all very innocent, I assure you.'

Preston ignored this cosy account of tea with the family.

'Do you have a current girlfriend, Michael? Or, working in a boys' school, does that suggest your sexuality is more aroused by boys rather than girls?'

I was shocked by the question. I said I had no current girlfriend, but boys or men did not interest me in the way he was inferring. I told them my passions were my hobbies of ornithology and photography, especially capturing shots of birds in flight, but also butterflies and moths were equally fascinating. They looked bored.

'Thank you, Michael. We may have further questions. We will try to trace who was with her in the pub. Can you describe him?'

'She was with an older man, broadly built, like a rugby player, and he had wavy blond hair and piercing blue eyes. He was standing at the bar sideways on, but when I waved to Michelle, he looked across at me coldly. Then he moved away, out of sight. He prised her away from the bar to move out of my sight. Check with Jones. He could help with a better description.'

'Thank you, Michael. We did ask Mr Jones, and he could not recall seeing a stranger on the other side of the bar with Miss Gagneux, such as you describe. We will follow up and ask the pub landlord and any of the regulars in case they can throw some light on this person. Have you seen him before?'

'No, definitely not.'

'We'll print a copy of our taped conversation to make up a statement. You will need to check and sign. It's our normal procedure. Is that alright?'

Preston seemed to have all the information he needed. He asked Inspector Bishop if he had questions, but Bishop just shrugged. As far as he could see, Preston was going over the same ground. They had learnt nothing new from interviewing the young teacher. They should follow up at the pub to see if any of the locals recalled this tough-looking character with piercing blue eyes talking to the French teacher. And a visit to Michael's parents. Surely, they would recall their son driving home after the pub. Bishop reckoned these were the dull tasks Preston would delegate to the Pulborough force, but he was wrong. Brighton would handle the case.

Preston turned off the tape recorder; Michael smiled and told him he was very thorough. Something about this young man rang false.

I was feeling uncomfortable after this interview as I had misled the police into thinking I had no relationship with Michelle. This was not true, strictly speaking. In fact, our day trip to Brighton started with a bracing stroll along the seafront, photographing seagulls and a pleasant walk around town, followed by a few drinks and a hot curry from an Indian restaurant. Rather than drive home over the drink-drive limit, a safer option was to book a bed-and-breakfast hotel on the seafront. It was out-of-season. We checked into the first half-decent looking establishment—an old Victorian townhouse converted to many small bedrooms, the majority with shared bathrooms down a draughty corridor. A bad-tempered woman in her sixties wearing a nylon dressing gown and with her hair in a hairnet put us in a pokey attic room with a giant old wardrobe and dressers. The old furniture hemmed in a small double bed covered in thin nylon sheets and an old blanket in emerald green. On the wall was a picture of flying mallards. Michelle thought it was charming.

I think we had set out with innocent intentions. Clearly, it was an economic necessity to share the small bed. She was not used to alcohol and giggled a lot as we shared a cheap bottle of red wine before she fell asleep in my arms. In the morning, the smell of frying bacon and sausages drifted upstairs. Michelle, who was a vegetarian, screwed up her nose in disgust. It was such an endearing sight that I gave her a quick kiss and that led on to longer kisses and we gave breakfast a miss. Of course, I did not intend to share this experience with the police. It would only heighten their suspicions. But who had killed her, and why?

I was in a daze at lunchtime, lost in my thoughts, so the conversation rolled over me. Jones brought me back to reality.

'Don't forget it's the Parents' evening tomorrow night, Michael. We know you like to escape to your country house as soon as you can, but the mummies and daddies need to be reassured that their money is being well spent.' Jones loved to mock me. On this occasion, it was helpful, as I had forgotten about the dreaded Parents' evening. These periodic encounters were normal in the State-run school sector but had infiltrated the private schools. Most of our pupils were boarders whose parents would not travel large distances for an update on their child's academic performance, but the parents of the day boys were very keen. The democratisation of learning meant we shared the boys' progress in exams, coursework, sports, and even activities and hobbies with parents to focus on the best way forward to pass the Common Entrance exam and step on to the next stage in life's exciting journey.

'Most of my pupils are boarders. So, few parents to see. The trouble is I can never remember their names. We see them so rarely.'

'Mona has a master list,' said Miss Cresswell. 'Ask her for a copy. It gives the names of the parents or guardians. I have been doing this so long I know all their names and all the parents know me and Trueman!'

'You need to keep an eye open for Charlie's mother,' said Jones. 'She is a real stunner. I believe her name is Laureline—very French!'

Charlie had recently joined the school after his family had moved to the UK from Hong Kong. He was a polite, shy boy and had done badly in the January school exams. This was not unexpected, as the syllabus and the style of teaching differed from his previous school in Hong Kong. It intrigued me to hear about his mother, Laureline. A glamorous parent was as rare as a good school meal. However, Jones' idea of 'a stunner' and mine might differ.

'Jones,' I said, as we were leaving the refectory. 'I have a favour to ask. Would you mind if I put your name down as a referee? I am applying for another teaching job for next year. I doubt the school will follow it up, but just in case.'

'Happy to oblige, Michael. Although I may not be the best person—I understand you wouldn't want to approach the headmaster. Has this dreadful case brought this on?' he asked.

'No, I feel like a change and a new challenge.'

'I will recommend you highly.'

'Thanks. I'll buy you a pint. And stress my coaching skills at cricket and rugby.'

'Can I ask what school is offering you this dream job?'

I looked uncomfortable. 'No, I find it's the kiss-of-death to reveal anything. I can tell you that the school is abroad.'

'Understood. And good luck. Anything else I can do to help?'

'Well, there is one other thing. I need to give two referees and I am stuck on whom else to ask.'

'The school has appointed a new governor—a best-selling novelist if that is the right word. She writes those Mills and Boon romantic books teenagers love,' Jones said dismissively.

'Really, that is interesting. What is her name?'

'Camilla Flockhart.'

'Camilla Flockhart,' I repeated the name to see if it unlocked any key in my brain, but it was no use. I had never heard of her.

'You can ask her yourself tomorrow night,' said Jones. 'She will be at the Parents' evening. No harm in asking her, but unusual to apply to one of the school governors for a reference to a different school.'

'When you put it like that, it does sound odd, but I am stuck. I can't ask my father for a reference, and he wouldn't give me one.'

'A dilemma,' said Jones. 'But I shouldn't worry as I doubt you will get the job.'

Chapter 3

There was tension in the air you could cut with a knife. I helped myself to coffee in the staff common room. No one seemed keen to talk about our deceased French teacher, but I gathered the police had completed the staff interviews and were waiting for results of the post-mortem. This did not restrain the press from wild speculation.

I sat down next to Jones, who looked subdued.

'Why is everyone so quiet this morning?' I asked.

'Besides our murder, we now have a hospital emergency. The day boy, Whittington, is in St Richard's hospital in Chichester,' said Jones. 'He caught measles and his parents kept him home all last week. Now he has pneumonia. We are hoping he will pull through. The lad is only eleven.'

'From measles?' I was incredulous. In my school days, there was no vaccination. It was common to get a fever and rash, but recovery was quick.

Matron was sitting close by, puffing on a cigarette. Her stylish teacup was an original WWII British Red Cross teacup and saucer, which she always kept with her. No one would ever dare borrow it.

'I have told the headmaster before *all* children need the measles jab. It's been available for years and our ineffectual government needs to make it mandatory for school children to be vaccinated in schools. I can administer it and inoculate the entire school in one afternoon. We have six cases in the sick bay right now. It's highly infectious and could bring the school to a standstill. You staff are not immune either.'

'Matron, I believe the complications are very rare, aren't they?' asked Jones.

'That's no excuse for inaction,' she said, grinding her cigarette out in the ashtray.

'I agree with you. I mean, if the vaccine is safe, we should all get it done. Can I go along and get a jab from my doctor?'

'Yes, of course. All the local doctors should ensure everyone at risk gets the injection.'

I knew Jones was humouring matron and would refuse any vaccination. He asked her if it was true that they developed the vaccine from the embryo of aborted foetuses, and she went ballistic. She ticked him off for spreading false rumours and explained that the vaccine used the embryos of dead chicks to give a mild form of the disease to avoid a serious infection. I kept out of the conversation. My parents were of the same mindset as Jones and left me to catch everything possible, including measles, mumps, and chicken pox.

He asked how my interview with the police had gone. Strange that they needed us to vouch for each other—almost as if they suspected a conspiracy.

'Jones, can you remember seeing Michelle in the public bar?'

'No, boyo. Never go into that bar.'

'I saw her with someone in there.'

'Can't say as I noticed. Odd thing. Why go to that bar?'

In fact, that was strange. We avoided it as it had a rougher element, with coarse language and local troublemakers. Fights fuelled by too much alcohol were common. What made Michelle change her normal routine? Was it to meet someone she didn't want us to see? Jones had something else to say.

'I saw her at school before I went down to the pub, and she said to make sure I brought you along as it was her birthday and she hoped you would buy her a drink.'

'Her birthday? She never mentioned it. Oh, My God, I think I screwed up. Whoever was with her had remembered, but I hadn't.'

Just then, Miss Cresswell arrived for morning coffee. Trueman rushed through the door, straining at his lead, with his tongue lolling about. It was a funny sight, and I could not help laughing. Miss Cresswell glared at me.

'I'm sorry. Trueman looks like he is in a hurry for a drink.'

'Yes. The poor darling has a brand-new lead, which I don't think he likes. Or maybe it's the collar?' she rubbed her hand around his neck.

'It's a bit too tight,' she eased it off a bit.

'Is that better, Trueman?'

'It's very smart. Is it real leather?' I asked.

'Yes, it's much more expensive than his old chain one. The silly dog broke it last month when he ran after a rabbit.'

'A passing car could have run the poor dog over,' said Jones. Matron and I suspected he was being sarcastic, but Miss Cresswell accepted this at face value and looked across warmly at Jones, thankful to find someone who understood her and Trueman.

'It's no good having an unreliable lead. The link snapping was a surprise, so I had to buy a cheap replacement from the pet shop as soon as the shops opened after Christmas. Trueman was fed up with his lack of exercise, but we didn't like it, did we, Trueman? It was too short.'

'This latest one looks very sturdy, Miss Cresswell. And I hope it lasts a long time of rabbit hunting. We have a chain one at home for our dog.' This silly conversation wasting so much time talking about Trueman was a bore.

'Poor Trueman,' she cooed. 'Don't chase the naughty rabbits. I didn't know you had a dog, Michael?' she enquired in a friendly voice as she welcomed me to the dog owners' fraternity.

'Yes. He's an old black Labrador called Nelson. A very lazy dog that spends most of his time asleep by the fire.'

'Dogs are such a blessing,' she simpered. 'Guess what, I have just seen the headmaster, and he seems even more unbalanced than usual.'

'How is that possible?' asked matron.

'HMI are visiting us in March for the school inspection. For an entire week!'

'Sorry, who is this HMI?' I asked.

'Her Majesty's Inspectorate of schools. They inspect all schools every six years.'

'Even with two months' notice, we are bound to fail,' said Jones.

Parents' evening was like the launch of a new exhibition at an art gallery. Parents sipped wine and made awkward small talk in the centre of the room. The staff sat at small desks faced by two empty chairs, waiting in anticipation of a parental visit. The headmaster mixed with the parents and school governors with self-congratulatory fervour, oblivious of the loss of their French teacher. At his side was the ever-helpful Mona, eager to keep him on message and extract him when conversations lagged. The parents were targeting the wine and canapes with grim resolve. They reserved better claret for the governors and important persons, and this select group congregated around a small table set aside, which they sought to defend from passing parents. As a school governor, my father was always keen to attend events with free wine and had attached himself to this group, like a limpet, and did his best to avoid me. The hierarchical system sickened me, and I grabbed a plate of sausage rolls and a beer to eat alone at my desk.

These open evenings were a trial. A parent might descend on me and need instant answers on how their boy was progressing. After a few fumbling, difficult visits, I was sweating with tension, my head buried in the class list, when an attractive dark-haired woman sat down, smiling, at my desk. I had never seen her, but at once felt a strong rapport. She stood out as someone different, a loner, unfamiliar with the school. Other parents liked to fraternise with their own circle of friends. They ignored any newcomers.

'Hi, I'm Charlie's mum. We haven't met before. My name is Laureline.' She held out her hand over the table. I shook it awkwardly, half standing in embarrassment. Charlie's mother—of course, Jones had mentioned her yesterday. Her English had a strong and attractive French accent. Charlie had joined the school after his family had left Hong Kong. Into the deep end of a strange country with alien topics of English history and language, a mystery to him.

'Hello, I am Mr Fletcher—in fact, Michael Fletcher. Michael is fine. We are informal here, apart from the headmaster, of course. He is a stickler for formality.' I was burying myself in confusion, but her smile encouraged me to press on.

'Of course, I teach Charlie—a talented boy. He has settled in very well. A sensitive and shy lad, which is only natural. It would be good if he could contribute a bit more in class.' I was glancing at his January exam marks, which were so poor I did not feel it wise to reveal them.

Laureline pulled her chair closer, and I covered the results page with my hand. His score in the English exam was 35 percent and well below the class average, but in mathematics, he was top of the class. She accepted my praise for this excellent performance.

'That is a subject they teach very well in Hong Kong. But English is much harder for him. I thought his essays were unimaginative and lacking in flair, and I saw one you had marked quite low. Is this something we can improve on?'

'Oh yes—it's not something that comes straight away. He must develop a style.'

'Why thank you. I will encourage him. Is it possible he could aim for a scholarship?'

Of course, nothing was impossible, but I did not want to give her any misplaced optimism. 'He has only just started and is unfamiliar with our syllabus. He will catch up and then the sky's the limit,' I said with all the enthusiasm I could muster.

'It was a culture shock for him to come here after Hong Kong. He was at an excellent expat school with boys and girls of all nationalities. Before that, he attended a local school with Chinese boys and girls, and they were horrible to him. So, we had to withdraw him. Why are most of your schools in the UK single-sex only?'

'Well, I couldn't agree more. Soon schools like this will have to admit girls.'

'Have to? You make us sound like second-class citizens.'

'No, sorry. That is not what I meant. We are so rooted in tradition it takes time to change. Most of the staff would favour a mixed school.'

She sighed. 'The system needs fixing. For Charlie, this is a foreign country. It is his first time in England apart from vacation visits.'

'I understand. Our weather is horrible. He was very lucky to have that experience abroad. He needs time to adjust to a different experience.'

'I hope so.'

She looked sad. I wondered if I had said something to upset her. Unaware of her history, I had indeed put my foot in it, as I would discover later. She had talked of 'we' so was there an unseen husband, or an ex-husband, I wondered.

'It has been nice meeting you, Michael.'

Laureline rallied and gave me a shy smile.

'And I was sorry to hear about your loss.'

'My loss?'

'Michelle Gagneux. I hear she was a good friend of yours.'

This comment knocked me off balance. Everyone assumed we were very close friends.

'Yes—a very sad case. All the staff loved her. She will be hard to replace. We are waiting to see how the police investigation proceeds.'

Another parent was waiting to see me, so she vacated her chair with a parting smile.

'Maybe we can arrange some extra tuition for Charlie?'

'There are agency tutors for home schooling. They charge by the hour and are quite expensive.'

'I wasn't thinking of going elsewhere. Couldn't you help me? My home is nearby, and we could agree on a generous hourly rate for your services.' The waiting parent shuffled her feet and gazed up at the sky, her impatience soaring. I gulped. Extra work would be useful, and tutors could earn up to four pounds an hour.

'I would be happy to help. Let's see how Charlie does in the end of term exams.'

She looked downhearted. The end of term was weeks away, and I could sense she needed help as soon as possible.

I wanted a chat with the new governor, the lady novelist, Camilla Flockhart. It was easy to spot her, a very short plump lady with a loud laugh who had been demolishing the red wine with gusto. Her straw-coloured hair was close-cropped, and she wore a worsted jacket and a light blue cotton shirt with the school tie. A tartan skirt enclosed her broad girth and the dramatic outdoor look continued with long green socks and walking boots, ideal for mountain climbing.

My father was doing his best to avoid her, spending most of his time chatting to the bursar and the headmaster so it did not look the right time to ask her for a job reference. Besides, she didn't have a clue whom I was.

However, my luck was about to change. Mona had taken charge of Camilla and was introducing her to Miss Cresswell. I crashed in on the group. Seeing me hovering close by, Mona did the helpful thing.

'Miss Flockhart, this is our English teacher, Michael Fletcher. He is the son of Major Fletcher, one of our governors.'

'Oh yes, the major,' she glanced across the room at my father.

'These former soldiers are so important in upholding our traditions. I see them as a link to a more romantic, but more violent past. Just a pity they get dotty as they get older.'

Mona also thought this was funny. *Ha ha ha*, she trilled. Aware I was standing by, looking unamused, Miss Flockhart turned to me.

'Ah, the handsome son of the major, splendid show, charmed,' she shook my hand in a powerful grip, which was a struggle as one hand gripped a glass of red wine and the other a cafe creme cigar. She put the cigar in her mouth, inhaled, and dispelled the cloud of smoke over us.

'As an English teacher, you are no doubt familiar with my books?'

'Oh, yes by repute,' I lied.

'Unfortunately, I am constrained to teach only approved books on the syllabus, which does tie our hands a bit. A pity with so many great modern novels I would love to share with our boys.'

'What can you expect when old dinosaurs control the examination boards?' she grumbled.

'No matter, I will donate my complete *opus* to the school library. I had a chat with your father over a drink at my governor's inauguration thingummy and told him I am the author of twelve best sellers, you know. Of course, one understands these ex-military types never read a book, so I look to you to educate the younger generation.'

'How kind of you—that's very impressive and I will recommend your books—highly— to my class.'

'Geoffrey, that is very good of you. Be a sweetie and bring some more wine.' She handed me her empty glass. Mona's glass was also empty, so I took hers as well to give her more fuel for her hysterical laugh.

'Was that red?'

'Of course, white wine is for gals,' she laughed that loud horse-like guffaw, *Haw, Haw, Haw,* which silenced the room. Mona joined in with her higher pitched *Ha, Ha, Ha.* I left as quickly as I could and ordered a large glass of the vintage plonk from the upper table. My father scowled as I approached, so I quickly made it clear to the steward that it was for the special guest with the loud laugh and the Chablis was for Mona. He smiled and filled three large glasses and put them on a tray for me. After some witty chat with Camilla, I dared mention my need for a reference for my job application to the school in Singapore. This prompted her to reveal her next book was a romantic love story set in the Tropics. I promised to keep an eye out for suitable material such as newspaper articles to give authenticity to her novel and she appeared pleased at my offer. I think we struck a deal, provided she could remember my name.

Wandering around the room, I searched for someone I could relate to. Around the perimeter, the teachers were busy receiving parents, and I noticed one or two waiting at my desk. With luck, they would get bored and move away. Just as my conscience was tugging me back to duty, Jones approached. He looked at his watch and sighed.

'One hour to go, Michael. Did I tell you they are changing my syllabus?'

'Who's they?'

'The head. He says Latin is too difficult for our boys' age group. I explained they would fly through the O level at their next school if they learn a bit now. But he wouldn't listen. The pass rate is worse than all the other subjects. My results are bringing down the school, so they want me to teach a watered-down version called "Ancient Classics." It's a broader syllabus and the pupils will learn about ancient Greece and Rome. This will debase the Latin language—the key to all other languages.'

'Shocking,' I said.

'Listen, Fletcher, if you get your dream job abroad, please remember me and tell the school they need a good Latin teacher.'

'Of course, it's a deal. And Camilla Flockhart, author of twelve best sellers, has promised to give me a glowing reference in case the school in question shortlists me!'

I could see Jones reckoned I had no chance of escaping from St Wilfrid's school.

Chapter 4

Just over a week after the discovery of Michelle's body in the school pond, I attended a further interview with Detective Inspector Preston at Brighton police station.

Brighton, alone with my memory of Michelle, was a cruel place. I recalled walking arm-in-arm along the windswept seafront—a reminder of that happy and carefree time two months ago. Once I had entered the drab police station, they led me into a small interview room where, once again, DI Preston started his tape recorder. A young lady police officer with short blonde hair and an elfin-like face sat at the table next to Preston. She looked at me with an unnerving stare. Preston opened the proceedings.

'Michael, thank you for coming to Brighton at such short notice. Did you have a pleasant journey?'

'It took me about an hour as the traffic was quite heavy. I came by the A27.'

'Yes, it's the only feasible route. Early afternoon is the best time to travel to avoid the morning rush.'

'They will miss me at school, so the sooner we start, the sooner I can get back,' I said, to end the pleasantries.

Preston opened a case file and scrutinised it.

'Michael, I wanted to share some things with you. The pathologist has completed the autopsy report on Miss Gagneux with a preliminary report on the manner of her death, the cause of her death, and the time of her death. It's a mystery who killed her and why. Isn't it amazing what science can do these days? The toxicology results will take two more weeks, but they are not important. We don't suspect any drugs or poison in her system. Best to look anyway, isn't it?'

He looked up at me, judging the impact of his words.

'How do you think Miss Gagneux met her end, Michael?'

'All I know is they found her dead in the pond.'

'Do you think she drowned?'

I shrugged my shoulders. It seemed dangerous to say anything, as they would misconstrue my words.

'Michael, this pub that you all frequent. Explain how that works?'

'It's an informal meeting place away from school where we unwind with a few drinks on a Saturday evening. If a colleague is leaving, we might meet on a weekday lunchtime. It is only the younger staff who turns up.'

'On Saturday 15th January, when did you go to the pub?'

'I already told you. The rugby game I was refereeing ended at about half past three. It was still light, but cloudy and freezing. The boys went to the refectory at five for the evening meal. The food is pretty horrible, so I prefer to get something when I get home or sometimes a bar snack from the pub.'

'Michael, can you remember what time you went to the pub?'

'It was late. I think about nine, I was working in my study marking essays from my class—I like to set aside a quiet time for this as it's time consuming. Some of my students are very bright, so I enjoy seeing how the class performs. I like to praise all the work and encourage those less talented. I went to find Jones to see if he needed a lift, but he had already left. If the weather's good, I like to walk but I planned to look in briefly and drive home, so I took my car.'

Preston looked thoughtful.

'You never thought to check on your friend Michelle. As she had no car, she might have appreciated a lift?'

'I assumed she would be at the pub, especially as it was so late. We had a chat earlier just after games and agreed to meet. However, you must understand she always preferred to walk. Even in bad weather. She didn't like to impose. Or maybe she didn't trust my driving.'

My attempt at a joke misfired. Preston asked after my drinking habits. Did I often drink and drive and exceed a safe limit?

In fact, the police once stopped me for a taillight not working. Fortunately, just a warning. I had to produce my documents at the local police station, so maybe there was a record. The police noticed I had been drinking, and I admitted having a few beers. In those days, things were more laid back. I decided not to mention this case.

'So,' said Preston. 'We presume, with no evidence to the contrary, that your friend walked to the pub alone along the track from the school. At this time of year, it gets dark at five.'

The young police officer interrupted Preston. She was looking at her diary.

'On 15th January, sir, the moon phase was a waxing crescent.'

'Thank you, Tracey—a useful detail. Therefore, it was *very* dark for that walk past the pond and through the woods. She would have needed a torch. And when she returned following the same route, she must have traced her way once more using her torch. In fact, the torch was like a beacon, revealing her progress to anyone hidden in the trees or following her from the pub—a journey that led to her death.

You drove to the pub via the main road, and, after a few drinks, you went home. You saw your friend was in the public bar with a stranger. Although that was a surprise, you did not tackle her. Do I have all these facts correct?'

'Yes.'

'What time did you leave the pub, Michael?' said the policewoman.

'Around ten—Jones could confirm that. It takes me about half an hour to get home. I told you this before.'

'And was Michelle in the pub when you left?' said Preston. 'You didn't check because you were in a jealous rage.'

'No, that's not true,' I protested. 'I was a bit put out because her behaviour was so unusual. But it was none of my business.'

After a long silence, DI Preston changed tack, 'I will level with you. The killer hit Miss Gagneux with an object like a rock. Just a single blow, but hard enough to knock her unconscious. He dragged her into the pond and positioned her face upwards in the water. The doctor found traces of water in her lungs, so it is likely that she struggled, and the killer pushed her down and drowned her. It has all the hallmarks of a sudden impulsive act—a crime of passion.'

Preston's vivid description shocked me.

'Did you find a rock close to the pond?' I asked.

'No, but such an object would be consistent with her head injury,' said Preston. 'We found nothing, and the ground shows no sign of disturbance.'

'Maybe the killer parked in the school car park and walked through the woods to the pond area—a psychopath who saw her torch and accosted her. It's just a theory,' I said.

DI Preston looked annoyed. It was his job to do the interviews. Suspects should not try to do his job. The school employed no security guards. Preston doubted they bothered to lock the front door. This lack of security was surely obvious, even to the staff. For Michael, to suggest an imagined suspect lurking in the car park was disingenuous—a step a clever criminal might make to convince them of his innocence. Two could play at that game. Preston congratulated Fletcher for his suggestion and said they would follow up on that scenario.

'Now, to move to the time of death. This is harder to establish as rigor mortis had worn off, but the pathologist estimates it was 20 to 30 hours prior to the discovery of the body at seven Monday morning. That puts it at late Saturday or early Sunday morning. You admit to seeing her at about nine on Saturday night in the Three Horseshoes, which makes you the last person to see her alive.'

'Sorry. I have nothing else to add. I'm happy to give you fingerprints, a blood sample or whatever else you need to establish my innocence.'

'We need to check your prints against the criminal database and for any we lift off the body,' said Preston. 'You can check known local criminals for a match to the man you saw in the bar.'

'I did see him. I'm sure if you ask around in the pub someone will back up my story.'

The police must consider me their prime suspect. Although they had discovered a lot, there was no solid evidence to link me to the crime. Using a rock as the murder weapon was only a guess. Even if they found a rock encrusted with blood, I doubted they had the technology to lift fingerprints. It must have happened when she walked back to school from the pub. Maybe someone followed her—some chancer who tried it on with her and, when she fought back, hit her with a rock. During the brief silence, Preston and his assistant looked at each other. She opened a folder, reading through the contents. Preston stood up to leave without explanation. The icy blonde spoke.

'Michael, my name is Tracey Smith. Shortly, we will take your prints and show you our database to check out this man you say you saw in the pub. I want to share our theory for a plausible motive for the killing.'

Preston returned with two cups of coffee for himself and Tracey. He checked the tape recorder was still recording and gestured Tracey to continue the interview.

'Michael, the pathologist discovered Miss Gagneux was pregnant. Very early stages—just about two months. Are you the father?'

'Two months, you say.' This was a shocking revelation. 'If that's true, she never told me.'

'So, you admit you are the father?'

'Well, it's possible, I suppose. But highly unlikely. She was in France at Christmas. You should check in case there was a boyfriend.'

Preston came to my rescue with news of a new test called DNA profiling, which could prove paternity to a high accuracy.

'It's a new-fangled test and no doubt very expensive. We have never used it. I imagine you don't object to taking a test?'

'Of course not. If the test proves I can't be the father, that's fine.'

'When Michelle said she was pregnant, and you were the father, that was a tremendous shock. A bombshell, in fact, because you were not ready to accept that responsibility,' said Tracey Smith.

'Look, that's pure conjecture. Sure, my first reaction would be surprise, but we would have talked it over. I would have been supportive.'

The police officers looked dubious. It was clear I was in the frame with the proximity and motive established. They led me through to the records office and retrieved several box files.

'Look at the mugshots and see if anyone matches the mystery man in the pub. In the meantime, where did you park your car?' asked Preston.

'It's in the station car park. Is that alright?' I had visions of a parking ticket for over-staying.

'No, that's okay, you won't get a ticket. Give us the car keys. We need to check if Miss Gagneux has been in your car.'

This was startling. Apart from the November trip to Brighton, she had travelled in my car many times. I handed over my keys.

'It's an old green Morris Minor. I gave her a lift to town once for shopping in December. You may find her prints on the door handle. In fact, I seldom give lifts, so you could well find some.'

'Thank you, Michael, for being so honest,' said Preston. I felt everything I said was confirming I must be the killer with both opportunity and motive established. I hoped they were ready to let me go, but the lady detective had other ideas.

'It's fascinating the details we get from an autopsy,' said Inspector Tracey. 'We had a similar case from a murder in Littlehampton. The killer had suffocated his girlfriend and then rifled through all the drawers to make it appear like a robbery. The girl was pregnant, which was a great shock. In that case, the girl was promiscuous and someone else was the father, not him. Do you know how we caught him?'

I looked blank.

'Fibres,' said Tracey.

'As he was suffocating her, squeezing the life out of her with a pillow, she dug her nails into his back and a fibre from his pullover caught under her nail. This was enough to implicate him, and he later confessed to the crime.'

She stared at me with unblinking eyes. I held her gaze, trying to remain expressionless.

'Michael, would you object if we asked a male officer to conduct a strip search to look for any signs of injuries, such as scratches on your body?'

'That's extreme, isn't it?'

'At this stage, if you refuse, we cannot force you, but it is in your interest to comply.'

I had little choice. An older officer took me to a small toilet and asked me to strip off. A humiliating experience as he examined every inch of me. Worst was the cold, wet floor and the noisy drip from a tap in the washbasin. I concentrated on looking ahead, trying to avoid the eyes of the police officer scanning my body.

He noticed a thin scar on the back of my right hand. I explained it was from pruning roses. I told him my mother would remember as I had come into the kitchen dripping blood. At the weekend two weeks ago. In fact, on Sunday the 16th January. Nice weather that day and a chance to catch up on the gardening front. He disappeared to return with Preston.

He gripped my hand and turned my wrist over to reveal the thin scar.

'We will need a photograph of the mark. Anything else?' Preston asked the older police officer.

'No sir, nothing untoward.'

After that experience, I wanted to leave, but they made me trawl through loads of mugshots of local criminals. Inspector Tracey returned to the room. Her manner had relaxed a tad. She sat at the table, watching me flip through the files. But it was a waste of time. To re-focus my attention on the remaining files, I examined each photo closely. There were very few blue-eyed, blond lads with a criminal record, and none matching the man I had seen.

I could not face going back to school. After the police had finished with me, I drove down to the beach and parked my car on the front near the Metropole Hotel. Normally, I would enjoy the mild January day and lack of crowds as I walked along the promenade. But everywhere I went reminded me of Michelle. I retraced our steps to where we dropped to the beach. She stopped to pick up plastic bottles and place them in the bins. It was one of her pet hates—plastic litter everywhere—a threat to the seabirds and marine life. I walked on alone. The derelict Victorian pier, closed to the public in 1975, stared back at me, deserted now except for a few dog walkers. Everywhere the sound of the waves pounding the beach and the drag of gravel pulling back and forth. Overhead, gulls searched for easy crumbs from discarded fast-food containers flapping by in the wind. The screeching seabirds soared around me, hostile to the lone visitor to the beach, who came with nothing. I lost track of time and did not notice DI Preston watching me from the other side of the road.

Chapter 5

Two weeks had passed since the murder of the French teacher with no sign of progress. SIO Preston only fed the Pulborough police crumbs of information as the Brighton force kept a tight rein on the case. Inspector Bishop and PC Jimmy James knew the prime suspect, Michael Fletcher, had attended another interview with Preston, but since then press interest had waned as life returned to normal.

Bishop had the bright idea of dropping by the Three Horseshoes on Saturday night. Informally, of course—this was not a pub to arrive at in uniform. The pub was the last sighting of Michelle alive. It made sense to call in two weeks later to check the regulars; many of whom, from force of habit, only visited the pub on a Saturday night.

'Hasn't Preston done this already?' said Jimmy.

'Yes, after a fashion,' said Bishop. 'I think they drew a blank. No one could remember seeing the French teacher because it was busy with a darts match. Besides, the locals are more likely to talk to us.'

'Don't let Preston know. He'll think we are interfering.'

'We'll go in undercover posing as normal customers. Book a table and have a meal.'

'Won't that look odd? Just us two. Strangers to the area. We would stick out like a sore thumb.'

'Yea, I see what you mean. Well, we can book a table for four. I can bring along Sheila. Is there a girl you can invite along to make a foursome?'

Bishop knew Jimmy had several girlfriends, none of whom stayed with him for long. Jimmy's latest was a trainee hairdresser called Sandra, and she could join them. Her hair was normally blonde, but she liked to experiment with new fashions and colours. This week she was sporting a purple spiky punk style, and it had bowled over the customers in the hair salon. Next step would be a piercing, perhaps a metal ring through her septum. So cool.

The two groups arrived in separate cars at 8.30 p.m. and met up in the car park, which was already busy. Inspector Bishop was with his wife, Sheila—a reluctant party to the investigation, and PC Jimmy James was with Sandra, glad to assist in the special operation with a free dinner and drinks on offer.

The landlady frowned as the non-regulars asked for a table in the restaurant. Last orders were at nine in theory, but the chef left sharp on nine.

'You haven't booked?' She asked as she weighed up the pros and cons of taking a late booking. She looked at the dinner reservation list, shielding it from view. The list was empty apart from one no-show. The restaurant had just three occupied tables with sad-looking couples. But the raucous darts match was in full swing, and they had to provide sandwiches for the teams, plus copious refills of beer. There was only herself, her useless husband, an alcoholic chef, and the part-time waitress. Catering to the public was a daily nightmare.

'Hmm, I suppose we can squeeze you in,' she conceded. The younger couple looked relieved, so she handed over two a la carte menus and the wine list as she led them to a table close to the log fire. They didn't look like big spenders. Hopefully, in and out fast.

'Can I interest you in an aperitif?' she asked.

'Very nice,' simpered Sandra. 'Rum and coke for me and a pint of bitter for my Jimmy. That's on the rocks for mine.' The young couple seizing the initiative put Inspector Bishop out, but he quickly recovered.

'I'll have a pint of bitter. What about you, Sheila?'

'Just a glass of tap water.'

'Leave the wine list and menu with us for a couple of minutes, love.'

They studied the menu in subdued whispers, conscious of an elderly couple who stared across but averted their gaze when Sheila stared back. The men opted for medium rare steaks, chips, and a mixed selection of vegetables. It was tempting to order starters, but the atmosphere was unwelcoming, and the service was certain to be slow.

'I fancy scampi with a side salad and chips,' said Sandra. 'With lots of tartare sauce—I love tartare sauce. And a glass of wine.'

'The house white or something sparkling?' asked Sheila.

'I *love* Mateus Rose, but it's only available by the bottle. Perhaps you will share a bottle with me?'

'Sorry, love. I don't drink alcohol. No choice for me,' said Sheila. 'I am a vegetarian, so I will have to go for the mushroom risotto.'

'Oh, I so admire you,' trilled Sandra.

'Although I can't abide cruelty to animals, I don't have the discipline to be a strict vegetarian like you. I hardly ever select meat and prefer fish, so I am *nearly* vegetarian.'

'She thinks fish have no feelings, so that's alright,' laughed Jimmy.

'And the wine? We don't do rose, I'm afraid, but there is a very nice Spanish white by the glass.'

'She'll have that,' said Jimmy. 'A large glass.'

Sandra was a sport. She didn't mind being made fun of. Unlike the inspector's wife, who was a miserable battle-axe, but Sandra was used to dealing with people like that. Jimmy was only a humble PC, but so what. He was a giggle and quite attractive in an immature, boyish way.

The pub landlady cut their banter short, returning with their drinks and taking the food order.

They were surprised by the fast service. The chef was determined to be out of the door by nine. Once the mains were served, he would be away. The waitress could throw any simple dessert orders together. Anything more complex was off.

'That was a lovely meal,' Bishop congratulated the young waitress who had taken over from the frosty landlady.

'You were lucky to get a table. We have been so busy.'

'I expect the murder of that poor teacher is attracting the ghoulish element?' said Sheila.

The waitress looked around nervously. Their table was in full view of the bar where the landlady lurked, wiping dry the glasses but always alert and listening, like a hawk. It wasn't the done thing to gossip with customers.

'I can't say. But she was a lovely lady.'

'I expect teachers from the school visit the pub often?' asked the inspector.

'Sure, there are some regulars. They always drink in the posh lounge bar and never eat in the restaurant.'

'So, you are saying the French teacher never went to the public bar?'

'She would never set foot in there. Why are you asking all these questions, Mr?'

Aware of hostile stares from the landlady, the waitress hurried off like a startled rabbit, rushing to its hole.

A bald man walked over aggressively from the bar, clutching a damp T-towel in his hand. Inspector Bishop produced his identity card and introduced himself and PC Jimmy James. The man relaxed a little but remained on guard, adopting an overly polite manner.

'Gents, Pulborough police are always welcome here. It's those bastards from Brighton we're not so keen on!' The police declined his offer of drinks as the landlord pulled up a chair in front of the log fire and agreed to answer their questions.

'I guess you want to know about the French teacher murdered and thrown in the pond. My wife and I live on the premises, so we are always here. If it's a quiet night in the week, we leave the staff in charge, but most Fridays and Saturdays, it's full on. Apart from tonight, mind you. We had a sizeable group booked, but they let us down and didn't turn up. That sort of thing is always happening, I'm afraid to say—sign of the times we live in, isn't it? Mind you, that weekend, two weeks ago today I took the ferry across to France from Newhaven, leaving on the Friday afternoon crossing and not getting back until the Sunday afternoon. Just a mini break for the weekend. We often go to Dieppe on impulse.'

'No doubt you stock up on cheap wine and spirits?' said Inspector Bishop.

'For personal use only. I'd be a fool not to.'

'So, you can't corroborate the report from a witness that the French teacher visited your pub on Saturday 15th January? We need to question anyone who saw her in the pub that evening.'

The landlord stared into the fire at the fading embers. His bulk blocked the heat from the group and the ladies shivered, impatient to leave. He drank from his pint pot.

'Funny thing that. Since the story broke in the *Daily Mail*, none of the regulars can recall seeing that woman in the public bar. Many of our customers don't care for the public cos of the cursing and like. We use the lounge bar for the posher folk, but the only ones who go there are them junior teachers on Saturday night. We call it "Teachers' night" and the locals scarper to leave that room free for them. I told the coppers from Brighton this already.'

'Is there a bad feeling towards the school?' asked Bishop.

'Nah, not really. It's them and us, in 'it? The well-off fee-paying families send their kids to these places, which are like concentration camps. The head is a stickler for discipline. I feel sorry for the children. Some as young as seven cry themselves to sleep at night cos they miss their mother.'

'And the teachers? Do they seem reasonable types or does the system corrupt them as well?' The landlord had enough of the questions. He suggested they visit the lounge bar and see for themselves.

'Well, thank you for your help. If any of your regulars recall seeing the French teacher in the pub or have information, that would be a great help. Contact me, Inspector Bishop at the Pulborough station.' Bishop handed over his card.

'Certainly will, inspector. We are always happy to help the police.'

As the couples returned to their cars Bishop remarked how it was odd that no one could recall Michelle's visit to the pub two weeks ago.

'Not really,' said Sandra. 'Who remembers occasional drinkers? And is so stuck up she only goes to the lounge bar.'

'Don't talk of the dead like that,' said Jimmy, shocked at his girlfriend's outburst.

'But what you say is right. Your average punter won't be able to describe a stranger unless there is something distinctive about him or her. There is no conspiracy of silence. Besides, if you don't believe the landlord and his wife, we can always ask for proof of their ferry ticket or receipts from their spending spree in France.'

Sandra looked at Jimmy with a growing respect. He thought of everything. He should be in charge of the investigation instead of that dull inspector.

An icy drizzle was falling from the dark night sky. The drops lit up as the inspector switched on the car headlights. The police officers were keen to visit the lounge bar to see which teachers were present, but the ladies were dead set against wasting any more time. Jimmy volunteered to check while visiting the toilet.

'Don't hang about in the rain,' said Bishop. 'Thank you for your help. No positive leads. Hopefully, something will develop.' He drove off without waiting for Jimmy to return, leaving Sandra standing in the rain. She shivered and drew her raincoat around herself, seeking some warmth from the freezing January night. Jimmy ran back, disappointed. The only teacher in the bar was Jones, drinking alone at a corner table. No sign of the chief suspect.

'That's significant,' said Sandra. 'The English teacher can't face going back to the scene of the crime. Imagine, that poor girl was sitting in the pub with some mystery bloke two weeks ago. Perhaps they left together and walked across to the woods. But something happened. Either the man she was with or, maybe some pervert hiding in the trees, jumped out and killed her before sliding her dead body into a nearby pond.'

'Don't think about it. It's my job to find her killer. And I will.'

Jimmy reckoned his statement of intent would impress Sandra and it had the desired effect as she kissed him passionately, blind to the renewed force of the rain and the purple dye running out of her mangled hair. Close by came a strange, high-pitched cry from the woods. Startled, Sandra pulled away in alarm.

'What was that?'

'Just a fox. It's the mating call of the vixen,' said Jimmy. 'Anyone living in the countryside would know that.'

'Are you sure? It sounded human to me.' She shivered. 'Jimmy let's get out of here. I want to go home.'

As they headed for the car, a figure draped in a black raincoat with a hood blocked their path. They recognised the pub landlady.

'I know who you are. Local bobbies following up on the murder of the French girl. My husband talked to you. But don't believe all he says! Did he spin you a yarn about us going to France and away from the pub that night?'

'You mean that was a lie?'

'Yes, and no. He was away that weekend, but not with me. He met up with his lady friend in Dieppe. I was here all weekend. I saw the girl in the public bar like that teacher from the school said. But I bet he didn't mention they had a row after he spotted her in the bar with another bloke. He went into a jealous rage. She and the other guy backed off and went into the snug, so he thought they had left. He drained his beer in one, banged his glass down on the counter, and asked for a whisky. I served him a double, and he downed that in one and left.'

PC James agreed this was important fresh evidence. He asked her to come down to the station and make a signed statement.

'I don't want to get the young lad into trouble. He has always been very polite. Maybe I am exaggerating a bit—just a lover's tiff. I can't waste time going to Pulborough. And if Harry found out, he'd go mental.'

PC James wished he had an official card to hand over for her to follow up, like in the films.

'You should report what you saw,' said Sandra, touching the hooded figure on her arm.

They left her there in the rain and drove home to Jimmy's flat in town.

Chapter 6

The temperature plunged overnight to seven degrees below freezing. The ill-fitting sash windows let the dull heat from my bedroom radiator escape and the frozen air outside wrapped around my huddled shape as I buried myself under the bed covers. I resisted the urgent message from my bladder to visit the toilet as I yearned for sleep. I doubled up in a foetal position to thaw out my numb toes and waited for the annoying repeater alarm to drive me out of bed. At last, it rang, and I stabbed the stop button, sending it skidding to the floor, where it continued ringing and turning in circles like a yapping dog until the clockwork mechanism stopped. Peace at last. I noticed a crust of ice had formed on the glass of water by my bedside. A minute later, my mother was knocking at the door, interrupting the only deep sleep I had enjoyed all night.

'Michael, are you awake? It's a lovely frosty morning and nearly eight. You will be late again!'

Mona knew the chances of my being on time for the school

assembly on a Monday morning were remote. When I arrived twenty minutes late, she was waiting inside the chapel porch. The morning hymn sounded far away until Caldwell-Brown opened the thick oak door, and the hymn startled me with the wall of sound stopping me dead. Confused, I headed for the open door, gazing inside the chapel for an empty seat at the back.

'Fletcher, you're late as usual,' he said. 'I am making an early escape. Join me for a hot tea to counter this freezing weather. Assemblies nearly over—no need to go in.'

'Mr Caldwell-Brown, I am afraid we have other plans for Mr Fletcher,' said Mona in her strictest tone. The Science teacher shrugged his shoulders, and his eyes showed me sympathy and understanding.

'Mr Fletcher, the headmaster has instructed me to pass on a message. Would you go to his study and wait for him? As soon as he finishes assembly, he wishes to talk to you.'

My first thought was how odd. What is going on? Perhaps Singapore had requested a reference, and he wanted to chat about that. Yes, that was it. As a popular and competent English teacher with an excellent record of sports training, it would disappoint him to discover I wished to leave. No doubt, he would implore me to stay and even increase my salary. I was thinking these warm thoughts sitting alone as I studied his cluttered study—a room I seldom entered.

Along one wall, ancient leather-bound books of the unread classics filled the bookcase under a thick coating of dust. The headmaster's desk was large and messy, with an in-tray, an out-tray, and a telephone for outside calls plus an internal phone for summoning Mona. He operated a system of lights outside the office. A glowing green light meant he was in residence and open to visits from staff and pupils. If the headmaster was away from his study attending duties within the school, such as his morning walk or inspection of the dormitories, the lights were turned off. When the dreaded red light was on, it signalled that he did not wish to be disturbed. An alternating sequence of red and green lights was the usual sequence if a queue of boys waited outside in the passage to be caned.

A small window behind the desk afforded a view across to the sports grounds and distant woods. It had a southerly aspect, and, in the summer, the sun shone into the study with pleasant warmth. At such times, the sun blinded any visiting parents seated opposite the headmaster, which was an effective measure to discourage their petty complaints. On rare occasions, when the parents or visitors were welcome guests, he could draw the blind to cut out the glare.

The walls were bare apart from some framed certificates and a cheap reproduction of the death of Nelson at the Battle of Trafalgar. In a corner by the door, a cluster of various canes and a cricket bat stood inside a tall Chinese vase decorated with angry dragons.

The headmaster's study displayed an ornate Victorian fireplace with a black slate hearth, which had fallen into disuse. The large wooden mantle clock with Roman numerals set on a dark slate mantle piece was a pretentious Edwardian antique. All heating was via inadequate radiators plus an electric bar heater for back up on bitter winter days.

Apart from the threadbare cord carpet there was an unpleasant dirty hearth rug upon which rested a black leather chair. A curious smell pervaded the room: a mix of stale cigarette, lavender furniture polish and the frightened sweat of small boys. Upholding discipline was very important to the headmaster and instilling fear and obedience was the first step in the character development of St Wilfrid's boys to uphold the highest standards to progress to useful careers in the armed forces, government, and politics.

After a long wait, the headmaster arrived with Mona. He sent her off to make tea and asked me to take a seat on the black leather chair as he sat down behind his ample desk. No chance of sun on this frosty January morning, so I made myself as comfortable as possible in the upright, armless chair as I stared across at the short, balding figure of the headmaster who busied himself opening a folder containing indeterminate paperwork. It was quite a thick wad so unlikely to be a response to my job application. More likely, it was a folder with outstanding letters and bills. The strains of keeping such a school running smoothly!

'Michael, there have been several unfortunate press reports singling you out as the chief suspect in the incident which took place with poor Miss Gagneux. True or not, and I know an Englishman is innocent until proved guilty, but there has been pressure from some parents to ask you to step down from teaching until the police force has time to resolve this matter. It places us in an awkward situation.' He glanced down at his paperwork now, as if reading comments from irate parents.

'But the press reports are untrue. Certainly, the police interviewed me along with some of the other teachers, but I can assure you I am innocent of this horrible crime and the police have not charged me.'

'You must understand there is also the moral dilemma. The police autopsy report found Miss Gagneux was pregnant, and you were in a relationship with her, outside marriage. That is not the sort of example which we can condone in a Catholic school.'

'But I am an atheist,' I protested.

'Nonsense, your family is devout Church of England. Your father attends all our services when he can. Our Anglican brothers are all part of the Christian fold, and they uphold the same values as us. Mona and I have considered the matter and feel you should take the rest of the term off to let the matter die down. You will still be on the payroll. This will give time for the police to complete their investigation. Prior to any possible reinstatement, I will seek the approval of the Board of Governors. In the long run, it might be in your best interest to seek another position in the teaching profession elsewhere. Occasionally one hears of a private school desperate for an English teacher of your calibre and, if

I hear of any suitable leads, I will recommend you. If that is a course you wish to take, I can give you a positive reference unless the police investigation proves otherwise. Regrettably, the sort of salary you can expect after such an incident, even when proved innocent, may be less than ideal.'

There wasn't any more to say. I looked dejected at the floor, as if hit by a blow, and then up at the ceiling, noting the stark light bulb staring back at me from a brown stained lampshade.

'Mona has cleared out your locker.' He pointed towards a sports bag on the floor by my chair, which I noticed for the first time.

'If there is anything else we have forgotten, we can send it to your parents.' The headmaster stood up and followed me towards the door as if guiding a sheep from a pen. We were both embarrassed. He offered me his hand, which I shook loosely like a limp lettuce. I left just as Mona was returning with my cup of tea, which I refused. She was flustered as I walked past her in a daze.

As I returned to my car, the shock of my expulsion raised fresh possibilities. I could not face returning home in disgrace. No doubt, they would inform my father, as a governor of the school, of the headmaster's decision. How could I fill the void from now until returning home at my usual time? To kill time, I wandered into town and took a coffee in a newly opened cafe. It had Italian pretensions with a professional espresso machine. The local women on their shopping trips favoured weak cappuccinos and carrot cake, so I ordered a double espresso.

'Is that black?' asked the young girl serving behind the counter.

She poured me a large black coffee. I picked up two of the free papers to stop other customers noticing that the front page of the *Daily Mail* featured a picture of me, holding a tennis racket and smiling shyly after I won a local tennis tournament when I was an awkward 18-year-old. At age 23, I looked much the same. The headline ran 'Is School Teacher and former Tennis star a Cold-blooded Killer?'

After that shock, I had to get out of town. I drove to the nearest countryside—a pleasant, wooded track, which led to a large pond. There were a few couples out walking in the crisp air and most of them greeted me with a cherry cry of 'Hallo' or 'Good Morning,' as if I was their greatest friend. I mumbled back an indistinct greeting or an idiotic smile, holding my hand to my face, pretending to adjust my scarf. This was more stressful than town, so I gave up the paths and strode through the wooded undergrowth, tripping over branches and scratched by brambles. I felt like a fugitive and kept stopping and listening in case I was being pursued. After an hour of crashing through the trees, I was bleeding from several cuts but felt exhilarated. I must hang on to reality. I was innocent. If the police could not prove it, then I would have to do their job for them. A plan for action took shape in my head.

If there were a sunset on such a dull day, it would be at 5 p.m. One of my lights had failed, which made me nervous that the police might stop me on my drive home. I still had not installed seatbelts in my old Morris Minor despite the new law, which made them mandatory. Rather than pay for an expensive fitting of anchoring points in an old car, it was time to trade it in and get something more modern.

'You are back early,' observed my mother, looking up from filling the kettle.

'Bit of a headache,' I lied. 'I rearranged my classes to get away early.'

'That's a pleasant surprise. Would you like a cup of tea? Your father and I are keen to watch the evening news. We want to see the item about the serial killer Dennis Nilsen. It is a shocking case. Apparently, he stored the bodies under the floorboards in his room until the smell got too bad. You would think someone would notice,' she remarked with glee.

'You can't let this Nilsen case panic you,' I said. 'The *Daily Mirror* says Nilsen cut up the bodies of his young victims and flushed bits down the toilet. He lived in the top flat, but he blocked the drains of the entire house so the other tenants couldn't flush their toilets. They complained to the Water Board, and that is when the plumber found the drains clogged up with human flesh and bones.'

'Yes, I have read the gruesome accounts in the papers, and it says he realised he was sick in the head after the first killing and thought of going to the police, but he was very fond of his dog and worried who would look after it. So, he does have some decent feelings.'

'You're joking, I hope. You mean he carried on killing because he couldn't bear to be parted from his dog?' How could my mother see anything good in such a man?

'There was a call from the garage. The man said they have got the Morris Marina in, whatever that may mean,' said my father, collecting his cup of tea and heading back to his study. Clearly, the school had not been in touch, and he did not know of my suspension.

'Yes, I know about that. They were expecting a 1980 model. I think it will be too expensive. I only need a car to run around.'

'A reliable car to get to school on time,' said my mother. 'The Morris will go on forever, but it's not a young person's car. You need a nice little sports car like an MG or a Mini Cooper to attract the ladies.'

So far, I had managed my social life away from my parents' scrutiny and it was best to let them believe in my boring predictability and lack of friends. My old green Morris Minor still had some life left in it. Even Michelle's sudden death had not shaken them, and they remained loyal and outraged at the tone of the press reports suggesting I could be involved.

'Some small-minded people in town have been quite petty and adopted a superior air, disapproving glances and such-like,' said my mother. 'But it is only the ignorant few, and it has been heartening the support from the local shopkeepers. Many back you up and say how unjustified the press reports have been.'

'I'm sorry for all the trouble I have caused you. Don't worry, the police will find the culprit, and this will be like a bad dream.' The fact that I was now retired from the teaching profession was a shock I would hold back until another day.

Chapter 7

Four weeks since the body in the pond case captured the press interest the search for the killer had stalled and the papers had moved on to other crimes. A regular from the Three Horseshoes public bar had turned up at Brighton police station to report seeing a couple in the pub on Saturday 15th January matching Michelle with a broad-shouldered man with long blond hair. This backed up my version of events so the pressure from the police relented and they stopped calling me for interviews. However, it was not enough to push the police into action. All leads led to a dead end.

DI Preston had been convinced I was not being totally transparent. The police suspected I was downplaying my relationship with Michelle. I admitted taking her to Brighton and spending the night with her. The timing of the pregnancy fitted so it was likely I was the father although this had come as a surprise. She had never mentioned it. Preston suspected it was a casual relationship meaning nothing to me, but he was wrong. I had genuinely loved Michelle.

Preston had nothing but contempt for me. I had no alibi for the night of 15th January because my parents did not back up my story. But this was no surprise. It did not prove I was the murderer just because they did not hear me drive home. School had forgotten about me too. Out of sight meant out of mind. There had been no contact from the headmaster or any of my teaching colleagues. Since it was nearly a month since the murder, I decided to visit the Three Horseshoes to meet Jones and catch up on the gossip. I was in no hurry to return to school while they continued to pay my monthly pay cheques. The break gave me an opportunity to roam the local countryside alone with my thoughts. On such trips, I always took my camera and a pair of binoculars and recorded bird sightings in a notebook. Sometimes I attempted amateur drawings of special sightings such as sparrow hawks or kestrels if I had been too slow to get a decent photograph. An absorbing hobby helped take my mind off the present trouble.

My father had been appalled by the headmaster's quick decision to suspend me and threatened to resign as a school governor unless I was reinstated. The school called his bluff and ignored the threat, knowing the perks of the post meant more to him than standing up for me. Other friends told me to consult a solicitor and bring a case of unjust dismissal. Not to do so, in fact, made me look guilty. I should go on the offensive. After all the head had strongly suggested I get another job. If my job application were successful, that would solve everything. I could disown the whole affair and start with a clean sheet in Singapore. This nightmare would be over.

At 8 p.m. I parked outside the pub and was relieved to see Jones' car in the car park. At least I would have someone to talk to provided he was still my friend. Entering the bar, I was met by a welcome wall of warmth from the log fire. I was wearing a heavy overcoat, a scarf, and a grey wool hat to hide my identity. Fortunately, the young man behind the bar did not know me. Neither the landlord nor his wife was over-friendly, but they were busy in the public bar. Knowing I was still a suspect of Michelle's murder, they might refuse to serve me.

'I should keep your head down if I were you,' whispered Jones, not fooled by my disguise. 'The locals are hostile to all the staff and if they see you there will be a scene.'

'I won't stay long,' I said gulping my pint of bitter. 'Just after an update. You know the police have no case against me.'

'Trouble is they have no one else to pin it on,' said Jones. 'Unjust, I know. Let's move around the corner away from the bar. Matron said she might look in. She is loyal to you like all the staff. We all think the headmaster over-reacted. I am sure it's only a matter of time before they reinstate you.'

'I don't care anymore. I am enjoying my leisure time.'

Jones shrugged his shoulders. But before he could say anything the door blew open with a crash and matron marched up to the bar. Jones quickly offered to buy her a drink plus two more pints for us.

'Michael. It's good to see you.' Aware that I may not be welcome in the pub matron approached very close and lowered her voice, which immediately attracted the rapt attention of the adjacent tables. 'I was *appalled* by the headmaster's stupid decision to force you to take a sabbatical. Nervous breakdown, indeed! What a lie. As an innocent young man, I am sure you are more than able to weather the insinuations of the gutter press!'

'He told you I had a nervous breakdown?'

'That's right, he claimed you asked for some time off. I said that was unlikely, knowing you, and he admitted he was under pressure from some of the parents. Just the normal troublemakers complaining about exposing their precious children to a suspect in a murder case.'

'I blame this Nilsen business for getting everyone on edge,' said Jones returning from the bar with our drinks.

'Michael is hardly a serial killer.'

'Thanks, Jones for your support,' I said sarcastically.

Matron downed her whisky in one and I half rose to order more drinks when Jones said he would get another round in. I passed him a fiver and he left with enthusiasm.

'Now we are alone I need to pass on a useful lead. A contact of mine, who must remain anonymous has tipped me off that on the night Michelle was last seen in this pub she was definitely in the public bar watching the darts match.'

I was amazed. 'As far as I am aware she had no interest in darts. But the police told me a regular from the pub actually saw Michelle in the bar with a man matching the description I gave them.'

'There you go! Two witnesses backing you up.'

'Was this witness in the bar at the same time as Michelle?' I asked.

'No. He heard about this from someone else. I know it sounds a bit shaky, but I have followed up on the lead and I can tell you the darts game was a league match between the Three Horseshoes team and the Royal Oak from Graffham. Graffham are top of the league, so it was a one-sided affair, quickly over and gossip has it that Michelle got chatting with a young man from their team—a man who is not a regular but filled in for one of the others who was off sick. Apparently, this guy was a talented player.'

'It must be the person I saw.'

'No, I don't think so. The man you saw her with left. Then the lad from the darts team got chatting with her.'

'The police should be pursuing this. It can't be that difficult to trace these people, surely. I'm tempted to drive over to the pub in Graffham and make my own enquiries.'

'Best not, Michael. The trouble is my informer won't go to the police himself. Apparently, there is some trivial motoring offence on file, so he dares not. He hoped I could pass on the information but there is no point as I have heard this second or third hand. The police would suspect me of filing a false lead to distract them. I *did* try an anonymous call to Brighton police dealing with the case but that was a waste of time. They said they had tons of crank calls and they would only follow it up if I came down to the station to lodge a formal statement. I don't have time for that, I'm afraid.'

'We might have more joy with the Pulborough police. I get the impression that they resent Brighton interfering.'

Jones came back with our drinks. Both matron and I had the same idea. After we explained the situation, he agreed to pass information to the Pulborough police.

'Only thing worries me is that they may recognise my Welsh accent, because they interviewed me at school and asked loads of questions about you. However, I can give it a go. Try disguising my voice or talk posh.'

'Exactly,' said matron. 'They will listen to a man.'

I knew that Mona had been arranging a memorial service for Michelle at the school and asked matron if this had gone ahead yet.

'Last Saturday the school put on a lovely service. It was Requiem mass and Michelle's mother and her sister, Giselle, came over from France. In addition, she has a brother who lives and works in Southampton, would you believe. He is a few years older than his sister but has lived in the UK ever since his parents divorced. His father is English and lives in Hampshire. Both attended and I had a very useful chat with Mark—that's her brother's name, which I will tell you all about. First let's talk about the service. They had hoped to arrange the repatriation of her body back to France. But unfortunately, the police were still waiting for some of the test results from the autopsy so they would not release the deceased for a dignified burial.'

'Even I was impressed by the service Father Roderick arranged,' said Jones. 'The choir sang *Ave Maria* with a solo from Giselle to a packed chapel. Not just school but people from the French embassy came along to pay their respects. During the Offertory, there was a tear-jerking performance of the *Dies Irae* followed by a final hymn—a traditional and inspiring rendition of *In Paradisum* which completed the Mass with an uplifting theme.'

'For the *Dies Irae* to be effective I feel you really need strong bass voices of mature men such as you hear in the Gregorian chants,' said matron. 'The tenor voices of young boys lack that hopeless, gloomy feel of Death.'

Jones agreed with matron. He was always happy talking about choirs.

'As you know I am not exactly high church, Michael. In Wales, we are more rooted in cheerless Methodism rather than the Papal fripperies, but the performance of *Ave Maria* by Giselle Gagneux was spine-tingling. And the *In Paradisum* was beautiful and just right to celebrate the life of a young, pure lady taken from us by a deranged killer. What a tragic business.'

We all sat silent for a moment before Jones recovered to tell me about the reception in the school library attended by staff, parents, senior boys, and the family after the service. No expense was spared, he assured me. With a buffet spread and decent wines rather than the usual cheap Spanish plonk from the local Co-op Mona seemed to like. Detective Inspector Preston was also present observing the proceedings with alert attention to those present.

'No doubt looking for me,' I laughed.

'I imagine the headmaster wanted to avoid the potential embarrassment of having you attend along with Michelle's family,' said matron.

'They say that sometimes depraved killers will attend their victim's funeral in a show of bravado,' added Jones.

'I can understand that. I have never met her family, but I would like to someday. Maybe I will write to them.'

Matron agreed that was a good idea once more time had passed and said she would find out their address in France.

She also promised to put in a good word for me with the headmaster and recommend they reinstated me after half-term.

'Half-term already?'

'It starts next Friday, and the break is ten days. Honestly, Michael *every* teacher knows the holiday dates. Of course, you are already on holiday, after a fashion, so I imagine the days glide by with your parents looking after you, feeding you regular meals and...'

'That's enough,' I knew she was just joking but I couldn't stand people pointing out I still lived at home with my parents.

'And I don't need any help to make the headmaster change his mind so please leave it.'

'What did you mean when you said her brother raised some interesting questions about his sister?' said Jones.

'Indeed, he did. He told me that Michelle had a doctorate in Chemistry and used to work at a research laboratory at the University of Nantes. Her thesis was a study into the stability of plastic water bottles and detection of harmful chemicals leaching from plastic into the water. Apparently, this can upset our hormones and even cause cancers in later life.'

'That's ridiculous,' I said. 'I knew she was obsessed about waste plastic bottles, but plastic is in use all over the world without any obvious detrimental effects.'

'Both of them—Michelle and Mark—were researching this in detail. Mark runs a testing laboratory in Southampton mainly for soil and core samples collected from the North Sea for the oil companies. But he also has equipment to analyse water quality and has discovered some worrying results.'

Matron said she was initially sceptical but when she looked over Michelle's belongings in her room at school, she came across loads of research papers and some letters from Michelle to the press and government officials. It seemed she was a whistleblower and had amassed a lot of evidence.

'Of course, the police looked, but they weren't interested so I took the files home for safe-keeping and to read through all the material. Then, just last week a man claiming to be a solicitor for her family came to the school and asked for all Michelle's personnel effects. Mona bagged up all her clothes and belongings and handed them over. But the man asked for any files or papers she was working on. Mona said she thought everything else had been passed to the police and the solicitor did not look happy!'

'I smell a rat,' said Jones. 'I doubt if that man was a bona-fide solicitor.'

'My thoughts also,' said matron.

'Michael, can you look at her papers and make photocopies? I can't do so at school without raising suspicion.'

'Can you pass them to me tomorrow? We could meet at the George & Dragon at lunchtime. It's not far from my home.'

'Oh, yes I know it. A very nice pub, especially in the summer with the beer garden. A great idea but I am away tomorrow so let's make it in a week's time during half-term. I would like to finish reading all the files first. Sunday midday, shall we say?'

I could not face returning to that school so soon. Even if they wanted me back, I knew there would always be a shadow hanging over me. Parents would point me out to new arrivals as the teacher who got away with murder. 'Yes, of course he is guilty, but the police can't find enough evidence to make it stick.' Or 'The school suspended him, but his father is a governor and threatened to sue them if they didn't reinstate him.' No, I would only return after I was proved innocent, and the killer was behind bars.

Chapter 8

Friday dawned on a crisp, sunny morning. My mother was up early. Since the start of BBC Breakfast Time in January, she liked to be up for the 6.30 a.m. start hosted by Frank Bough. She had seen Frank in the press box at the Wimbledon tennis finals one year, admired his rugged looks and relaxed style. The new format presentation with weather reports, traffic updates and innovative interviews was a recent innovation, although many other countries in the world had been doing this for years. At least it gave me an incentive to get up early rather than lying in bed late feeling sorry for myself.

'Michael, I am surprised to see you up. Even your father doesn't stir before eight.'

'I wanted to see the early morning news programme you are so keen on. And I plan to drive to Brighton today.'

'Whatever for? Your car is not very reliable, especially in cold weather.'

The Morris was like a venerable old lady, and she hated the cold. The garage had offered me an expensive Marina with a good trade-in price for my old Morris. I was considering their offer, but something made me hold back. This week I must decide whether to go ahead. That's why I thought of Brighton. A walk by the seaside to clear my head and then the bold initiative of an unannounced visit to that horrid police station. I hoped to find Preston and that cold police officer with the elfin-like face who had made me undergo that humiliating strip search. What progress had they made? Had they located the mystery man in the pub? Were they aware he a member of the visiting pub darts team from Graffham was a witness? Had they done any research in France to discover whom Michelle had been so keen to visit in December? Many questions and I needed answers, and the best way was to go on the offensive. I was about to leave the house around 10 a.m. when Nigel Caldwell-Brown phoned.

'Hey Michael. I hear you met up with Jones and matron at the weekend. We are right behind you, supporting you all the way. It's only a matter of time before the head will reinstate you. Since you have been away, they have appointed a temporary English teacher from some agency. However, he is a complete disaster. Seldom sober. Even first thing in the morning. He is like a character out of that Evelyn Waugh book. I can't remember the name.'

'Decline and Fall?'

'Maybe. It was about some misfits teaching at a school in Wales.'

'That's right—just like St Wilfrid's. A dark satire about the teaching profession set in the 1920s and based on the school Evelyn Waugh attended.'

'You would know that sort of thing. How are you keeping?'

'Fine, thanks, Nigel. Considerate of you to call. I feel a bit ostracised and cut off from reality, so I wish the police would buck up and find Michelle's killer. I have a few leads to pursue and a plan of action, starting today.'

'Good on you. Keep positive. Listen, I am ringing about another matter. I heard you are looking for a new car. I have one for sale. It's a red 1970 Triumph Herald 13/60 convertible.'

I imagined myself driving a powerful red convertible, changing the gear, and smiling at the beautiful blonde with the windswept hair by my side. The dappled sun flashed in and out of the tree line as I sped down a steep hill, but we only had eyes for each other. She laughed at some memory, her arm reached out, and her fingers rested on my thigh...

'It has always been an excellent runner,' continued Nigel, bringing me back to reality. 'And very reliable, so Jane is sad to see it leave. But with baby Hannah, we need a more practical car.'

Nigel said his wife's car was in immaculate condition and only used for shopping trips. He could get a better price by advertising in the *Argos,* but, as a favour, he would sell it to me. It seemed expensive for a thirteen-year-old car, but I did not like to haggle, as he was doing me a favour.

'Sounds great. When can I see it?'

The trip to Brighton was my way of saying goodbye. My forced absence from Michelle's requiem was a cruel blow, but I did not need to attend a formal ceremony of pretence and hypocrisy. We had all failed her, especially me. I retraced our steps from only a few months ago, gazing at the seabirds. Perhaps some seagulls were the same as then. A fatal fascination drew me to the Indian restaurant where we took dinner. But it was desolate and empty.

I could not remember the name of the bed-and-breakfast establishment where we spent the night. We had tried so many, tipsy and giggling, posing as man and wife, and all had refused us except for the sour woman with peroxide hair. Turning back pages in time was too painful and then I remembered the pub off the sea front where we went before the restaurant. I ordered a beer for myself and a glass of red wine for Michelle, just like then, but I drank Michelle's for her as I thought of her smiling eyes.

My watch told me 2 p.m. It was time to visit the Brighton police. I parked my car in the same spot in the police car park. The Desk Sergeant looked up curtly, annoyed that a member of the public should need attention when he was enjoying a mug of tea.

'I wonder if I could speak to Detective Inspector Preston or Miss Tracey Smith. Sorry, I don't know her rank.'

'Inspector Smith, you mean. Are they expecting you?'

'No, I was just in the area. They know who I am. I am just after an update.'

'An update? And what is your name, sir?'

'Fletcher, Michael Fletcher.' At the mention of my name, the penny dropped. Even he knew the name of the chief suspect for the murder of the French teacher. He called an assistant to man the desk and hurried to a back office to relay my message.

I wandered over to the well-worn bench beside the door. The seat had a patina from years of nervous use by those waiting to report a crime or come to bail out an imprisoned relative or friend. It smelt of urine and disinfectant. Even as I waited, a middle-aged couple approached the desk to report a missing teenager. The bored policeman placated them with a few reassurances and took down some brief details to add to the Missing Persons file, which he then lodged in a box file for the current year. Some junior officer would trawl through the entries, checking names against any recent bodies washed up at high tide from the popular suicide spots. They listed open cases in a ledger where the weight of subsequent entries soon banished them to oblivion. He looked at his watch, wondering why the Desk Sergeant was taking so long and I noticed a fixed camera behind the desk aimed at me. I could imagine Inspector Smith staring at me, looking for give-away signs such as nervous twitching, sweating or deep sighs guilty persons could not control. Should I smile like an idiot? Wave at the camera or maintain a Stoic stillness? Getting impatient, I started walking up and down the room. I passed a door, which suddenly opened, and Preston motioned me inside as if expecting me.

'Mr Fletcher. The sergeant tells me you were just passing by and popped in for a chat. Is that so? Or do you have anything new to add since we last spoke?'

'Indeed, I do. Thank you for seeing me. I have some fresh evidence and want to check if my informant has been in touch to pass it on.'

Preston sat up, attentive. He asked me to wait a moment and called Tracey Smith in to record any startling revelations. Tracey sat opposite me with a notebook and pen poised in expectation.

'At the weekend, I visited the Three Horseshoes and met up with some teachers. One of them—I won't say who at this stage, but a trustworthy member of the school staff—told me there is a witness from 15th January who backs up my account of Michelle talking to a man from a visiting darts team. This was *after* they saw her talking to a mystery man with long blond hair and piercing blue eyes.'

'Yes, we recall your description,' said Smith. 'We checked out both darts teams at the pub that night and there was a man on the Graffham team who got chatting with the French teacher. Unfortunately, he is away now. He works on an oil rig in the North Sea, but we talked to him via a satellite phone, and he admits chatting to Michelle and buying her a drink. She was upset about something. The darts player is short and dark with a ratty moustache. The Graffham team showed us a photograph of him winning some competition. So, he is *not* your mystery man.'

'That's what I said. There were two men who saw her.'

'We were wondering, Michael, if she was trying to avoid you?'

This news shook me. It made little sense. She had told Jones it was her birthday, and she hoped I would buy her a drink. Unless there was someone else, she was trying to avoid.

'I need to clarify one point,' said Preston. He made a play of reading from his notes. 'Back when we interviewed you on the second occasion, I think you said you had seen your girlfriend in the public bar when you were at the serving counter in the lounge bar.'

'Yes,'

'And you waved across and called out to attract her attention. Is that right?'

'Yes.'

'But, then this unpleasant looking fellow scowled at you and pulled her away. A person we still have not located as the darts player does not match that description.'

'Correct. That's what happened.'

'What would you say if I told you the owner of the pub says you got quite heated, ordered another drink—I think a whisky—downed it in one and stormed out of the pub? Is that a correct account?'

'No, I was with Jones. I think you must be referring to the owner's wife. She has misrepresented the situation. I admit I was bad-tempered, but that was only because of her slow service. The landlord's wife is notorious for serving the regulars first and ignoring the teachers. I drank up my whisky in one and left in protest at her unfriendly attitude.'

'Not a jealous outburst from seeing your girlfriend with another man?'

'No, it surprised me to see Michelle talking with a stranger, but it was none of my business. I ignored the situation. You and other people keep inferring she was my girlfriend, but that was not the case.'

Tracey Smith came back into the attack.

'Not your girlfriend! We have a report from a lady who runs Mon Repos in Brighton—an upmarket guest house—that a couple looking like Miss Gagneux and yourself spent a night of passion at her establishment back in November.'

'I don't deny we stayed at her very crummy place. We stayed there because I was over the drink-drive limit. A night of passion is her imagination gone wild. It was a scruffy room, and after a long walk birdwatching along the coast, we shared a few glasses of wine and collapsed exhausted. Miss

Gagneux was not used to drink and fell asleep. She was a friend. We knew it was not a good idea to get involved.'

'You see how the evidence is building up against you,' said Preston. 'I think you went into a jealous rage when you saw the girl you deny was your girlfriend with another man. After a few drinks, you left the pub and debated whether to confront them in the public bar or wait for them to leave. I believe you hung about in the car park and waited. Michelle left with the other man. They were on good terms and maybe kissed before he drives off alone. That inflames you! Your jealousy is like a red flag. Michelle is heading back to school by the shortcut through the woods and you run after her. You confront her and argue. She tells you she is pregnant, and you are the father. This is such a shock. At once she realises you will not stand by her. Her words sting more than any blow and you can't stand it anymore. There is a tussle, and she falls to the ground beneath you. There is a rock close by and in your blind rage, you smash it down on her head. You think she is dead. The pond is close by, and you drag her to the edge and roll her in. You notice she is struggling to escape, so you push her head under the water and hold her down until she stops fighting. You take the rock you stunned her with back to the car to dispose of far away. When we ran forensic tests on your car, we found several sets of Michelle's prints, which prove she was a frequent traveller in your car and your girlfriend, even though you deny it.'

'Of course, I told you that. I used to take her shopping because she didn't have a car.'

'Forensic tests can detect blood even after you wipe a car mat or carpet clean,' said Inspector Smith.

I knew their tests would not detect bloodstains in my car, so I just let them run on with their fantasies.

'We noted a scar on your right hand which could be a scratch wound inflicted in self-defence,' said Preston. 'A fresh wound consistent with the time of her death.'

'For the record, please make a note of what I say, Miss Smith. The story narrated by DI Preston is pure conjecture, unsupported by evidence or facts. The sequence of events leading to Michelle's death is unknown and does not involve me. You do not have a shred of evidence to link me to the murder scene. Now unless you plan to charge me, I intend to leave and wish you success in finding the killer.'

The police asked me to wait. I think they were debating whether to hold me overnight for further questioning. I heard a muffled phone conversation. Perhaps they were consulting a more senior officer on what steps to take next. They kept me waiting for another hour and night was falling when they said I could go. They cautioned me not to leave the country as they were still reviewing the evidence and it was possible they would need to interview me again.

Chapter 9

It was the first weekend of half-term with ten days of freedom for staff and boys. However, the school still banned me, so I could not benefit from the break. I was getting used to the new regime of sleeping late, with no need to rise early and rush in, with no lessons to prepare, no morning assemblies and, best of all, no rugby in wet and freezing conditions. I felt like the unwelcome lodger impinging on my parents' routine. They would tolerate some idleness, but soon I would annoy them.

'This is not a hotel where you can drift down for breakfast at any hour you choose. You had better sort yourself out with tea and toast. Your father and I are going to the morning service at Saint Mary's.'

'Oh no, is it Sunday again?'

'I presume you won't be joining us at church?' My mother looked at my unshaven face, and shrugging her shoulders, passed me the *Sunday Telegraph*.

'There's nothing much in the papers,' she said. 'Apart from Princess Diana visiting some old folks' home in

Wandsworth and the Nilsen murders. Thank goodness, the murder of your French teacher is no longer news. The press is obsessed with Princess Diana. Why do we need to know that Jaeger made her burgundy velvet suit and someone else made her a hat decorated with ostrich plumes?'

'It must interest you to remember that.'

'And this afternoon will you be joining us for lunch?' she asked. 'It's a good day to go for a long walk in the countryside and get some fresh air. Take your camera and see if you can get more pictures of birds like you used to do every Sunday last year.'

'Yes, it is a nice day, but too early for barn owls, although maybe suitable for photographing raptors. I plan to take it easy today—a visit to the pub to see who is around.'

'I will assume you will be back for lunch unless you call and tell me otherwise.'

My parents headed off for church. Peace at last. I would make myself a strong cup of coffee and read the Sunday paper.

I had put the Triumph's battery on slow charge overnight, and the car started straight away. The half-term on a Sunday and our local pub, the George & Dragon, would be busy. I phoned matron to remind her of our plan to meet up for a drink at midday. She sounded flustered. Before I could say anything, she stopped me.

'Michael, are you phoning from home?'

'Yes, why?'

'As agreed, I will meet you at midday. Goodbye.'

This was most unlike matron. Normally, she would chat for ages. I hoped she would remember to bring me all the files and correspondence that Michelle had been working on. I left early to catch a drink before her arrival.

The smoke-filled bar of the George & Dragon was humming with activity. It still ran on traditional lines with a public bar, popular with the local lads of the village, and the lounge bar for the weekenders and country gentry. I entered the crowded lounge bar full of the London set down for the holiday, forming a human phalanx engulfing the bar in a party atmosphere. An old school friend, Michael Cox, thrust a pint into my hand and introduced me to his friends, the twins, Julie and Lizzie. Both girls wore tight denim jeans with checked shirts and Jaeger sweaters with their long legs encased in knee-length tan leather boots. They had blonde hair down to their shoulders but were uncombed and rough looking. Maybe they had slept late and rushed to the pub without a care in the world. Both smoked in quick puffs without inhaling. Everything they did was in tandem. They had the same laugh and the same friends.

'Hi,' said the nearest twin to me. 'I am Julie, and this is my sister, Lizzie. I don't think we have met before, have we? But you are a friend of Michael, right?'

'Yes, Michael and I went to the same school. My name is Michael Fletcher.'

'Oh, wow. What a hoot, two Michaels. That's *soo* amazing.'

'Michael is an English teacher at St Wilfrid's,' said Michael Cox.

'Lizzie, what is the name of that teacher you know at St Wilfrid's?'

'Nigel Caldwell-Brown. I babysit for him sometimes. They have a lovely baby girl and a puppy.'

'Oh, I am *soo* jealous,' said Julie. 'A baby *and* a puppy.'

I had never met Caldwell-Brown's baby or their puppy.

'Wait a minute,' said Lizzie. 'Wasn't it you in all the papers suspected of murdering a teacher last month?'

'Yes. It was very unfortunate. Just because Michelle was a friend of mine, the police plods think I must be the cold-blooded killer. And the press said some horrible and inaccurate things without a shred of evidence. They make things up to sell more papers! It was a dreadful case, and I am trying to put it behind me. Some parents have taken their children out of school.'

'How stupid of them,' said Julie. 'I mean, it's not as if it's likely to happen again, is it?'

'No, it's nice you are so understanding about it.'

'Typical of our press,' said Michael Cox.

'They finger the wrong chap and don't even have the grace to apologise. If I were you, Michael, I would sue them for libel and get a huge pay-out in compensation. Losing one's good name is a serious matter.'

The girls nodded in agreement and looked at me sympathetically. Just then matron arrived, so I gave my apologies, and we went to a quiet table at the back.

Matron ordered a double gin and tonic because the weather was warmer. Winter was so unpredictable, but once the snowdrops and daffodils were in bloom, you knew spring was on the way and optimism returned.

'Michael, I'm sorry I had to keep it brief on the phone. The fact is, last week Mark—Michelle's brother—drove over to the school to see me. He looked through all her papers and research and said there was nothing new he did not already know. They were working together to shed light on issues that concerned them. He thinks someone murdered her to shut her up and stop the research. According to Mark, we are all at risk.'

'You mean there is some clue in her correspondence who is behind this?'

'You must be extra vigilant. It is likely the police will tap your phone, so only use phone boxes to make calls. He said he is happy for you to read the files. He wants you to visit his laboratory in Southampton, and he will explain everything.'

She fumbled in her purse and found a business card from Dr Mark Carter of the Carter Soil and Rock Testing laboratory based at an address at the Solent Industrial Park, Hedge End, Southampton. She could see the different surname confused me.

'Yes, I know he has a different surname. It's because his parents divorced when he was a teenager. The family lived in Nantes. Father and son moved to the UK where Mark went to university and followed in his father's business, which is the laboratory where he works. Michelle, after graduation, studied at the University of Nantes for a PhD in Chemistry and two years later moved to the UK and ended up teaching French at St Wilfrid's. Michelle's mother and sister, Giselle, still live in Nantes with her grandfather. Very complicated! Mark can explain it all better than me. Read all the files as soon as you can and go and meet Mark.'

I looked forward to a trip to Southampton. The case was intriguing. It confirmed the police had no case against me, but this new revelation from her brother was appalling. Who had killed her? Pursuing her research and leads might expose me to danger as well. But I owed it to Michelle.

'I should see him sooner rather than later. School may reinstate you, so best use your paid leisure time,' said matron as she passed me the bundle of correspondence and research papers. I promised to get them photocopied on Monday. We agreed I should take all the original correspondence with me and pass them onto Mark and keep a copy back for our own reference. Matron downed her second double gin and tonic and left.

I picked up the package and returned to the bar to see my friends. They were too polite to ask about my sudden cloak-and-dagger meeting, although they kept eying the thick package of papers, I kept a tight hold of. Soon time was called, and the bar thinned out, ready to close. I drove back home without enthusiasm for Sunday lunch.

My mother served up a large plate of roast beef with Yorkshire pudding, roast potatoes, and mounds of overcooked carrots and cabbage. Since his retirement, my father was using his generous army pension on buying up expensive wines. He reserved the best ones for Sunday lunch.

'Try this one,' he poured me a taster of a red wine, which had been adjusting to room temperature. 'It's a Château Montrose Saint-Estèphe 1970.'

'Nice.'

Nice! Michael, the wine is a grand cru from a legendary year. 1970 was one of the best vintages in Medoc. And all you can say is nice!'

'I am sure he was just lost for words,' said my mother. 'It is a very fine wine, but not all of us have the palette to appreciate the best quality.'

Nelson rolled over on his back, roasting himself from the burning logs on the fire. He hadn't a care in the world. I had another sip of the wine, and this tasted better. I had a pleasant daydream about Julie and Lizzie. That was a tricky thing with twins. If they were identical, how could you fancy one more than the other?

'Michael, it's the phone for you.' My mother waking me from my dream world.

'He says he is an old school friend, Michael something-or-other.'

I started up in surprise and rushed for the phone in the hall.

'It's Michael, Michael Cox. How's it going?'

'Fine, Michael. It was nice meeting up with you at the pub this morning.'

'Yes, well, you made a good impression on Julie and Lizzie, and they would like you to make up a foursome playing tennis. I seem to remember you were quite a useful player at school.'

'That would be great. But when are you thinking? It's freezing cold outside.'

'No, we play at the indoor court at Ranville's club. We booked for five tonight but one of our players has dropped out. That's not too late for you, is it? I expect you have lessons to prepare for tomorrow?'

'No, we are on half-term, so that's no problem,' I lied. I hadn't revealed the school had suspended me. 'I have never played at Ranville's—it's quite new, isn't it?'

'Great, it's just south of Pulborough on the main road. You can't miss it. I think it is best if you partner Julie. Both the twins are about the same standard—not too flash. It's a bit of fun and gets us all out of the house. There's a club bar for a drink after the game. See you there.'

I was in a daze at this sudden switch of fortune. How was it that my daydreams were becoming reality? But I remembered that Michael Cox was a first-class tennis player with a fast serve and hard-hitting groundstrokes.

It seemed incongruous getting ready to go out and play tennis in winter darkness and with the outside temperature below zero. The Triumph Herald didn't like the idea and refused to start. How annoying. The fallback plan was to use the Morris Minor, but I couldn't face that. What if Julie and Lizzie witnessed my arrival in that ancient car, beloved by midwives and eccentric matrons. My father's car was a solid Rover 175—another old person's car—but better than the Morris Minor.

'Pa, you are not planning to go to the golf club tonight, are you?' I tried as an opening ploy.

In summer, he was a regular at the club. But in February, the club was as welcoming as an out-of-season hotel in Torquay. He looked surprised.

'I hadn't thought of it. Why is there a function on tonight?'

'No, I should think it will be dead quiet—especially on a frosty night like this. It was just that if you aren't using your car, I wondered if I could borrow it.' I bumbled on. 'I have a tennis match—a foursome. And the Triumph has a flat battery again.' My father did not look pleased.

'What's wrong with the Morris Minor? Why can't you use that?'

'It's illegal. It hasn't got seatbelts fitted. Driving at night, I am more likely to be stopped by the police.'

'You are not insured to drive my Rover. What happens if you crash it?'

'I'm a very careful driver. If anything happened, I would pay for the damage.'

'Oh yes, I have heard that before. No doubt you will be drinking and driving?'

'No, it's just a tennis game with some friends—Julie and Lizzie—they are identical twins. I can't let them down. They depend on me.' He thought about this.

'Tennis in winter is mad. Where are you playing?'

'Ranville's club near Pulborough. Of course, it has indoor courts.'

'Well, that's different. Why didn't you say? Here,' he reached into his pocket and threw me his car keys. 'It might need some petrol.'

After the game, we sat at the club bar.

'I thought you played very well,' Julie consoled me after a three-set defeat to an ebullient pairing of Michael Cox and Lizzie. We were alone, as the victors, after a quick drink, had left on some pretext. Splitting the twins, like splitting the atom, had thrown me into unfamiliar territory and the ready repartee of the foursome was now flat and more restrained with just one of them to talk to. Her long legs wrapped around the bar stool as she puffed on a cigarette alternating with sips of a coke and lime juice distracted me. She shifted them restlessly, as if aware of the potent spell they cast. We had come straight to the bar in our tennis clothes, which was not the 'done' thing, but some sweaty squash players were also propping up the bar. They were on friendly terms with the staff, so they tolerated our dress violations. Besides, the bar was thin on customers on this chilly night.

We discussed our cars. Julie had a red Triumph TR6— a powerful six-cylinder model capable of reaching 60 miles per hour in just 8.2 seconds. This was impressive.

'It's short of space for passengers,' she gushed. 'I mean, it's not the sort of car to go shopping or take the family in. You have a more respectable Triumph Herald, I hear.'

'Yes, I bought it off Nigel Caldwell-Brown. It's quite old but I like it. It takes about half a minute to reach 60 m.p.h and top speed is 70 m.p.h. Tonight, it refused to start, so I had to borrow my father's car.'

'Oh, how funny. And what does he drive?'

I looked mortified to admit our family possessed such ancient cars.

'A Rover. I think it's a Rover 175 from the mid-1970s. Pa has old-fashioned taste and is too mean to buy a new car.'

A pitying smile, before she over-ruled it.

'Can you show me?'

'Well, it's a very dull car with a doggy smell, but if you want to, I can.'

'Lizzie took my car, so I am carless. Can you take me home, please?' she smiled and the little girl in distress voice had the desired effect.

'Oh, that's no problem. Just show me the way.'

'Michael, I'll just get a quick shower and meet you back here in a jiffy,' she left the bar, her long legs striding purposely and her short tennis skirt flapping provocatively. Every male eye in the room followed her progress, and the conversation ceased.

Julie lived close to Burpham.

'I don't know anyone this side of the village. It's only a small hamlet. There are no shops, so no reason to come here.'

'Maybe when you were small you went trick-or-treating or had a paper run or dropped in leaflets for a lost cat or something?' I guessed.

She laughed. 'I wouldn't waste time in Burpham doing anything like that. Take the next turn on the left outside the village. It's a sharp turn.'

We drove up a long drive towards her parents' house, the house where Julie spent her weekends to escape from

London. It was a large Georgian pile with outhouses and racing stables surrounding formal lawns, which extended to distant meadows and farmland. The family was well off. She ordered me to pull into the side and turn the headlights off. Leaning over smiling, her face looked up at me and we kissed, nervously at first, but with growing intensity.

'I can walk from here.' she gave me a parting peck on the cheek and gathered up her tennis kit. 'Thanks for the game. It was fun.' Then she was gone.

Chapter 10

I was enjoying the freedom of the south coast road as I drove the Triumph Herald past the Portsdown Hills, north of Portsmouth, and headed along the M27 towards Southampton. The new motorway was open apart from roadworks at some junctions. The road surface was very odd. Maybe they had run out of money, but it was a concrete track which produced an annoying whining and vibration through the tyres and the separate blocks had expansion gaps which gave a rough ride, as if my tyres had gone flat. As instructed by Mark, I left at junction seven and in less than an hour, door-to-door, arrived outside his workshop at the Solent Industrial Estate at Shamblehurst Lane.

Mark Carter's business premises were a two-storey mid-terrace industrial unit housing the laboratories on the ground floor and office space above. It was a typical trading estate but softened by nearby houses and tree-lined streets with several shops, a supermarket, and a school nearby to establish a vibrant community. He greeted me with a warm handshake, apologising that the reception desk was unmanned as Paula, who he called his front-of-house, was off sick with measles. A tall man—at least six and a half feet, with thick, wavy dark hair and a lean frame. There was a similarity to his sister with his dark hair, firm set of his mouth and steady gaze. When Michelle listened to my idle chatter, she was always attentive and amused. I sensed Mark was the same.

'In fact, we get very few callers either in person or by phone. We don't really need a receptionist, but she doubles up as a laboratory technician because we are short of people. Everyone has to learn new skills here.'

Mark showed me around the lab, which was a conventional soil and rock testing facility but specialising in marine sediment samples collected by survey contractors working on North Sea oil and gas projects. His staff were young and smartly dressed in white laboratory coats. He employed inexperienced personnel from the local technical college or youngsters on apprenticeship schemes. For me, it was opening a door on a new world. I was impatient to get down to the purpose of our meeting. Mark led me through to an empty room, which he called the hydrographic lab.

'In here we run a chemical analysis on water samples using a chromatography method which we have developed. Our focus is in on detecting BPA—Bisphenol A, which is common in plastic water bottles but also occurs on the inside lining of cans.'

Mark explained his major concern was with BPA used in the manufacture of polycarbonate—the clear plastic used for water bottles.

'Toxins can leach from the plastic water bottles into your drinking water. Our mission here is to conduct the research to proof this and move industry to a rethink on their plastic usage and a ban on proven toxins such as BPA.'

'An ambitious agenda,' I said. 'I know Michelle was against using plastic containers and bottles, but I thought that was because of the pollution to the environment and harming marine life from ingesting plastic.'

'Of course, that is the most obvious aspect, but the chemical leaching factor is a more subtle and invasive form of an attack on the body. This BPA is a synthetic substance that can disrupt the hormonal balance, especially in children and young adults. BPA and many other chemicals found in ordinary water may even cause cancers to develop. It's a nightmare scenario, and no one wants to believe it,' said Mark.

'First, my commiserations about the loss of your friend and my sister. I know she was very fond of you. It's unjust how the police have tried to pin the killing on you with no evidence. That is why I wanted to see you in person to explain what Michelle and I were doing with our research. I realise we have upset certain parties who dispute the results of our studies. We are challenging vested interests and the status quo. These people would prefer the public stay in ignorance. Previous researchers in the US have had their evidence for BPA and other toxins in water discounted as minor and unlikely to cause any harm in the minute traces detected. I want to ask if she talked about her research with you.'

'No, I can't recall her ever talking about it. I expect she thought I might not be a sympathetic listener.'

'I can understand she might not want to involve you. Being a whistleblower and lifting the lid on the reality behind the plastic bottling industry is likely to upset many people. It's a billion-pound industry worldwide, which is slowly poisoning generations. She was writing to the media and concerned individuals to alert them of the dangers. Beating her head against a brick wall as there are too many people bent on reassuring the public that there is no appreciable risk.'

'From what you say, you were a team working together on this issue.'

'Yes, Michael. We phoned each other every week, and I sent her copies of the research results. Her task was publicity. To educate the public on the dangers. There were confidentiality issues, so we couldn't be too specific on the detail. It was a long-term project, and we built up a network with cooperation from researchers in UK universities and even hospitals.'

He led me upstairs to his office. The room was light and airy, with a pair of windows looking out onto the busy car parking area at the front of the office. Several large pot plants with variegated leaves softened the harsh lines spreading out towards the windows.

'Sorry, I was full on back there. It puts people off if you are too dogmatic.'

He motioned me to a comfortable sofa and poured me a glass of Hildon water—a natural spring water from Hampshire.

'This is a pure product straight from an underground chalk aquifer and they bottle it in glass bottles.'

He watched me as I sipped it.

'Very good. I drink little neat water. I prefer to get my liquids from beer and wine.'

'For excellent beer, you need good water. The same goes for all drinks. Look at whisky, for example. Half the mystic over a malt whisky is the peat infused water, perhaps with added flavour from a dead sheep in the river.' Suddenly, he switched the subject.

'How was your trip?'

'The traffic was light; it took me an hour.'

'The motorway has made a tremendous difference. I live in Swanwick in an old cottage, which is just a short commute, and I use the back roads and avoid the M27. If I must travel to Southampton, I join the M27 at junction seven. Don't join the motorway at junction six. That's a local joke because they never built it. Junctions five and seven yes, but they abandoned junction six. Funny thing is, when they looked at the plans, they could see if they *did* add junction six, all the junctions from five to seven would be too close together. Apparently, there is some separation ruling that you must adhere to.'

'So, as they had already built junctions five and seven, they had to cancel junction six?'

'Exactly. There are many examples of skipped or cancelled junctions on other motorways, such as the M1 and the M4. The motorway building programme in the early days was chaotic.'

The strange conversation had run its course to be replaced by an awkward silence. Mark looked at his watch.

'There's a good pub I know called the Jolly Sailor, so let's get a beer and some lunch. Leave your car here and I can drive. It's a lovely spot next to the Hamble River.'

Mark's car was a white Peugeot 305 estate, which he had bought new in 1981. It was the ideal car with plenty of space for transporting samples and equipment. Mark drove a leisurely route along the country roads, passing the Fox and Hounds in Hungerford Bottom, then the Vine Inn via a narrow-wooded lane before descending by the Land's End Road to Old Bursledon. We stopped close to the pub sign on the hill. The pub was beside the river, and we descended via steep stone steps to enter the old, flagged bar with low set timber beams. A stunning view stretched out over the placid River Hamble crowded with eager yachts heading out to the Solent, jostling for space with tired yachts returning to their berths in the marinas. Inside the Jolly Sailor, a warm glow hit us from the wood burner, radiating its heat through the packed crowd. The yachting fraternity defied the winter chill with sporty tops and shorts exposing their pink bare legs. Many nautical artefacts such as models of boats and coiled ropes reinforced the boating theme. It felt like being on a wooden boat moored beside the jetty, waiting for a fair wind. The high tide was lapping up to the pub and the pontoon supporting the restaurant extension over the calm waters was already full up with customers.

'There is a spare table on the terrace,' remarked Mark, giving an involuntary shiver, 'But we might be best getting a bar snack inside. A pint of bitter and a ploughman's lunch, okay for you?'

We settled down at a table away from other diners, so I felt secure in opening a discussion about Michelle. Two enormous platters arrived heaped with local cheddar, chunks of homemade bread, local butter, and chutney, so we paused to concentrate on the delicious food.

'This business has been a nightmare. As I was one of the last people to see Michelle, the police think I killed her! I am sure you have read the press articles with their vile and inaccurate insinuations. We *were* good friends because we saw each other every day at school. Recently, we had developed more of a romantic attachment. But I am shocked and appalled at this crime. My school has asked me to take leave while the police continue their enquiries. Fortunately, all the staff, apart from the headmaster and the school secretary, is right behind me. From what you say, there is a motive for someone wanting to silence her. I can offer you any help I can. I have read all her correspondence, so maybe I can follow up on some of her contacts with the press and other bodies for you?'

'Michael, that is the sort of help I need. You see how busy we are in the laboratory?' he fumbled in his pocket and extracted a folded sheet of A4 paper.

'Here, this may help you. It is a contacts list of all the people she wrote to and there is a reference back to the specific letter she wrote. Interestingly, she contacted many societies and pressure groups. For example, she wrote to the Friends of the Earth about plastic pollution of the oceans and there was a campaigner there she was friendly with. Who else, let's see—WaterAid? But they are more about providing clean water to those who have none, so their concerns are greater than ours, and I don't think Michelle made any headway with them.'

'Do you have any suspects yourself?' I asked.

Mark looked uneasy. He lowered his voice.

'There is an odd connection. Two years ago, a scientist visited me at the laboratory. He was from a major oil company active in the North Sea, which I am not at liberty to divulge. We had an order for some core sample testing from a drilling operation. This man started asking about plastic bottles. In the US, studies show leaching of chemicals like BPA and phthalates out of plastic and into the water. He wanted to know if we could test for these chemicals. I said, sure, if we had the right chromatography equipment. He asked me to look into the cost of buying the equipment that could do the job and put a proposal together for the purchase and testing of samples he would pass to me.'

'How strange. You'd think an oil company could do their own testing. Unless it was something they wanted done undercover.'

'That is what I thought!'

'Well, I submitted my proposal, including the cost of installation of one of the best and most expensive models I could find, plus a sample testing rate when everything was up and running. Moreover, within a week, the oil company approves the plan, sends me a Purchase Order, *and* sends an advance payment to get the ball rolling. I had to guarantee the water analysis work was for their sole use and I could not conduct tests for other clients for the first year. After that, I was free to do what I liked.'

'Brilliant. A happy story.'

'Indeed, everything went well at first. They sent batches of drinking water in their original plastic bottles every month, and I tested them. These were well-known brands available in the supermarkets. The results were always quite consistent with low levels of BPA. Then a curious batch was delivered with unusual chemistry. It showed elevated levels of BPA, many toxins and chemicals which you would not expect, such as DEET.'

'What is DEET?'

'Diethyltoluamide—a mosquito repellent.'

'What did you do?'

'I submitted my reports as usual. I pointed out the result on one sample was unusual because of possible contamination. There was no label on this bottle, so we called it Brand X. The oil company scientist said nothing, and the company stopped sending samples for testing for the next three months. All very odd. When testing resumed, the results were all back to normal levels of leaching.'

'Why should an oil company be so interested in plastic bottles?' I asked.

'That's easy,' said Mark. 'To manufacture a one litre water bottle needs a quarter of a litre of oil. Just to service the U.S market with enough plastic bottles this year will need about three million barrels of oil. But production growth is exponential. Since plastic water bottles first became established in the 1970s, there has been a five-fold increase. Imagine the situation in 40 years' time in 2023? It's a massive problem worldwide!'

Chapter 11

An air of depression hung over the school. Outside, icicles draped the rainwater pipes. Inside, radiators groaned as lukewarm water slowed to a trickle. A week before, the weather had been mild—a false dawn promising the end of winter, or a pause in its attack like the rasp of coarse sandpaper across wood grain stops before resuming its jagged thrust.

'How was your half-term, headmaster?' asked Mona, as she handed him his morning cup of tea.

'You forget life goes on even though the boys are away. The catering staff, the groundsmen, the bursar and my secretary all clear off so my wife and I have to survive alone.'

'Well, I offered to stay on. But you said you could manage.'

'Indeed, I did. I went to the Three Horseshoes one night, but since this incident involving Fletcher, the atmosphere at the pub is quite frosty. They did *not* make me feel welcome, and the food was dull and tasteless.'

'I think the pub is over-rated,' said Mona. 'The teachers only go there because it's so close to school. The Royal Albion is a much better option.'

The headmaster admitted he wasn't the pub frequenting type, but if the Royal Albion offered better food than the average pub staples, he would love to visit it one lunchtime and perhaps Mona would like to accompany him. He confided that during the half-term holiday he loved to take long walks around the deserted pathways in the woods.

'A certain peace descends on the school when you are alone with only the trees and birds for company. My wife doesn't like the quiet. It unnerves her, so after two days she left to stay with her mother in Surrey. Since then, I have been on my own with the two cats. However, I do my best thinking when I am alone and have no interruptions.'

'You are so right, headmaster. Walking, especially in the winter cold and wet, is so rewarding and good both physically and mentally.'

'We agree on that. And one thought that hit me is that discipline is far too lax at this school.'

'Oh, you are so right!' It fascinated Mona that both had such similar views and could identify the problems.

'You look around and our boys are badly dressed—some indeed cannot tie their ties or even their shoelaces and they never clean their shoes. They cannot make their beds, are late for classes, lark around in class, and are rude to their teachers. Why do you think this is Mona?'

'Poor example?' she said. The headmaster motioned with his hands that she should expand her theme.

'Selfish behaviour—only thinking of themselves.'

'Indeed, that's part of it.'

'Disrespect!' she had found the key word. The headmaster smiled.

'Exactly, Mona. Disrespect and all those other aspects of poor character you mentioned. And what is the key to dealing with the problem, I wonder?'

'Discipline,' she said. 'Strict discipline.'

'Of course, you are right! And why do we have this problem? This is not a popular view, but I blame the parents! If the family cannot set a good example and bring up their children properly, then we already have damaged goods when the boys arrive here! And our teachers make the problem worse by not enforcing discipline, because *they too* are also the products of bad parenting. They cannot get their act together. The problem is self-perpetuating. Look at Fletcher, for example. Since I agreed to reinstate him after half-term, I noticed that on his first day back, he has all the faults we are trying to eradicate. Even before the unfortunate incident with Miss Gagneux, he was late in the mornings and used to dress scruffily as if he had just thrown on yesterday's clothes. And this morning, after bowing to pressure from the staff and the governors, I allow him back and he thanks me by turning up to school wearing jeans and some sort of military looking jacket! His classes have no structure, and he encourages the boys to chat about any subject they care. As for religion, he tells the boys to question everything. Is it any wonder they lack discipline with such a role model?'

'I think you are exaggerating a bit, headmaster. Don't forget he had an awful time being made a suspect in the murder of Michelle and the papers printing such lies about him. And we cannot blame Major Fletcher for the faults of his son!'

'Hmm,' said the headmaster. 'He is not as innocent as he pretends to be. If you throw enough mud, some of it sticks. This DI Preston from Brighton had a quiet word with me and revealed they did not have enough evidence to take the case any further. Two of the requisites were in place: Fletcher was at the scene, and he had a motive as the poor woman was pregnant, a responsibility he could not accept. Nevertheless, without a witness or material evidence, the police cannot proceed. We need to keep a careful eye on that young man.' The headmaster waited for some response from Mona, but she stayed silent.

'Have you reached a decision on the agency teacher who replaced Mr Fletcher? He is still teaching, and we can't afford to pay for two English teachers.'

'Good point, Mona. Thanks for reminding me. That man was a disaster at first with his drinking problem, but since I had a firm talk with him, he has improved, and he assures me he is a reformed character and put his problems behind him. And he is quite popular with the boys.'

Mona was not pleased. At least he was only teaching the Remove class, made up of the densest, most backward pupils, so he couldn't do too much harm. She knew it was only a matter of time before he reverted to his habitual drunken stupor.

'Anyway, back to my ideas on discipline: We will call a staff meeting next week to ensure all staff report cases requiring discipline to me and I can deal with the offenders the same day. Day pupils will report to me at five, before they go home whereas I will deal with boarders after dinner.'

'By deal with you mean...'

'It will depend on the offence, Mona. The usual range of punishments such as writing out lines for minor stuff, detentions, loss of privileges and an instant caning for everything else.'

'So, no change—just as we are doing, anyway?'

'Yes, but more of the same and to emphasise this new regime, I have prepared a list of offences we will crack down on.' The headmaster handed Mona an A4 sheet of paper for her to study. 'See what you think?'

'Hmm. No student, apart from sixth form students, may lounge about with hands in his pockets.'

'I thought that was a good one to smarten them up.'

'We do not permit any student to walk on the grass in the quadrangle—of course so logical, headmaster to stop the grass being damaged by muddy shoes.'

'Quite right. They walk across to look at the fish in the pond and ruin my lawn.'

'We will not tolerate boarders talking in their dormitories after lights out. I think that is difficult to enforce, headmaster, unless a prefect witnesses it.'

'No problem, Mona. I will instruct the prefects to catch offenders and bring them to me.'

'All pupils will be on time for classes, sports, and morning assembly. Tardiness is a serious offence.' Mona saw the list extended to twelve items. To avoid reading the complete list, she reassured the headmaster they looked fine and would improve standards.

'It is a splendid plan, headmaster.'

'I'm glad you approve. I am sure it will work.'

'Your wife will be proud of you when she comes back from Surrey.'

'As you know, Mona, she can be a difficult woman—never satisfied. She would prefer a modern comprehensive school in a large town—somewhere near the shops or close to London. She thinks I am wasting my time in such a traditional school out in the sticks.'

'It's no fun dining at the pub all alone,' she remarked. 'You should have called me for company.'

'Mona, how nice of you to think of me. You are my rock. I would be adrift at sea without an oar if you were not at my side to navigate a safe passage through the stormy seas.'

Mona blushed with embarrassment. Such a poetic turn of phrase! During their conversation, Mona had moved next to the headmaster and was sitting at his desk with her legs crossed. Very fine legs, thought the headmaster, showed to best effect in sheer tan tights. She wafted the list of discipline offences in the air, forcing the headmaster to slide his chair closer to retrieve the list. By chance, his legs touched hers during the retrieval of the list.

A loud knock at the door startled them.

'Sorry to disturb you,' the door swung open and matron marched in. 'I have three cases of lice infestation. Lee Minor, Lee Major and Cuthbert.'

This appalled the headmaster. Hair lice could jump from head-to-head in no time and soon the entire school would harbour the nits. 'What do you recommend, matron?'

'We must do a hair check of all the boys using fine combs. If I detect hair lice, then I can apply a dimethicone spray to kill them. Molly from the kitchen has volunteered to help me.' Matron's orders were explicit.

'That sounds a good plan, matron. When do you want to start?'

'We must cancel games this afternoon and deal with it. Let us do it class by class, using the gym as the treatment centre, starting with the youngest. Once a class is lice free, they must be isolated in their classroom until the entire school is clear; otherwise, the chain of lice infestation may recur.'

There was another knock at the door. It was the sports master, Mr Higgins. The headmaster found Higgins to be pushy, aggressive, and unpleasant. To be effective at sports training, it was beneficial to bully the boys to train harder, and he was performance driven and ruthless in pursuit of victory.

'Is it true, headmaster, that you have cancelled all games today?' he fired off angrily, his eyes staring out like the stalk eyes of a prawn.

'We were just discussing it,' said the head. 'Some children have hair lice, and the priority is to eradicate them. The lice, not the boys,' he attempted a feeble joke, which they ignored. 'The games period this afternoon is the best chance to do this.'

'With due respect, headmaster, the school has the inter-house rugby matches coming up in under two weeks' time and we need all the practice we can get. After half-term, the boys always come back lazy and over-fed and it takes time to get them fit again. Surely, we could do this treatment now. If we wait until this afternoon, the lice will have jumped from the boys to the staff.'

The headmaster looked doubtful and scratched his head. All this talk of lice infiltrating the school was unsettling.

'Matron, Mr Higgins has a point. Wouldn't it be better to get started on the treatment as soon as possible?' The contemptible Higgins was challenging her authority.

'Have it your own way. It's less efficient going around the classrooms and it may delay lunchtime. I doubt if practice will make a blind bit of difference to the Under 13s who have yet to win a game. Besides, with the heating on the blink, no one will get a hot shower after sports.'

'I think Mr Higgins will agree with me that cold showers are character-building and economical as the boys will not waste water.'

'True enough, headmaster,' said Higgins, with a self-satisfied grin. Matron stormed off like an angry hen and Higgins left the study.

'Discipline and obedience—these are the values we uphold. Soon the lefties will ban corporal punishment in schools, and we will be powerless to enforce discipline. I can foresee a bleak time, in the future, when classes will be out of control. Teachers will live in fear of assault from their students. Their parents will have no power over them, either. A "Brave New World" of undisciplined bedlam,' forecast the head.

'Hopefully, long after we retire,' said Mona. 'Would you like another cup of tea, headmaster? First, I must see if the post has arrived. No doubt that will bring more problems to deal with.' The headmaster sighed.

'It's nice to be understood by *someone*. I sometimes feel isolated. Like the last of the dinosaurs defying the odds as new smaller species such as rats take over the world.' Mona understood what he meant.

Despite being forewarned by matron, it was a surprise when I received a letter from the school governors informing me I was free to return to school after half-term. There was no apology, just some phrase about how the school was required to run a due diligence check considering the ongoing enquiries by the police about the recent tragic death of a staff member. The situation was still unsatisfactory. The school governors had not cleared my name. However, I would not let matters rest. I planned to visit the village of Graffham and find the pub with the celebrated darts team. They posted a fixtures list for all to see, and I would be very interested in witnessing the next fixture between Graffham and the Three Horseshoes. Next, I needed time to assimilate all of Michelle's files to understand what she had got involved in. Meeting Mark at his laboratory had left me puzzled. It seemed a giant step to believe their enquiries into the plastic water bottling industry could have led to her killing. Far more likely, it was some pervert lurking in the woods. The key for me was still to locate the man I saw talking to Michelle in the pub.

On top of this, I was aware of a growing infatuation with Julie. I knew the symptoms, which were both welcome and unwelcome. Only once before had I experienced deep feelings for someone and knew it could be shattering if the feelings were not mutual or, fate, in its many guises, intervened to end it all.

With identical twins, it was a challenge to tell them apart. I only had Julie's word that she was Julie and not Lizzie. For a joke, they could pretend to be each other and then gather two views of any potential boyfriend. Julie had hinted that there *were* ways to tell them apart—some physical difference she did not want to share with me.

Had the kiss after tennis meant anything, or was it just a polite thank-you, a parting gesture to say great game but no need to see each other again? Was she attracted to me or not? The silence over the last week was disconcerting. On the other hand, was she waiting for me to call her? I had looked in at the George & Dragon at the weekend in case the girls were down from London, but there was no sign of Julie, Lizzie, or Michael. It was as if they had never existed.

Chapter 12

Three weeks had passed since I met Julie and three weeks of silence. The weekend loomed, and I was tempted to visit her parents' house and try the bold approach.

At school, there were other distractions. The school was busy presenting its best face, as the HMI School inspectors had been busy intruding into every class. This was not a short one-day visit but an in-depth scrutiny and the inspectors were keen to talk to the boys who did not hold back on graphic accounts of the severe discipline regime of the headmaster, awful food and too much religion. I just hoped they appreciated my efforts at teaching. Jones explained these inspections were always a whitewash affair, and it made no difference how bad the school was as the inspectors always sided with the school. Any criticisms or suggestions for improvement were minor.

Before that, my afternoon was about to get worse. Higgins had finished his lunch and was coming over for a talk.

'Michael, we need you to referee some of the inter-house rugby matches this afternoon. All four houses will kick off at two, so you can take the matches on the main pitch, and I will referee those at Newton field.'

'Which game do you want me to referee?'

'Moore and Fisher, and I will cover Campion and Howard. The winners will play off for the final and the losers for the final places. You can take the losers.'

'And, Michael, I know you are always keen to get away early, but it will be half an hour each half, and a fifteen-minute break, so you won't leave school till after five. Stay for supper, I would like a few minutes to review the teams' performance.'

'There's no hurry. I must do something at school tonight so I can give the rugby my full attention. Moore house should do well this year.'

Despite myself, I was looking forward to the matches, which pitched all age groups together to make up the best team for the houses. I favoured Moore house but any house other than Fisher where Higgins was the housemaster would be an excellent result. He walked off with a dismissive shake of his shoulders as if I was someone to be tolerated but compared to him was just a rank amateur.

Early March, and there was a sense of spring in the air. It was a perfect day for the annual house matches with the playing fields bathed in a blue sky as the players ran onto the pitch larking about, throwing the rugby ball erratically until someone marshalled them together for practice runs, passing the ball. I could imagine this timeless scene unfolding many years earlier with other schoolboys in long baggy shorts and a heavier rugby ball going through identical rituals before their service in the First World War ended at the Battle of the Somme.

Fast forward to May 1940 when a new generation, running on these same playing fields, would retreat, under fire, from Dunkirk. Perhaps these boys in 1983 would die in some other conflict, yet to come, as war seemed a never-ending constant. Or present conflicts, such as 'The Troubles' in Northern Ireland, might drag on for many more years still claiming victims. The cycles of the past turned and turned and here was new fodder for slaughter, more deluded minds following in father's footsteps, more parents setting in course the paths of repetition, more teachers like me to mould conformity and obedience.

The first match was very close, but Fisher ran out eventual winners in a tight, low-scoring game. Most of the boarders in my class were in Moore house. During the break at the end of the first game, Higgins came gushing over, full of himself, as usual.

'Excellent result, Michael—Fisher versus Campion in the final and I fancy Fisher will run out winners.'

'It was a close game, but I would say the best team won on the day.'

'A sporting loser—here comes Howard for the runners-up playoff. They might be too strong for your Moore house.'

During the next game, Howard tackled like a team possessed. They had a tall boy from Nigeria called William Obote, who looked about 18. Every time they threw him the ball, he barrelled through, scattering any boy who tried to tackle him. He was unstoppable, and the score racked up in favour of Howard. How they had lost their previous game with this ogre on the team, I wondered. Moore house was outclassed and in awe of the Nigerian, apart from Charlie from Hong Kong, who took on the role of marking the giant. With an astute and well-timed tackle, he flattened William and stopped a certain try. This made William angry. Shortly after, the studs of his rugby boot cut a neat scar across Charlie's cheek as he lay prone on the ground from a push off. It looked deliberate, but there was no time for recriminations. I stopped the game, and we took Charlie off.

Jones looked at the wound.

'He will need some stitches, Michael. If you run him over to the hospital in town, I can referee the rest of the game. I would do it myself, but the wife has taken my car to go shopping.'

'Of course, no problem.'

I bandaged the wound, but it was obvious this would not stop the flow of blood. No sign of matron when we needed her. She was probably at the bookies in town putting a bet on the horses; her habitual pastime whenever she could get away.

The A & E department at the hospital was twelve miles away. Caldwell-Brown said he would ring Charlie's mother and tell her what had happened. No need to delay, I drove as fast as the law allowed, plus faster.

'Does it hurt?' I asked Charlie.

'No, not much. It looks worse than it is.'

'I think it will need some stitches, but it should heal without leaving a mark.'

At the hospital, the nurse stitched up Charlie and prescribed antibiotics in case of infection. We were just waiting for his prescription when Laureline, arrived, breathless.

'Mr Fletcher, how kind of you to bring Charlie to the hospital. Caldwell-Brown told me you were the referee in the game, and you saw the whole thing. What happened?'

'It was nothing mother—just one of those things,' said Charlie 'This guy's boot studs caught my cheek. I fell in his way, and he could not avoid me. He is a giant and was winning the game for Howard single-handed. I don't mind about the injury. It's more upsetting that we will lose the game.'

'It was a very brave tackle you made on him,' I said. 'I think Moore house would have won but, as you say, Obote made all the difference.'

'It's a terrible, rough game. It may scar you for life,' said Laureline.

'The nurse thinks it will heal but maybe leave a thin scar, like a duelling scar.'

The nurse arrived with the prescription and after a brief chat with Laureline; we were free to leave.

'Mr Fletcher. Sorry, it's better if I call you Michael. Michael, the school is breaking up for the Easter holidays on 26th March and they don't have to go back until mid-April so I was wondering if you could manage a few hours tuition for Charlie during the holidays to help him catch up. Please?'

I certainly could use the money. Two hours a week would not be a significant burden.

'What day and time would suit you best?' I asked.

'Charlie, what do you think?'

'Not weekends. Maybe Monday or Tuesday mornings would be good?'

'That would be ideal for me. I don't have your address. Do you live far away?'

'Write your home phone number and I will confirm later. Monday will be the best. We live just outside Burpham.'

'Burpham.'

'Why does that surprise you? It's a quiet little hamlet.'

Leaving Charlie in expert hands, I felt tempted to skive off home early, but I headed back to school to update Jones. I found him with matron pacing outside the locker room.

'I'm so sorry I was called away,' said matron. 'How is the lad?'

'Fine, they stitched him up, and he's in good spirits.'

'His poor mother must be beside herself. What a stupid accident!'

Jones and I exchanged a glance. Both of us suspected it was a deliberate act. Best to say nothing, of course.

'Yes, she's a bit upset,' I conceded. 'But Charlie refuses to blame Obote.'

Matron looked relieved. Jones had given her a full account of the accident and it was best to downplay it. She admitted she could have stitched the boy herself, but it was better for the hospital to take care of him. Her stitching skills were rusty. She would close out the report and update the headmaster that it was an unavoidable accident. In her opinion, rugby was too dangerous for young school children to play. Especially this scrum business where everyone pushed, shoved, and then collapsed in a heap. The chances of a serious injury to the back or neck were huge. And then the idea of running full tilt and have someone tip you over onto the hard ground with embedded flints. It was madness. It was a waste of time talking to Higgins, but she had raised her concerns with the headmaster. Serious concerns. He fobbed her off on how it was an outlet for their natural aggression. A traditional English sport great for character building. What a load of rubbish.

'Higgins was cross you didn't stay until the end of the match,' said Jones. 'Fisher won, by the way. So that was a lucky escape for you. Matron and I have some interesting news. Tonight, we plan to visit the Royal Albion—our new venue for drinks.'

I looked confused. 'Why change the day from Saturday? That's our normal day for our end of week socials?'

'True enough,' said Jones. 'You see matron has discovered that the Royal Albion darts team is playing a home match against the Graffham Royal Oak darts team tonight at seven. For obvious reasons, we thought we should see the match. Also, we think a young man like you should use his Saturday nights more profitably. Matron tells me that the George & Dragon has some attractions.'

Was I so transparent? I frowned at Jones and matron but they both started laughing.

The short young man with a thin moustache had just landed three darts in the triple twenty.

'One hundred and eighty,' an annoying voice boomed out.

A slight smile cut across his thin lips, but he ignored the applause and stood aside to let the Royal Albion's star player take his turn. Matron leant across the smoke engulfed table in the small bar.

'Graffham are about to win. We need to catch that young man before he leaves. Jones, you know all about darts. Congratulate him and offer him a drink and say there's someone wants to meet him.'

'Just like that, matron. The heads on approach. It's not subtle.'

I noticed the darts champion was heading for the bar and followed. If I chose my moment, it should work. For my opening gambit, I told him he played like a professional.

'Not really,' he said. 'There were just worse than me. Mind you, I enjoyed the attempt at distraction Albion put on.'

He was referring to the first pairing—an attractive teenager in tight jeans who represented Royal Albion in a pairing with 'Big Jock McFee' from Graffham. A twenty stone player who had a keen aim and a concentration so total that a bomb could have exploded, and he would carry on as normal. Annie, as the girl was called, sprayed her darts all around the room and insisted on bending over to retrieve the loose darts from the floor, which, with the tightness of her jeans, was difficult to achieve. Her technique was to adopt a provocative wriggle before each dart retrieval, followed by a hearty giggle as her elegant fingers closed around the shaft of the dart. This gamesmanship put big Jock off, and those triples and doubles became elusive. But it was the first act in the ploy. Annie, who was a good darts player and junior champion, tightened up her game and went onto win her match. Graffham got their revenge later and Annie was Albion's only winner.

'I should introduce myself. The name's Michael Fletcher.' The man with the rat-like features looked surprised, so I rushed on.

'We've never met, but I believe you saw my friend, Michelle, our French school teacher at the Three Horseshoes back on 15th January.'

He turned pale and made to get up from the bar stool.

'I just want a quick chat. At first, the police tried to pin her killing onto me, but we now suspect someone else was involved. We know you got talking with Michelle, so anything you can tell me is useful.'

'The police have already been on it. They called me by satellite phone to the oil rig, which didn't go down well with my boss. Then this young policewoman called Tracey came to see me at my home, which annoyed the wife. I told them everything I knew.'

'Let me get you a drink and meet my friends,' I pointed over to the table where Jones and matron sat. 'Just five minutes.' I caught the barmaid's attention. 'One double gin and tonic, two malt whiskies with ice—the Glenfiddich will do. And Ron, what about you, a whisky?'

'No thanks. It's the one drink I can't stand. A double vodka and lime on the rocks if you please.'

I led him to our table and made the introductions. Having the same surname as our Latin teacher made Ron relax. He explained how he had noticed the lady talking to a French bloke.

'He was a tough-looking man, broad-chested with wavy hair like Gerard Depardieu. In his thirties with piercing blue eyes. Looked like a rugby player. From what I could tell, they were talking normally, but in French, so it was difficult to follow. Besides, I was busy playing darts. Then she raised her voice and seemed angry. He got up, pushing the chair aside with a squeak, and left the pub. The lady looked upset, so I ambled across and said something like "Cheer up. It can't be that bad. How about a drink?" I put on the charm a bit and said *"peut-être que vous aimez un dubonnet."* She was surprised I could speak the lingo. Laughing, she refused, as you do to a total stranger, but finally she agreed to a glass of red wine.'

'The house wine at the pub is very good,' I said. 'The landlord buys it duty free on his trips to Dieppe. Michelle always drank the same red wine—a red wine from Chinon, which they kept for her.'

'You're right. It was a red wine. That's about it. We got chatting. She said she knew this man from the past, but he was not welcome. Fortunately, he got the message and left.

She was happy now and could relax. Anyhow, I quite fancied her and tried it on, but she wasn't interested. "Don't talk to me about love," she said. "A man I used to love in London doesn't love me. And another man loves me, but he is too immature to know it." She laughed a sad laugh, finished her drink, and said au revoir. That was the last I saw of her.'

Chapter 13

After the revelations from Ron Jones at the darts match, I knew I had to call Mark. A Saturday morning, but I was sure he would be in his laboratory working away. In fact, the phone rang for ages without a connection. I rang back. This time, Mark answered at once.

'Yes. Who is it?'

'Sorry to disturb you. It's Michael.'

'Michael, I'm sorry. I assumed it was a wrong number. We have been getting a lot. Double glazing sales reps and other charlatans. On Saturday, it is usually phone-free and a good day to catch up, undisturbed.'

'There's been a development. Yesterday some friends and I tracked down the darts player who talked to Michelle on the night she was in the pub. His name is...'

'Michael. Are you ringing from your home?' From my guilty silence, he assumed I was.

'I warned you not to. You may think no one is listening in, but they may be. Call me over-cautious but the police or the security forces are interested in us and may monitor our calls. Of course, it's illegal and they need a court warrant to tap your phone, but there are ways round it, such as hiring a private investigator to gather intelligence or apply to the Local Council or HMRC. Well, it's too late now. If it's that important, we should meet up today.'

'Okay. It *is* quite urgent. Can you come over and talk? There's a pub I know, but it's difficult to find and I can't tell you the name because of this secrecy thing. I could meet you somewhere nearby. Do you know the train station at Arundel? There is a car park next to it. Can you get there at eleven to eleven-thirty?'

'No problem. I can lock up here and be with you at eleven sharp.'

I had picked a busy time. The London Victoria train was due just after 11 a.m. and the car park was full of those waiting to pick up the arrivals. Any sleuth rushing to track us down after my phone intercept would have had one and a half hours to react and follow us. Out of caution, I scanned all the cars and parked at a far point where I could see new arrivals before they could see me. I imagined any security people would use an unmarked car, so I scrutinised all the cars in the car park. From the registration plates, I could recognise the area codes for the local counties and discount them, but I was not sure how London registrations worked. Was it by county or was there a specific London code? And why should I assume any suspicious car would originate from a London address? My checking revealed most of the cars had Sussex plates plus two from Hampshire, and some from further afield.

Bang on eleven, Mark's white Peugeot 305 turned into the car park. There were two other Triumph Heralds, so I sounded my horn to attract his attention. He changed direction and drove towards me.

'Hop in, it's my turn,' I offered, sweeping the passenger seat clear of piles of homework and textbooks. As we left the car park, we looked in the mirror to see if we were being followed.

'All clear,' I said. 'Do you think the police will go to the trouble of tapping my parents' phone line?'

'Not really. Cases of terrorism, political activism, treason, anti-government tendencies, left-wing leanings and so on, it's certain they will. However, a suspect in a murder case is most unlikely. But best to be cautious, Michael. I'm surprised you have the time off. I thought private schools kept their staff busy on Saturdays.'

'True enough. There are no home games this afternoon—some away matches which I don't have to attend. I had one geography class to sort out. I rang matron to tell my class to get on with their prep. She agreed to make sure they don't run riot.'

'Geography? I thought you were an English teacher.'

'My degree was in geography and that is my genuine interest, but the school wanted an English teacher, so I agreed to the dual roles. Plus, teaching rugby and cricket and general dogsbody.' As we chatted, I had been studying the wing mirror to see if any cars had followed us from the car park.

'It looks like we gave them the slip. The George & Dragon is about a twenty-minute drive. Quite pleasant and many tables; we should find a quiet spot.'

'I'm intrigued to hear what you discovered from this darts player.'

'Yes, he is quite a character. Fantastic with the darts. He scored one hundred and eighty with three darts in the triple twenties. I have never seen that done. His name is Ron Jones, which gave us a laugh as I was with two of our staff—Jones the Latin teacher and matron.'

'I met your school matron at Michelle's memorial service, and I visited her again recently, as you know, to explain my concerns about Michelle's death and the issues this has raised. She is a very intelligent person who was friendly with my sister and knew a little a bit about our research.'

'Of course. Did you meet Jones? He is from Wales.'

'Yes, I think so. Your school organised a beautiful service for my sister. She wasn't religious, but I appreciate the school's effort and it impressed our French relations.'

As they had banned me from attending, I did not know what to say.

Saturday lunchtime at the George & Dragon was very busy and today was no exception, with loads of families milling about like lost sheep trying to find room in the busy restaurant. No sign of anyone I knew, although I was only searching for the elusive twins. Never mind. Easter was not far off, and I was sure they would be around for the holiday. Neither of us was hungry, so we grabbed a beer from the bar and nabbed a quiet table by the log fire. I updated Mark with the conversation we had with Alan Jones. Of prime interest was the new information that Michelle met up with a French man in the public bar, a former friend who appeared unannounced. When I had finished my account, Mark sat back in his seat, alert and focused.

'Very interesting. I can't think who this French person is. Maybe a contact from her university days in Nantes. Do you recall any correspondence in the files?' asked Mark.

'No, nothing. She was meticulous. For example, she kept a copy of her letter to the *New Scientist* in early December.'

'I think the obvious step is to make a call to the *New Scientist* office on Monday to follow that lead.'

'Would you like me to do this?' I asked.

'Michael, it's not fair for me to call on you the whole time.'

Mark reached into his jacket pocket and took out his wallet.

'We should get this on a more professional basis. Here is £100 to cover your time and costs so far. I can see you have the enthusiasm and drive to sort this out, so please take it. First call is to check out who she saw at the *New Scientist* if she ever went there.'

'That's unnecessary,' I objected, handing back the money. 'The school was paying me in full during my suspension. Since they reinstated me, I can only devote time outside school times like in the evenings and weekends, but the Easter holiday is not far off so I have more availability.'

'Great, so you will have some free time.'

'I have some tutoring for one boy. He recently arrived from Hong Kong. His mother is very insistent, but I think it will only be for a few hours a week.'

'Hong Kong. That will be a culture shock changing to an English prep school in deepest Sussex.'

'I am sure it's an upheaval,' I was thinking of our authoritarian headmaster and some of the eccentric staff. 'At least he is a day boy and can escape home. A bit like me. I have one foot in the school and one at home. The live-in staff become institutionalised.'

'Were you aware of Michelle's boyfriend in London?' asked Mark. 'The love interest that the darts player mentioned?'

I looked downcast. This had come as a terrific shock. That there was someone else in her life was bad enough, but it was her comment she had feelings for someone else who was too immature to realise it. That worried me.

'His name is Dominic,' said Mark. 'He is a laboratory technician working in the clinical chemistry department at St Thomas' Hospital in London. I do not know how they met, but it was a few years ago. He is an amazing person. Unique, full of energy, fun, great to be with. But also, a dedicated worker. From my point of view, he is a great asset because he conducts routine daily chemical tests on blood and urine samples from patients and weekly tests on drug addicts, undergoing methadone treatment, for any other addictive drugs they are taking. As a result, he has access to very sophisticated equipment. During routine testing, he discovered an unusual chemical was present in many of the urine samples. On further research, he discovered it was BPA. Imagine that! You test for cocaine and find nothing, but you discover traces of an artificial oestrogen you never knew you were ingesting, and it has come from leaching from plastic bottles.'

'Amazing. But the amounts must have been tiny.'

'Yes. Very low in parts per million, and it is rapidly excreted from the body. But it is an involuntary additive and there may be cumulative effects we don't know about. Because Dominic is in an ideal position to help us, we have been using his expertise. He is happy to assist within the obvious limits.'

'What limits?'

'NHS employs him, so he is not free to undertake any external work. If BPA and other toxins show up during routine testing, that is a matter he can mention to senior staff to flag it up.'

I was worried about the direction this was taking. Mark then dropped another surprise and told me that Michelle had visited Dominic in London in early January during the school holidays.

'I believe Dominic had tickets to a matinee of "Cats" by Andrew Lloyd Webber. She loved musicals. She had a pleasant break taking in some shopping at the January sales and visiting a few museums. I think she took at least three days off. I wonder if you could visit Dominic in London and find out if they discussed his research. It's possible there is a lead that could be significant. I phoned Dominic. He is happy to meet you and show you his work at the hospital. He told me his relationship with Michelle was friendly with no romantic attachment.'

After dropping Mark at the train station, I headed back to school. I wanted a chat with matron to discuss the latest revelations about Michelle. Did she know about Dominic in London? I seemed to be the last person in the picture. My friend had led a complex double life I had no inkling of. The Michelle I knew was a stranger to me. This dedicated researcher and whistle-blower was someone I would have respected if only she had shared more with me. But was it likely that her actions had precipitated her death?

Drawing into the car park, I encountered Father Roderick and Miss Cresswell with her annoying little dog all wrapped up against the cold. This included the dog that had a coat on. They greeted me politely, but with no warmth. Since returning to school, these two had ignored me before grudgingly acknowledging me when they could not avoid it.

'Off for a walk?' I enquired.

Embarrassed, they looked at each other before Father Roderick spoke up.

'Indeed. Such a pleasant afternoon—shame to waste it.'

I noticed them heading for the path through the woods towards the pond.

'There are still a few snowdrops left by the pathway,' I said. 'There was a lovely display in February, but they are fading fast.'

'Sic transit gloria mundi,' said Roderick.

I was sure he meant this as a pointed reference to the death of Michelle but wrapped up in his clever Latin. Miss Creswell gushed at the comment but kept to the point.

'Too early for the bluebells. Another two weeks and the first ones will peer through, and we know spring is on the way.'

They wandered off with Roderick helping Miss Cresswell over the stile, steadying her waist in case she should slip in the mud.

I made a point of walking along the path outside the headmaster's study to prove I was on the premises just in case they had noticed my absence in the morning. Out of necessity, I attended most of the lunches but few of the dinners. The food was so appalling that many of the staff bought in their own sandwiches and flasks of tea at lunchtime. I glanced across at the study and caught the eye of Mona, mouth open and staring back, so I gave her a cheerful wave. Immune to their criticism. Roll on my job application to Singapore which, any day now, should pop through the letterbox with a grateful invitation to join them in the Tropics.

I went straight to matron's study. She would be there, at the infirmary dealing with the sick, or down at the bookies in town. Fortunately, she was sitting behind her desk with her unstockinged feet resting on a chair and scanning the *Sporting Life*.

She looked up, startled, but relaxed when she saw me. She motioned me to sit down and removed her feet from the only available chair. I felt guilty for disturbing her leisure time. Her door was ajar, but I pushed it shut just in case Mona or any other staff might intrude. I filled her in on all the latest developments with Michelle. After I had finished, matron looked thoughtful.

'I knew all about Dominic,' she admitted. 'I think there had been a romantic involvement some time ago until that changed last year, but they were still on good friend terms and kept in touch. She used to catch the train to London Victoria and meet up from time to time. From her perspective, she wanted to keep track of his work because he had access to specialist laboratory equipment for liquid chromatography, mass spectrometry and electrophoresis techniques.'

'But he is just a laboratory technician.'

'In my experience, the technicians are sometimes more knowledgeable than the doctors who order pointless blood and urine tests with minimal understanding of what is the most suitable test in any situation. Too often they order up unnecessary tests and then start patients on medication which they have no need for and may even harm them.'

Chapter 14

The Easter holidays had started. In the afternoon, there was a constant stream of parents arriving to collect their children. The coach to Arundel train station dispatched more boys to catch trains far and wide. Unattended by teachers, they purchased cigarettes at the station cafe and gathered in cheerful groups on the station platform, showing off to schoolgirls as they waited for their train connections. Private taxis and limousines transported the foreign students to Heathrow and Gatwick for flights abroad. Soon the only sad pupils left were those with delayed departures or those waiting for late pickups from unreliable aunts or other complications, such as marital rifts and miscommunications.

Charlie was still waiting for his mother at 4 p.m. and I was debating whether to drop him home when his face lifted with a huge smile as he saw her hovering behind me.

'Michael, I'm sorry I am so late collecting Charlie.'
'Oh, no problem. I was just about to give him a lift.'

'How sweet of you! Charlie, get your things. We will wait here. Do you see his face is much better? The scar is very faint. It makes him look quite distinguished.'

'Has it put him off rugby?'

'No. He is very stubborn. He wants to get his own back. The boy who hurt him was much bigger than him.'

'Yes, William Obote is very tall and looks older than he is. In fact, he is the same age as Charlie.'

Laureline yawned.

'Well, Michael, I didn't want to talk about that horrible sport. Will you be free to come along on the first Thursday of half-term to give Charlie a tutorial? That would be the 31st March. Just an hour to start with. Please say yes.'

'Of course—I can do that. I will bring along some of the set books. I know Charlie has had some trouble understanding Macbeth.'

'Thank you. Will five pounds an hour be alright, or should I pay you more?' She had an imploring voice that ensnared me. I would be happy for half that rate.

'No, that is very generous.'

'I am so pleased. Would you be mind if I listened in for a bit? I remember that play is very violent, so Charlie will love that!'

'As long as Charlie doesn't object—but he might prefer a one-on-one, at least to start with. Your presence might inhibit him.'

'Of course, you are right. I will stay out of your way.'

'What time would you like me to arrive?'

'Not too early. Shall we say midday?'

'Okay. I will look forward to it.'

Jones had told me the staff planned an end of term party at the Three Horseshoes kicking off at six, so I had a couple of hours to fill in. Since I had been allowed back, I was keen to attend all the events to dispel any lingering suspicions.

To unwind, I drove into town for some shopping. My mother's heavy meals, with their emphasis on traditional

English cooking, were becoming repetitive, and I longed for lighter meals and some healthy snacks such as fruit, yoghurt and nut bars. Afterwards I dropped into my usual cafe for a strong coffee. The staff had learned to master the coffee machine after attending a barista course and the quality and choice was much improved. As I still had an hour to kill, I rang Michael Cox from the phone box near the town garage.

Within the first minute, I sensed it was a mistake.

'Hi Michael. It's Michael Fletcher.'

'Oh. Michael. What's up?' he sounded as if he was half asleep.

'Not a lot. I was wondering if you fancied any tennis this weekend or next.'

'Michael—this weekend is impossible. I must attend a wedding—somewhere in Hampshire. Well, to be accurate—I plan to miss the church business and join the reception later for the food, drinks, and boring speeches. It's a former girlfriend of mine called Bunty Bulstrode, marrying some guy in the marines. Can't think what she sees in him. Must be the uniform—some girls go wobbly at the knees when they meet some weak-chinned prat all dressed up and trying to impress. Then again, he's probably from a suitable family. Frankly, I would much prefer a game of tennis with you, old boy.'

This had a hollow ring, so I felt a comment about the loss of Bunty might be in order.

'They sound well-suited couple, so maybe you have had a lucky escape.'

'You are *so* right. I am too young to settle down and my fling with Bunty was ages ago. It's water under the bridge, as they say. Of course, we are still the best of pals.'

'No good for tennis tomorrow then. What about next weekend?'

'Hmm. Next week is hard. The parents have arranged a shoot, so I had better make myself available to pour the drinks. They send an annual invite to a select group of the country set. I can't stand killing birds for sport, can you? Well, old boy, great to hear from you, but must rush. We *must* sort out another date soon.'

I put the phone down, depressed. That he hadn't mentioned the twins was suspicious. Maybe, my tennis was not good enough. I was not part of the inner circle.

The school teaching staff packed the Three Horseshoes. Even the headmaster and Mona had turned up to dispel false notions that they were stand-offish and superior. It was a chance for them to observe their colleagues in relaxed mode. Mona had even ordered a finger buffet. The standard presentation for wedding reception and wakes included finger rolls with three flavours: tuna spread, real grated cheddar cheese and tomato with cucumber for the vegetarians. Also, the pub's own sausage rolls and cocktail sausages on sticks. All generous portions plus plain or salt and vinegar crisps.

Mona glowed with goodwill even when Michael joined the party. The headmaster chatted with the bar staff to avoid any awkward welcomes as Michael drifted past him.

'Glad you could make it,' said Jones, who was the first to guide me to the bar and sort me out with a pint of bitter. 'Matron had saved you a place, but Miss Cresswell and Caldwell-Brown moved in so best not say anything about the case until we can speak.'

'Not a lot has happened in the past few weeks. It's like a game of snakes and ladders—one moment there's a good lead and then we are back to square one.'

I allowed myself to be led to a table at the back of the lounge bar. Around the small bar table, matron, Miss Cresswell and her dog, Nigel, and his wife, Jane, occupied the four chairs. Jones and I stood sipping our beers and Jones created a smoke cloud from his cigarette, where he could shelter in a happy haze.

'A good turn out,' said Jones.

'Indeed,' said Miss Cresswell. 'A wonderful show. Sadly, no sign of Father Roderick, but he said he might look by after Benediction.'

All of us knew this was unlikely. Miss Cresswell was always loyal to Father Roderick and wouldn't hear a word against him.

'How's it going, Michael?' said Nigel. Jane woke up from studying her half pint of bitter and I was aware all eyes were on me. I was sure they were not asking about their old car.

'Yes, there have been some developments. I went to the Royal Albion along with matron and Jones during a darts match when the visiting team was from a pub in Graffham. In fact, the same team that played at the Three Horseshoes on the night Michelle was last seen alive. We had a chat with Alan Jones—one of the Graffham players—who confirmed talking to Michelle in the pub. This was after Alan saw her in animated conversation with a French man who looked like the person I saw in the bar. The conversation between them became quite heated, and this man stormed out of the pub. We have passed on all our findings to the Brighton police for them to pursue further.'

They all looked amazed. Matron was the first to speak, sensing I needed backing up.

'Michael is correct. This Alan Jones is a credible witness. Maybe the account he gave us is more detailed than the one he gave the police. Or more likely they have just ignored it as they remain convinced it is an open-and-shut case. They never mentioned the mystery man is French.'

Nigel broke the stunned silence.

'Michael, you are an innocent victim.'

'Nigel. This has been obvious from the start and not helped by the stupid gesture of our headmaster in forcing Michael to leave the school,' said matron.

'No, you can't blame him, matron,' I said. 'He was under pressure from some parents. He had no choice.'

'It's a fascinating story,' said Jane. 'Nigel has mentioned your case and I know all about it.'

'Michael bought your Triumph Herald. He is very pleased with it, aren't you?' Did I detect a warning glare?

'Yes. It's a very nice car.'

'Of course, you did. Nigel told me you needed a new car. With baby Hannah and our puppy to consider, we needed a more family-friendly motor. But I still miss the Triumph, especially in summer, cruising about with the open top and stopping off for a picnic on the Downs.'

Matron felt trapped at the small table and overcome by the trite conversation about a baby and a puppy. She hauled herself up and headed for the bar, beckoning us to follow her.

'Sorry, but I couldn't take any more of the Caldwell-Browns.' she said when we had reached a safe distance. 'Now tell me, have you contacted the *New Scientist* to see who Michelle was in touch with?'

This was proving tricky. None of the regular staffers recalled seeing the initial letter from Michelle describing Mark's research, and they believed a freelancer must have picked it up. Being an international science weekly, they had freelance correspondents all over the world but especially in America and Australia. For me, they produced a list of freelancers active in their office who might fit the bill and invited me to their London office to check their photos. I explained this to matron and Jones and said I would visit the *New Scientist* in London during the Easter holidays, which I would combine with a trip to see Dominic at St Thomas' Hospital.

'Who's Dominic?' asked Jones.

Matron and I looked at each other and both came to the same conclusion, to say as little as possible. Matron took over.

'Dominic was a friend of Michelle's. We know she was up in London just after Christmas for a shopping trip and she went to the theatre with her friend Dominic. He has agreed to see Michael and pass over any useful information because she might have contacted the *New Scientist* at the same time. We have to look at all potential leads, as the police are proving so useless.'

Further explanations paused as the headmaster pushed through the crowd at the bar and headed for Michael.

'Michael, I feel we owe you an apology for the unfortunate way things developed with the police investigation. As you know, I was under extreme pressure from the governors and some of the more vocal parents. The police inquiries have stalled, so we can put a line in the past and move on.'

'I agree that's in the past,' I said. 'But it's a concern that the police don't follow up useful leads. I even visited their SIO in Brighton, to pass on new information from a witness in the pub as to the mystery man, but it was a waste of time. Preston and his assistant, Tracey Smith, do not welcome my help.'

Mona had joined the headmaster. She was eager for him to leave after spending quite long enough with the staff. Arranging a tab for staff drinks had been a mistake as one look at Jones' glassy expression and over-familiar attempts to be friendly confirmed. She had paid the very large bill and they could pay further over-indulgence themselves.

Chapter 15

SIO Preston had summoned the Pulborough police team to an important meeting at the Brighton station.

'I bet it was that piece in the *Daily Mail* that has got them upset,' said Bishop.

'What piece was that?' asked PC James, undoing his seat belt as they parked behind the police station.

'The article saying we have messed up and failed to locate a vital witness while wasting time trying to implicate an innocent teacher. Jimmy, I showed you the paper last week.'

'Oh that. Yes, I remember. Didn't you say their source was a friend of the teacher, so likely to be biased?'

'Yes,' said Bishop. 'But they also alleged some tosh about a conspiracy to shut the case up because the French teacher was involved in industrial espionage. They hinted whatever she knew was highly sensitive and hush-hush.'

'That could be why someone murdered her,' said Jimmy helpfully.

The Desk Sergeant scarcely bothered to acknowledge the Pulborough men, and he kept them waiting as he prioritised dealing with an elderly couple who needed everything repeating loudly. The sergeant was the epitome of tired patience and reassured the couple, who left slowly looking puzzled.

'Sorry about that, gents. Ah, yes, the Pulborough force. You are here for a meeting with SIO Preston, aren't you? Let me just check his phone.'

After more delay in locating Preston and Smith, the meeting finally convened.

'Grab a seat,' said Preston as they gathered around a large table in a Spartan meeting room. On the wall was a photo of Michelle, smiling shyly and looking very young, and one of Michael, which was an unflattering police mugshot.

'After two and a half months, those photos show the extent of your investigation.'

He directed this attack on the Pulborough police.

'To be fair, sir, our station has had no remit to conduct any investigation apart from surveillance on the English teacher. We understood Brighton was taking the lead.'

'That is correct up to a point, inspector, but I have discovered you two had other ideas and visited the Three Horseshoes to interview the staff and any witnesses, but never passed this information back to us. Am I right?'

Preston pinned some photos of the bars of the Three Horseshoes on the wall. He also added a photo of Michelle in a lab coat taken at the research laboratory where she formerly worked in Nantes. In chalk on the board, he wrote 'Nantes' under Michelle's photo.

'Well?'

'Yes, sir, we reconnoitred the pub on a Saturday—two weeks after the murder. We visited in plain clothes so as not to arise suspicion and the staff were more amenable to talk. The landlord claimed he and his wife were away that weekend in France, but his wife told us he went on his own and she stayed behind.'

'And you never reported that. It might be significant. Are they hiding something from us? What about witnesses?'

'No one admitted seeing the French teacher,' said PC James. 'Except the landlady reported there was a confrontation between a lady in the public bar and the English teacher. There is a point where you can look across from the lounge bar into the public bar. According to the landlady, the English teacher went into a jealous rage when he saw his girlfriend chatting to someone else and stormed off.'

Tracey Smith's mouth dropped open in surprise.

'I wish we had known that information before,' she said. 'You should have sent us your report.'

'No, she said the same thing when I called straight after the crime,' confirmed Preston. 'And Fletcher denied it was like that. He said he was impatient and angry with the landlady at her slow service and poor attitude.'

'A likely story!' said Tracey.

'Rather than rake up old ground, I want to know what the force in Pulborough has been doing over the last month. What about the surveillance of the teacher? Did that give anything useful?'

Bishop opened his notebook and slowly turned the pages, relishing updating the arrogant SIO with some positive results.

'Indeed. Very interesting. In February, the POI purchased a second-hand Triumph Herald, number plate...'

'Don't bother with that. Carry on,' said Preston, impatiently.

'On Sunday 20th February the POI left his parent's house at eleven-fifteen in the morning, and I followed him in my personal car so as not to arouse suspicion. I observed him park outside the George & Dragon at midday. Careful to avoid being recognised, I entered the pub after him, suitably disguised in a long coat, scarf, and deerstalker hat. As the weather was cold, I blended in well with the locals. I noticed Fletcher was chatting to a young man of a similar age to himself and two young ladies in jeans who were, in fact, twins.

On this visit to the pub, he used the Triumph Herald. I should add that is an improvement on his previous car, an old Morris Minor.'

PC James laughed and received a winnowing glare from Preston and Smith.

'At a quarter past one Fletcher left the pub, and I followed him all the way until he reached his home. I should add that the young man had drunk at least three pints of beer and I could have stopped and breathalysed him for suspected drunken driving but as I was not in uniform, it seemed more sensible not to reveal my identity considering the more important surveillance mission.'

'Quite right,' said Preston. 'But next time nab him anyhow. Just make sure you have the testing kit with you and your hat. Plain clothes are no problem as you are a bona fide officer.'

'Yes sir. Thank you. There is a bit more. On the same day in the evening, he tried to give us the slip by taking his father's car, an old Rover, to a place called Ranville's, which is a posh sports club. There he met up with the same group I saw him talking to in the pub—the other man and the twins. These four persons engaged in the sport of tennis for a one-hour session.'

'Tennis, in winter!'

'Sorry, I should have explained. Ranville's has an indoor court. It's very grand and there is a bar there as well.'

'Good work, inspector. How did you infiltrate this private club?'

'Easy, sir. We had a view from the road into the bar and saw the group still in their tennis whites, sipping drinks and appearing to be on friendly terms. The POI was with one twin and the other couple left after five minutes in a separate car. Michael Fletcher and his young friend stayed drinking at the bar for another 40 minutes. As the girls appear to be identical twins, I could not ascertain which of the two is most friendly with the POI.'

'Probably Fletcher doesn't know the difference,' said Preston. 'This teacher sounds like a sexual predator. Are the twins younger than him, Bishop?'

'Yes, sir. I should say so. Late teens or early twenties. Tall, blonde, and attractive. Dressed provocatively in tight blue denim jeans, as is common with the younger generation.'

'Keep up the surveillance on the parents' house and Michael Fletcher. Types like this will try to repeat patterns of behaviour so the two triggers will be this pub—the George & Dragon and Ranville's club. I think over the Easter holiday these friends will meet up again.'

'With Easter coming up, we don't have enough persons for surveillance. We need some support from Brighton, if possible.'

Preston and Smith broke off to discuss this and agreed to send two junior officers and an unmarked car to the Pulborough station to beef up the operation. Inspector Bishop thanked him and then told the team of one other interesting occurrence on Tuesday 22nd February.

'Just two days after the successful surveillance by the Pulborough team of the two meetings just described, PC James was on duty in the morning outside the Fletcher residence when he observed the Triumph leaving at some speed and heading west to the M27. PC James followed at a discrete distance and observed Fletcher leave the M27 at junction seven, close to Southampton. His journey continued in the suburb of Hedge End, Eastleigh and ended at an industrial estate where he parked outside one unit and entered the ground floor office where he stayed to attend a meeting for about one hour. He then left with another man in a white Peugeot 305 estate driving along back roads near Bursledon and the Hamble River.'

'Unfortunately, whilst tailing the car, PC James was impeded by a slow vehicle and lost contact. As he was low on fuel, he returned to Pulborough. The address of the office Fletcher went to is as follows.' Bishop flipped through the pages of his notebook and finally found it.

'Carter Soil and Rock testing laboratory, Solent Industrial Park, Shamblehurst Lane, Hedge End, Southampton. The unit is on two levels. I think the ground floor is a testing laboratory and the administrative offices are on the first floor, which is also the top floor.'

'As well as being an English teacher, Fletcher is a Geography teacher, so we wondered if this was a visit connected to his teaching,' said James. 'Otherwise, we can see nothing relevant in the visit.'

'It may be significant.'

'Perhaps there is more to this than meets the eye,' said Tracey. 'The article in the paper hinted at some conspiracy theory.'

'You can forget that rubbish,' said Preston. 'If that was the case, the government would have slapped a Schedule D notice on the press and forbidden any reporting. They haven't done so. The newspaper report is speculation with vague conjecture and quotes from anonymous sources. I still think Fletcher is in the frame, but we need to double down on this missing contact in the pub. Tracey, you went to interview the darts player, but you haven't flagged up anything unusual, have you?'

'Correct, sir. I visited Alan Jones at his home when he was back on leave. He works on an oil rig on four-week rotations. That's offshore for four weeks and then home for four weeks before returning to the platform.'

'Thanks, Tracey. There is no need to spell that out. We all know how the personnel on oil rigs work.'

'Alan Jones was very helpful, and his story correlated with that of Michael Fletcher in that Jones observed the French teacher talking to a man matching the description given us by Mr Fletcher. After chatting and sharing a drink with this mystery man, the man departed, and Miss Gagneux stayed in the pub. Alan Jones bought her a drink and got chatting. His game of darts had finished, and he offered to drive her home as the pub was closing, but she declined, saying it was just a short walk back to the school where she worked. That was all. She left the pub before Alan, who stayed on for a further half an hour. He seemed an honest witness, so I think we should discount him.'

Preston went back to the board and wrote on 'Alan Jones' and then inserted additional columns for 'Man in the pub' and 'Man at Carter's laboratory. Looking pleased with himself, he added, 'The Twins'.

'Going forward, we need to speed up the investigation and keep all our options open. Some of you may think this is a straightforward case, and that Fletcher did it, but there is not enough evidence to charge him. My view is we cannot discount the darts player. He could easily have followed Michelle when she left the pub, and we only have his word that he left later. Contact other members of the Graffham darts team to check out his version of the timings. Next we will release the identikit picture of mystery pub man to the media to take that line of enquiry further.'

'Sorry to interrupt, sir, but we could try to get the picture shown on ITV's "Police 5",' said PC James. 'You know. It's that five-minute programme hosted by Shaw Taylor.'

'Good idea,' said Preston. 'It can't do any harm and shows we are still looking for the culprit. I will make enquiries how we do this.'

'What about this Carter fellow and the twins?' asked Bishop.

'I explained before. Keep up the surveillance. Now we have the address for Carter's laboratory, we need to find out what sort of testing they do and who their customers are. Try the direct approach, phone them up, and ask if they have a price list for the tests they perform. Just because it's called Carter's laboratory doesn't mean this man is called Carter. The person Fletcher met could be anyone working there. You have done a good job despite our limited resources. Any questions?'

'You mentioned the landlord at the Three Horseshoes was a bit fishy. Maybe he knows more than he is telling us. I met him and he was very cocky and lied to me,' said Inspector Bishop.

'That's right,' chimed in Jimmy James.

'His wife made out he went to France to buy booze and meet up with a mistress.'

'Individuals can bring in tax free liquor from France for personal use, so maybe a call to Customs or Weights and Measures to check out his bar supplies is a good move. I bet the house wines will be cheap French plonk in a more expensive bottle. The threat of action might loosen his tongue.'

'You have put a column headed "Nantes" for the French teacher's work in France where she was a research chemist at the university,' said Tracey Smith. 'Possibly this needs more investigation. What was her field of research? Why did she stop and come to England, changing her career direction to become a French teacher?'

'I agree it's important,' said Preston.

'I met Michelle's mother and sister at the school memorial service in January so I can visit them to update them on progress and fill in the details on Michelle's former employment. Any of you speak French?'

Tracey Smith raised her hand.

'I worked as an au pair for a family in Paris when I was younger. My French is rusty, but I am sure I can pick it up again.'

'Excellent,' said Preston. 'I will get approval and plan a trip after Easter to Nantes.'

Chapter 16

After a leisurely family breakfast, I was helping my mother wash up the dishes in a manner of speaking. I had started the hand washing routine until she relegated me to drying the cutlery. She stacked the dishes and cups in a drainer and told me to leave them alone. I sensed she did not want my help, but I wanted to prove I was able and willing in the daily chore business.

It had snowed overnight, and the thin morning sun shone from a dull blue sky, flooding the kitchen with light. My father was busy sweeping snow and ice off his car screen as he had a doctor's appointment. Pure snow drifts lined the drive like cotton wool and some of the country lanes would be impassable unless the Council had scattered grit and salt.

I explained a parent, called Laureline, had booked me for tutoring her son—a single parent recently moved to the UK from Hong Kong. Hopefully, conditions would thaw before I had to leave the house for the appointment at midday.

'Laureline, what a lovely name. Of course, now you mention Hong Kong, I know whom you mean. The headmaster informed your father about her case. I don't think she wanted sympathy from anyone. It happened. That for her was the end of it and only the future was important.'

'What are you talking about? What happened?'

'Very tragic. Someone killed her husband during a break-in at their apartment—very traumatic for her and Charlie.'

'How terrible! I put my foot in it at the Parents' evening when I said what a great experience it must have been for Charlie and her living in Hong Kong.'

'You were not to know,' my mother dismissed my concerns. 'She had to leave Hong Kong, and she settled in the UK because her husband had family connections in the area. I suppose the other option was to return to France, but the family felt the son needed a traditional English education. You must ask them over for tea sometime.'

Laureline's house was at the end of a long gravelled drive bound by massive mature trees. The snow hid the gravel, but the tyres slipped on the mixture of snow, slush, and stones as I slid up to the front door of an imposing Georgian house at midday. Laureline was already waiting for me on the porch, dressed in blue jeans. To keep out the cold, she wore a thick white polo neck pullover.

'Michael, I thought the snow would stop you coming. It's so cold. Quick, come into the warmth. We have a splendid log fire burning. Charlie has been so looking forward to your tutorial,' said Laureline.

'It's a beautiful old house,' I remarked in awe.

'It's very grand, isn't it?' she said. 'But we are just renting it for the year. It dates from the mid-1700s in the reign of George III, so it is older than modern America. No wonder the heating is so bad. It's impossible to keep the complete house warm so we live in the ground floor rooms relying on the log fire backed up by a few radiators.'

'You mean there is no central heating? My parents' house is the same, although much smaller. They rely on an Aga for the kitchen and log fire for the sitting room and little electric bar heaters for the bedrooms. I think it's a thing with the older generation.'

'Yes. It's the British war spirit thing combined with thrifty living. I think schools like yours breed that attitude into the children.'

'The hardships and examples of the grandparents rub off on the parents and then on their children in a self-perpetuating cycle.'

'Something like that,' she agreed.

'You have lovely views over the garden.' I had wandered over to the large bay windows where I could see the thick expanse of snow-covered fields rolling out in the distance ending at a coppice of trees with bare frozen branches at the edge of the property. It was a desolate but beautiful sight.

'No doubt you must think we are wealthy to live with such opulence. But the executors of my husband's estate arranged it all before we left Hong Kong and the rent is very reasonable. They cannot sell these grand houses and the owners can't afford the upkeep, so I am doing everyone a favour by living here. My husband was a successful fund manager for a bank and his success was the curse that killed him because a gang broke in one night when we were asleep. Someone had tipped them off. We had valuable paintings and a safe. He resisted them, so they killed him in front of me. Fortunately, Charlie slept through it.'

This account was even more shocking for her flat, unemotional expression.

'I am so sorry. My mother told me some of this, but I was not aware of the details. I can't imagine how awful it was.'

'Yes, it was horrific. They sentenced the gang leader to death, but the courts commuted it to life imprisonment. I agree with that. I don't hold for a life-for-a-life, and it would never bring my husband back. I don't want to talk about it anymore.' She went to fetch Charlie.

Charlie came into the room looking sheepish and less than enthusiastic at the prospect of work. We settled down in the drawing room: a large formal room with a grand piano and an Adam fireplace. Bookcases lined the walls from floor to ceiling, all packed with pristine leather-bound volumes that looked unread. We sat at a low table. Laureline disappeared to fetch tea and biscuits.

Macbeth was one of the exam texts, so I made a start at Act 1, scene 1 on the desert heath with the three witches. We each played one of the three witches, with Laureline joining in the fun. After that, Laureline wanted us to act out the three witches in Act IV, the famous cauldron scene, where the witches add disgusting ingredients to their cauldron as they confront Macbeth and foretell his future.

'Double, double toil and trouble.'

'Fire burn and cauldron bubble.'

After completing a one-hour lesson, it was obvious Charlie loved the play. When I left, he was so absorbed in reading he ignored me when I left.

'I hope you will come again next Monday at midday?' said Laureline as she led me to the front door. The snow had thawed in the sunshine with just ribbons left near the hedge. I hesitated because I needed to fit in a meeting up in London with the *New Scientist* and it would be useful to visit Dominic at St Thomas' Hospital on the same day.

'I think that day is free, but I have to be in London for a day or two. Let me get back to you when I know for sure. It is still during the school holidays.'

'Monday at noon, then. Any change, call me.'

She wrote her phone number.

'Will one hour be enough?' I asked.

'I would think so. Charlie's attention span isn't great. No point overloading his brain. Afterwards, you can stay for lunch. I have discovered the house has a cellar with a few bottles of old wine. Perhaps you can help me choose a few suitable ones for guests.'

'Thank you, I will look forward to next week.' Generous to a fault, Laureline gave me ten pounds for the tutorial.

As I drove away from Laureline's I noticed a blue Ford Escort parked in a side road that turned and followed me, keeping about 200 metres between us. Instead of returning home, I headed for a nearby village and parked outside the village shop next to a phone box. I placed a call to Mark.

'Hi Mark. I think I am being followed. It's a blue Ford Escort, and I first noticed it this morning when I went out for a private tutorial. When I left, the same car was waiting and has followed me all the way. I turned off to a village I have never been to and when I stopped, he pulled in by the church about 50 metres away. What should I do?'

'Why not walk past the car and go into the church as if you are a tourist? Don't look at the car until you are close enough to see the occupant or occupants. Take it slowly and gaze into the shop windows as if you are killing time. Call me back later and let me know what you discover.'

I noticed there was a convenient side road leading to the back of the church, so I could make a circuit out of sight of the car and approach from behind. As I walked up, I could see the driver reading a newspaper as he watched my car ahead. At once, I recognised PC James from the Pulborough police station. I turned and retraced my steps and returned to my car and drove straight home. Sure enough, the blue Escort followed.

At home, my mother was cooking dinner, and my father sat in front of the television with a large whisky. Nelson lay in front of the log fire. I supposed the predictability of habit was something that crept up on you as you became older. I hovered about in the kitchen, watching my mother cooking.

'Looks lovely, ma. You know many of my married friends share the domestic tasks, so the man may cook the meal and let his wife put her feet up with a drink by the fire. Is that something you have ever considered?'

'Don't be stupid. Your father could never do that. Toast and marmalade are his limit. Besides, we don't hold with this equality business. Sit down, dinner's ready.'

'Delicious, as usual,' said my father.

She had cooked duck a l'orange—another Elizabeth David recipe which was not a great success being as tough as old shoe leather. My father and I picked at it, concentrating on the vegetables, and making small inroads into the duck by hacking off slivers of flesh from the edges.

'Will you be alright on your own over Easter?' my mother asked. 'We are going to Norfolk to see our friends, Charles and Davinia. They have invited us to stay for the Easter holiday. Charles was in the army with your father in Malaya during the Emergency in the 1950s. It will be quite a reunion for him.'

This sudden turn of events was a surprise. The contemplation of the house to myself filled me with expectations, an opportunity to relax without censure or disapproval. 'I will be fine,' I said, trying to suppress my joy. 'But what about Nelson? You will not take him with you?'

'Poor Nelson would love the exercise. But I am afraid Charles and Davinia are anti-dog and it's a long journey for him to put up with at his age. Would you mind looking after him? It will only be for a few days.'

'No problem,' I said.

'Last time we left you alone at Christmas was a disaster,' complained my mother. 'Rubbish was everywhere, mud on the floors and nothing washed up. You are old enough to behave like an adult.'

'Yes, sorry mother. I had some friends over after the Boxing Day hunt.'

'And very boisterous friends too,' said my father. 'You have never been fox hunting, so I don't know how you got involved.'

'It was quite a laugh. It was a chance encounter with a school friend, and we all had too much to drink.'

'Oscar Wilde had the right idea about hunting,' said my mother. *'The unspeakable in pursuit of the uneatable.'*

In fact, I had invented the whole scenario about the hunt. There was a local hunt, but my riding ability was poor. I spent most of Christmas Day asleep recovering after a late night and Boxing Day drinking and watching TV. The whole of Christmas was a blur. I had no energy left even to clear up the mess of takeaway meals and beer cans. Worst still, my complete memory of Christmas seemed to be wiped out apart from occasional flashbacks. Since November, when I had persuaded Michelle to join me on a birdwatching trip to Brighton, our mutual attraction had become apparent, which was strange as we had been working at the school and seen each other almost daily for the last two years. I had hoped the Christmas holiday would be the best time to get to know each other better. But when she said she was returning to France for the holiday, I had sunk into a depression.

'We intend to leave by zero-nine-hundred,' said my father. 'It's a long drive and I want to get there in daylight. Good Friday is busy on the roads. Are you going to the Easter Sunday service at St Wilfrid's?'

This gave me a shock. The headmaster expected the staff to attend the Easter Sunday service at school even though it was the holidays. Many of the parents came along for the service. In his role as a governor of the school, the school would also appreciate his presence at the service. What a dilemma.

'I suppose you won't be able to go if you are travelling?'

'Please offer our apologies. I am sure the headmaster will understand.'

'Yes, of course.'

The prospect of a long sung Mass by Father Roderick filled me with dread. Thinking back, I had only attended this rite of passage once, in my first year at the school. But this year I could see no way out unless I became ill.

'I hope that means we can count on you to be at Mass at St Wilfrid's, representing the Fletchers?'

'Definitely possible,' I agreed.

Chapter 17

My parents departed on their trip to Norfolk, and I felt a warm glow walking around the empty house. Nelson had stirred to say goodbye, and I gave him a large bowl of food and let him play in the garden. Yesterday's snow had melted, and the weather was mild and cloudy.

Mid-morning, I drove over to the George & Dragon. The Saturday before Easter Sunday would be a busy time for the London set to reconnect with their friends. Throngs of excitable youths and giggling girls packed the lounge bar. They were standing three layers deep, vying for the attention of the harassed bar staff. Queuing for a drink was not my priority. I was scanning the faces for anyone I knew. The worst situation is to be in a pub full of strangers. Standing alone looks sad and lonely, friendless, and ignored. My eyes searched only for her, so when a hand touched my shoulder, it startled me. I turned to see Julie smiling up at me. But I was wrong. It was Lizzie.

'Hi, Michael. We haven't seen you for ages. Come and join us over in the corner. Julie was just saying the other day we should see what you are up to this Easter,' she pointed over to a far table. I caught Julie's eye, and she smiled and gave me a shy wave.

'I'd love to. I was just going to the bar. Would you like a drink?'

'Thanks. Could you get me a gin and tonic?'

'I guess Julie will have the same?'

'God, no. We may be identical twins, but we have opposite tastes. Get her a coke and lime. She prefers soft drinks.'

I thought identical twins had the same likes and dislikes. Today, they were different—Lizzie wore a short skirt, blouse, and trainers whereas Julie wore a stone-washed denim jacket with blue jeans and black knee-length boots.

'Michael,' Julie greeted me with a dazzling smile. 'Where have you been all my life?'

'Well, you know, busy at school with the usual stuff. I haven't seen you since that game of tennis a few weeks ago. I meant to apologise as I haven't played tennis for ages. Your sister and Michael Cox soundly beat us.'

'That was fun. Michael Cox is annoyingly good at tennis, isn't he? He seems to forget it's only a game. But I thought you played very well.'

'Thanks. What else? Yea, school has been better, and I have picked up some tutoring work, so all good.'

'Is it like that old Pink Floyd video?' said Lizzie. 'Another Brick in the Wall? Does your school have a horrible headmaster?'

'Yes. It's extreme, but there is a lot of truth in it. Education is like a factory routine churning out identical sausages at the end of the process, just like in the Pink Floyd song. And our headmaster is a very firm disciplinarian.'

'You mean he canes the boys?'

'He delights in finding loads of petty rules which are caning offences if not obeyed.'

'But St Wilfrid's is an excellent school,' Julie added. 'That song is more about State schools, I think. And everyone has forgotten about the unfortunate murder of your French teacher.'

'St Wilfrid's is an old-fashioned Catholic faith school, so religion is central to them. Passing exams is less important, so the teaching is more relaxed. We *do* encourage pupils to think for themselves.'

'Do you have to be a Catholic to work there?' asked Lizzie. The popular view of Catholics was to treat them with caution, or you might end up trapped in a mirthless marriage with countless children.

'No, many of the staff are not. In fact, even anti-Catholic or agnostic, but we are all tolerated.'

'I think it's creepy the way religion interferes with young people's lives and makes out anything enjoyable is some sort of mortal sin,' said Julie.

'You know a bit about it?'

'Of course, our mother sent us to her old boarding school in Berkshire. It's a famous Catholic school and very refined and expensive. So, we know *all* about it.'

'Please, let's not reminisce about school. It's an episode of our lives we dislike being reminded of,' interrupted Lizzie. 'Are you doing anything special for Easter, Michael?'

'Not really. Nothing planned. My parents are away visiting friends in Norfolk, and they have left me to look after the dog.'

'Oh. How sweet. I love dogs. What breed is it?' asked Julie.

'He's an old black Labrador called Nelson. He lies in front of the fire all day. If a burglar broke in, he would just get up and wag his tail. He is a waste of space.'

'What about you two? Anything exciting planned?'

'How we wish,' said Lizzie. 'Michael Cox asked us over for a shoot. We don't want to go. We are bad shots and hate killing pheasants.'

'I spoke to Michael last week, and he mentioned the shoot, but it's not my thing,' I said. 'He was in a hurry to attend a friend's wedding in Hampshire. Someone called Bunty.'

'What a tart,' added Lizzie.

'Let's change the subject,' said Julie.

'Can I get you girls another of the same?' I noticed Lizzie had finished her gin and tonic already, whereas Julie's coke and lime was untouched.

'I fancy a change,' said Lizzie. 'The barman makes a marvellous Tom Collins. I love the way he adds a lemon slice and maraschino cherry garnish. So stylish,' she pointed out the young man behind the bar, who was the only member of staff capable of creating this masterpiece.

'Go on. I'll try one as well. I don't drink, but Lizzie has led me astray. If I drive home, there is no telling what might happen. A fast car on narrow country roads and a deer might rush out. My natural reaction would be to slam on the brakes and next thing I might skid and hit a tree.'

'If you are over the drink-drive limit, leave the car here. I would be happy to drive you all home.' The girls agreed this was a good plan. They sipped their Tom Collins like cats with a saucer of cream. It was an expensive drink for a small measure of gin, soda, and some lemon juice. I suppose the cherry on the top justified the price tag, but it was worth it to see them happy.

'When is this shoot at Michael's parents' estate?' I asked.

'Easter Monday,' said Julie. 'We will give it a miss as Bunty Bulstrode and her new husband may be there. And some others we do not want to meet.'

'That crowd is so predictable,' said Lizzie. 'It's all those hunting types. Worst of all is their obnoxious little boys. You see these 12-year-olds firing off both barrels of a 12-bore shotgun in all directions—so unsafe.'

'No doubt the same boys will join the army and end up shooting people instead of pheasants,' I said.

'Peasants instead of pheasants,' said Lizzie, which they both found hilarious.

'Is that one of your sports, Michael?' asked Julie. 'You look the sporting type.'

'What shooting? No, I feel the same way as you do. And fox hunting is even worse.'

'We think it's barbaric and disgusting, too,' said Lizzie, smiling at me. 'But one should be tolerant. There are those who say it's upholding the country's traditions and is needed to control excess foxes and game birds. Of course, that's just an excuse. Most of these hunters are cowardly bed-wetters.'

'Drink up my dearies, the bar is closing in ten minutes,' the barmaid, a large lady with muscular arms, tried to whisk away our glasses. The girls held on to their drinks, but my pint glass was empty, and she grabbed it in triumph.

'But there are still people drinking in the restaurant,' I complained.

'They are *eating* and entitled to carry on drinking until three. Drinkers,' she added with disdain, 'have to abide by the licensing laws and the bar is now closed.' She folded her arms in case I needed a push towards the door.

'You said it was closing in ten minutes time.'

'That's the drinking up time, love. I see your glass is empty, whereas the young ladies have some left. It's two for last orders.' With a self-satisfied smile, she moved on to harass other customers.

'What a cow. The licensing laws are so stupid, aren't they?' Julie tossed back the rest of her Tom Collins and sucked on the maraschino cherry. 'Erm, this tastes *soo* good.'

'I am happy to drive you home in case you are over the limit.'

'Two weak Tom Collins is *hardly* over the limit,' said Lizzie. 'I am quite sober enough to drive.'

'Yes,' agreed Julie. 'But you didn't bring your car. I gave you a lift, remember?'

'You had at least three Tom Collins each and I have only drunk one beer, so it would be best to leave your car here. I can drive you both home.'

Lizzie agreed it was the best plan, considering meeting such a strict upholder of the law. After all, it was a quick trip back to the pub later when she was more sober to drop Julie back to rescue her car. In the car park, I noticed the blue Ford Escort and wondered who was on surveillance duty.

'The blue Escort following us is, I suspect, an unmarked police car. He may stop and breathalyse me, but by law he has to have a reason to pull me over such as a light not working.'

'I think you are driving awfully well,' slurred Lizzie. 'Although a bit on the slow side.'

'It's a forty limit, silly,' said Julie. 'How do you know he's the police?'

'He is a policeman from Pulborough, I am sure. Let's see what happens if my driving becomes erratic.' I swung the wheel towards the centre of the road and then swung the car back again, causing the girls to fall about. As expected, the head lights on the Escort flashed on and the car overtook us and flagged us down. Inspector Bishop walked over to speak to me. He presented his warrant card as ID as required by law. The girls giggled, which was not helpful.

'Excuse me, sir. I notice your car was all over the place back there. Have we perhaps been to the pub and been drinking?'

'It was my fault, officer,' said Julie. 'It was a bee. It must have flown in the window and scared me and then it flew right into my friend's face and made him lose control just for a moment.'

'That's how it happened—a bee attack. But ask me to blow into your bag if you wish. I am innocent.'

Bishop asked for my driving licence, which I did not have with me, so he requested I present it to a police station within seven days. He asked my name, address, and date of birth and when I gave them, he acted surprised and said of course he was sorry for not recognising me, but I was that teacher friend of the poor murdered French teacher.

'The one thing you failed to mention, Inspector Bishop, is that I was a friend of Michelle's and innocent of the crime you and Brighton police have been keen to pin on me. I am also aware of your constant police surveillance, which has no justification, and I will be approaching my solicitor to discuss the continued harassment, including this uncalled-for act of stopping me without due cause.'

Poor Bishop was unsure what to do next. His mouth gaped open in surprise. Whilst I had been talking, he produced the breathalyser and decided he had better go ahead with the test. He showed me the procedure for blowing into it. I did as he said and recorded a zero reading. The girls asked if he would breathalyse them as well. He replied he had no jurisdiction over inebriated passengers. This set them laughing, so I motioned them to calm down, as the police might invent a new offence for them. Deflated, he asked where I was driving to, and I explained I was giving the girls a lift home to Burpham. He asked the girls' names, but I said it was irrelevant and he had no right to ask for passenger's names when there was no evidence of them committing a crime.

At the girls' house, they invited me in. Their parents were out. They were unsure where, but agreed it was probably shopping or walking the dog. We discussed the pros and cons of parents and agreed they were a necessary evil. Lizzie discovered a half-empty bottle of white wine and some cheese and biscuits. Julie made some coffee, and it felt normal. We discussed jobs, and I learnt the twins worked on London's go-to guide *Time Out* for the best places for food and drink, events, attractions, and things to do. Like any job, it had upsides and downsides. Of the former were free offers to test out new restaurants and write up reviews, free entry to theatres, cinemas, and exhibitions; on the downside, excessive research was boring and repetitive. Lizzie loved the total scene, but Julie savoured more serious investigative journalism. *Time Out* did some of this, which was rewarding.

I told them a little about Michelle's background as a research chemist in France and her cooperation with her brother in Southampton, looking at the effects of chemicals from plastic leaching into water and food stuffs. Hostile forces were at work trying to stop the research and it was possible her activities had led to her violent death.

'The editor at the *New Scientist* is adamant that none of their staffers met Michelle. In fact, they cannot trace the letter she wrote even though there is a polite reply, unsigned. I am due to meet him in London next week. As the police have been so useless, I have been working with Michelle's brother, Mark, looking through her research for any clues.'

'Wow, it's cloak-and-dagger stuff,' said Julie. 'Is there anything we can do to help?'

'In fact, there is. After the meeting at the *New Scientist,* I have a contact at St Thomas' Hospital I want to see. I may stay in London overnight and wonder if you can recommend any cheap hotel or bed-and-breakfast place?'

'Hotels in London cost a fortune. No need to waste money, Michael. You can stay at my flat in West Kensington,' volunteered Julie. 'One girl has left, so there is a spare room.'

Chapter 18

Most of the staff, with their families, had turned out for the 11 a.m. Easter Sunday Mass, celebrated by Father Roderick. The boys usually packed the front row, but it was the holidays, so the church was nearly empty apart from a sprinkling of day boys and their parents, looking awkward and self-conscious. The parents stared at every new arrival, hoping others would join them, but none did. The staff hung back, favouring the seats as far from the altar as possible, apart from Miss Cresswell, who sat alone on the front pew watching Roderick celebrate the Mass with no disturbance from coughing parishioners. It was one of those rare occasions when she had left her annoying dog behind. I was pleased to see Laureline and Charlie in mid-chapel and joined them rather than stay with my over-dressed colleagues at the back. Amazing how important the seating conventions were. I had breached some protocol by sitting with a parent.

'Michael, happy Easter,' said Laureline in a hushed whisper. Everyone had stopped chatting to listen to us. 'I forgot that tomorrow's Easter Monday. No need for the tutorial.'

'No, tomorrow is fine. I can be there for midday as we arranged.'

'Midday then. As it is a holiday, I believe I should pay you twice the normal rate.'

'No, that's unnecessary. Hi Charlie, how's Macbeth?'

'It is an interesting play exploring the way Macbeth and Lady Macbeth are so obsessed with power. They believed the witches and look what happened.'

He was so serious both Laureline and I laughed.

'If you liked Macbeth, read Hamlet next,' I said.

A bell rang and Father Roderick and the servers entered from the vestry with a medieval flourish. Everyone stopped talking and stood up to welcome the priest, dressed in white vestments as opposed to the purple hue of Lent. The organ burst into life with *'Jesus Christ is risen today'* and everyone opened their hymn books with military precision, ready to sing the hymn. Roderick was at his most efficient. He sensed the congregation wanted a rapid service with a short sermon and nothing too thought provoking. The major festivals, such as Christmas and Easter, attracted those lapsed Catholics and non-Catholics who liked to turn up for the occasion. He had not seen most of them since the Christmas Midnight Mass. It must tick some box with them. With less attendance would follow a slow decline of these magnificent buildings until, in the distant future, nature would encroach and eroded by rain and storm, the roof would fall, leaving jagged walls and hidden memories. But today the altar was awash with flowers and dust particles danced in the sunbeams slanting through the stained-glass windows. Roderick searched the rows looking for regulars and noticed the absence of some staff and families he expected to be present. He was aware of Miss Cresswell smiling back from the front row—such a loyal supporter. A few sympathetic faces were a relief, but it was the predictable crowd that stared back, each with a void within, seeking a reassurance he found harder and harder to fulfil.

As the final hymn *'Thine be the Glory'* set to the tune of Handel's Maccabaeus rang out, he felt his tension release like a spring uncoiling. The Mass was over, and the congregation departed slowly, stopping to have a word or two at the door, where he struggled to remember parents' names. Many dropped a few coins into the plate rather than a £1 note, which was the least one should expect. Then again, the school fees were exorbitant, and he sympathised with the middle-class parents struggling to survive in these troubled times. There was a reception in the school library, another painful duty to perform.

I hated these social occasions, but I had to appear on behalf of my absent father. The drinks and snack spread were some compensation.

'Surprised to see you here today,' Jones sidled up, a glass of red wine in one hand and a sherry in the other. 'Just getting the drinks in,' he motioned towards a large lady with a bold beetroot-coloured hat standing beside the fireplace, who I guessed was Mrs Jones. She had cornered Father Roderick and was in deep conversation.

'I am here as the official representative of my father. As a school governor he is expected to be here.' I needed to clarify that I was only here out of duty—a painfully boring duty.

'Of course, Michael, as you claim to be a dedicated atheist, I understand your sacrifice. Your father will be proud of you. But none of them want to deal with the problem.'

'Problem. What problem?'

'Can't talk. Catch you later.'

What was he about to divulge? I looked desperately for someone else to talk to. Nigel Caldwell-Brown was over by the bay window with his wife. Closer to my age but, despite that, middle-aged and dull in outlook, as if weighed down with constant worries. Their young baby slept contentedly in a pram beside them. They were pleased to see me, fed up with being ignored by the little cliques of the contented as opposed to the rest of us gauche and friendless souls.

'Michael, my wife, Jane. Oh yes, you met at the bash at the pub.'

'Oh, hi. And this is…' I was looking at their baby, uncertain if it was a boy or a girl. Jane sensed my confusion.

'This is dear little Hannah. She is just six months old. It was her first Easter service, and she slept right through it. What a good little girl,' she trilled. 'Are you married, Michael?'

'No, not yet. I haven't any plans in that direction.' I squirmed, hating questions like this.

'But I feel pretty married to your old car.' It was a joke, of course, but Jane just looked at me in horror.

'Michael bought your Triumph Herald,' Caldwell-Brown reminded her. 'He loves it like a woman, don't you, Michael? That's what you meant.'

'Yes, sorry, it was a bad joke.'

'No, hilarious, and I see what you mean. I felt the same way about the car before I met Nigel.'

Fortune sometimes helps at difficult moments and the headmaster loomed into view dressed smartly, for him, in a formal dark suit with a matching waistcoat. Ill-fitting, so I suspect an old suit reserved for formal occasions. The waistcoat bulged under the strain of his belly, exaggerated by the bottom button left open to relieve the strain.

'Michael, it is good of you to come. Is your father here? I have not seen him for ages.'

'No, my parents have gone away for the Easter holiday, visiting friends in Norfolk. They are getting quite adventurous. At Christmas, they went away to Devon.'

'World travellers,' he joked. 'Perhaps they have popped into Sandringham?' I took him literally.

'No, I don't think so. They left me the dog to look after.'

'Probably less trouble than this little one here,' he said. Jane gave him an icy glare and he moved on to chat with other victims.

'You looked a bit puzzled by the allusion to Sandringham,' said Nigel. 'It's where the royal family goes during the holiday, but I believe they only stay there for Christmas, not Easter.'

'That's right,' said Jane, an expert on the monarchy. 'Everyone knows the Queen stays at Windsor Castle at Easter. This year Diana and Charles are away in Australia, so it will be dull for the press with no one to hound. Obviously, the head thinks the Queen and Prince Phillip favour Norfolk at Easter. He is such an ignorant man.'

'I don't care where they stay, the whole concept of royalty is an anachronism—a quaint and old-fashioned tradition, a bit like this school when you come to think of it.'

'Steady on,' Caldwell-Brown looked offended. 'The Queen does a great job. Without royalty, this country would be some ghastly republic like France.'

'Well, I agree she plays her role very well, but you shouldn't run down France like that. At least they have a written constitution, which we don't; and ideals of "Liberty, Equality and Fraternity." President Mitterrand seems quite reasonable, and we all get on fine together in the Common Market.'

'Our entry into the Common Market was a disaster. The sooner we get out and run our own show, the better.'

Clearly, Caldwell-Brown was insular and bigoted. The conversation was not in his comfort zone. It was obvious he had little knowledge beneath his pre-conceptions, just bluster. He left abruptly—a sign that I should move on. I sampled the appalling cold buffet of cocktail sausages, chunks of cheese and pineapple on sticks, bowls of potato crisps and sandwich rolls filled with Kraft cheese slices, Spam or sandwich spread. If you were a child of the 1960s, it was the sort of party buffet a group of flatmates might throw together in a flat in Earl's Court according to Jones who, unlike me, had experienced that period in our history. I remember Jones had hinted at some mysterious problem. Before I left, I tracked him down and asked him what the issue was that no one wanted to deal with.

'Possibly I spoke too soon,' he said. 'But there is a rumour that the headmaster wants to downgrade the Latin syllabus to a Classics option. Forget learning Latin verbs and replace with Greek and Roman history.'

'You mentioned this before, Jones. What's different?'

'Before it was only a suggestion. Now the rumour is that it *will* go ahead.'

'No more *amo, amas, amat?*'

'Precisely. The thin end of the wedge. In due course the head will announce his new initiative to make Latin fun.'

I reassured Jones that I was on his side and would help resist this march into populism. I had put in a decent appearance, gave my excuses, and left. I was in a hurry for my lunch appointment.

On arrival at Julie's, I parked alongside her red TR6 on the wide gravel chipped driveway. She had retrieved her car from the pub. The front door was ajar. I let myself in. I could hear music playing from a drawing room to the right. I walked through this large room, which had doors opening out to the garden veranda where a planter lounge set caught the brief afternoon sun. The room had several sofas and armchairs, all faded, as were the curtains, but the overall impression was of comfortable elegance. Sounds came from the kitchen, set down a corridor off the hallway, and this is where I found Julie and her mother preparing lunch.

They say that many children end up looking like their parents and even morph into clones with the same attitudes and prejudices. If that was the case, then the twins' parents were a couple I felt I could immediately relate to. The mother was warm and friendly, the father more restrained, as if I was another one in a long line of former boyfriends. They asked the usual questions and were interested in my honest impressions of the school. I was cautious in my replies and not over-critical except to say I was against single-sex schools.

This set up a lively debate with everyone except their father favouring change, whereas he was a stickler for the status quo.

'Just the four of us. Lizzie is with her boyfriend,' Julie whispered as she handed me a glass of sparkling wine. 'They are not too happy, so try to distract them.'

Lunch was a large roast chicken with roast potatoes, leeks in cheese sauce, carrots, plus the usual trimmings of sage and onion stuffing, chipolata sausages, and bread sauce. It was delicious. The sparkling wine for starters was a Moët et Chandon champagne and there was an old claret and another white wine with the meal.

'I read in the *Daily Mail* that the police have been on the wrong track with the killing of the French teacher at your school. The way the media was targeting you was disgraceful,' said Julie's father. 'It must have been a dreadful experience.'

'After the negative press reports, there was some hostility from parents at the school and the headmaster suggested I take some time off while the police completed their investigations. They suspended me on full pay for half the term. The police are reluctant to consider other suspects even though we have good evidence of a person of interest. The police call that a POI.'

'I hope you don't mind,' said Julie. 'But I filled them in about all the weird stuff that has been happening and how the police keep following you wherever you go. I bet they are even listening in to your phone calls!'

'Maybe, but they need to apply for a court warrant for tapping private phone lines. All they would hear is my mother arranging games of bridge or my father chatting to his friends from the golf club.'

'Seriously,' said Julie's father. 'The police get up to a lot more snooping than they admit to. If you need an excellent solicitor to get them off your back, just ask. I know a firm who specialises in police harassment cases.'

'Michael says it's pointless waiting for the police to find her killer. He has been busy investigating it himself and making significant progress.'

'Not just me. Michelle's brother, Mark, is researching drinking water contamination by plastic. His discoveries have stirred up powerful people in the water industry. Is there someone alarmed enough to suppress the research or even commit murder?'

'Contamination by plastic?' This issue concerned Julie's mother more than the threat of murder.

'Apparently, all those drinks you see packed in plastic bottles are leaching harmful chemicals into the water, milk, or whatever it is. Some of them, for example BPA, may upset the hormone balance in young adults and even cause cancers,' said Julie.

'Scare talk,' Julie's father dismissed the claim. 'The quantities are minute and will have no effect on a normal, healthy individual. Do you really think governments all around the world don't monitor the drinks and packaging industry? Plastic packaging has been in use for years. Are you saying it is only now any dangers are being flagged up?'

'I thought the same way,' I said. 'But Mark at his research laboratory has identified some worrying results. Also, we have a contact at a hospital in London who has detected BPA in samples during routine sampling of urine. According to him, BPA is ubiquitous and likely to be ingested every day by most of the population. Michelle became involved as a whistleblower to raise public awareness.'

'Anyone for pudding?' asked Julie's mother.

Chapter 19

The phone ringing downstairs in the hall sent a jolt of electricity through me. Some automatic reaction sent me scurrying down the stairs, grabbing a towel on the way with a vestige of modesty.

'Hello, hello.'

'Yes, mother.'

'Michael, you took ages to answer. I can't believe you are still in bed at ten.'

'Sorry, mother—I was in the bathroom.'

'The snow drifts have closed a lot of roads, including the A10. We are trapped in Norfolk. We cannot leave today. I hope it thaws out so we can travel tomorrow.'

Gazing out of the window, I could see the snow had thawed.

'There is no snow here.'

'Oh, dear—the car can't handle the snow. Your father is a bad enough driver as it is.'

'There's no hurry. Just come back when it's clear. Take your time.'

'Father wants to know if you went to the Easter Sunday service at school and did you offer his apologies?'

'Tell him yes. And I spoke to the headmaster to explain you are both away in Norfolk. There was the usual buffet spread, cheap wine, and a good turnout from the staff. Fortunately, Father Roderick kept the sermon short, so everyone was happy.'

'Oh, good—and how is Nelson?'

'Nelson is just fine. I have taken him on long walks every day.' As I fibbed again, I wondered where Nelson was. I hoped I had not let him run in the garden and forgotten to bring him back in.

'Well, it must be very boring for you stuck at home. You ought to have someone over for tea—maybe that friend of yours, Michael Cox.'

'Don't worry about me, ma.'

Julie appeared in the hall and tried to distract me. She tugged at my towel, unravelling it, so I was bursting with laughter as I put the phone down. She ran back upstairs, giggling. I went into the kitchen, made some coffee, and rummaged about for things for breakfast. It confused me as I tried to piece together the events of the night before.

After the Easter lunch at her parents, I remembered I went home to clear up and feed Nelson. The evening was an anti-climax after the busy Easter Sunday, and I was falling asleep in front of the TV when Julie called to say she needed rescuing from the George & Dragon. She and Lizzie had looked in, but it was quite dead with none of their friends there apart from Lizzie's boyfriend, Jack, sitting at the bar. After a drink, they left for another pub, but Julie stayed on. She had hoped that I would drop by, so she waited longer, just in case. On impulse, she called me from the pub's pay phone and apologised for disturbing me so late. I was tired and grumpy.

She explained how she had left her car lights on and drained the battery. The car would not start. She was stranded friendless and alone. I perked up at the prospect of filling the role of the knight in white armour rescuing the damsel in distress. I complained how it was very late, rubbing the sleep from my eyes, and agreed to meet her in twenty minutes. Best to stay in the pub to keep warm.

I suspected the girls had planned this, so I drove back to the Old Rectory. Telling the girls my parents were away for Easter made me complicit and keen to take advantage of the opportunity.

Compared to her parents' estate, our house was a more modest old Victorian farmhouse. Once, it had several acres of farmland, but previous owners had sold much of it off to developers. The present plot was only an acre of garden and a surround of mature trees. We were not over-looked by neighbours. At night, the house looked enormous and imposing. If I left the lights on, then the warm glow stood out against the dark trees.

My visitor excited Nelson, who bounded about like a puppy. I offered her coffee, but she said she fancied something stronger, like a Tom Collins or vodka. The night was still young, and she was grateful to escape the pub. For a teetotaller, she knew all the drinks to ask for, but she could see cocktail making was not one of my skills and accepted a Bacardi on ice with a cold bottle of Coca-Cola. We sat by the fire with Nelson at our feet, listening to music. Her knee-length black leather boots seemed a bit too formal, and she asked me to pull them off.

Julie lit up two Rothmans and passed one to me. It felt decadent, like being players in an avant-garde film with no script. I flung more logs on the fire and prodded it back to life with the poker. Soon, welcome flames shot out, throwing dramatic stabs of light and shade across the room. I pushed the sofa nearer to the fire, forcing Nelson to get up and move out of the way. This created a womb-like shelter enveloping us. The glowing fire had a hypnotic force warming us, relieving the stress of the day. Julie stretched her legs out towards the fire, warming her bare toes. There was no need for words, but at last, I broke the silence.

'It must be so amazing to be identical twins. Do you have a rapport where you know what each of you is thinking and feeling?'

'Maybe, when we were younger. Our parents liked to dress us alike, and at Christmas, our presents were the same. Then we rebelled, and we tried to be different. We still dress the same when we feel like it, but no, we are separate individuals. That is why she went off with her boyfriend, Jack, and abandoned me in the pub. Lucky she did.'

'And you work in the same office in London? Do you share a flat with Lizzie as well?'

'Yes, to start with. But she moved out last year. Now we get along much better.'

'I hope she is okay. Do you want to ring her to put your mind at rest?'

She looked surprised at the suggestion and reclined back on the sofa.

'As you are both twins, I was wondering if there is any physical feature different between you. Some subtle detail perhaps?' With a mischievous grin, she pulled herself up so her face loomed close to mine.

'I have a birth mark in an interesting place. It's just a small blemish.' She pulled the top out of her jeans and leant forward, revealing a small light-brown pigmentation about an inch across on the left-side of her lower back.

'Just below my bikini line, so no one can see it unless I am naked.'

'Very charming and distinctive,' I said.

After a few more drinks, it was too risky to drive her home, so I offered her my parents' bedroom. Not used to drink she had to be assisted upstairs, and I dropped her on the bed where she passed out like a grounded whale. After a couple of rum and cokes on top of drinks in the pub with Lizzie, it was enough to knock her out.

After the wake-up call from my mother, I made some coffee and a basic breakfast loaded onto a tray to share. The master bedroom had the best view over the garden and the sunshine filling the room made it look inviting. We sipped coffee and ate buttered fingers of toast and marmalade in bed. I had found Nelson, and he came into the bedroom wagging his tail. Julie looked thoughtful; a frown creased her brow.

'Michael, it's so boring for me to be working in London with you down here at your school. We need to have more time together.'

'You come down on weekends so we can meet. And there will be more opportunities during the school holidays. I plan to be in London for a few days so we can look forward to spending more time together.'

'But you *still* live at home with your parents. When I am down here, I stay with my parents. God, *what* shall I say when they ask where I was last night?'

'Just tell them the truth. Your car broke down. I rescued you and after a few drinks, we both decided the safest option was for you to stay here—in the spare bedroom, of course. That's what happened after all.'

'I don't drink. At least I didn't until you and Lizzie led me astray. Did you put me to bed? I must have been out like a light. When I woke up this morning, I was under this thick, warm quilt. Did you do that?'

'Yes, it's a freezing house. I didn't want you to catch hypothermia. You were tired, plus just a few too many drinks. Quite understandable. My room upstairs is even colder than this one.'

'Maybe I'll call mum in case they are worried about me—can I do that?'

'Lizzie might have set you up with an alibi, best check with her first.'

'Life is so complicated when you have to lie, isn't it?'

'Don't think of it as lying. It's just saying things to avoid complications. The truth can be over-rated. We are adults and no longer little children. Parents forget that.'

'Could I have another cup of your delicious coffee? Afterwards can we look at the garden or just laze about all day?'

But I remembered something important.

'I have to give a boy a tutorial at midday. I'm sorry I arranged it some time ago.'

'At midday. It's eleven-thirty now. You will be late.'

'True. I'll give Laureline a call and see if I can make it an hour later. That will give me time for a quick shower and freshen up.'

Downstairs, I made some fresh coffee and explained the situation to Laureline with my apologies. I mentioned my friend Julie was visiting over Easter. Laureline said not to hurry, and suggested I bring Julie over and we could all have a pleasant lunch after the tutorial session.

When I returned to the bedroom, Julie was coming out of the shower and asked me for a hair dryer.

'That's good. Laureline says to take our time. She said it is her fault for expecting me to work on Easter Monday and she is eager not to interfere with your holiday plans.'

'My holiday plans?'

'Yes, I said you are visiting me over the Easter holiday. She suggests I bring you over when I have the tutorial with Charlie and stay for lunch. You will like Laureline. They are new arrivals to the school from Hong Kong. If you like, of course. If you would prefer to go straight home, then I can drop you off. Laureline's house is just outside Burpham.'

'I accept her kind offer. After, can you drop me back at the pub to pick up my car?'

I remembered her car had a flat battery and went to look for jump leads from the garage. She looked sheepish and suggested we could try to start it first. Maybe the car had recovered during the day, as it wasn't so cold.

At 1 p.m. I resumed reading Macbeth with Charlie and Laureline. Julie took over Laureline's part when she left to attend to the meal—a simple dish of chilli con carne and rice.

At the same time in Norfolk, the Fletchers walked gingerly up to the shops along the icy pavement. The salt grit had melted some of the snow, but it was still slippery underfoot. Litter of discarded plastic bottles and takeaway food containers buried by the snow re-emerged as the snow and ice melted into rivulets coursing across the pavement.

Charles and Davinia had been hospitable, but after two days stuck inside the house, eating, drinking, and recalling the Malaya campaign, the urge to escape was strong.

'Let's go to the pub,' said the major in desperation. 'The east coast is always worse in winter than anywhere else. I'm worried this snow may not melt for days and trap us here for ages—just like the big freeze of 1963.'

'But we said we would get them a bottle of wine from the supermarket.'

'That can wait. I need a proper drink first. I can't stand another of their glasses of sherry before dinner.'

It was a cheerless, new-build pub on the edge of town geared towards the young in the neighbouring housing estates. A large television was showing a football game, and the customers gazed at the screen with disinterest and downed pints of lager. The Fletchers opted for a double whisky and soda and sat by a simulated log fire, eating salted peanuts past their best-by date.

'I think Michael had a friend with him when I rang this morning. I am sure I heard a female giggling in the background.'

'Well, good for him. A female, you say. That is encouraging. It's time he thought about the future. He can't stay with us forever.'

'We shouldn't read too much into it. Perhaps he had a party of friends over.'

'What in the early morning?'

'You know what young people are like. They have sleepovers. They don't want to be driving home after a few drinks, so they "kip" down for the night in a sleeping bag. It was probably a girl he put up overnight.'

'As long as they haven't been drinking my booze and being sick everywhere. Honestly, we go away for a couple of days, and he is busy having wild parties and orgies in our house. Look at the mess he caused at Christmas. This is an awful pub. Another drink here or should we go to the supermarket?'

Chapter 20

After the holiday, I expected the editor of *New Scientist* would be busy, so I left it until midday before calling him. My parents were travelling back from Norfolk, so I was keen to use the house phone to set up meetings for the coming week without the disruption their return might cause. After several attempts, I spoke to the editor.

'Ah, Michael, I was meaning to call you. I am pleased to say we have made some progress. It appears one of our staffers, Peter Fowler, remembers Michelle's letter. He invited her to meet him at our office. This meeting went ahead in early January. Peter says she fixed it up just after returning from France and before she had to return to her teaching post at school. The same school as you are working at, so maybe you already know this timeline?'

This was a surprise to me. Then I remembered she had visited Dominic and stayed for a few days, so the meeting at the *New Scientist* was logical.

'I think it was all last minute,' said the editor. 'The upshot was she presented some of her findings about the status of plastics in the food and drinks packaging industry. I should add that none of this is new to us as there have been concerns and several studies in the USA and elsewhere for many years. We all know about the factor of chemical leaching of BPA into drinks such as water and milk. However, she did present an alarming result from a testing laboratory on a sample called Sample X which did have unsafe levels of some toxins. As she wasn't at liberty to name the test laboratory or identify where it originated from, our hands were tied.'

'I may help you with that, but I will have to clear it with the testing laboratory first. I am aware of this case.'

'Peter has been working for us since we started the *New Scientist* in 1962. He came to us straight from Cambridge University where he got a first in chemistry. He is in his 50s, but very fit as he goes by bicycle everywhere.'

'I plan to be in London sometime this week. Would there be a chance to meet Peter Fowler and discuss this further?'

'I don't see why not. Let me talk to him and see when would suit him. What day will you be in London?'

'I was planning on catching the train up on Friday morning, so Friday afternoon would be best.'

'Will get back to you and see if that works. If you can get more information about the test and its provenance, that would be brilliant. Bye.'

After this development, I was very confused. I paced about the house, trying to work out what to do next. Were we on the wrong track? I looked through all Michelle's files once again in case I had missed something. She kept a record of her correspondence in date order in a ring file with annotated notes for the date of any replies or phone contacts. But there was no mention of her trip to London to see Peter Fowler at the *New Scientist*. Presumably, she had visited Dominic at the same time. It was getting late, and my parents would be back soon, so I wanted to be away from the house to avoid any inquisition about Julie's visit. My efforts at tidying up were impressive. I had even bought another bottle of Bacardi to top up my father's bottle to the halfway point. I felt confident that the house and contents were back in their normal state, and I had removed all evidence of our time together.

The ever-reliable Mark answered my call at once and reassured me he enjoyed a pleasant Easter break.

'I just spoke to the editor of the *New Scientist,* and they have identified the person Michelle was dealing with. Apparently, she visited their London office in early January. Did you know about this?'

'No. I knew she planned to see Dominic, but she never mentioned going to the *New Scientist*. Their office is in New Oxford Street, so I expect she caught the tube direct from Victoria.'

I still felt uneasy about using the house phone and volunteered to drive over to discuss the latest news with him. He agreed, and I gathered my things together and headed for my car.

When the Fletchers arrived back home, it surprised them at how tidy the house was. Michael had washed up the dishes and left the house spotless. This was a first. His mother looked upstairs and noticed that there were fresh sheets on the bed in the master bedroom, but Michael's bedroom was in its usual state of untidiness. She detected a lingering aroma of a musky amber perfume, which was Calvin Klein's *Obsession*. However, she was not aware of the names of modern perfumes. She was fond of the classic and timeless richness of Chanel No 5. This strange perfume was quite unsettling, and she conjured up an image of the sort of woman attracted to this as someone brazen and very young, rather than a mature woman. Her suspicions were confirmed when she discovered long blonde hairs in the shower. With a sigh, she took Nelson for a walk. It would take her mind off things. Best not to meddle. Whatever Michael had got up this time, he was mature enough to deal with it.

The major had gone straight to the drinks cabinet and noticed the whisky bottles were untouched. The Bacardi bottle was about half full. It was not a drink he liked, but he kept it for guests, especially younger people. As he closed the door, he noticed there were two bottles of Bacardi, both half-full, which was very odd.

Since the episode with Inspector Bishop, the police had suspended surveillance, so Michael did not notice the black BMW following him until he was on the motorway. The car was still on his tail after the Portsmouth and then the Fareham exits. At junction seven, he slowed down sharply. This caught the BMW unawares, and the car approached so close he could make out two males looking startled before they eased back. Michael drove past the Solent Industrial Estate and headed onto Shamblehurst Lane south. Passing St Luke's church, he noticed a parade of shops and pulled into an available parking spot. The BMW found a parking spot next to St Luke's at a point where they could see Michael's car when he left the shopping parade. They had trapped him in a cul-de-sac with nowhere to go.

'Mark. I have a problem.' Luckily, I had noticed a phone box outside a Tesco Express. 'I have a tail, but it's not the usual Pulborough police. Two people followed me all the way on the motorway in a black BMW.' The phone line was about to break off. I searched for more coins.

'Give me your number,' said Mark. I looked along the pavement at the pedestrians searching for the men from the BMW. I think they wore suits, but it reassured me to see only families and pensioners going about their shopping. The phone rang, and I answered it with relief. I told Mark where I was, and we worked out a plan. I was to walk back along the row of shops and identify where they had parked the BMW and if both the guys were still in the car.

'Take your time. Light up a cigarette. If there is a paper shop, buy a paper. Let them see you. What are you wearing?'

'Normal stuff—shirt, tie, grey trousers and a dark green cardigan.'

'Great. Meet me inside Tesco's in ten minutes. I will bring along a jacket and a hat and you can ditch the tie and cardigan into my shopping bag. I will leave first and return to my car, and you can slip out as I am leaving and get in the passenger seat. Okay?'

'What if the men follow me into the supermarket? They may see us together.'

'One man may come looking for you and the other one will stay in the car. That's standard for MI5. Just keep alert.'

'MI5!'

'Yes, we are not dealing with country cops. These guys are professional. Once you are in my car, we have the advantage of surprise and can leave before they notice.'

Mark's plan went like clockwork. As we pulled away, I noticed one man standing by my car, a puzzled expression on his face. Mark confirmed their car was still in the church car park and no one was looking as his white Peugeot estate sailed past them. As an added precaution, he squashed me onto the floor of the passenger seat.

In the business estate, Mark parked several units away from his laboratory in a small parking space behind some skips as an added precaution, just in case the BMW entered the Solent Business Park. The ground floor laboratory was a hive of activity, but Mark directed me to the upstairs office, pausing only to order up two cups of coffee from Paula.

'How do you know those people are MI5?' I asked.

'It's the Spooks. Since the *Daily Mail* article revealed there is more to this case than the opportunist murder, the police are trying to frame you. We both know that, so it is logical the security forces are following you, as they suspect you and Michelle were working together. Tell me what the *New Scientist* fellow said.'

'I thought one of their freelancers was dealing with Michelle, but a senior staff member called Peter Fowler contacted her. She met him in London in January to present your joint research results. The editor explained they are well aware of the issues with plastic and PET bottles and the leaching problem but welcomed the new research. He said the high levels of toxins in Sample X were alarming, He wanted more information on the water source and bottling plant. You told me an oil company scientist, supportive of your work, passed it to you. I think the way forward is to find out the provenance of this sample.'

Mark paced about the office, looking thoughtful before returning to his desk and searching through a bunch of business cards.

'Let me see. Yes, here it is. Dr James Ridley, Ph.D., CGeol., FGS. He calls himself a geoscientist for Phoenix Oil. It's a new start up. They are looking for opportunities in the North Sea. Frankly, I cannot understand their interest in analysing water samples. When I noticed the high levels of BPA, I suspected a contaminated sample. If we leave water in a plastic bottle for a long time or subject it to high temperatures such as being left in the sun, this can speed up the leaching. But I kept about 250 ml of the sample for further analysis. I ran additional tests using chromatography, electrophoresis and sent some more to a colleague for mass spectrometer testing. The results showed trace readings for heavy metals and toxins, including arsenic, which could have a serious cumulative effect if the affected water has the same profile over a long period to show consistency. Frequent drinking of a few glasses a day could lead to serious health concerns and, in the worst-case scenario, even death.'

'How could that happen?' I asked.

'It suggests the water catchment area used for the water bottling has industrial pollutants such as industrial waste. Instead of fresh Spring water, someone is bottling and selling a harmful product to the public. Of course, in London we are all happy to drink water from the River Thames, but it conforms to UK and EU guidelines for potable water after filtration and chlorination to kill off the bacteria.'

'But London water tastes disgusting.'

'Maybe,' said Mark. 'But it is not harming you, unlike Sample X.'

Mark looked at a folder on his desk.

'I see we completed the latest tests on a batch of water samples from Phoenix Oil last Thursday, so I will follow up with James Ridley. Fortunately, they all look to be within normal parameters. I can't just ring him; I need to speak to him in person, so I will deliver the results to his office.'

'Which is where?'

'Not far away in Epsom. The other thing that concerns me is this journalist, Peter Fowler. If we can discount him as the man talking to Michelle in the pub, then we can trust him, but we need to be sure.'

'I will go to London this week—perhaps on Friday—to interview him, but the editor told me Peter doesn't match the description, and he is much older than the man I saw in the pub. The person Michelle met on Saturday 15th January was not Peter Fowler and was not from the *New Scientist*. It is also likely he was her killer.'

'Think of a way to give MI5 the slip. Were you planning to drive to London?'

'No, I will catch the train from Arundel. I can either drive my old Morris to the station car park or get a lift from my father. If I don't use the Triumph, I should get away with it. These people can't be hanging about outside my house at all hours.'

'Having lost you today, they may stop the surveillance. When you get back to your car, I suggest you check for any trackers stuck in the under carriage. From here to your car is only a short walk. That is the best option. I don't want them to see my car again, as they may work out the connection. It's important we keep my research laboratory off their radar.'

'What about the *New Scientist*? Can I mention your laboratory testing programme?'

'Oh, yes. It is a well-respected magazine. Here, take my business card and tell Peter Fowler he is most welcome to get in touch. However, the oil company work for Phoenix is confidential and we must not divulge their name even if tortured!'

'I hope it won't come to that,' I said.

Chapter 21

When I recovered my car from outside Tesco's, the black BMW had given up tailing me. I looked under the car for any tracking spy devices but could not find anything suspicious. As an extra precaution, I studied my rear-view mirror constantly on my trip back home from Southampton.

Early Friday morning I drove into town to buy a paper to check whether I was still under surveillance from the police or MI5. Reassured, I left the house an hour later to catch the morning train from Arundel to London Blackfriars. This was convenient as it dropped me within walking distance of *Time Out* magazine's London office in Covent Garden.

Twenty minutes later, Julie welcomed me into the crowded open-plan office where the team were busy working on the next week's issue of the magazine. I sat down on a sofa and waited while she finished an earnest conversation with the film critic. Unknown to me, London had a vast range of cinemas running special release late-night movies besides their regular showings. The programmes for the coming week had to be completed for the next Tuesday print run. At last,

Julie had some free time, and we left the office to grab a coffee in Covent Garden.

'Can I drop off my overnight bag for safe keeping? I have an appointment at one-thirty in Holborn with Peter Fowler at *New Scientist* and then I will see Dominic at St Thomas' Hospital. He says after three is best. He will issue me a white lab coat and give me a tour of the Clinical Chemistry lab and then have a chat.'

'That's brilliant. I'm not sure what time I can get away from the office. Tonight, will be frantic. Not likely before five-thirty at the earliest. It sounds like you have a lot to do. Call me at the office and we can arrange something.'

'Dominic says the laboratory technicians like to go to a pub under the viaduct at Waterloo Station after work on Fridays.'

Julie groaned. 'That will be the Hole in the Wall—a popular pub for CAMRA enthusiasts and rugby supporters before games at Twickenham.'

'I am impressed. Yes, he mentioned that pub. But you don't sound so keen?'

'No, it's not my sort of place, but I can meet you there. We don't have to stay long. You may discover more about Michelle's London visit in an informal setting.'

'Great. What is that CAMRA thing?'

'CAMRA stands for Campaign for Real Ale—an organisation which recommends pubs all over Britain which serve real cask conditioned ales rather than fizzy, artificial alternatives. I thought you would know that.'

'Yea, it rings a bell. I didn't see Lizzie in the office?'

'You just missed her. She has gone out with the restaurant critic to test a new restaurant in Soho. Undercover stuff and paid on expenses. Our wages are miserable, so we need to take all the perks we can. Until two years ago, the magazine worked like a cooperative with all the staff on equal pay. That was before I joined the magazine, of course. The editor changed all that to appease the advertisers, so the magazine stopped the equal pay cooperative idea and became respectable and less left-wing. All the best staff resigned. They formed a rival magazine called *City Limits*. Their format is like ours but more agitprop, so we have a fight on our hands to keep hold of our customers. To be honest, quite a few left, especially when we increased the price by ten pence. Most of the advertisers are staying with us and the editor says new ones are keen to try us. He has promised better pay and conditions once things settle down. Anyway, I like it here so hang on in! Lizzie feels the same, but if it fails, we can find another job. Maybe with *City Limits*!'

'It all sounds very cut-throat. I would love to see a copy. I hear it is a very useful magazine for Londoners and visitors.'

'Normally you have to pay fifty pence, but I will see if I can get you a free one.'

Next stop was the office of *New Scientist* in Holborn, a ten-minute walk via Neale Street and Shaftesbury Avenue. Compared to *Time Out,* this office was much larger. Although open plan, the desk space for each staffer was generous and there was an air of quiet efficiency.

The editor bustled over to the reception desk and led me off to meet Peter Fowler. From his name, and the editor's description, I was expecting a white Caucasian person in his mid-fifties. I guess my face registered surprise because Peter was a tall, well-dressed, and bespectacled middle-aged man from a black West-Indian ethnic group.

'Michael, good to meet you,' he had a firm handshake and a deep voice, as he drew up a chair from behind his desk so we could sit side by side.

'I was sorry to hear of your loss. Miss Gagneux was an informed researcher, and her detailed coverage of the BPA leaching issue impressed.'

'Thank you. I am trying to establish the details of her trip to London in January. Besides seeing you, she had other business in town. What day and time did she meet you?'

Peter checked his desk diary.

'Yes, I thought so. Our appointment was at ten on Tuesday 4th January. She was a few minutes late which is understandable when you are unfamiliar with the Tube system and the road directions. Coming from the calm county of rural Sussex to the hustle of London must be an eye-opener. She told me she had caught the train up from Arundel the previous day and stayed at a friend's overnight. We reviewed the papers she had sent me and discussed the anomalous results from the water sample.'

'The one she called Sample X?'

'Yes, a sample which was contaminated. No, natural water could have portrayed such a footprint.'

'You mean the analysis was so extreme it was unique? One hypothesis is that the sample was contaminated from industrial pollutants,' I suggested.

'It's possible. What I found interesting is that the BPA level was fifty times higher than normal, so plastic leaching was greater than expected. That might be down to an issue with the PET bottle manufacturing, and I suspect they had added some recycled plastics to the mix. If they do not clean the recycled material, harmful toxins could contaminate the new plastic bottles.'

'You are saying the use of recycled plastics could cause a problem?'

'Maybe. Very little plastic recycling takes place as the commercial plastic bottling industry is only about thirteen years old. However, in the future, it is an obvious step to recycle old for new for environmental concerns and minimise use of plastics overall. As you can see, it is a complex issue, and we should not be getting side-tracked by one anomalous result.'

'I'm sure you saw mention in the papers about Michelle's death on Saturday, 15th January, after talking to someone in a pub near our school. According to a witness statement, she had a meeting with a French man. Given the timing shortly after visiting you, are you aware of anyone else from this office going to see her on that day? From the description it was a guy with long blond hair looking like Gerard Depardieu.'

'As you can see, I am of Black Caribbean ancestry, despite my English sounding name, which I think rules me out. I don't read the daily newspapers. I find them too depressing. However, the editor filled me in on the details of the crime. We had no follow up meeting planned. I would not wish to rush down to some pub in the country to see anyone on business. I hope that puts your mind at rest.'

We were no further on. I had learnt nothing new. As I got up to leave, he stopped me.

'Did Miss Gagneux mention a book she was writing— an exposé of the plastic industry?'

'No. News to me. I'm surprised if she had time to write a book. And her English was not fluent.'

He looked thoughtful.

'I was interested in which laboratory ran the tests to detect BPA. The Americans are much further ahead of us, but this country needs to catch up, so any UK company with the right equipment interests us. When I asked Miss Gagneux, she said there was a possible confidentiality issue. Is that still the case?'

'Partly so. I have been in touch with the testing laboratory and their Chief Scientist is happy to talk to you and discuss their methods. They have an ongoing private contract, which is confidential, so none of Miss Gagneux's research studies, which are based on that source, may be used without their permission. The laboratory is a soil and rock testing laboratory based near Southampton, but they have chromatography equipment for water testing.' I reached into my wallet and found the business card.

'Dr Mark Carter runs the laboratory, and the owner is his father, so it is a family concern, although I have never met Carter Senior.'

Peter Fowler studied the card with interest and thanked me for my help. It had been such a quick meeting I felt let down. They had not even offered me a cup of coffee. After I had left the office, Fowler reached for his phone and put a call through to a number in the Boltons, an affluent 19th century street in Kensington and Chelsea whose opposing grand houses face inward to a private communal garden. It is one of the most sought after and expensive streets in London.

I took a leisurely 30-minute stroll along the Embankment from Temple tube station to Westminster, following the course of the River Thames towards the heart of government at the Houses of Parliament overlooked by Big Ben. A cluster of tourists was gazing up at the dramatic statue of Queen Boadicea, spear in hand, and her daughters mounted on a chariot attacking the Roman invaders. In Parliament Square, there was the sound of a noisy demonstration as a crowd of anti-nuclear protestors gathered on the green mingling with the tourists snapping pictures amid stern looking police officers. The statues of Winston Churchill, Benjamin Disraeli and other political leaders stared down with the same indifference as the modern members of Parliament scuttled by, looking away to avoid the protestors and media seeking interviews. I was in no hurry, but it was time to cross Westminster Bridge and meet my appointment with Dominic at St Thomas' Hospital.

Dominic was a short, energetic man with a ready smile and a trace of an Irish accent. His face was clean-shaven and hair brown and thinning, so I reckoned him to be about 35 years old. Well, about ten years senior to me. After the usual pleasantries, he handed me a white laboratory coat.

'Best wear this. You will blend in. We have a lot of visiting medics and clinicians from all over the world, so the other staff will ignore you. If anyone asks you your business, leave me to do the talking. I will give you a quick tour of the Clinical Chemistry Department, where we run tests on blood and urine samples from inpatients and outpatients. Just to give you an idea of how it works. Then you can follow me around, as I must visit the wards to get blood samples from diabetic patients, we are monitoring for their glucose levels. After that, it's time for a cup of tea and we can have a chat.'

In the laboratory, Dominic showed me a system for automated sampling with small samples of blood, each one from a different patient, rotating on a carousel with a needle aspirating a sample for testing, then being cleaned in a water blank before testing another sample.

'Once we load the carousel, the equipment does the hard work, and we get a read-out of the blood sugar level in each of the samples. If levels are too high, we can adjust their insulin levels to stabilise the patient. Sometimes we get incredibly high values. The mornings are the busiest time as the doctors need to get the results by ten. Then there is another busy time early afternoon. When it's quiet for glucose testing, there are loads of other tests to keep us busy.'

They conducted additional specialist tests in a separate Haematology lab, and he led me to a small extension lab where they could test kidney stones and run titrations on faecal specimens—an unpleasant task handed to new recruits. He pointed to a machine not in use.

'Whenever there is a major operation, like heart surgery, the team takes blood samples every twenty minutes and sends them to the lab for instant testing of sodium and potassium levels. The values give the surgeons a warning if anything is going wrong. Time is of the essence if we are to save the patient's life.'

After the brief tour, we visited diabetic patients on the hospital wards for routine tests conducted three times a day using small blood samples taken by pin-pricks into a finger or thumb and squeezing the blood drops into a small capsule with heparin for preservation. Most of the patients were cooperative, used to the routine, but in the children's ward, a teenage girl with adolescent diabetes put up a struggle to cause Dominic to stab his own hand instead of hers. She smiled defiantly and the Ward Sister asked us to leave for upsetting her patients.

'That's the first time I've done that,' said Dominic. 'I respect her for her spirit. Diabetes is a horrible disease. It is a slow killer unless we can get it under control. Every day, I see patients depressed because they know they will need a leg amputated or their eyesight is failing.'

Finally, we sat down to talk. Dominic said he was very sorry to hear about Michelle. She had been a friend for many years after a chance meeting at a medical conference in Paris. Her joint research with her brother into the analysis of water samples from plastic bottles excited his interest. He told her he worked once a week at a hospital attached to the St Thomas' group, which had specialist equipment for analysing urine samples for drug monitoring. Drug addicts undergoing methadone treatment to wean them off opioid dependence had to submit periodic samples for testing to make sure they were not taking other drugs. The equipment was sensitive enough to detect caffeine from tea or coffee. Dominic had noticed BPA was showing up with increasing frequency and at higher concentrations compared to previous years. Leaching of BPA from plastic water bottles was now commonplace. He wondered what other artificial endocrines and toxins were present in our drinking water.

'When Michelle showed me Dr Carter's results for this Sample X that rang alarm bells. Where had the sample come from? Was it the water supply or the plastic bottle causing the contamination, or both? Was it poor testing technique or contamination during the testing? Do not forget the reagent bottles used in the testing are plastic, so they may also influence the results. What we needed was to identify the source and run repeat tests.'

'I believe Mark Carter repeated the tests and got comparable results. He also sent a sample to another laboratory and found additional heavy metal contaminants and toxins such as arsenic.'

'Arsenic. You must be joking!'

'It's best if you liaise with Mark rather than me,' I said. 'I wouldn't want to misinform you. My concern is not over the water business, but who killed Michelle and why?'

'They must tie it in to her work,' said Dominic. 'Sample X is the key.'

I called Julie at 5 p.m. from the hospital to give her an update. Dominic said he would be at the Hole in the Wall at 6 p.m. for the usual Friday staff de-stress session. He had some theories he wanted to discuss, and I felt I needed to warn him about the continued interest from the police and the security forces. Julie said she would meet us there. If she was late, to go ahead without her.

Chapter 22

Julie rented a spacious first-floor flat on Charleville Road in West Kensington, which she shared with two other girls. Lizzie had also lived here but moved out, which was the best move for both. Proximity at work was one thing, but sharing every evening together was excessive.

Her flat contained three large bedrooms, a vast sitting room, and a kitchen with a bathroom down a flight of steps on the stairwell. The downside was the inconvenience of one bathroom for three girls, all wanting to use it at once. By a weird design quirk, the shared stairs connected to an upper flat of a similar size rented by three young men. This led to a lack of privacy when the girls dashed to-and-fro the bathroom as the men were passing up or down the stairs. The boys found this amusing.

Julie's flatmates were away most weekends, and she liked to go home in summer to escape the oppressive heat of London. In winter, daylight was so short it was pointless to rush down to rural Sussex after work on Friday.

The first-floor apartment had a balcony overlooking Charleville Road, a quiet road, with only minor traffic. It had once been a Georgian family house, but rapacious property owners had converted the houses to flat rentals to service the burgeoning demand for cheap lets in the capital. Similar flats formed a mirror image on the other side of the road. When looking inward at her world and her space; she saw her flat was dull and lifeless—a room typical of many similar rental flats in London, with narrow twin beds, small bedside-tables, and a wardrobe for hanging clothes with a single coat hanger. There was a worn threadbare carpet in a dull grey cord. To brighten it up, she had purchased a small rattan chair and an antique dresser with a mirror.

Of course, there was the usual clutter of postcards and photos, including a colourful poster of West Pier, Brighton, by Dave Thompson, to give her bedroom a personal touch. But it needed more imagination than she was prepared to give the room.

We had arrived at her flat late. The after-work drinks in Waterloo had started in a restrained fashion. As more and more office workers crowded into the pub, a party atmosphere developed. Dominic liked Julie, but he seemed more attracted to a youth who wandered in a bit later. Michael was worried the couple might leave soon. It was important to discover what else Dominic could tell him about Michelle. Michael and Julie cornered Dominic on his way back from the toilet. Had he any idea who had killed Michelle? He appeared unsteady and his speech was slurred after too many drinks downed in too short a time.

'It's obvious he was a hired hit man,' said Dominic. 'Chances are you'll never find him. The surveillance stuff you told me about is all part of it. *They* know about it, and they suspect you know as well.'

'Who's *they?*' asked Julie.

'MI5 of course. If the threat is to British security, or if it is of international interest, it would be MI6. You two need to accept that this dirty water is a deliberate creation. Imagine there is a foreign power that would have no compunctions about selling water to kill you and you have a source of chemical warfare. Do you want a concrete example? Look no further than Colonel Gaddafi in Libya, a man surrounded by enemies: the Israelis, the Americans and, in his own country, the Kurds. If you have a supply of bottled water such as your Sample X then supplying it to select targets such as the Kurds could be an effective, low cost, low-risk strategy to eliminate your enemies. A tweak to the chemistry to make a slow killer or a quick killer. An indiscriminate weapon.'

'That's very far-fetched. Why do you suspect the Libyans?'

'I don't. It could be anyone. Maybe the IRA. This business might be a feasibility study. If so, we can rest easy and hope they forget the whole thing.'

After this revelation, Julie and I felt confused and deflated. The enormity of what Dominic had suggested was too appalling to consider.

On Saturday morning we both felt more relaxed and inclined to ignore Dominic's theory as an alcohol induced paranoia.

'Let's stay in all day,' said Julie. 'I need rest after a hectic week and unwind, doing nothing.'

'That sounds a good plan. It's great that we are alone, and no one can bother us. Can I get a cup of coffee?'

'Coffee, huh? So impatient. I can make you a cup of instant. And my mother may call,' said Julie as she leapt out of bed and headed to the kitchen. 'Don't answer the phone. It's the Grand National this afternoon and I want to see what horse she fancies. Can you buy some papers so we can study the race card? There is a newsagent nearby on North End Road. The race is at three-twenty, so we can watch it on TV. I think the William Hill betting shop is near the Tube station, so let's put a bet on. I won last year on Grittar, and he is running again this year so he could be worth a wager.'

She had made the coffee already and passed me a cup in the bedroom.

'What papers do you want?'

'The *Daily Telegraph* and the *Daily Mirror* are best for the racing.'

On Julie's instructions, I placed a win bet of £5 for her on Corbiere at odds of 13 to 1 to win the Grand National at Aintree. I thought this was a long shot. Grittar, who had won by 15 lengths last year, was attracting the punters. This year he was favourite again, at odds of 7 to 1. I opted to support Delmoss with an each way bet. He was the front-runner in 1982 and unlucky to come in fourth. His odds were an attractive 50 to 1, so if he got a place, my moderate bet of £2 each way would be worth the gamble.

'Why did you pick Corbiere?'

'There are three reasons, first Corbières in France is a very nice red wine, second Jenny Pitman trains the horse in Lambourn, and third the going is heavy, which will suit it.'

The first reason was illogical and the other two reasons were not convincing. She ignored my objections. Did I not think a female trainer could be as good or better than any man? Was I also an expert on ground conditions? She was arguing just for the sake of it.

'Delmoss is a good bet, but I think at thirteen-years-old he is past it.'

'My God. I didn't realise that. Your horse is an eight-year-old, so maybe he is too young and inexperienced.'

'Sounds like you. But you are learning.'

At that moment, the phone rang, and Julie ran off to answer it.

After a long conversation, she returned. She sat down on the rattan chair and lit up a cigarette, blowing the smoke across to me.

'See, I was right. My mother rang just as predicted.'

'What did she want?'

'Oh, just a chat. I told her my bet for the Grand National is Corbiere and she dismissed its chances.'

'So, who is she backing?'

'The favourite, Grittar. She says he was a big winner last time out. This year will be easier as he has done it before. The going is heavier, so I am not so sure. My horse is lighter and younger, and it won the Welsh Grand National in December. Too late for a change of heart—we have placed our bets. Just time for a late snack lunch.'

Sometime later, we sat on the floor in the lounge sharing a cheap bottle of red wine and eating a pizza. Half-an-hour before they came under starters orders. The TV was on with the volume turned low.

She was contemplating me. Was I eating the messy pizza grossly or knocking back the wine a bit too fast? I felt self-conscious under her scrutiny.

'Sorry, I am a greedy eater.'

'No, your manners are fine. I am just curious about you. You are a dedicated teacher, but do you have any other hobbies or interests?'

'I am a keen amateur ornithologist and I specialise in the birds of Sussex.'

She fell about giggling. 'You are having me on.'

'No. I combine my birdwatching with photography. I have a Minolta X-700 35mm SLR camera that I bought last year. It's a brilliant camera. Last year I won Best Bird of the Year photograph from the Sussex Wildfowl Trust for my photo of a barn owl.'

She collapsed in more laughter because I was deadly serious.

'The judges were impressed that I actually caught my picture of a male barn owl in flight *inside* a barn. I waited two hours buried in straw to get that picture. There was a nesting mate in the rafters, so I knew the male would return at some point.'

Strangely, she thought, this was even funnier. She was laughing so much that I went to the kitchen to fetch a glass of water. Grateful, she spilled half and drank the rest. Composing herself, she sat in front of the TV.

'Look, it's about to start. Forty-one starters lining up at the start. Only a few horses will complete the race as the jumps are fiendishly difficult.'

We sat enthralled at the ensuing dramatic race. Her predictions were spot on. Only ten horses finished. Corbieres won by three-quarters of a length in a tight finish. My horse, Delmoss, came in last. She netted £65 plus her stake of £5.

'See, you have been lucky for me. Can you pick up my winnings from the betting shop while I take a hot bath? Then we can go out for dinner.'

'That would be great. But I would like to pay for dinner.'

'No way, stupid. We can share my lucky win.'

When I came back half an hour later, the mood had changed. Julie was pacing up and down angrily. The editor at *Time Out* had phoned. He wanted her to attend a launch party at the Royal Garden Hotel in Kensington for some new book.

'I don't work weekends. They don't pay me for it, but because no one else wants to go to this boring event, they said let's ring Julie. It's pointless. My only role will be to see who is attending and chat with the author.'

'Who is the author?' I asked.

'Someone called Dick King-Smith. Apparently, he is a farmer who has written a book about a talking pig who thinks he is a sheep dog. It's called "*The Sheep Pig*." I must be there at seven at the latest for a session of about two hours. How can they talk about a book for so long? We can share a taxi. Wait for me at a pub nearby. I just hope Toby doesn't want me to go out for a curry.'

'Who is Toby?'

'Oh, just someone at work. I will meet him at the hotel. They need both of us. We went out for a meal after work once and then he invited me to his flat for a coffee. I shouldn't have agreed, as he had another agenda in mind. He was drunk, so I escaped and got a taxi home. It's not good to get involved with people you work with and see every day, is it?'

'Was this when you first started at the firm or more recently?'

'Soon after I joined last year—I think he has forgotten all about it.'

'He sounds very creepy. No wonder you don't like him.'

'The Elephant & Castle in Holland Street is a friendly pub where you can wait. It is quite close to the hotel. We must get our skates on to be on time. It will be good if you can come along and protect me.'

The launch event at the Royal Garden drifted on longer than expected. It was ten before Julie and Toby breezed into the Elephant & Castle pub. Meeting King-Smith and his wife, Myrle, was a thrill. Especially when he gave her a signed copy of the first edition. She promised to read it in time for a puff piece for *Time Out*. There was a slide presentation during the book launch of Dick's life explaining key events and his progression to becoming a successful author: How he had served in WWII and been active in the Italian campaign until wounded. Then after the war he returned to farming where he loved his animals so much that he hated to have to send them to market for slaughter. He admitted his business dealings were poor and mathematical skills zero, so his family was always struggling to pay the bills. Eventually, he took up teaching qualifying with a teaching certificate at the same time as his daughter and then worked at a local primary school for some years writing children's books in his spare time. Dick had already produced books for children and his latest book, '*The Sheep Pig,*' was likely to be an enormous success. Late in life, he had become a popular and well-known author.

'He told me he loved working with children and writing books to make them laugh, but he found their parents harder to get on with,' said Julie. 'He is a very sweet man!'

Toby, who looked bored, ambled off to the bar to buy us all drinks. I bought another round before the pub called drinking-up time. I was keen to escape back to Charleville Road, but Toby wanted us to join him at Annabel's nightclub in Mayfair. The members' only club is the most exclusive in London. The roll call of the rich and famous that frequent it includes the royal family, film stars and even US President Richard Nixon. I had never heard of it, but the way Julie's lip quivered, I could see she was wrestling with a tough decision. In the end, her dislike of Toby or loyalty to me won over, and she offered the excuse of extreme tiredness after such an action-packed day.

Rather than take the Tube, we hailed a taxi back to West Kensington and collapsed, exhausted.

As Sunday loomed, our union would end. A coming week of separation would be a flat return to normality and a humdrum existence. For me, it was four last days of freedom before the start of the summer term on Friday. Teaching sessions would wind into motion, without enthusiasm, with resignation. That was the end of my weekends. I would be on duty for match days on the Saturdays. Sundays would be my only free day each week. There was no prospect of a weekend in London until half term in six weeks' time. Julie would go home some weekends, so there would still be a chance to meet. At this stage, the investigation into Michelle's murder seemed to have reached a dead end, and I was ready to step back and leave it for others to pursue the solution.

Chapter 23

I was completing another tutorial for Charlie. Laureline had popped out to the shops to get something for lunch.

'What do you like to read in your free time?' I asked Charlie.

He smiled shyly. 'Well, now I'm reading *"The Secret Diary of Adrian Mole, aged 13¾"* by Sue Townsend. It's funny. I know it's not great literature. I also like novels by Stephen King and the books of Roald Dahl are great.'

'So, you have quite an eclectic taste?'

'I guess so,' he agreed.

'That's wonderful. The more diverse the literature, the better. When I was your age, I was a great reader. I shouldn't say this, but you can get more from reading than from some teachers. Some you like and get on with, but others you don't like. Yet other boys will get on okay with those teachers.'

'Yes, it's a dilemma,' said Charlie. 'At our school, I think all the teachers are fine, but the headmaster is really mean.'

With Laureline away, it was a chance to be informal and find out a bit more about Charlie. His likes and dislikes and what made him tick. 'It must have been a shock switching from your school in Hong Kong to St Wilfrid's—a very different lifestyle.'

'In fact, I felt more of an outsider in Hong Kong. I was the only *gweilo* in my class. And my classmates could be very cruel. The teachers always treated me like a foreigner. G*weilo* is the insulting term the Cantonese call us. It means "Ghost" because we are white and scary. My dad told me that in Singapore they call white people *Ang Mo,* which means red-haired devil, so that is even worse. Then my parents moved me from the local school to an expat school, which had students of all nationalities. I loved it there.'

'I was sorry about your father. It must have been such a shock for you and your mother. I am amazed how well you are all coping.'

'We can't change the past. Only the future is important. You know my mother likes you very much. I just need to find her another husband, and she will be happy again,' he laughed. I was quite stunned by this confession.

'Charlie, your mother is a lovely lady, so I am sure she will find someone. I have a very nice girlfriend up in London and I am too young and selfish to settle down. First, I must make sure you pass the exams and get a scholarship.' I looked at my watch. 'We have done little work today, but I'll leave you some books to read.' We heard Laureline's car in the drive and resumed our studies.

'Mr Fletcher has just finished,' said Charlie, who felt an hour's tutorial was enough.

'That's good,' said Laureline. 'Will you stay for a simple lunch? I have a range of cheeses and the shop in town makes a fair baguette so we can have a typical French lunch. Michael, choose some wine. There's white in the fridge, or perhaps you prefer red wine?'

'White is fine, thank you.'

'Same for me,' said Charlie with a smile. 'Do you know Mr Fletcher has a girlfriend in London?'

Laureline looked surprised, and I blushed.

'Well, a good friend, yes. But it is early days. I had to visit London over the weekend following up on some leads in the Michelle case and she put me up in her flat. She works for the London magazine *Time Out*. Her parents live down here in Sussex, and that is where I first met her a few weeks ago. Of course, how stupid of me, you met her already when I came over here for my last tutorial with Charlie!'

'Yes, she is a delightful girl. Charlie, you confused me by saying Michael had a *new* girlfriend in London. I was wondering what had happed to that beautiful girl, Julie!'

Laureline wondered if there had been any further developments in finding Michelle's killer. I needed someone else to confide in, so I tried to explain some of the complexities of the case.

'It's quite a mystery,' she conceded.

'Charlie, you are not to mention any of this to your friends at school. Understand? Michael, you have unearthed a conspiracy, so maybe now is the time to place all the evidence in front of the police. After all, they have the resources to investigate further. It proves they were wrong to assume you were the guilty party.'

'I didn't tell you the police were tracking my movements. The police from Pulborough used an unmarked police car to follow me. After they gave up, there was a more sinister move when a black BMW followed me all the way to Southampton, when I went to see Mark Carter. Fortunately, I noticed, and Mark met up with me and handed over a coat and hat as a disguise and then he drove me in his car to the laboratory. We fooled them. Mark is sure the team tracking me was from MI5. That is why I can't trust anyone and certainly not the police.'

'Wow!' said Charlie. 'Maybe they are outside our house right now, waiting for you to leave?'

In fact, Charlie's prediction proved quite accurate. As I was about to turn into the driveway at home, the black BMW appeared from the opposite direction and pulled up across the drive, blocking the entrance. Two men leapt out and ran up to the driver's door, instructing me to wind down the window. They dressed alike with hoodies and jeans.

'Mr Fletcher, it's nothing to worry about,' said the first man as he flashed a warrant card. 'We would just like a quick chat. Is there a hotel or pub nearby we can go to?'

'What's this about?' I asked.

'As you know, the police have you in the frame for the murder of your girlfriend, Michelle. We have nothing to do with the local police investigation. We would like to share some of our mutual findings. That may give you closure for the murder of your friend.'

'I may refuse to come with you. I mean, you wave some card and give me a story, but I don't know who you are or whether I can trust you.'

The two men looked at each other. Clearly, they could just bundle me into their car and drive off. I was in unchartered territory.

'You are quite right to be suspicious,' said the first man. 'My name is Gary Smith,' he looked at his younger partner, 'and this is Wayne. It impressed us at how you gave us the slip in Southampton. You have talent and the service needs men like you. Have you ever considered working for the security services?'

'By which you mean MI5 or MI6?'

Both men smiled but said nothing. I still didn't trust them but felt it best to comply.

'There's a pub called the George & Dragon not far away,' I said. 'You could follow me.'

The MI5 men located a quiet table and sat down, still hooded, with their pints. If they wanted to remain anonymous, this was a mistake. Among the glances they attracted was one from Michael Cox. I hoped he would stay away for his own good. If he came over, how could I explain the situation?

'You might fit in better if you took off your hoodies,' I suggested. 'Some regulars know me, and they are giving us some odd looks.'

Reluctantly, they removed their head covers to reveal identical black tracksuit tops, black cord jeans, and white shirts with plain navy-blue ties and well-polished black shoes. Their dress code uniformity was startling and intimidating. Gary, the taller of the two men, had a pale, pinched face, a weedy-looking moustache, and a prominent incisor, which gave his mouth a sneering, unbalanced look. Wayne was shorter and broader, sporting a ruddy complexion marked with unshaven stubble and a silent air of menace from unsmiling eyes. They shifted about, looking awkward and out of place. Michael Cox approached with a broad smile on his face.

'Michael. We meet again. Not seen you or the twins for ages,' he hovered, waiting for me to introduce my two minders. I was inventive.

'Gents, this is a good friend of mine, Michael Cox. We were at school together. These guys are a couple of security guards from St Wilfrid's school that have just started. This chap is Gary Smith,' I explained to Michael Cox. 'They wanted to know a good pub nearby, so I said just follow me as I was heading this way. Now the weather is getting better. We must have a return game at Ranville's.'

'I'm up for it. Just call me. Bye, guys.'

Wayne, the one who never spoke, looked up and ignored Michael Cox. I felt confident and relaxed on my turf.

'Explain why you stopped me?' I asked.

'Who did you visit in Hedge End near Southampton last Thursday 7th April?'

'It's none of your business.'

'Why do you still maintain there was another man in the Three Horseshoes who you believe, with no evidence, was her killer?'

'I saw him with my own eyes and gave a description to the police. And I talked to one of the Graffham darts team who backed up my evidence. He told me Michelle met up with a French man, someone she knew from the past. These are facts. If you doubt my word, speak to him yourself.'

'We planned to do that, but he died in a motor accident on the A3 on Easter Monday. He left the road near Hindhead, and his car plunged into the Devil's Punchbowl. He was over the drink-drive limit. It's lucky his wife wasn't in the car.'

This news was hard to absorb. How had this accident happened? How did they know about it?

'If you can't share information with us, I suggest you pay our superior a visit. He scrawled the name Sean O'Connor and wrote an address and a phone number on a scruffy piece of paper. It was an office in Battersea, which made me even more suspicious. MI5 Central HQ was called Thames House, but maybe they had a place in Battersea.'

Gary opened his wallet and placed a £50 brown Christopher Wren design note on the table. It was the first one I had seen.

'Take this for your travel expenses. The service can use people like you. You have two options. You walk away from this business and stop your detective work and this conversation never happened, or you agree to help us. Michael, we know everything there is to know about you, your family, and your life. There is more to this case than meets the eye and we wouldn't want you to come a cropper like Michelle.'

I left the note on the table as I played for time.

'I don't believe you. My life is very dull, and I am no threat to anyone.'

'But Michael, did you not express the view that the monarchy is an out-of-date institution, and you would like to abolish it? You seem to hold some anti-establishment, left-wing views. Mind you, some of our best agents are on the fringes and are considered extreme, so that is no problem, although we demand total loyalty and confidentiality. If you agree to join us, then you will have to sign the Official Secrets Act.'

I struggled to remember running down the monarchy. Of course, it was at the Easter Sunday reception at school, and I had been talking to Nigel Caldwell-Brown and his wife, Jane. Was Nigel working for MI5? Alarmed, I tried to remember if I had shared any information with him. Although I had talked about the darts player to close friends, I had been very careful not to mention Dr Mark Carter to anyone at school apart from matron. And what about my visit to the *New Scientist* and Dominic? Again, I was sure no one else knew the entire story, which meant Nigel Caldwell-Brown was the mole. If so, I must not let them know I suspected him.

'I often make immature comments like that. If you don't mind, I would like to think about your offer. But I don't need that,' I said, pushing the £50 note back across the table.

'Fair enough,' agreed Gary, putting on his hoodie once more. 'Only don't take too long. There are other options we can consider which I hope will not be necessary.'

The men left the pub. Their parting comment rattled me. On the grounds of national security, the Spooks could do anything they liked. I conjured up disturbing images of the empty eyes of the younger man as he sucked on his cigarette to ignite the embers before delicately lowering the burning tip onto my bare inner arm securely tied to a chair in some dark cellar. The other man stared from dead eyes and waited for my scream. I felt Gary was dangerous and unpredictable, the one with a masochistic streak, whereas the other man would obey his every command.

Chapter 24

Before formal classes started for the summer term, the staff were required to turn up for what the headmaster called a TD Day—a teacher development day. Depressed, we gathered to chat in a stilted fashion over a tense morning coffee. This was the precursor for a formal session also held in the Staff common room. I studied Nigel Caldwell-Brown closely. It was tempting to concoct some wild story about my trip to Southampton to make sure MI5 did not discover the true reason. If the intelligence made its way back to MI5, then this would prove his guilt.

'Did you have a good Easter break?' I asked him.

'Yes, thanks. What about you?'

'Oh, a dull time. As you know, my parents were away in Norfolk for a few days, so they left me in charge of the house and looking after the dog. Very monotonous.'

'But your last chance of freedom at the weekend and the last few days. Did you get away anywhere exciting?'

'I wish! I have been doing some tutorials for a boy and I need to prepare the material the day before, which is time consuming. That and helping my parents at home has been all I have been doing apart from a trip to the pub.'

'Did you see *Police 5* the other day? They showed the Identikit picture of the man you saw in the pub. They have received loads of sightings.'

'I suppose it's worth a try. Great, if it's successful, but I bet most contacts will be dead ends.'

I moved off before he asked me any further questions. After sufficient tension had built up, the headmaster and Mona entered and after a few platitudinous greetings, he got down to business.

Subjects covered in a brief introduction covered exam results, the visit of the HMI in March which he expected to be a glowing report, news of children expelled for serious offences, withdrawals for family reasons, a revised policy to enforce discipline with greater vigour, and any new student arrivals. The headmaster introduced a young exchange teacher from Wellington in New Zealand. His name was Dale, and they arranged that Caldwell-Brown would take him on a guided tour of the school. With regret, the head cancelled a planned upgrade to the antiquated communal showers in the changing rooms because of a shortage of funds.

Next, Higgins gave an upbeat report with a gloss over past sports results. He considered the cricket outlook for the coming term to be bleak since Shaw Major's parents were relocating to Dubai. Their son, a star player, would move to an international school in Dubai. Higgins maintained cricket coaching was not one of his strengths and volunteered me to take charge of all teams. This was flattering, but it would have been nice to ask me first. It meant I now had no chance of escaping early on Saturdays.

Matron got up to speak. She warned us to be on the lookout for hair lice. A few weeks holiday and we could expect an epidemic unless quickly dealt with. Not to mention colds, flu, scarlet fever, measles and sundry viruses and vomiting sickness, which were always threats. A visiting doctor would call for an annual inspection of all the boys to make sure they were developing in the right direction in terms of maturity and not displaying any malignancies, incorrect attractions, or alarming practices. Miss Caldwell lowered her eyes, looking embarrassed.

After the group meeting, we had another tea or coffee we did not want and tried to conceal our yawns. Some took a quick look around the classrooms to make sure their lockers were still intact, our teacups to hand and pencils, pens, writing pads, chalk, duster, textbooks ready for action. Time dragged and tension mounted. Each teacher had an individual time slot with the headmaster to review his or her performance over the previous term. Which students were under-performing and why? If an entire class were doing badly, then we would have some explaining to do. Having survived my review (apart from a rebuke about my unpunctuality, poor example, ill-disciplined teaching and nil enforcement of the school rules), I was back in the Staff common room at teatime, wondering why I had not been sacked. It was empty apart from Jones at one end of the room and the new exchange teacher, Dale, at the far end. As formal teaching did not start until the following day, the rest of the staff had left. Dale, looking lost, was a spotty youth with boyish features, short ginger hair and a too-intense stare and fixed grin. In fact, he was someone I could dislike. He seemed ill at ease in conventional long trousers, shirt, and tie.

I avoided him and took my time getting a cup of tea. Jones was the only option. Sitting alone, he would welcome my company. Tempus fugit, I tried as an opening gambit. Jones looked appalled, but decided I was harmless.

'Indeed, it does, boyo. And I have been here far too long.' He glanced about the common room, focusing his glare on poor Dale. 'I have worked at this school for ten years and need a change. The teachers look younger than the boys.'

'I am sure there are many jobs for Latin teachers if you felt like a move somewhere else,' I suggested.

'That would be more of the same. No, it's teaching I hate. I don't want to teach ungrateful pupils anymore. I want to do something different.'

'Have you anything in mind?'

'My wife misses Llandudno. Her parents run a bed-and-breakfast business on the seafront. It's a steady trade, in the season. She's keen to find a suitable property and try the same thing. Our eldest two have left home so it would be a good time to make a move. Mind you, the youngest is at Cardiff University, so he only sees us during the holidays. I'm worried he will stay with us for years. No get-up-and-go. No girlfriend.'

'Well, I'm sure he will find his feet soon. I expect there are excellent schools in Llandudno where you could work,' I guessed.

'I could get a job teaching Latin again. Trouble is, although I'm Welsh, I'm not so keen on that part of North Wales. If it were down to me, I would prefer Swansea in South Wales. I think I need a complete change.'

'It's a dilemma, isn't it? Once we have ties, our options are more limited. Forgetting about your wife and family. If you had total freedom, what would you do?'

Jones laughed bitterly.

'That's easy; I would be off to the Far East to Singapore. I was in the navy as a young lad and our ship stopped off in Singapore. It was only a few days to take in the normal tourist spots like Bugis Street and Orchard Road. I loved Chinatown as it looked unchanged—a chance to embrace the past with its traders plying forgotten trinkets and the murky Singapore River swarming with boats.' It surprised me to see his eyes mist over.

'Maybe, somewhere to visit on a holiday, but I doubt if there would be job prospects for a Latin teacher in Singapore.'

'No, you are wrong to think that. Latin is not a dead language. It is the root of all languages and I expect some schools in Singapore will have it on the syllabus or maybe something like classical studies. I am more than likely to stay put here. It's better the devil you know—anything to avoid Llandudno.' His voice trailed off sadly. Was ten years of teaching so numbing? Strange, to think that Singapore should resonate with Jones. I doubted if my off-the-cuff job application would come to anything but, at that moment, I focused my total attention on Julie—so much so that the Singapore job was dead and buried. Jones brought me back to the present and out of my daydreams.

'Have you heard about that teaching job you were chasing abroad?' he asked.

'No, nothing yet. I think nothing will come of it. Anyway, I am not so sure I want to change jobs now.'

'Change of heart—maybe some romantic interest?' he probed.

'No, it's early days. You know me—boringly predictable and still living at home with my parents.' I thought it was a good idea to change the subject.

'As you mentioned, Singapore, I admit the English teaching post I applied for is in Singapore. It is at an independent school called Dunearn Academy. I think they would have contacted me by now if I had a chance. Even if they offered me the job, I don't think I want to leave anymore.'

'Michael, you are a man of mystery—that's one secret you have confessed to. I wonder how many more you are hiding beneath that cool exterior. If the school in Singapore asks me for a reference, I will let you know. That reminds me you still owe me a pint for my agreeing to that. By the way, how did the inquisition with the head go?'

'Oh, he tore me apart. I thought I was going to be sacked.'

'Yes, he really hates you, but he can't let you go, as all your sports teams do well, and your classes are out-performing all others. Whatever you are doing, you must be doing something right.'

'Well, thank you, Jones. I wasn't aware of that.'

Jones and I headed for the door burdened by the thought that lessons would begin the next day. We were the last to leave, lost in our private thoughts.

SIO Preston and Inspector Tracey Smith had visited the Prefecture of police in Nantes to explain their mission. Michelle had completed a PhD in the Chemistry Department of Nantes University. Preston was eager to discover the nature of her research and to speak to any staff or colleagues still in the department. The prefecture had assigned them a commissaire equivalent to the rank of a superintendent in the UK to help with the language.

At the university, they tracked down Michelle's supervisor, who explained Michelle had worked in interdisciplinary chemistry, synthesis, analysis, and modelling, specialising in gas and liquid chromatography. Both Preston and Tracey Smith looked confused and unable to see any link to teaching French to schoolboys at an obscure school in Sussex. Michelle had been a talented researcher and was popular with both the staff and students. One man, a post-doctorate research student, remembered her well and said he recalled her reason for moving to England was two-fold. First, to move near to her English father's side of the family. She was close to an elder brother who ran a research laboratory in Southampton, and the second reason was she wished to escape from a persistent admirer, almost to the point of being a stalker. This was helpful intelligence. But if her brother ran a laboratory, why had she not gone to work for him?

'I think that was her original intention until she met Dominic in Paris,' said the researcher. 'She was keen on this man. I think he was Irish, and he worked in a Clinical Chemistry lab at a London teaching hospital. I can't remember its name. It all happened fast. She went over for a visit. Someone showed her the advert from a school wanting a French teacher and she realised she was the ideal candidate, as her English was adequate, and the school was not far away from both Southampton and London. They were happy to find her.'

'Thank you,' said Preston. 'That explains a lot. Did she have any enemies, anyone who would wish her ill?'

'No. Quite the reverse. She was attractive and good company, not a staid academic like me! But this besotted admirer was annoying her.'

Preston produced the identikit picture of the mystery man from the pub.

'Does this admirer look anything like this eyewitness reconstruction?' he asked.

'Facially, the general shape is quite similar, but Marcel does not have long blond hair like that anymore. True, he used to look a bit like that.'

'This Marcel. Do you know where we can find him?'

'Sure. He is our senior laboratory technician, Marcel Fouché. He looks after all the equipment such as the X-ray diffraction, the mass spectrometers and so on. Even a scanning electron microscope. He is the expert in everything.'

'And is he here today?' asked Preston.

The researcher looked at his watch.

'You can try. It's after four so I expect he has left. But he should be here tomorrow morning.'

Fortunately, for the Brighton police, the laboratory technician had not left. He looked up from his desk with surprise at the three visitors. The commissaire explained their purpose and introduced Preston and Tracey Smith to Marcel.

'Monsieur, parlez-vous anglais?' asked Tracey, keen to show her language skills in front of Preston.

He gave a reluctant nod and agreed he knew a little.

'Can I ask where you were on Saturday 15th January?'

The commissaire translated, but Marcel showed he understood the question and replied in English.

'Certainement. I was at Twickenham in London watching the rugby between England and France. France won by 19 points to England's score of 15, as I expect you know—a brilliant victory.'

'Are you a friend of Michelle Gagneux?'

'Yes, a good friend. She was a student here at Nantes, but two years ago she left to work in England.'

'And have you kept in touch with her, by letter or by visiting her in England?'

'No, we lost contact. I do not know where she lives now.'

'Lived. Sadly, she died under suspicious circumstances. The pathologist determined the date of death was likely to be on 15th January, the same day you were in England.'

'What! You tell me she is dead. This is awful news. How can it be possible?'

Marcel seemed to fold inward with shock. Sitting at the table, he buried his face in his hands as he tried to wipe away his tears. Was this a genuine reaction or was he a talented actor? Preston was not sure. His dramatic meltdown looked contrived. Surely, a normal reaction was to ask how your friend had died. He didn't ask because he knew the answer.

'We are sorry for your loss,' said Tracey. 'After the match finished, did you travel straight back to France or stay in a hotel overnight?'

'How can you ask me this? I stayed in some cheap hotel in Victoria and then returned to France on the Dover to Calais ferry. From Calais, another train to Paris and a train from Paris to Nantes.'

'Can you remember the name of the hotel you stayed in, Marcel?'

'No. no. I tried so many. They were all alike and full up. At last, I found a small room in an attic—very expensive at £10 for the night.'

The Brighton police stayed one more night at a hotel in the town centre. They planned a courtesy call to the prefecture and a request for the French police to follow up with further questions to Marcel. Unless he could provide evidence of his story and travel, he was a suspect based on the amazing coincidence of being in the UK on 15th January. He could have caught a train to Arundel and a local taxi to the pub to surprise Michelle on her birthday. And there was eyewitness evidence of a man talking French to Michelle according to the darts player plus Michael's physical description. If he sported long hair back in January and had since cropped it, that would be a powerful indicator of his guilt. On balance, the evidence was not overwhelming, but they had hanged people for less.

Chapter 25

The first day back at school was a sunny day in early spring and a carpet of fresh green grass and delicate flowers of yellow cowslip carpeted the Sussex Downs, so harsh in winter.

Most of the boarders had arrived the previous day, but because of late arrival of pupils from abroad and the dilatory return of some of the day boys, the school abandoned normal morning classes. The headmaster kept the morning free to talk to influential parents and the governors, so the staff settled the boys into their classrooms and got them busy writing essays on what they did during their holiday. These could be factual accounts or imaginary capers. Matron, assisted by a visiting doctor, was busy with medical inspections and recording weights and heights of all the boys to update the records. A few weeks of school food and healthy exercise would soon shift those extra pounds.

The staff lunch served in the refectory, with its scrubbed pine tables and benches, was a humble Irish stew. The thick gel of overcooked sliced carrots, whole potatoes and chunks of lamb was one of the cook's favourites. She liked to make it the day before and give the tough old meat a long cooking time. If she had taken the trouble to taste it, she would have discovered that the meat was still as tough as the Berlin Wall. The amount of indigestible fat clinging to the meat was more typical of a very elderly sheep. Mutton dressed as lamb was all the school could afford and the staff struggled through it with as much enthusiasm as condemned prisoners eating their last meal. Father Roderick was the first to push his plate away in disgust. Without a word, he left to light up a cigarette. We could see him pacing up and down outside, smoking furiously.

'Roderick left before his apple pie and custard,' said Jones. 'I wonder if that is a sin.'

'I can't say I blame him. The stew is disgusting. Even the headmaster has skipped lunch.'

'He took Mona to the pub,' said Jones.

'It's usually a Saturday fixture with them. I suppose the start of the term is a good reason. More sense than putting up with this garbage. Horsemeat would taste sweeter.' I pushed my half-empty plate away in disgust.

'Anyone fancy a pint?'

Jones looked at me with surprise and respect.

'Good idea. Let's get out of here.'

A streak of sympathy tempered Miss Cresswell's sniff of disapproval as we abandoned lunch. But she continued to eat her food without complaint.

'No one for pudding?' Molly looked in horror at the pile of plates stacked with leftovers.

Our arrival in the Three Horseshoes annoyed the headmaster. He was sitting with Mona in the restaurant annexe. She was enjoying scampi and chips with a glass of white wine, and he ate a steak and kidney pie with a pint of bitter. It wasn't haute cuisine, but it hit the spot.

However, this was a trifling annoyance compared to the bombshell letter he had received this Friday on the first day of term. The HMI inspection in March had produced a damning report critical of his stance of strict discipline, which was deemed excessive. The teachers were all rated highly, which was frustrating, and showed how the inspectors had the wrong priorities. How could they praise slackers like Michael Fletcher, for example? He had shared the findings with Mona, who felt so upset he suggested a visit to the pub as soon as he completed various meetings with troublesome parents.

'I don't think the teaching staff should drink at lunchtime, especially on the first day of the summer term,' remarked Mona, frowning over at the pair, as she sipped her wine.

'Well, it's acceptable in moderation,' said the headmaster. 'Like anything, it's bad when it's abused. If it becomes habitual, that's another matter. Like the bursar, for example, is in here every day.' Mona searched the bar but couldn't see him. Maybe he was in the snug bar.

'I suppose we need to be tolerant,' said Mona. 'As long as they are sober when they take their class. My husband is a teetotaller, you know.'

'Is that for religious reasons? Is he in the Salvation Army?'

'Oh, no. He over-indulged at a party, when he was a young man, and vowed never to drink again. At home, he won't allow any alcohol in the house. If friends visit, they must put up with a cup of tea or a soft drink. That's why it's such a refreshing contrast to be having lunch with a connoisseur like you.'

The headmaster sympathised and stretched a shy hand over the table to squeeze Mona's hand as a sign of reassurance. She smiled and let him continue, allowing her fingers to respond and squeeze his hand back. A gesture noticed by Jones, who nudged me in the ribs.

The barmaid persuaded us to have more drinks. As she turned away to use the till, something caught my eye. Next to the till, there was a thin yellow torch. I asked her if it belonged to the staff or had someone lost it.

'I wouldn't know, love. Let me ask the boss as I only started here last week.'

She disappeared to the public bar where the landlord was sitting by the log fire, running through the accounts. She came back and told me they found it in the public bar in January and they were waiting for the owner to claim it. I recognised it at once as Michelle's torch. The barmaid passed it to me. So, on the fateful night when she left the pub, she forgot her torch on one of the darkest nights of the month.

'She's a good-looking lass,' said Jones, more interested in the new girl than the torch. 'Talking of which have you found anyone that takes your fancy? Young lad like you should have some action.'

My natural sense of caution warned me not to reveal any details about Julie, but he had put me on the spot. I admitted I had a friend, one of identical twins, who worked in London, so I only saw her on the weekends when she came home to see her parents in Burpham.

'Burpham—a posh area. Father Roderick has a cottage there, or maybe it's in Wepham. When he first came here, four years ago, he invited some of us over for a glass of sherry after Sunday Mass. It was a regular thing, but it was a bit of a strain with the same people making small talk. Why should I go to church just to get a drink afterwards? I soon gave up that caper.'

'I didn't know he had a house in Burpham,' I thought Roderick lived in the school.'

'Burpham is cram full of teachers from our school,' remarked Jones. 'Higgins and his wife and their ghastly boys live in a former council house on the edge of the village. And Miss Cresswell has a very nice cottage there. She is always popping round to see Roderick with her homemade cakes. If you visit your lass in Burpham, you will meet half the staff down in the George & Dragon.'

He wanted more information, but I said as little as possible. I made a silly joke about how I wasn't sure which of the twins I was seeing. After this flippant remark, I felt guilty about discussing Julie behind her back.

'Must be difficult for you. Each of you is still living at home with your parents. But at least she can escape to the nightlife of London during the week.'

When he put it like that, it made our romance sound doomed, so I sprung to her defence.

'She doesn't have much time for socialising after work. She shares a flat with two other girls and they all seem to be stay-at-home types.'

'What you need is a place of your own to get to know her. That's the thing these days. Young couples cohabit to see if they are compatible. Bloody stupid to get married first, like I did. But then back in Wales, when I was a young man, that was the only option. Still, we found ways if you know what I mean.'

'We better drink up and get back to work. I see the head has gone to the till to pay his bill.'

'What is the name of your girlfriend?' said Jones.

'I didn't say. She wants to keep our relationship secret.'

'But there are two of them, you say. Twins.'

'Yes.'

'Tricky situation. How can you tell them apart?'

Practice cricket games had already started ahead of the first inter-school matches in early May. The crack of cricket ball against bat followed by the high-pitched cry of the fielders rang out, disturbing the peace of the headmaster in his study. Athletics training was also underway with running events, long jump and high jump competing for space with javelin throwing.

The headmaster's foul temper would not budge. He dragged his cigarette down to the tip, before throwing the butt carelessly out of the open window. With no one to watch, it felt pleasant to rebel and the sight of Michael

Fletcher shouting encouragement to the Under 12s during afternoon cricket coaching was guaranteed to darken his mood. The trouble with Fletcher was that he had an annoying air of superiority and questioned all the school rules. He never enforced simple disciplinary rules that all the children had to obey. In these so-called more enlightened days, teachers like him had become far too tolerant of misdemeanours. Fletcher had even caught boys smoking behind the bicycle shed or bullying and let the culprits off with a warning. Bullying was a difficult one, as the person being bullied probably deserved it and might have provoked it. In cases like that, the head would punish everyone involved.

Clearly, Her Majesty's Inspectorate of Education thought differently and would like ill-discipline and chaos to rule.

Later that afternoon, after games, I was walking down the corridor near the headmaster's study heading for the exit. I had nothing to do and no classes on the first day and hoped to escape early. But Mona bustled out of her office like a spider on its web. She looked flustered as she removed her reading glasses, left on in the rush. They were for near-sight vision, and she wanted to see the reaction on my face to what she had to say.

'Mr Fletcher, I am sorry to bother you, but I just received a peculiar call from a gentleman in London. He just said, "Tell Mr Fletcher that following my chat with him on Tuesday, we need him to decide by next week. He said you would know what he meant." I am afraid he didn't leave his name.'

This was a shock. I had tried to put the memory of the run in with the Spooks out of my mind, but it was easier said than done.

'That's okay, Mona. Thank you for passing the message on. I know what he means.'

'The headmaster does not encourage personal phone calls to or from the school, as you are aware. It's a distraction we can do without.'

I was sitting in my car in a state of paralysis. I was in a hurry to escape from school but had no wish to return home. Julie was staying in London for the weekend but promised to come home the following week. Her parents were off for a weekend break in Florence, so we might have the house to ourselves. She wasn't sure about Lizzie. Her plans were always changing at short notice. As an extra incentive, Julie planned to cook dinner. She sounded so happy that I didn't dare mention my encounter with MI5. It was too unbelievable.

Lost in daydreams it surprised me to see Mark's white Peugeot estate pull into the car park with such urgency that gossiping parents stopped in their tracks. He noticed me at the wheel of my car.

'Michael, I'm glad I caught you,' he said through the open window, spinning the wheel and parking alongside me with a sharp jab on the brakes. 'Hop in. Let's head off for a drink at your local hostelry and catch up on the news. There has been a development. You can come in my car if yours is still hot.'

Mark drove off with a squeal of the wheels, leaving the staring parents clutching their boys in a defensive huddle at the edge of the car park.

The George & Dragon was my usual pub for assignations. Even the recent tense meeting with the hooded security force at my favourite waterhole hadn't put me off, and I looked forward once more to a friendly welcome from the bar staff. I filled in Mark about MI5's barbed offer to recruit me. If he was surprised, he didn't show it.

'Standard practice, Michael. They flatter to deceive, as someone famous once said. I think it was Shakespeare.'

'No. It was Sir Walter Scott. It was in a poem called a "Tale of Flodden Field" and the correct quote, if I remember, is "O what a tangled web we weave when first we practice to deceive".'

At 5 p.m. the pub was quiet but began filling up as office workers arrived for Friday sessions. I steered Mark to a quiet corner, where we sat with our backs to the wall and with a good view of all arrivals.

'I had a break in at the office,' he said. 'A professional job with no sign of damage—a mystery how they got through the locked door. It has a secure mortice lock. There is no way in via the windows, which are double-glazed and secure. They have rifled my office files. Nothing missing apart from an invoice to Phoenix Oil accounts for the last order of water sampling.'

'That's weird. Why break in to steal an invoice?'

'It must be someone trying to discover information about the oil company. I forgot to tell you I went to see Dr James Ridley at Phoenix Oil. He gave me a logical explanation for their testing programme. As you know, the oil industry is a big supplier of crude oil to the plastic manufacturing industry. He wants to test how stable the final plastic bottle is in terms of leaching with different oil mixtures. His objective is to achieve greater stability and minimal potential for leaching and he feels the type of crude oil may influence the result. Phoenix wants to develop a zero-emissions plastic bottle. That is the mission. There is nothing sinister. It's a welcome first to find an oil company showing concerns for the environment.'

'But what about Sample X?'

'Ah, yes, the famous Sample X. He said they got it from a source in the Soviet Union, provenance unknown. He says to ignore it, as someone may have contaminated it to discredit the manufacturer. It's a one-off anomaly. However, that gives me cause for concern because of the break in. I think I need to get back to Phoenix Oil and tell James what has happened. During your sleuthing, have you given my address to anyone?'

'No. I have been very careful not to. Matron is the only one at school who is aware of your connection to Michelle because Michelle confided in her. Even Julie doesn't know about you specifically.'

'What do you mean by specifically?'

'Well, I told her Michelle has a brother who runs a test laboratory. But I never mentioned your name or the office location. Don't forget you gave me permission to pass on your business card and details to Peter Fowler at the *New Scientist*.'

'That could be it. Perhaps it is a coincidence that stuff happens after confiding in that man. Someone kills Michelle a few days after meeting Peter Fowler in London and my office is ransacked after you leave him my business card.'

I found it hard to believe Peter Fowler was suspicious. I reassured Mark he was a long serving professional of a respected scientific journal. More likely, the police or security service had followed us.

'It could have been the first time I visited your office. If the police were following my car I would not have noticed. If you remember, you showed me around the laboratory and then we travelled in your car to that pub next to the Hamble River—without a care in the world.'

'Not true. I had already warned you not to use your house phone. The police are up to many tricks. Now, there is something very important to tell you.'

He reached into his jacket and pulled out a slim brown envelope addressed to me. I recognised the handwriting to be from Michelle.

'Michelle gave me this letter just after she returned from France in late December. I am the executor of her estate. She instructed me to hand you the letter in the event of her death. Did you know she had a hereditary heart defect? She was convinced she would die young like one of her sisters. It's a gene-related condition, which affects the female side of the family only, so I guess I'm safe. She was involved in lifting the lid on the big players in the water bottling industry. As a result, she received threats and advice to cease her crusade.' He could see I wanted to say something, but with a raised hand, he showed he wanted to finish.

'The pressure made her more determined. She told me she had completed a book examining the exponential growth in the use of plastic in food and drinks packaging and the results of the stockpile of huge amounts of non-biodegradable plastic waste polluting the seas and environment. Nothing new there, you may say, but with her chemical knowledge, she could take a fresh look on the microscopic level and the harm plastics are doing to our bodies. In the package is a key to a bank safe at Barclays in Arundel. She wanted you to collect her books, proofread the English version and find a publisher.'

'You say books. You mean there is more than one?'

'No, it's the same book. She wrote the original in French and then translated the English version. As you are an English teacher, she said you were the ideal person to make sure it is correct in grammar and spelling. Her personal letter to you will explain everything. You know, Michael, she was very fond of you and who knows what the future may have been for you and her. With everything that has happened, I am convinced there are forces out there that will stop at nothing to prevent the publication of this book.'

Chapter 26

The Brighton force had called for a catch-up meeting at the Pulborough station. Usually, they requested Inspector Bishop and PC James to travel to Brighton for the periodic case review, but they needed to revisit the school to check some details with a staff member—a task they preferred to manage themselves. Preston looked in distaste at the red brick police station as they pulled into the front car park off the London Road.

'Typical Sussex town full of retired colonels and their memsahibs,' Preston joked. 'Care homes and tea shop territory for the retired.'

'A Tory stronghold. But pleasant countryside and interesting small shops.' Tracey was prepared to keep an open mind. Preston looked at his watch. Just before eleven. If they could wrap up the meeting by midday, a chance to catch a drink at one of the local pubs and then visit St Wilfrid's school on the way back to Brighton.

'Let's get on with it,' he said without enthusiasm. 'They are expecting us.'

Preston kicked off the meeting to give the local force an update on his visit to France and the discovery of a new suspect. Marcel had been in the UK on the weekend of the teacher's murder at the England and France rugby game at Twickenham. There was history between them, and he was an obsessed stalker of the poor girl and would not accept her lack of interest.

'When we saw him, he had no alibi for the Saturday night apart from staying in some crummy hotel in Paddington—the name of which he could not remember. Therefore, we believe he travelled down here after the match, met up with the girl in the pub and killed her. Better still, the French police have been on to me at the end of last week to say that Marcel admits trying to contact Michelle on the Sunday. He says he got the phone number of the school from Directory enquiries and called from a street phone box in London at about nine on Sunday morning. According to his testimony, someone at the school answered and went off to find Michelle in her room. Remember, she had live-in accommodation at St Wilfrid's—a miserable single bedroom with a desk next to the infirmary and close to matron's day room.'

'Sounds like we've got him,' said Inspector Bishop. 'Obviously, he killed her the evening before and made the call to establish an alibi.'

'My thoughts exactly,' said Preston.

'Whoever he spoke to, assuming the call is genuine, checked Michelle's room and told him she was out. He says he gave up trying to see her and returned to France.'

PC James pointed out that the phone billing for the school would show the number of all the incoming calls. If there were a London number from a call box, it would prove Marcel was innocent.

'Not so fast, lad. You are assuming he made the call, but he might have had an accomplice ring on his behalf. It is also not impossible that the school received other London calls that morning from other innocent parties. On our trip back to Brighton, we will visit the school to check out his story. It is feasible he caught the train down from London, met the girl in the pub and was walking her back to the school when, on the spur of the moment, he killed her with a rock and dragged her into the pond. Panicking, he took a taxi to the station and returned to London by the train. He was miles away when they found her body. I am assuming there is a late train. Does anyone know?'

'We can check the times,' said Bishop.

'It's far-fetched. Why assume a train? He might have hired a car, which would have made the logistics much easier.'

Preston drummed his fingers on the table with impatience. Why did they all have to make it so complicated? Forcing himself to stay calm, he pointed out the man had a motive. He was an obsessive stalker with a past fixation on Michelle—a condition documented two years ago by the police in Nantes. He admitted being in the country on the key date and trying to contact her. They just needed his confession, and it was done and dusted.

'I seem to remember you said much the same about Michael Fletcher,' said Bishop.

'Yea, the inspector and I wasted hours following his car because you ordered full surveillance. My girlfriend, Sandra, left me because I was never free to take her out.'

The Pulborough men annoyed Preston and were always trying to score points, but he kept his cool.

'It was correct to keep Mr Fletcher as a POI. That is how policing works. You follow the suspects like a dog with a bone. Michael Fletcher is *still* a suspect. He has been up to something, which has alerted the security forces in London. I will let Tracey explain.'

'He called me on the phone last week,' said Tracey. 'He complained he was being trailed by a black BMW, which he said was an unmarked Q car. This is the funny bit. He claimed two men in hoodies stopped him and forced him into a nearby pub where the guys admitted they were MI5 officers and offered to recruit him.'

'He's deluded. A crazy fantasist,' said Preston. 'According to Michael's account, some mystery person killed his girlfriend because she uncovered some mad conspiracy theory—something to do with toxic water and big business trying to suppress her results. No details. It is all supposition and guesswork.'

Inspector Bishop looked thoughtful. He suggested they should interview Michael to get it all on record, as a phone conversation alone was never satisfactory.

'After all, we should investigate all leads, however crazy they may seem to us.'

Preston said he had made discrete enquiries with the security forces and there was no record of any surveillance by their officers. They admitted using unmarked BMWs for operations, but usually in the London area. Who else might use unmarked fast cars?

'Good question,' said PC James. 'I know you can buy personalised number plates like 007 but driving with no plates is illegal unless you are on an official undercover job. So most likely it was someone pretending to be MI5.'

'I agree. Michael claimed the men wanted him to meet their superior officer; someone called Sean O'Connor at an address in Battersea. Clearly a made-up name.'

'Or the IRA,' said James. 'They are still active.'

Preston looked at his watch.

'If we are finished, I suggest we take an early lunch. I hear good things about the White Horse Inn just outside town. They stock Gales HSB from Hampshire.'

The mention of the famous Horndean Special Bitter put a spring in their step, and they piled into Preston's Cortina.

I was heading back to my study after cricket practice with the Under 12s when I saw Preston and Tracey Smith heading towards the refectory with Mona. What were they up to? I was tempted to follow them when Jones walked past, giving me the ideal excuse to follow him over to the refectory. Normally we went to the Staff common room for our tea and kept well away from the chaos of the school meals.

'Jones, I've just spotted the police from Brighton heading this way with Mona. Let's see what they are up to.'

My plan was to walk past the refectory and head over to the ground floor reception room, which was out of bounds to the boys but used by the staff as a smoking room. As we entered the corridor, we came face-to-face with the police, led by a startled Mona. She gave a nervous laugh and backed against the wall, hoping we would pass by. With Jones blocking progress, all five of us came to a standstill like a rugby scrum. To ease the tension, I tried to lighten the mood.

'Ah, the Brighton force! Any further news on the Spooks from London? Are you making any progress in locating Michelle's killer?'

Mona gave her excuses and left in a hurry. A faint smile creased across Preston's face. He looked relaxed and took his time before replying.

'Mr Fletcher, we have discovered nothing about the security forces engaged in covert surveillance of your movements. Both MI5 and M16 deny any interest in you. However, I do have some welcome news for you. We have located a new suspect. A French man called Marcel, who was a friend of Michelle's. In fact, he developed an unhealthy obsession with her despite receiving no encouragement from your girlfriend. Is this a surprise?'

'Not entirely. Michelle had mentioned a man back in France who was obsessed with her and became a bit of a pest. I suggested you look into him.'

SIO Preston and Tracey Smith exchanged a look. He had put them on the spot.

'It was always our plan to follow up on some questions in France, but it took a bit of time for the Prefecture in Nantes to approve a visit. It's not possible to barge in asking questions on their turf. Last week the French police said we could visit the laboratory at the university where Michelle worked as a PhD student. Tracey and I arranged our travel immediately and visited Nantes. Naturally, most of Michelle's fellow researchers and colleagues have moved on and left the university. Those that remember her recall her as an impressive student and a postgraduate researcher in the Chemistry department. She had some problems with one of the laboratory technicians, called Marcel. He became obsessed with her and was always following her around and she reported him to the university for his unwelcome and intrusive behaviour. Our informant seemed to think he backed off and things returned to normal. The technician still works in the Chemistry department, and we interviewed him through an interpreter, even though we believe he speaks quite good English.'

'Marcel admitted he was in London on 15th January to attend the Five Nations rugby match between England and France—the same day as someone murdered Michelle on Saturday night or the small hours of Sunday. He had the opportunity after the match to travel to Sussex.'

'Has he got an alibi? Where did he go after the match?'

'He maintains he stayed overnight in a hotel in the Paddington area, but he can't recall the name and has no receipt. He says he paid in cash. The French police have also questioned him, and he confessed he hoped to visit Michelle. He says he phoned the school on Sunday morning and one of the staff went to check Michelle's room. Of course, it was empty. He says he gave up and caught the ferry to France.'

'And you believe this story?' said Jones, who felt I needed some moral support.

'Mr Jones isn't it?' said Preston. 'The police always listen to the statements from POIs on their merits and seek to establish the truth.'

Jones looked confused. Preston apologised for using police slang. By POIs he meant Persons of Interest, of course.

'In pursuance of our enquiries,' said Tracey, 'we have established that the French POI did call the school at around nine-thirty Sunday morning and spoke to the head cook. At the weekend, the school secretary is off duty, so the catering staff deal with any calls. The cook checked Michelle's bedroom and saw that her bed had not been slept in. But this was no surprise as she was often away visiting friends at the weekend.'

'Thanks, Tracey,' Preston butted in. He was not happy sharing this information, standing around in a school corridor with loads of small boys rushing past them.

'So, gents, this French man is in the frame for the offence, and we hope he will confess soon.'

'Great news, but does he match the description I gave you?'

'Not exactly,' said Tracey. 'His facial features are quite similar, but he doesn't have long, blond hair. We think he has cut his hair and dyed it a darker brown recently. And witness descriptions are often not very reliable. At least he has blue eyes, so that fits your observation.'

'Don't get your hopes up,' added Preston. 'Unless we find some solid evidence or he makes a confession, we don't have enough to charge him. I will welcome two inspectors from Nantes next week and, as I explained to the school secretary, we will visit the school, the pub, the murder scene and anywhere else that may help our enquiries. I don't hold out any hope this will turn up anything new, but the French police wish to see the scene of the crime. You are the key witness. You witnessed the suspect in the public bar of the Three Horseshoes talking to Michelle. We will be in touch as you may have to attend an identity parade to see if you can pick Marcel. He is in France, so would you be free to travel to Nantes? Of course, we will pay your expenses.'

'I expect the school will allow that. And I have no objection to helping your enquiry. Possibly you can get the security agents off my tail meanwhile.'

Chapter 27

I left the unopened letter from Michelle on my mantle piece at home, for over a week. Most people receiving a letter like this from beyond the grave would open it immediately, but I held off because I felt afraid of what it might say and because it would be the last link from her to me. Julie had invited me to dinner at her parents' home. She said they were away for the weekend and Lizzie was staying in London. She invited me for the weekend, so I packed an overnight bag with a few essentials. I couldn't delay opening the letter any longer. It was the ideal time. My parents had left to go shopping in town and would not be back for over an hour. Inside there was a long letter and a key to a safe deposit box with instructions on how I could open it at the bank.

samedi, 8 janvier

Dear Michael,

It is a week before my twenty-fifth birthday. Why, I hear you say, are you writing me a letter only to be opened in the event of my death? Well, I hope to live many more years, but I have to tell you I have a hereditary heart defect just like my eldest sister, Elena. She died from this condition on her twenty-fifth birthday in Nantes when I lived at home and studied at the university before I came to England two years ago. The heart business doesn't bother me most of the time. I get tired and must rest and take some medicine, so I hope you are not reading this letter!

Maybe we are married. I loved our little outing in your old Morris car to Brighton to look at the seabirds. As you know, I don't drink, so I am sorry if I got a little tipsy. But then again, I felt pleased as well!

Now, I must tell you a bit about my secret life. If you are reading this letter, it will mean my worst fears are reality and you will have met my brother, (I know that sentence sounds odd!). In France, an executeur testamentaire deals with one's affairs after death. The role is like an executor in the UK, but less formal. As I have no property, no children and hardly any money, there is only one thing I leave behind, and this I will leave for you!

With the enclosed key, go to Barclays Bank in Arundel and withdraw a package. If the bank gets stuffy, I enclose the receipt and just tell them you are picking it up on my behalf. The manager, Mr Johnson, is very nice. Inside the box is a thick manuscript, which I have typed up with double spacing twice! Once for the French version, which I wrote first and then my English translation, which took ages as my English is so poor, as you know. I leave it for you à faire ça bien. You are my English teacher! I am not sure of the title. I thought it could be 'The Plastic Planet' but I'm sure someone has used that already, or maybe 'The Plastic Shroud.' As you know, I was very anti-plastic, and this book is all about how plastic usage in food and drink packaging is growing out-of-control. As a result, more and more non-biodegradable plastic waste is polluting the oceans and clogging up landfill sites all over the world. It doesn't have to be like this! It is only in the last ten years that plastic has become ubiquitous (omniprésent in French, which sounds better, n'est ç'est pas?)

But it is the more subtle chemical pollution of humans which worries me. Organic chemicals are leaching out of plastic into the water we drink. Bien sûr only in tiny traces. The scientists know that BPA (bisphenol A) is harmful, and they could remove it and use alternatives, but nowhere has banned it yet. So, Michael, my mission is to get my book into print. Please proofread it and correct my awful English. As to the French version, maybe pass it to St Wilfrid's next French teacher for checking (joke).

On a serious note, there are organisations and people out there who will go to <u>any</u> lengths to suppress this book. Knowledge is dangerous and the big bottle manufacturers and oil companies will not want to change their ways! Pressure must come from the People.

With eternal love,
Bisous milles

Michelle

Arriving at Julie's, I heard sounds from the kitchen, set down a corridor off the hallway, and this is where I found her preparing dinner.

'Sorry I didn't hear you arrive. The Eurovision Song contest is on the TV. Pour yourself a glass of wine and watch if you can stand it.'

'The music is so predictable, and the voting is all fixed,' I said. 'The only things I like are the really terrible songs and Terry Wogan's commentary. What's the English entry this year?'

'Oh, you missed that. They were on quite early. It was by a teenage group called Sweet Dreams with two girls and a guy called Bobby something. He was quite cute, and you would have liked the blonde girl. She was very bouncy. They are just like Buck's Fizz, but they won't stand a chance.'

I settled down to watch with a glass of red wine. The compere kept translating every comment into three languages, so the 20 contestants took ages to complete each song. Distracted, I walked around the room with its high Georgian ceiling, and studied the books in the bookcase, antique leather-bound box sets of famous authors such as Dickens, John Milton, Jane Austen, Rudyard Kipling, and Arthur

Conan Doyle. There were very few contemporary authors, so I guessed that the bulk of the collection was inherited from family. A grand piano displayed family photos of the parents and the twins as young girls on their horses or in family groups. It was a solid family house with a lived-in feel much larger than my parents' home.

'We can eat at the little coffee table in the corner,' Julie pointed to a charming mahogany round table with a white marble top next to the piano. 'It's called a *Kopitiam* table. My father bought it at an auction of Asian furniture in London. I think it is from Malaysia or Singapore.'

After I sat down, she served up two cottage blue Denby stoneware bowls, hot from the oven. I lifted the lid to reveal a small tartlet stuffed with mushrooms in a cream sauce.

'They have lots of garlic,' she said. 'If one person has garlic, and the other doesn't, then a kiss may be repulsive for the non-garlic eater, so I thought we could both have lots of garlic and then try kissing.'

'Maybe, if this is a scientific experiment, we should try a control kiss first without garlic?'

'Yes, that makes sense. In pursuit of scientific research...,' she closed her eyes, pursed her lips together, and leaned over the narrow table so I kissed her at which point my glass of wine spilled over the table. Red wine poured in a rivulet and spilled onto the expensive carpet. She laughed and rushed off to the kitchen to apply warm water and salt on the stain.

'Our quick survey with no trace of garlic was quite pleasant, except I noticed a metallic acid taste of the *Rioja,* which was interesting. It introduced a subtle overtone,' she giggled.

Meanwhile, the Eurovision Song Contest ground on relentlessly in the background.

'That was a very nice starter,' I complimented her on her cooking.

'I stole the wine from my father's cellar. He won't miss it.'

She was wearing a light top, but a breeze had picked up, rattling the shutters. She shivered. 'It's getting chilly. The sun has gone down. You can't trust the weather at this time of year.'

As I finished the first course, she shut the veranda doors, drew the curtains, and lit some lamps. She cleared the plates and ran off to prepare the main course. I poured myself more wine. In no time, she was back, bearing two large dinner plates with small but elegant servings.

'That was fast. You are a skilled waitress and cook. What is the main course? Does this have more garlic?'

'You ask too many questions,' she said.

'I worked in a small restaurant in London when I was a teenager. Doing everything! Waitress, cook, dishwasher, general dogsbody! It is obvious the dish on the plate is pan-fried breast of chicken with a lemon sauce with French tarragon and thyme. You know it is quite tricky to buy French tarragon? Mostly the type they have in the shops is Russian tarragon, which has an inferior taste. And before you ask, yes, it has more garlic. Is that a problem?'

I looked nervous but laughed along with her

'Sounds amazing. I look forward to tasting the tarragon!'

After a delicious meal, we sat on the sofa, drinking more wine. We had switched to a French white as a better match for the chicken and more suitable to spill on the carpet. The last song of the evening on the Eurovision was a French song from Luxembourg "*Si la vie est cadeau*" by Corinne Hermès.

'Now that's a lovely, romantic song. I like that. What do you think?'

But the song had brought back memories of Michelle. My eyes were watering, and I excused myself to run off to the bathroom. Once I had composed myself, I returned. I explained a little about Michelle's letter and her bequest of the book. Julie said she wanted to read the book and cooperate in finding the best publisher. With her contacts in London, she was sure it would be a best seller.

Much later, after the never-ending voting completed, the winner was '*Si la vie est cadeau*' with Israel second. The UK entry came in sixth.

'I have a knack for picking winners. The Grand National two weeks ago and now the Eurovision Song Contest. And you as well, of course,' she snuggled up before breaking off.

'It's been a very tiring week at work, so I am going to take a quick bath and go straight to bed. Help yourself to more wine. Isn't this fun without boring parents around?' She gave me a cheeky smile and ran upstairs to fetch me a towel.

'There is a second bathroom upstairs you can use. My bedroom is first on the left and I have an ensuite bathroom.'

I sipped my wine slowly to give her time for a bath and then went upstairs. The rooms above were all furnished with a feminine touch. Julie's bed was not as small as she implied, but the room itself was small so that the bed took up most of the floor space. I walked along the corridor to the guest bathroom, an inviting room with a generous antique Victorian bath with noisy plumbing. I half expected cold water, but it was boiling, so I was glowing pleasantly after a relaxing bath when I joined Julie in bed to be swallowed up into a soft mattress. It was just then that we saw the beam of headlights from an approaching car coming up the drive. Frozen in fear, the lights flashed across the room before the car stopped with a sound of crunched gravel.

'It's my parents!' Julie jumped out of bed and slipped on a dressing gown.

'Get dressed. You can go into the spare room on the next floor. First on the right, up the stairs. They will have seen your car, so I'll head them off.'

She scuttled to the bedroom door, listening for their arrival. We both heard the front door opening, and she pointed me in the right direction as I retrieved my clothes, and as an afterthought, my shoes, and socks.

She called down to them in an over-eager voice. 'I thought you were going to Florence?' Quickly, she bustled downstairs. Her parents looked up in surprise. It was unusual for her to go to bed so early. Perhaps they hadn't seen my car. I was safely out of sight, but Julie was anxious in case they heard creaking floorboards or the pattering of nervous footsteps.

'Your father made a mistake on the booking. He booked 23rd May instead of 23rd April. We drove all the way to Heathrow for a night flight a month too early. The flight was full, and we couldn't change the booking. Really, I am so cross. What a disastrous birthday.'

'I am quite certain I asked the travel agent for the correct dates.'

'And they sent you the tickets. Why didn't you check them?' she fired back.

Just then, Julie's mother noticed the empty dining plates left on the table and discarded wine glasses. 'I see you have been entertaining whilst we have been away.' She was already in a bad mood, and it was getting worse. 'In a grand style, by the looks of it.'

'Yes, Michael came over to watch the Eurovision Song Contest.'

'Michael? Is this a friend we know?' asked her father.

'Pa. He is the English teacher from St Wilfrid's! You both met him at lunch at Easter.'

'Of course, your father's being stupid. That nice young man who went to school with Michael Cox.'

'Correct,' said Julie in exasperation. 'Also, suspected of murdering his girlfriend by the police and the media. He didn't want to drive home after drinking. You know how hot the police are on drink and driving. So, I've put him in the guest bedroom. I hope that is all right. He's had a busy week teaching, and he is probably sound asleep already. No doubt, you can meet him again tomorrow over breakfast. I have a severe headache—probably from watching that silly song contest, so I am going back to bed. I am sorry your holiday in Florence didn't work out.'

'But did you air the bed?' said her mother. 'It's a frightfully cold room. You should have put him in Lizzie's room as she is away.'

She ran back up the stairs and collided with me on the landing. Glaring, she manhandled me towards the stairs to point me toward the spare room. We could hear her parents coming upstairs, so we rushed off to our separate beds. In view of the urgency, I clambered under the covers, partly clothed. In the rush, I could not account for my socks and pants. A small detail—hopefully I hadn't dropped them in the corridor. I pulled the blanket up to my neck, turning on my side, pretending deep, untroubled sleep. When Julie returned to her bedroom, she saw a discarded pair of navy-blue boxers on the floor. Hurriedly, she pushed them under the bed.

Chapter 28

On the last Friday of April, the French police invited me to attend an identity parade at a police station in Nantes. Considering the travel options, I decided the best plan was to use my car and cross to France on the Portsmouth to Saint-Malo Brittany ferry. Then a long drive to Nantes. To make the morning appointment, I travelled the day before and checked into a cheap hotel in Nantes overnight.

DI Preston had phoned me at school to set the appointment up. The French police had arrived midweek in Brighton and looked at the scene of the crime and the pub where they were keen to try out the local beer. They had talked to matron, the headmaster, and Mona but said they would talk to me when I attended the identification parade so as not to bias the case. According to Preston, he convinced them that Marcel committed the crime, so it all hinged on my identification. No pressure then. It all seemed too convenient, and I did not want to identify an innocent man. I knew how that felt. Whilst in Nantes, I planned to visit Michelle's mother, and I asked the police to call and check if she was happy to see me. I wished to offer my condolences on Michelle's death. When the headmaster suspended me from my post, he denied me the chance to meet her family.

At the appointed hour, I arrived at the Prefecture of Police address in Nantes where the identity parade was due to take place. Although I was on time, there was a delay and they led me to a nondescript office on the ground floor and left me for twenty minutes. A tough-looking commissaire came in and apologised for the long wait. He lit up a cigarette and hovered by the door. He then told me some of the background to the case, which he should not have done as it influenced what would happen next. It did not seem ethical, but I knew nothing of French law, so presumed this was normal practice.

'Thank you coming all the way from England,' he started politely. 'My name is Jules. They have assigned me to answer your questions. When they are ready, I will take you through to the identity parade. We have eight men lined up with similar appearance. You can walk past, study all the faces, and pick the person who matches the man you saw. It is just as you see in films or the TV. You understand?'

'Yes, it will be no problem.'

'You are right. We know Marcel Fouché. When your police visited us, Marcel had short, dark brown hair and his English was poor. However, when we showed your identikit picture to the students in the university Chemistry department, they all said straight away that looks like Marcel. Marcel is a long-haired hippy type with straggly blond hair and blue eyes—a person attractive to the young women. Michelle was not the first. He falls for all the young girl students. When he came back from his England trip in January, he cut his hair and dyed it a shade darker. Why so? I guess because you witnessed him in the pub near to the scene where Michelle died. Many say it is an open-and-shut case! But we cannot know for sure.'

After this account, I had no trouble in identifying Marcel out of the line-up. He alone had short, dark brown hair and all the rest of the rabble had long blond hair. For some perverse reason, I decided not to pick him. This enraged the police. I explained the man I had seen had long blond hair, but none of the men with long hair matched the person I had seen.

'But Monsieur, I told you Marcel cut his hair when he returned to France.'

'Yes, I know you said that, but you asked me to recognise a man matching the man I saw. And no one with their current appearance fits, so I can't in all honesty pick someone just on the police recommendation.'

'If you do not cooperate with us, a sadistic killer will go free and may kill again. Have you thought of that?'

As they were getting nowhere, they took me to see the chief of the Prefecture in a large office where he sat behind a vast desk with a bank of phones. They brought a secretary from another room to take notes of our conversation.

'I understand the logic of your position,' he said. 'Marcel wishes to confess. He cannot live with what he knows. I saw in his eyes that it amazed him when you failed to recognise him.'

'But you weren't in the room,' I objected.

He pointed at the mirror on the wall, and I saw it gave a view of the room I had just been in. The officer smiled.

'Perhaps we should try a reverse strategy and ask Marcel if he recognises you.'

'Is it allowed that I speak to him?' I asked. 'I think he might talk to me.'

The officer laughed. 'Why would a murder suspect agree to chat to the boyfriend of the girl he murdered? All he has to do is say nothing and we have no reason to hold him. An impasse, yes?'

He sat thinking for a minute. There was nothing to be lost, so he agreed.

'It must be a private conversation between us, with no one listening in. If he admits anything, I will inform you and you can follow up.'

'D'accord. We will arrange it for later this afternoon. I believe you intend to visit Michelle's family. One of my officers can drive you and bring you back here.'

'No, thank you. I have my car. I can find her house.'

'Well, I see you wish to be independent. Michael, we meet again at three. Are you travelling back to England today?'

'No, I am staying the night and catching the afternoon ferry, so no rush.'

Michelle's mother lived in a modern house in a quiet tree-lined avenue to the west of the city on the Boulevarde Auguste Peneau. I shook off the commissaire and drove to her house without too much problem. It was okay driving in France apart from roundabouts, which terrified me, as I never knew the correct exit and had to drive around twice, being pursued by angry little cars like buzzing bees. I think my GB plates bought out the worst and least tolerant behaviour in French drivers.

Meeting Michelle's mother and her grandfather was emotional for all of us. I tried out my student French, and they applauded my effort before reverting to English. Next, I updated them on the situation with Marcel, just to say he was at the police station while they build a case against him. I did not mention my deliberate ploy of refusing to identify him, as I could not explain it to myself—possibly a desire for fairness and an objection to the police briefing me before the identity parade.

'The poor man is harmless,' said Madame Gagneux. 'Michelle was an attractive girl. And she told him to leave her alone. He was a nuisance, and she reported his annoying behaviour to the authorities at the university. But they laughed it off and said she should just ignore him. Then another girl complained about him making crude and suggestive remarks so they told him he should see a doctor and get some advice or maybe medication to calm him down.'

'I am so sorry for your loss. I have no words to say what I feel.'

She raised her hand to acknowledge my comment.

'It's a cruel fate. You know both Michelle and her older sister; Elena, had the same heart condition. Atrial fibrillation, they call it. They tell us it is not a serious thing. The heart flutters, the pulse rate runs too high and then it returns to normal. But Elena died on *her* birthday two years ago. Now Michelle has also died on *her* birthday, two years later! Quelle sont le chances pour ça?'

'She left me a letter explaining this. It's as if she knew the same thing would happen to her.'

'The police assume Marcel murdered Michelle, but did the autopsy *look* at her heart? I think the English police have a closed mind.'

'They have to work with the evidence,' I explained. 'When Michelle came home for Christmas, did Marcel try to contact her?'

'Yes, he did. To apologise, he said. He visited me here one day when she was away and wanted reconciliation, but I told him she had a boyfriend in UK and not to bother us anymore.'

'Did you mean me?' I felt I had to ask because I l knew she was also fond of Dominic.

'Yes, of course, she was mad about you.'

I mentioned Michelle's book, which she had entrusted to me, and this was news to them. They were aware of her environmental activism, but they knew nothing of her research with her brother Mark. I decided not to go into too much detail and did not mention the covert surveillance I had experienced and the break-in at Mark's laboratory. It sounded too much like a spy story.

'Mark is very loyal to my ex-husband, so he never comes to France, which is a shame. At the school service for Michelle, he was very supportive, so I think things can improve for the future.'

I refused an offer to stay for lunch and headed back to the police station. Michelle's grandfather had said very little, but he followed me to my car and shook my hand. He said I must seek justice for Michelle and discover if Marcel was indeed the perpetrator, which he found hard to believe.

'Truly, it is a mystery what happened. Everyone assumes the worst. First, they made you the chief suspect, and now it's Marcel's turn. The case against him is very strong because he was in England, but I don't think the police have much to go on. Are you sure the man you saw in the bar was Marcel?'

'Yes and no. I am sure the man they call Marcel was the man I saw, but as he had long blond hair, I could not match him in the identity parade.'

'You mean you failed to identify him?'

'I know it's him, but the police were trying to manipulate me, so I refused to say. I am going back to the Prefecture as I demanded a face-to-face meeting with Marcel. No doubt, they will pressure me to change my mind, but I doubt you can repeat an identity parade until you get the right answer. I hope to persuade Marcel to talk.'

Friday afternoon in London in late April was a pleasantly warm spring day. Peter Fowler had left the *New Scientist* office straight after lunch to avoid the usual rush on the Underground. Instead of heading home to Ealing, he left the train at Earl's Court and walked to the church of St Mary The Boltons. He hovered outside as if waiting for someone. Which he was. Holding an umbrella and a copy of the *Evening Standard,* he felt out-of-place and conspicuous in this island of calm, with its oasis of wooded gardens surrounding the Victorian church. Beside the road a row of grand mansions painted white heightened his feeling of inferiority at the sight of some of the most expensive and desirable houses in London. Involuntarily, he looked across at the house where his contact would shortly amble across to meet him.

'Good afternoon, Peter,' said a voice from behind. The man he knew as Colonel Lane had materialised next to him, approaching unseen along the pavement perimeter outside the private park. Lane was a tall, lean man in his late 50s clad in a full-length black overcoat despite the mild weather. He still had a full head of black hair with a hint of greyness. The men walked along the pavement and stopped at the locked gate on the south of the park. The colonel unlocked the gate, and they followed the path towards the church, stopping at a wooden bench where they sat in total privacy.

'We looked inside Dr Carter's laboratory near Southampton. Not me, of course, but we now know Carter's client for testing water samples is an oil company called Phoenix Oil. Have you heard of them?'

'No, I can't say I have,' said Peter Fowler. 'They must be a small company.'

'Small, yes, but they have important contacts. They have acreage in a southern North Sea gas field where Shell is the major operator and a US operation in the Gulf of Mexico. The question is why this sudden interest in water. That is the puzzle.'

'To make plastic, you need oil. One litre bottle of water made with plastic requires about 250 ml of crude oil to manufacture the plastic.'

'Exactly,' agreed the colonel. 'It's fascinating to realise that all those people drinking healthy water are not aware of the manufacturing process requiring huge amounts of crude oil plus the fact that the plastic is leaching out various unhealthy chemicals such as BPA. Some consumers are waking up to the realities, so we need to keep this level of knowledge out of the scientific journals such as yours. You have been doing a great job, Peter, keeping the lid on the various research findings so the public stay in the dark. This French girl's research has alarmed us. Now the English teacher is proving troublesome. What's the name of her friend at that school in Sussex?'

'Michael Fletcher—the young man who came to see me.'

'Yes him. He is proving a concern. We believe he is working with Dr Carter and running his own investigation to find the culprit for his girlfriend's murder.'

'You are well-informed, sir.'

'One has to be, Peter. We tried to get him to cooperate with us, but he declined our offer.'

'So, we wait for their next move?' asked Peter.

'Yes, but we look for the book she told you she had written. We sent a man pretending to be a solicitor to the school and there was no sign of her research or any manuscript. Was she telling you the truth? Did she show you her book? These questions concern us. It is of vital importance we find the book and destroy it. We will have another meeting in a week or two. Call me if anything comes up your end or else wait for me to confirm the usual place and time.'

The colonel handed over a package. Without looking, Peter knew it was a cash payment of £500 in used twenty-pound notes. But he was worried. Colonel Lane remained seated, which was unusual. A creature of habit. In the past, the colonel would leave immediately after passing over payment.

'Peter, I have to stress the importance of our mission. If adverse research results or, worse still, a book is published exposing the plastics industry the impact could be a worldwide collapse of the market. At a stroke we will be plunged back to the past using glass for bottling and natural plant materials like jute, paper and cardboard for storage. A horrific step back into the dark ages.'

Peter sensed the situation was getting out of control. Apart from the girl's death, there was the harmless darts player, Alan Jones, killed in a suspicious car accident. How many more would die? If Dr Carter and Michael Fletcher were at risk, then his own position was also not secure.

Chapter 29

There was a strike by French dock workers at Saint-Malo, so I had to drive to Caen to get an alternative ferry back to Portsmouth, which arrived in the early morning on Sunday. I knew Julie was down from London for the weekend, so I drove to her parents' house to surprise her and, hopefully, get some breakfast.

Following my last furtive visit to their house to watch the Eurovision Song Contest, I was nervous about my reception, but they were friendly.

'Must be a relief that they have identified Marcel Fouché as Michelle's killer,' said Julie's father.

'Hold on, where are you getting that information from?'

'It's in the *Daily Telegraph*,' he said. 'So, it must be true. You get a mention for travelling to France to identify him as the man you saw in the pub,' he flashed the paper in front of me where the stark heading declared 'Mystery Man in Pub is French Stalker.'

I explained how I had failed to identify Marcel in the police line-up. Julie's father was a Justice of the Peace, so my story both horrified and amused him.

'I think you did the right thing, Michael. They were trying to lead you. Any good defence lawyer would have caused a stink even if you had identified the man. As I understand you correctly, the man the police are holding *is* Marcel Fouché, and he *is* the man you saw in the pub.'

'Yes, that's right.'

'But you didn't pick him during the identity parade and when you went to have a friendly chat with him to persuade him to come clean, he refused to say anything.'

'Yes, that's about it.'

'I feel there is something you are holding back from us, Michael.'

'I believe he is innocent. Michelle's mother feels the same way. I think the police should do another autopsy and look into the possibility of natural causes.'

I explained about Michelle's heart problem and her sister's death on her birthday from the same condition. Julie's father agreed there was just cause to conduct a second autopsy, but the request would have to be made by Michelle's family. Fortunately, the police had not released her body for burial or cremation, so this was still an option.

'It's a big decision. Mrs Gagneux and the family may not want a second autopsy. Neither the English nor the French police will want one either.'

'There is another concern. There had been threats against her life. She was a whistle-blower taking on the big corporations over what she alleged were unsafe practices in the food and drink packaging industry.'

'Yes dad,' said Julie, 'This is *really* interesting. Do you realise every time you drink a glass of water from a plastic bottle, some chemicals used in producing the bottle are passing into the water and into your body? Although it is only minute traces, some are toxins, carcinogenic compounds, and artificial hormones. No one knows the long-term effects of ingesting all this artificial rubbish.'

'You sound like an old record,' said her father. 'You told me this when you came for lunch at Easter, and I still believe this view is alarmist and without sufficient scientific evidence.'

'*I'm* convinced,' said Julie's mother.

'Anyone for wine?'

'At least no one suspects you anymore,' said Lizzie.

'Yes, it was unfortunate to be flagged up as a suspect. I was one of the last people to see her alive, and that was enough for the police. We were good friends. She came for tea with my parents and once I took her down to Brighton as she was a very keen photographer, like myself, and wanted to see the seabirds on the seafront. They blew this up to make out we were having an affair.'

'Michael won the best photograph of the year award for his photo of a barn owl from National Geographic, was it Michael?' said Lizzie.

'No, not as good as that. It was from the Sussex Wildlife Trust.'

'Yes, he's quite an expert at bird spotting,' giggled Julie with obvious double entendre.

'Well, jolly good it's all settled now,' said Julie's mother. 'How long do you have off for half-term, Michael?'

'Half-term is still three weeks away. I have ten days off. Julie and I are planning to drive up to Scotland and look around. Visit the popular tourist sites like Loch Ness and Loch Lomond and then drive further north to the Highlands.'

'I expect you will take the M6 motorway, but I would avoid Glasgow as it's best to get into the countryside,' said Julie's father. 'No doubt you will take tents as there are excellent camping sites with facilities like showers and shops. All you need is a couple of tents, a Primus stove and a sturdy pair of boots—marvellous walking country.'

Neither of us planned to camp. A cosy bed-and-breakfast establishment held more appeal than a canvas roof out in the rain. Lizzie saw our dilemma and came to the rescue.

'You can borrow the tent I used last year at Glastonbury.'

'Brilliant,' said Julie. 'Michael, if you haven't got a tent, you could buy one from Millets.'

'I have an old one from my time in the Boy Scouts, but it is a bit moth-eaten. Glastonbury last year was good. I'm surprised you didn't go with Lizzie.'

'Yes, I was so annoyed I missed out. Van Morrison, Jackson Browne and Judy Tzuke were in the line-up, but I couldn't get time off work.'

I felt left out of this festival talk and listening to wet Glastonbury memories. I had never fancied attending this music festival in the muddy fields of Somerset, held in June, but after camping in the Highlands, I would be ready for anything.

Julie's mother served us up a late brunch of a full English breakfast. She had already offered wine in a jokey fashion, so the girls made up some buck's fizz.

After breakfast, the girls asked me to drive them to the seaside for a walk. I agreed as long as they did not dress the same. Walking along the seafront, sandwiched between attractive identical twins, would invite loads of stupid comments. A fine sunny Sunday afternoon: so, we could expect dog walkers, family outings, cyclists, runners, and day trippers for the whole seafront from Brighton across to Bognor Regis.

It was about eight miles to the coast from Arundel. I took them via a scenic route, passing close to the Fox Inn near Patching where the outside beer garden beckoned, but the girls insisted we get some exercise, so we headed to Goring-by-Sea. The beach was typical of this stretch of coastline facing the English Channel. The foreshore was gravelly, and above the storm level, a line of identical beach huts gazed out to sea, looking like Victorian relics. Families occupied a few huts, grimly wrapped up in overcoats against the icy wind as they warmed frozen fingers on mugs of hot tea.

'Hardly the Riviera,' said Lizzie, turning her nose up in distaste. 'I bet those beach huts sell for a fortune. They are just wooden sheds with no electricity, running water or toilets.'

'I can't see the point,' agreed Julie.

'I think it's somewhere to change for the beach where they can preserve their modesty,' said Lizzie with a giggle.

Many groynes, made of wooden beams and uprights, separated the beach into little segments, forming parallel strips. These shore protection measures, erected as a vain attempt to stop longshore drift and erosion of the sand, were an unattractive feature unless you were a small boy jumping off them or a couple sheltering in the lee to escape the wind. If you fancied a swim, the warmest water was near to the outflow pipes, which the Water Board said was harmless run-off storm water. The sewage discharge pipes were located further offshore, well out of the reach of any but the hardiest of swimmers. There was a concrete path next to the beach huts, so we walked along to see where it led, dodging the mass waves of walkers crowding the narrow path.

'Michael, we have found a very good literary agent for Michelle's book,' said Lizzie. 'I passed him your synopsis, plus her first three chapters. His view is that it could be a publishing sensation. Her murder gives the book huge marketing potential, and that is even before we look at the content. He plans to approach three of the most promising publishers and says it is likely there will be a bidding war to secure the rights.'

'And that's the next problem,' said Julie.

'Mark Carter is the executor of her affairs and represents the family interests, whereas Michelle bequeathed her book to you to complete and market it. To avoid future disputes, we think you need to discuss this with Mark to sort out the contractual stuff.'

'That sounds sensible. Michelle was never thinking of the material side. I want the book published because that is what she wanted. I am happy not to take a penny of any profits.'

'Very honourable of you,' said Lizzie.

'But let's meet Mark to discuss it. If you would like me or Julie there, I'm sure we can manage that, but the weekend is best for us.'

On the way back, we stopped for a drink at the Fox Inn and looked at the menu to see if there was anything that appealed. I felt a knot of unease ever since the conversation about the book. I should have spoken to Mark before rushing into things, but the girls were confident that their contact in London would be the best way forward. I phoned Mark from the pub pay phone outside the toilet to update him on all the developments since we last met.

'Michael. It's telepathy. I have been trying to reach you all day. I phoned home and your mother said you were back from France but had gone out to see Julie.'

'Yes, that's right. We have been for a walk on the beach and just arrived in a pub called the Fox Inn on the way back to Burpham.'

'I'm glad I caught you at last. There is an urgent development. I can't speak on the phone,' Mark sounded rattled. 'Give me your number in case we get cut off.'

The beeps sounded as I was finishing reading out the number and I waited for him to return the call. I was right out of change and the bar was so crowded it would take ages to get served. I had almost given up when Mark called back.

'Sorry you cut off before I could catch the number. Lucky you mentioned the Fox Inn. Trouble is, there are four Fox Inns in Sussex, so I had to work out the most likely one was in Patching. Are you going to stay put for the next hour or two?'

'We may order some food. We are likely to be here for at least two hours, I guess.'

'Right, stay put. Fortunately, I am in Chichester Harbour today. I have been sailing, so I can join you at the pub in about forty minutes. Lucky you caught me. I moored up an hour ago at the marina and then met up with my secretary, Paula. We are in Birdham at the moment having a drink. Would it be alright if I bought her with me?'

We waited for Mark and his friend. The girls were excited to meet Mark for the first time. Mark, when he arrived, looked the very model of a casual yachtsman wearing a white Shetland pullover under a blazer with brass buttons and a navy-blue denim fisherman's hat. We had moved inside the pub out of the evening chill and Mark removed his formal blazer to blend in. He introduced Paula, who I had met before at Mark's office. Both were keen on sailing and their usual haunt was the Hamble River, but to try something different, Mark had sailed over from Hamble that morning.

'That sounds quite a trip,' I said.

'It's just a couple of hours with a westerly. I am leaving the boat moored up in Chichester for the week and Paula drove over to collect me. Then next weekend a friend is dropping us both back to our boat and we will sail her back to Hamble.'

'The logistics are complicated,' I said. 'I guess that's what happens when you rely on an outmoded form of transport.'

Paula sipped on a Pimm's and seemed thrilled. Mark addressed his first comments to the twins.

'I'll get straight to the point. I don't know how much Michael has told you, but since my sister's death, we have been aware of covert surveillance from the Sussex police following Michael everywhere and then a more sinister development was another team who purported to be from MI5. They even tried to kid him to join their organisation as an agent! Then things got more sinister. Someone broke into my office and stole a file and a key witness from the pub—a darts player from Graffham—died in a road accident, but no other vehicle was involved. Apparently, he was drunk. But I followed the case up. At the inquest, the police report stated that there was an open whisky bottle in the car and the car reeked of it. Obviously, someone planted the booze to make us think it was an accident!'

'What was the court verdict?' I asked.

'Insufficient evidence so an open verdict. That's lazy policing. I should say it's murder by person or person's unknown,' said Mark.

'Why did someone want him dead? When I met him and offered him a whisky, he told me it was the one drink he didn't like!'

'There you are! That proves it!' said Mark. 'Alan Jones alive backed up your version of this man in the pub talking to Michelle. Whoever killed Alan wanted *you* to be the suspect and not Marcel, because pressure on you might stop Michelle's book in its tracks. And what about your friend from the *New Scientist,* Peter Fowler? '

I was shocked. What was he saying?

'No, he's not dead yet. Don't worry. Fowler has been the weak link. When you gave him my business card, he passed it on to a contact who has been paying him over the years for information. This guy likes to keep abreast of new developments on all science topics, especially relating to the oil and gas sector. Peter Fowler has realised his contact is ruthless, and he plans to make himself scarce and walk away from a situation he can't deal with anymore. He phoned me to confess his involvement and to warn us we are at risk.'

'At risk from whom and why?' I asked.

'A straight question deserves a straight answer. The whom is a very rich businessman known as Colonel Lane. He lives in the Boltons in London—one of the most expensive streets for real estate. We don't know if that is his true name or a pseudonym. He is most likely acting for another client. The why is because Michelle's whistleblowing has upset some powerful people in industry, and they wish to suppress all her research results and stop publication of her book—the book that Michelle gave to you to complete. The logical conclusion is that her book could put pressure on the manufacturers of plastic in the food and drinks industry and that would be a disaster for the firms who rely on the status quo. You told me you intended to withdraw her book from the bank security box, so where is it now?'

'Yes, I collected it from the bank. I needed it for proof reading. When I finished, I wrote a synopsis and passed the first three chapters to Julie. There are still a lot more corrections to do, so I just concentrated on the first three chapters to rush something out.'

Lizzie spoke up. 'My sister and I work for *Time Out* magazine in London. You may have heard of it. It has a huge circulation. We have good contacts with publishers and agents, so last week we sent one of the best literary agents the synopsis Michael prepared plus the first three chapters, with no obligation, to see if he thinks there is interest from the mainstream publishers.'

'Yes, I know how it works. What's his verdict?'

'That it could be mammoth. The rights may go to auction if several rivals bid for it.'

'Or not. If Colonel Lane gets to know of this, he will try to suppress it.'

'How would he do that?'

'By destroying the manuscript. I suggest we think of separate secure locations to hide the original and a backup. The fewer people know about this, the better.'

Chapter 30

The next week went silent. Mark contacted the literary agent in London, a small firm called Frobisher Daniels in St Martin's Court, close to the *Time Out* office in Covent Garden. He spoke to Jeremy Frobisher, the senior partner, and stressed the need for total secrecy and discretion. Mark suggested holding back on any discussions with potential publishers or auction plans until he gave approval for action. He explained this was for copyright and contractual reasons but hinted at hostile forces trying to get hold of the manuscript.

The delay did not please Frobisher. He had already sent out the synopsis and sample chapters to two publishers, plus another set to the editor of *New Scientist* with a request to check out the science aspects to see if the research was valid. He better chase up his contacts to alert them of the need for security.

Mid-week I called Preston at Brighton to see if there was any update on the Marcel Fouché case and Preston told me they had submitted a formal request to arrest and extradite Marcel to the UK for official trial. Despite the lack of evidence, Preston felt certain that any jury would convict him. Once they had him in the UK, they would offer him a deal: Come clean and confess, and he could return to France to serve his sentence. They were more lenient with crimes of passion over there.

In another development, Michelle's mother had lodged a request for a second autopsy of her daughter because the condition of her heart had not been examined in the original autopsy. Michelle had a condition that put her at risk. The French police were not familiar with the correct procedure and suggested it might be best for Mark to make a formal request on behalf of the family to the UK police.

At school, the pace was quicker, with panic rising at the approach of exams. Half-term was less than three weeks away and Michael needed that break to escape as far from Sussex as possible.

Mark's positive lead from Peter Fowler naming Colonel Lane as the figure hell-bent on locating Michelle's book was confirmation of their worst fears. The book was hot property. The surveillance team of Gary and Wayne must be the ground troops—a ruthless team who knew where I lived and where I worked. They seemed content not to make a move directly. Every morning when I drove from home to school and every afternoon when I returned home, I checked the road for parked vehicles. When driving, I locked all the doors and tried different routes, driving as fast as possible. I even considered sleeping over at school during the week. Logically, it was only a matter of time before they came for me.

Since our meeting with Mark, we lodged the original manuscript in a new safe deposit box with a firm of solicitors in London. Julie had arranged this. *Time Out*'s editor as a favour held the access code to the box. He was unaware of the contents and knew better than to ask. For added security I lodged the backup copy at school with matron

At some stage, I needed to continue proof reading, but this was on hold as it was too dangerous to have any full copies in circulation. Likewise, for any interested publishers. They would have to wait. The best option was to do nothing for at least a month and to give time for police investigation into Colonel Lane to bear fruit. Peter Fowler knew the man's name, his phone number, and his address at the Boltons in Kensington. We urged him to go to the police and put in a report, but he said the time was not right. Peter was not under suspicion, and he would be most useful in making them think he was still working for them. We must not alert the police, which might make things worse, and drive the team underground. Also, it was possible the colonel was entrenched within the establishment and might be untouchable.

There was one other loose end I wanted to investigate. I suspected that Nigel Caldwell-Brown was our mole, passing information to Lane or his subordinates. After lunch, he liked to take coffee in the staff common room. A creature of habit. I developed a plan.

Lunch that Saturday was a cottage pie. A hearty meal made from minced beef, onions and carrots topped with a thick wodge of oven-baked, mashed potato and served with tinned peas. On a cold winter's day, all that potato, over-cooked meat and vegetables could fill a hole in the stomach, but on a warm early summer day before cricket, it was not appropriate. Cook worked to a timetable not to the seasons. Nigel Caldwell-Brown had finished his lunch. His plate was impressively clean, and he still had room for the rhubarb crumble and custard. I sat next to him and waited. I opened a paperback to read as I toyed with squashing the food to the side of the plate to make it seem less hostile.

'What's that you're reading?' he asked. I enclosed the outside cover in brown paper so he could not see the title.

'Nothing much. An old book by John le Carré called *"Tinker Tailor Soldier Spy."* Have you read it?' I asked.

'Years ago when it first came out. It's slow, I remember.'

'Often the case with books like that. Best to persevere to the end.'

'Talking of which I hear you have been working on a book written by Michelle to improve her English. Something about the environmental pollution from plastic, is it?'

'Oh, yes. Very dull,' I said. 'But it's a lost cause. It's far too technical—only suitable for an academic study for specialists. I'm afraid I had to give up on it.'

'Really. So where is it now?'

'What?'

'The book.'

I tried to explain how it was not in a proper book format. It was all loose leaf with the pages mixed up and a hell of a mess to proofread and correct.

'I sent it off to her university in France where she was a student. Hopefully, they can assign some post-doctoral student to make sense of it. I feel I have let Michelle down, as I know she wanted the book published. Wishing and achieving are different things are they not? One must be realistic. No publisher in the UK would touch it.'

After this chat with Nigel, I left school early and headed home as a heavy shower had soaked the wicket and they cancelled the afternoon game. I treasured days when I could escape early. The chances of surveillance were also less if I left at an unpredictable time.

The first thing I noticed as I threw open the front door at home was an airmail letter with a Singapore stamp on the sideboard. Doubtless, it was a rejection letter for the English teacher post at Dunearn Academy. I had applied back in January, so they had taken four months to reply.

It tempted me to open it, but I resisted. Maybe pour a powerful drink first to counteract the disappointment.

'Michael, there's a letter come for you from Singapore.' My mother called through from the kitchen. 'Aren't you going to open it?'

'No hurry, Ma. I'm sure it's nothing important. Cricket's off. I am home early, and the sun is shining. Would you like a gin and tonic?'

'It's a bit early for me. Well, if you join me outside, we can sit on the veranda.'

'Splendid,' I agreed.

'Your father is in the garden doing some weeding. I expect he will stop for a drink soon.'

We settled into two garden chairs and listened to the birds as we drank our gin and tonics. The tension was killing me I could delay no longer.

On tearing it open, it amazed me to see it was a letter to confirm my appointment with a request for me to arrive in Singapore on Thursday, 18th August 1983. They asked if I was happy to head the English Department as there was a new availability and I seemed best fitted to teach English rather than Geology. They had not even called me for an interview. I was realistic enough to think there must have been well-qualified candidates, so why had they selected me? Since my application, a lot had happened, and I was still in two minds whether to accept. The salary offered in Singapore dollars was huge compared to what the school paid me. The ratio was about three Singapore dollars to the pound, but when I divided by three, the total was still more than double, and they expected me to live in at the school, so my board and lodging were all free. It was an offer hard to resist. An escape from one school needing remedial measures, into another with new horizons and a fresh challenge.

St Wilfrid's was imploding with many of the staff no longer prepared to tolerate the headmaster's reign of terror along with Mona, his arrogant partner in crime. The only stable factor in my life was my relationship with Julie. Maybe that could survive a year or two away. After all, my income from just two years in Singapore would equate to over four years' toil if I stayed at St Wilfrid's.

My father had stopped his gardening and poured himself a whisky and soda. He glanced at his watch and relaxed. There was enough time for a drink or two before the evening news.

'I applied for a teaching post abroad, as I felt like a change. Amazingly, they accepted me.'

'Really?' my mother choked on her gin and tonic in surprise. 'Abroad?' She seemed to consider this with some amazement. 'Is that what that letter is all about?'

'Yes, in Singapore. It's okay, it's a decent school. I believe it has an excellent reputation. The position is for an English teacher, and they do the same syllabus as in the UK, so it should be straightforward. The money is very good— about double what I am earning now, plus they include my accommodation.'

'Singapore used to be a great posting for the forces before the war,' said my father. 'But, after the Fall of Singapore, all that changed. Now it's a republic under the control of that former communist, Lee Kwan Yue. He hates the British and now he is in charge of the show.'

'You appear to have a very fixed and old-fashioned view. Singapore is modern and tolerant of all races. I am surprised they offered me the job. There must have been better-qualified candidates. Maybe they chose me because I play cricket.'

As they greeted this with silence, I expanded my explanation. 'I saw an ad in the *Times Educational Supplement* and sent off my application and CV back in January and just forgot about it till now.'

'Yes, dear,' said my mother. 'But won't you need to speak Chinese? You are doing so well at St Wilfrid's. Why would you want to leave?'

'Well, everyone else seems to be. There is a rumour the headmaster is being suspended for undue violence to the boys and having a relationship with his secretary. Jones is so fed up he plans to move to Llandudno. Caldwell-Brown is looking for another job, although in his case something in the security forces might be more suitable. I could go on. The entire school is disintegrating.'

'I do think you are exaggerating,' said my mother.

'That school inspector's visit and his scurrilous report have unsettled the school. I was furious when I heard about that,' said my father. 'The headmaster is an old-school disciplinarian—nothing wrong with that. You should stay there until things calm down.'

'You don't understand. I *want* to move. If Singapore hadn't taken me, I would have tried something different—maybe a comprehensive school in Liverpool.'

'Liverpool!' My mother sounded even more shocked than when I mentioned Singapore. I gave up talking to them in exasperation. Best to let them absorb what must have been a shock. They were on a different page in the book of life.

'Julie might not stick around if you leave,' she forecast gloomily.

This seemed to cheer my father up.

'Young attractive girls like that, in London, soon move on to someone else. It's not like in the war when you could count on your fiancé waiting for you.'

'I have only just seen the letter. I will discuss it with her. It's a hard decision, but whatever happens, I can't stand another year at that school.'

'How long before you have to let them know your decision?'

'I don't know. I think they presume I will accept it.'

'All I'm saying is have a good think about it. I would leap at the chance to experience life in a different country. This was the best thing about being in the army, being posted to different countries. In my career, I was in Korea, Malaya, the Middle East, Germany, and Northern Ireland. I should write a book about it. Stay here in Sussex for the rest of your life and you will never know what you missed. If Julie loves you, she will wait for you or maybe join you in Singapore.'

'Thanks, Pa, that's a very helpful comment. And you remembered to call my girlfriend Julie.' His comments touched me.

Julie was staying in London for the weekend. I felt very unsettled by the offer of the job and reluctant to mention it until I had thought through all the implications. I called her flat and one of her flatmates answered. In the background, I could hear music and laughter before a breathless Julie picked up.

'Sorry, I was in the bath.'

'Sounds like you are having a party.'

'No, it's always like this. Just a quiet night. We may walk down to the Troubadour later.'

'The Troubadour, where's that?'

'Earl's Court. It's a night club with free live music in the evening. Back in the 1960s, Bob Dylan, Paul Simon and Joni Mitchell all played there. Tonight, they have some obscure folk singer booked so we may drop in. Next time you are in London I'll take you there, you'll love it. But if it's too busy, we may look into that gay pub nearby.'

'It's been an awful week. The school inspector condemned the school. The only good news is that they may ask the headmaster and Mona to leave.'

'Well, *that* is good news,' Julie said. 'We need to go somewhere, just the two of us, where no one can disturb us. Is it still on the cards to drive up to Scotland? We can stay at a little bed-and-breakfast cottage near Loch Ness and look for the monster, or better still; I can take you on the Glen Coe ridge walk.'

'That sounds a grand plan. At half-term, I can get away for a few days.'

'I'll ask for time off from work—they owe me some,' Julie sounded so young and enthusiastic, and my heart soared away from the sordid present to the peaks of the Highlands with the smell of heather. If I was more impetuous, I would have hopped in the car and driven up to London. However, I sensed this was more of a girl's night out. Nelson waddled down the corridor wagging his tail and I knew tonight would be a stay at home one for me.

Chapter 31

Mark Carter approached the coroner to request a second autopsy on behalf of the family. Michelle's doctor provided a report on her condition of atrial fibrillation and details of her medication and annual check-up. It was a surprise to the coroner that her medical history was not available before the first port-mortem. He approved the application to assist the French police, who were holding a suspect for the Sussex Pond Murder case. With the benefit of hindsight, the first post-mortem performed by the police pathologist was not fit for purpose. It had only involved a basic forensic autopsy. There was no documented examination of the victim's heart. Given the family history of atrial fibrillation, they should have carried out a cardiac investigation to check for SAD (Sudden arrhythmic death syndrome).

The original post-mortem had been free, whereas a second test would have to be paid for by the family. Mark agreed but specified he would source a well-qualified cardiac pathologist. Dominic at St Thomas' hospital recommended one of London's top forensic cardiac specialists, Dr Elizabeth Howard, who offered her service pro bono.

Elizabeth worked at Guys Hospital and had been following the Sussex Pond Murder case in the press with keen interest. She had trenchant views on the failings of inadequate police post-mortem investigations, which she judged to be cursory with haphazard standards and questionable results based on bias and police pressure. She had represented the police in several high-profile murder cases and was a dogged seeker of truth.

Conventionally, when there is an instruction for a repeat autopsy, the new pathologist is provided with the results of the first investigation and reviews the findings before agreeing with the results of the first investigation. No one loses face.

However, this was not how Dr Howard envisaged her role.

'This autopsy was piss poor,' was her opening comment. 'They have run a basic forensic examination of the cadaver with a focus on the head injury. The internal investigation has only looked at the respiratory and reproductive systems and there has been no investigation of the cerebral hemispheres—that is the brain to you,' she explained to Inspector Bishop, who attended. 'But worst of all, the pathologist has not undertaken a full clinical autopsy and has ignored the heart all together. He has not sent *any* specimens to histology. The photograph of the injury to the forehead looks minor—enough to daze the girl, maybe with loss of consciousness, but not fatal.'

'I don't think they knew about her heart problem,' said the inspector tactfully.

'In all cases of sudden death in a young person, cardiac arrest is a possibility. The evidence of a head injury prior to the discovery of the body in the pond is not a presumption of a deliberate killing. If you give me some space, I will conduct a proper post-mortem. I suggest if you feel sick, please leave the room.'

The police pathologist had performed a neat job of sewing up his incisions after the autopsy. Michelle's body was back to the same state as when the body was first discovered. Dr Howard started afresh with the second autopsy, almost like a clean slate.

First, she laid the body out for careful external examination of the cadaver and looked at the victim's clothes and belongings. The police had produced her shoulder bag, but it contained no identification. There was a purse with a few pounds and some shopping receipts. Mark Carter had identified the body. To Dr Howard's trained eye, the cause of death was not apparent. The forehead of the victim had sustained an impact just above the eyeline and centrally above the skull's metopic suture line, but the bruising was slight. A bash like that would stun, usually without loss of consciousness. The subject would get up and carry on as normal. Possibly, later concussion might develop.

'Very interesting,' said Dr Howard.

'Inspector Bishop, who first came up with the theory that a rock had been used to inflict the head wound?'

'I think it was the SIO Preston at Brighton first suggested it as a possibility. You would have to ask him.'

'The police pathologist's report doesn't mention a rock. Most rocks have a rugged, irregular outline unless smoothed by water action. I guess rocks in this vicinity might be sandstones or chalk. You would have to hire a geologist to look at the area where they found the body, don't you agree?'

'I suppose so,' said Bishop.

'If I hit you on the head with a rock it would make a nasty wound with lots of bleeding. Splinters of rock might get embedded in the wound. Does that look the case here?'

'No. it's very smooth.'

She approached the forehead closely and extracted what looked like a baby wipe from a sachet and carefully laid it across the wound and pressed down on it before using tweezers to place the wipe inside a plastic bag.

'That can go for chemical testing. I can smell terpenoids on her head coincident with the impact area.'

'Terpenoids. What are they?'

Howard laughed. 'It's okay; they are not some burrowing worm. Terpenoids are the resin produced by pine trees. I suspect a collision with a branch or trunk of a pine tree caused this injury.'

'So, she was hit on the head with a tree branch?'

'Maybe. I would like to visit the pond location. If someone picked up a fallen branch, I doubt if it would have much resin in it. It's more likely she collided with a tree, which stunned her. Now to discover what happened next.'

The pathologist probed under her fingernails, looking for any sign of defence against an attacker like dried blood or skin tissue. She opened the mouth, moving freely now. Four months after death, the body was relaxed without decomposition, as they had stored it in the morgue at about $2°$ C.

Prior to the internal examination, the pathologist placed a rubber block under the body's arch to flex the chest cavity. Next, she reopened incisions from the first post-mortem but extended the incisions with a scalpel in a Y-shape opening up the trunk with the arms of the Y extending from the shoulder blades, curving under the breasts to join over to a point in mid-chest. A long cut then extended all the way down the abdomen to the pubis. On completion of these deep cuts, the pathologist folded back the fold of the skin to expose the internal organs.

'What are you looking for specifically?' asked Inspector Bishop.

Normally the pathologist did not like questions as it interfered with her concentration, but the inspector seemed genuinely interested.

'As this is a criminal investigation, I am going to examine each of the organs in situ for any clues as to cause of death, so the first step is to remove the rib cage.'

She picked up a saw and began cutting to separate the rib cage from the cartilage, peeling back the whole frontal ribcage. The sound of the saw cutting through bone, horrified Bishop, but he admired her no nonsense approach.

'It is very much like turning the pages of a book. You never know what the next page is going to reveal. There—now we can see better. What do you notice about the lungs?'

'They look quite puffy. Is that how they should look, doctor?'

'Yes, the point is they are not collapsed. If someone pushed down on her when she was in the pond that would have expelled the air. Murderers do that to make the body sink. But the police report says her body was floating on the pond, buoyed up with air. Therefore, she did not drown in the pond. I will take samples of the lung tissue for histology.'

'Amazing what secrets you can discover from the body,' said Bishop

'I am now going to examine each of the organs using the Virchow technique, which is a slow but thorough method, so there will be a lot of weighing, sampling tissues and photography before the organs have to be stored in formalin. It will take another two hours to complete so you might like to go for a tea break and check back later.'

'Thanks, I'll do that,' said Inspector Bishop. 'So apart from the lungs, what else is important to check?'

'I will examine the stomach contents for evidence of her last meal. The first pathologist determined she was pregnant, so I will check that. And, after we have finished with the abdominal cavity, I will need to check the skull to look at that head injury in more detail. And finally, I will examine the heart because I think that will give us the answer we need.'

Inspector Bishop felt queasy. The realisation that a few months ago, this was a young, vibrant woman now reduced to a cadaver on a slab was hard to comprehend. He gave his excuses and left the room.

After two hours, she had got tissue and toxicological samples to check for poisoning and examined stomach contents as well as catalogued and photographed all external injuries. She returned the organs to the body and sewed up the large Y incision. She placed the brain back in the skull, so the body was ready for burial once the results of the tests and a second inquest had taken place. Until then Michelle's body would remain in the cold silence of the morgue. A timeless state of waiting for answers, but it was of no concern to one whose life had been cut short bluntly in a frozen past.

Inspector Bishop had returned just as she was scrubbing up. It surprised him to see Michelle put back together so quickly and efficiently.

'We'll see what the lab comes up with,' said Dr Howard, busy washing her hands.

'But it seems a straightforward case of SCD. That is sudden cardiac death caused by her inherited arrhythmic condition. Her heart size was under weight for her height and there was a clear thrombus within the left ventricle. For the layman, a heart attack. Causation was likely high stress and sudden overexertion. I think she was running away from someone, ran into a tree and toppled into the pond. The cold shock was fatal. It is impossible to say the exact time of death, because of the frigid conditions, but they are consistent with the police reports, that she was last seen alive on 15th January. Most likely she died the same day.'

'My interim report will be on your desk by Monday, but the full lab testing may take another two or three weeks. I am keen to determine if the chemistry of the pine sap from the tree and the residue on her forehead are the same, so I will ask the lab to prioritise that test.'

'In these cases, the convention is to assign the cause of death to one of three categories: Certain, highly probable or uncertain. I will wait for the laboratory test results so I will file my preliminary report as "Highly probable SCD." Feel free to share my opinion with your superiors.'

'And was she pregnant?' asked Bishop.

'Yes, about eight weeks judging by the foetal development. At such an early stage, the embryo is smaller than one inch—about the size of a large kidney bean. The pathologist did a good job to discover that. I suggest you get a DNA swab from the English teacher, and we can run DNA profiling to establish if he was the father.'

'Yes, thank you for a very thorough post-mortem,' said Bishop. 'Would you like me to drive you to the scene of the incident?'

Dr Howard looked at her watch. She was running late and needed to get back to London.

'Yes, that would be useful. As long as it's not too far away. I have a train to catch at five.'

The pathway from the school car park led through the woods for about two hundred metres. Most of the mature trees were tall beech trees showing their early season green leaf. The wind had heaped autumn leaves over the thin topsoil. There was a slight gradient, which became steeper beside the small pond, the edge of which skirted the pathway through the trees. Ahead, the outline of the Three Horseshoes pub was partly hidden from view by the early summer foliage. The trees near the top of the hill changed to smaller pine trees, which looked like a more recent planting. The ground in the vicinity was dry, crumbly, and not as damp as the path closer to school.

'This is the tree,' said Dr Howard. She looked at a pine tree of about 0.5 metre diameter close to the path and the pond. At a height of about 5 foot 8 inches, there was an abrasion on the trunk. Dr Howard took a sample of the tree surface, and she peeled off a section of the bark and placed it in a separate plastic bag.

'I bet we will get a chemical match of the sap from this tree to the terpenoid on Michelle's forehead,' said Dr Howard. 'I imagine the girl was coming back from the pub, maybe after too many drinks on her birthday. Possibly running in distress as she was being bothered by the French stalker the police are trying to put in the frame. It is a cold, dark, frosty night, and she runs to escape from the guy and crashes into this tree. She spins round, dazed, and falls into the pond. The shock from the icy water sets off the arrhythmia and she suffers a cardiac arrest. If the man chasing her had rescued her from the pond immediately, it's possible he could have restarted her heart and she would still be alive today.'

Chapter 32

Peter Fowler was paralysed with fear. Since his last meeting with Colonel Lane at the end of April, there had been silence. Peter was aware of developments with the case of Michelle, the murdered French teacher. The papers had accused an obsessed French stalker of the crime and demanded his arrest and extradition to the UK. This was a relief because he suspected that Lane and his squad were involved. But the newspaper reports of the road accident to Ron Jones had the colonel's signature all over it, although his team had left no evidence of foul play and the coroner's verdict was an accidental death. He bitterly regretted passing on Dr Mark Carter's details. Lane admitted they had followed up and raided the laboratory only days after Michael Fletcher had been to see him in London. Clearly, Michael and Mark knew he could not be trusted. Hence, his recent phone call to Dr Carter to apologise and warn him off. He was in so deep he did not know how to extricate himself.

The next problem was a folder on his desk passed to him by the editor for review. It was a two-page synopsis of

Michelle Gagneux's book and the opening few chapters. The chapters were expertly written, and the material was dynamite. Nervously, he had read it. The covering letter was from a respected literary agent called Frobisher Daniels and signed by Jeremy Frobisher, the senior partner. The firm often sent novels with scientific content to *New Scientist* for fact checking unless it was some fantasy or science fiction book where imagination was more important than reality. If, as seemed likely, the package had already gone out to the major publishing houses; it was already a done deal. The book would be a best seller and Michelle's family would make a fortune. And good luck to them. She deserved it. The book would force his hand. The last thing he planned was to pass on any information about it to Colonel Lane.

The phone on his desk rang. He looked at his watch. One hour before his departure time. He was aware of staff in the office staring at him. Why did he not answer his phone? The editor was looking across as well. He had no choice.

'Peter,' the smooth voice, with an undertone of menace. 'Colonel Lane here. Sorry to call right at the end of the week. I expect you will leave the office soon. Is it convenient for a quick meeting at six? Usual place outside the church.'

'No problem, sir.'

'Oh, and Peter, could you bring a copy of all the files or paperwork relating to Michelle and your subsequent discussions with this Michael Fletcher character? We need to file all our information in a central source for efficiency. That's what my secretary tells me.'

Peter thought this was a worrying request. As a precaution, he had asked his office to make a full back up on WordPerfect files for the office computer—a slow and complicated machine, but with an elementary knowledge of DOS, he could conduct all necessary Word processing tasks. For the colonel, he would provide paper files and only those that were non-committal and omitted names. He had also promised a set of files to Dr Carter, but that could wait until he had an exit strategy. He had no great faith in talking to the police.

Peter had been waiting patiently for the colonel outside St Mary The Boltons since 6 p.m. There was a service at the church. A steady stream of the well-dressed congregation walked past the tall man, pacing up and down with his umbrella. A black BMW drew up and the chauffeur politely told Peter the colonel was held up in a meeting and instead of hanging around in the road, he was to drive him to a nearby hotel off Cromwell Road.

'Cromwell Road is walking distance,' complained Peter. 'What an odd arrangement. What's the name of the hotel?'

'The Mulbury Court Hotel, sir—an excellent hotel.'

The chauffeur laughed as if he was enjoying a huge joke. Fowler's skin crawled. What was he up to? Why would Colonel Lane want to meet him at the Mulbury Court?

When they arrived at the hotel, a younger man was waiting in the lobby, obviously a subordinate, who handed the chauffeur the room key. Both men had close-cropped hair, dressed in identical suits, white shirts, black shoes, and navy-blue ties.

'It's on the top floor, like you requested,' he whispered, but loud enough for Peter to hear.

'Excuse me, but these gentlemen have made a mistake,' said Peter, marching up to the reception desk. 'I do not require a room and even if I did, I am partly disabled and can only stay in ground floor accommodation.'

'That's no problem, sir,' said the receptionist, a short young Asian girl with a warm smile. 'Your colleagues requested a quiet meeting room so I can offer you suite 101 on the ground floor. It is one of our best rooms. Would you like to see the room first?'

The abductors quickly grabbed the new key and hustled Peter into the room. The chauffeur now showed his true colours.

'I suppose you think you are being clever?' He pushed Peter into a chair while the other man searched the room as if to locate listening devices.

'How do I know you work for the colonel? Who are you?'

'All you need to know is that my name is Jon,' said the one dressed as a chauffeur.

'My colleague is Paul. Like the Beatles, John and Paul except I spell mine J-O-N. Now the introductions are over, Mr Fowler. I will get to the point. Colonel Lane would like you to handover all the files you have relating to our investigation.'

'I bought the files as he requested,' said Fowler. 'We normally meet every two weeks for an update and our relations are very formal and correct, so I am surprised by the hostility you are showing. When is he due to arrive?'

Jon ignored Fowler's question and wandered off into the adjacent suite with the file and used the house phone to call a number. Meanwhile, Paul sat down patiently.

After five minutes, Jon returned to the room. He was slightly taller than Paul and was clearly acting on the instructions from the person on the other end of the phone, presumably the absent Colonel Lane.

'Mr Fowler, when the French girl who got killed came to see you in January, did she mention a book she had written? The colonel thinks she did. He thinks you are withholding information from us. Where is the manuscript? Did she sell it to you, and do you plan to get it published?'

Fowler laughed. This was too incredible for words. But they didn't like this reaction.

'That's several questions and the answers are all the same: No—she never mentioned writing a book and there is no book.'

'We believe you are lying,' said Jon.

'Believe what you like, mate. It doesn't change a thing.'

The two men exchanged a look. Paul stood up and pulled out a small metal box from his pilot case. It looked like a battery charger with dials and two electrode tips. Peter's chair was close to the wall and available electric power. Paul connected the unit to the wall socket. It came to life with a hum and a green light. He carefully laid the electrodes, which had covers at the ends for protection, down on the table next to the chair and stood back, arms folded as he waited for further instructions.

'We work for the colonel on a full-time basis,' said Jon. 'We believe you are holding back on us. Imagine if the colonel was sitting here asking you these questions, I think you would answer straight away. As you say, he is a very polite man. We prefer more direct methods of persuasion to get the answers we need.'

'This,' he pointed to the metal box, 'is an ECT machine as used by psychiatrists for electric shock treatment. What does ECT stand for, Paul?'

'Electroconvulsive therapy.'

'Yea, that's right. It's a nifty little machine, but quite an old model. I think recent ones have improved. In normal use, the electrode pads are attached either side of the patient's head and small electric shocks are passed through the brain to target problem areas. Hey presto—a depressed housewife is changed back to a happy housewife. We burn the problem part of the brain that causes weird behaviour out and you have a new personality. At least that's the theory. No one really knows. It's a bit hit-and-miss this therapy stuff. To make the machine more effective, we have changed the electrodes on this model so that we have greater flexibility in how we use the machine. In this country, if the NHS recommends ECT, they give you a local anaesthetic, so you feel no pain. I expect they play music to keep you calm, but that's unnecessary because they first tie you up on a board so you can't move. Afterwards, they smile and give you a cup of tea.'

Paul gave a crooked grin and suppressed a laugh.

'Sadly, we haven't time for the niceties, so we follow the same method as they use in China. They don't waste time and money on anaesthetics in China. I believe the pain is terrible and the muscles go into convulsions but most of the patients survive. So, we would like to run a few tests using the Chinese method on your good self, a noted scientist working for the *New Scientist* which you are free to write up as a review paper. For everything to be done correctly, we need you to sign this indemnity form I have here. Basically, it gives us the authority to use ECT treatment without anaesthetic on yourself and you agree not to pursue us for any damages caused by said experiments.'

'You monsters. No way will I sign any form.'

'We thought that might be your reaction. Paul, in the file from Mr Fowler, I see a letter he wrote to Colonel Lane. Do you think you could copy Mr Fowler's signature and add it to the indemnity form?'

Paul studied the signature at the end of the letter.

'Piece of cake. Just give me five minutes.'

Paul went to the suite next door and practised Fowler's signature a few times. Once the men were happy with the result, Paul signed the form, which they proudly showed him. It was an excellent copy of Peter's signature.

'Now the paperwork is completed,' said Jon. 'We can get the experiment underway.'

Paul tied Peter's wrists to the arms of the chair. He struggled and kicked his legs, but the two men overpowered him and secured his legs to the chair with nylon cable ties. He was trapped.

'Next time bring something stronger,' said Jon. 'Metal ties are much better. When that machine is put on high voltage, he will kick about like hell.'

'But if we use metal ties, the primary charge will go to the metal and possibly bypass the victim,' said Paul—a man of few words and no emotion. He spoke with a cut-glass accent.

'Hmm. You're right. Best double up the cable ties or he will snap them. Sorry Peter, I didn't mean to frighten you. I'm sure you will talk long before we have to use the high-power setting.'

Peter told them they were wasting their time and he knew nothing.

'They all say that at first.'

The men went to the door to make sure it was quiet outside in the corridor. They also shut the windows, which opened to a small courtyard with an ornamental garden favoured by hotel guests, and drew the curtains shut. Peter raised his voice and shouted, trying to alert any staff passing by, but there was no response. After that, they inserted a plastic mouth gag, which they said was to protect his tongue in case he bit it off—a considerate touch. There was a pipe shaped extension allowing him to breathe as normal, but he could not speak beyond angry mumblings. Once they got started, they would calibrate the ECT equipment from Peter's reactions to the level of pain.

'As I explained,' said Jon. 'We have adapted this machine for specialist usage. It will please you to know we will not be passing shocks through your brain. We will attach the two electrodes to your wrists and see if a few bursts at low output range will persuade you to talk. If that doesn't work, we will repeat using the high output range. If you still resist, we can explore attachments to more sensitive areas of your anatomy and try increasing the power.'

The men left Peter strapped up and went into the adjacent suite for a cigarette. He could hear them talking on the phone. They confirmed the subject had said nothing, and they planned to move to the next phase. They were aware he could hear them, and one of them slammed the door shut. Peter pushed against the nylon cable ties as hard as he could, but they would not break. He threw his weight backwards and forwards, trying to get the chair to tip over. Maybe that might break the ties and he could make a run for it. If he didn't get home by 7 p.m., his wife would get worried. He was always so punctual. If he got a chance, he would ask the men if he could phone her to stop her worrying.

After ten minutes, they returned. Peter had shifted the chair a few feet towards the door. Another two feet and he would have been able to beat his head against it to alert the staff.

'Good try, Peter,' said Jon as he pulled the chair back to the table where the ECT equipment waited to be attached.

They were impatient to start. Peter felt reassured to hear their commentary about the ECT unit, but he suspected they were making it out to be worse than it was. After all, it was a standard medical procedure used all over the world. How bad could it be? That the duration of the shocks was set at six seconds was very helpful for him to know what to expect.

First, they turned on the machine to check the controls. The green light on the control panel glowed, and it kicked into life. Paul, who seemed to be the technician, looked pleased. He set the range of voltage and carefully removed the end covers protecting the electrodes. They terminated in nasty looking metal jaws, which could be adjusted to grab hold of large targets like wrists or smaller parts of the body, such as fingers. He turned the unit off while they attached the electrodes to Fowler's upturned wrists, ensuring a tight contact by wrapping duct tape around each wrist and the arms of the wooden chair. Once they were ready, Jon opened a notebook and recorded the test parameters. He switched on a recording device and spoke into a microphone:

'The subject is a middle-aged male called Peter Fowler. He has volunteered to take part in a series of experiments using ECT under controlled laboratory conditions. Following our normal practice, I have fully explained the procedure to him, and he has signed an indemnity form giving us instructions to proceed with no liability to the consequences appertaining to the technical team. We will run the first series of tests using the Chinese method, without anaesthesia at increasing voltages to monitor the pain threshold of the subject.'

He instructed Paul to throw the power switch.

Paul switched on and stood back, waiting for the first six-second shock cycle to surge through Peter Fowler's body. Jon recorded the start time. The first few shocks were unpleasant, but not as bad as Peter expected. He gasped and twisted about dramatically, which pleased them. They stopped and asked if he was ready to talk. Peter shook his head so there was no need to remove the mouth gag and they applied the cycle of six-second shocks again. Once more, Peter overreacted as he tried to find a way out of the situation. During the shock wave, it was impossible to talk, even if they removed the gag. He concentrated on trying to outlast the pain.

Peter's reliance on the six-second length of shock proved premature. After an adjustment, they doubled the shock length to generate a constant surging shock, sending his muscles into painful convulsions for 12 seconds. They were really beginning to enjoy their work.

After these first sessions proved unsuccessful, they soaked his hands in water to improve conductivity. Paul explained the body naturally contained about 60% of water but adding external water to the electrodes would give a much stronger zap.

'Let's try this bottle of Spring water rich in minerals,' said Paul, as the water glugged out, soaking Peter's arms. 'It is the best for super-conductivity. London tap water is a waste of time, as filtration removes all the minerals. I am interested if you notice a change.'

They repeated the shocks at the low level which before were bearable, but now they were absolute agony. They were delighted at the progress, which was wearing Peter into submission. A measure of the success was that the cable ties holding his wrists snapped as his whole body contorted in agony. They had forgotten to double up on them and, just to be sure, they triple wrapped them before resuming.

They removed the mouth gag, and Peter asked for a cigarette. Not because he wanted one, but he needed time to recover. He wanted them to realise they could not break him. Surprisingly, they gave him a cigarette. They knew the break from torture would make it doubly worse for him when they resumed.

This was a bluff. Peter was now ready to give them a partial confession. Michelle *had* mentioned writing a book in French and she had translated this to English and hoped her friend at school would check the manuscript, correct her grammar, and find a publisher. All she wanted from *New Scientist* was a favourable review. She said there was a bit more work to do, but she would make a point of asking her friend to complete it. She ran out of time, as she had to rush to catch her train, so we left it like that, just hanging in the air. Then after her death, unexpectedly, the literary agent had sent the first few chapters and the resume. Wow! The manuscript really existed.

Peter was close to talking when they pulled the cigarette out of his mouth and jammed the mouth gag back into place. He tried to raise his hand in surrender, forgetting he was trussed up like a chicken on a rotisserie. They were too busy playing with the equipment to hear his gargled cry of 'no more' as the young man checked the cable ties were secure. Peter closed his eyes and prayed.

'You know you will talk eventually,' said Paul. 'Why not stop the pain now?'

'Try the wet treatment again, but on maximum power setting,' suggested Jon. 'I think he will break soon.'

'I'm keen to try adding some salt to the water. A saline solution is very conductive,' said Paul.

Peter's eyes pleaded for them to stop but they ignored him. It was all a daze after that. Peter felt detached from his body and looked down from above at what they were doing to him. Strangely, the pain no longer bothered him. Maybe he had a strong tolerance. There was a long pause, and they applied some soft pads to the end of the electrodes. With horror, Peter realised their intentions. Paul roughly unbuckled the belt on Peter's trousers and tugged them down by pulling on the legs. Jon assisted as his pants followed suit, ending up squashed against the cable ties securing his legs.

At the hotel reception desk, a group of doctors had gathered for the annual reunion of the 1958-1961 Barts Hospital Medical School intake. At this stage of their career, many were eminent surgeons and physicians. They had booked a meeting room with a Drinks Reception at the Mulbury Court for 7 p.m. before heading to the Park Lane Hotel in Piccadilly for a formal dinner. It was a group of twenty former students plus assorted wives and girlfriends.

The owner of the hotel, who had just come on shift, gave the doctor in charge the key to Suite 101 on the ground floor. She recognised the group as yearly regulars and quickly got on the phone to order the drinks trolley for delivery to the meeting room. The doctors ambled along the corridor in a leisurely fashion, not wishing to appear too eager to enjoy the expected hospitality within the meeting room. Behind them, they could hear the tinkle of bottles and glasses as a waiter raced to reach Suite 101 before the group. In fact, it was a dead heat. Awkwardly, the waiter stood aside to let the doctor open the door.

'We always book this suite,' said Doctor Simms. 'It's so private and has a lovely view of the garden at the back.'

As he opened the door, they observed a seated man, half naked, with his trousers dropped and two men trying to attach electrodes to the poor man's genitals.

Chapter 33

Julie and I had left, later than planned, on the Saturday for our long drive to Scotland. My idea was to reach the area of Loch Lomond and spend a night in a bed-and-breakfast. I had phoned one in Balloch at the southern end of the loch, which was very expensive, but I booked it as, after a nine-hour drive, we would feel exhausted. We had packed camping gear, and the plan was to find campsites for the rest of the trip. As inexperienced campers, we did not fancy the idea of erecting a tent after arriving late on our first night. I had purchased a tent just big enough for the two of us, sleeping bags, a two-burner cooker, gas supply and assorted pots and pans. Suddenly, a vista of fishing for our supper, catching wild rabbits and lighting campfires seemed very romantic and attractive.

True to form, as we drove north of Manchester in the Triumph Herald, the clouds became darker and, as we entered the Lake District, heavy showers fell. It continued raining with variable intensity for the remaining four hours it took us to skirt around Glasgow, and arrive in Balloch, within sight of the majestic Loch Lomond. Our bed-and-breakfast booking turned out to be in a depressing residential street. The majestic loch was somewhere out of sight to the north. The only scenic spot was the bridge over the River Leven with its clusters of motor launches along both banks of the river. Balloch's row of guesthouses and bed-and-breakfast establishments along the Balloch road attracted many visitors, like us, expecting unspoilt views of Loch Lomond.

Too tired to care and stiff with fatigue, we hauled ourselves into our accommodation. The small room was furnished with the expected essentials such as a small double bed, a bedside table with a lamp, a Gideon's Bible in the top drawer and a large Victorian wardrobe looming next to the bed and looking down upon us with inanimate menace. Julie was quick to open the squeaky door and check for anything unpleasant hiding within, but there were only a few wooden clothes hangers and a spare eiderdown for chilly nights. I did notice some mouse droppings under the wardrobe but kept the observation to myself. The interior decor ran to a worn dark brown carpet overlain by a small rug to hide burn marks and old flock wallpaper. There was a single radiator, turned off for the Scottish summer. The ensuite bathroom contained a huge and ancient long bath and the water was piping hot, so we were prepared to overlook the dowdy room and agreed we were possibly not the target audience, being too young and critical.

Late up the next morning, and after a typical hearty Scottish breakfast of porridge, fried eggs, bacon, black pudding, baked beans, and thick hunks of soda bread all washed down with sweet tea, we both felt strong enough for the day ahead. We were the last guests as the annoying sound of the vacuum cleaner and heaps of linen hinted. The friendly lady owner told us it had been a full house overnight with every room let. Mostly tourists like us, plus a couple of soldiers on exercise.

'What, they were in uniform at breakfast?' I asked.

'No, they were in plainclothes—two young men with close-cropped hair and not very talkative. I asked them if they were here for hiking, and they said no, just for recreation and maybe some fishing. So, I mentioned Donald McPhee. He's awfully good. He runs fishing trips in the loch. But all the fellow said was they didn't think they had enough time.'

'How could you tell they were military?'

'Aye, it's because of their secretive manner,' said the owner enigmatically, returning to the kitchen to top up our teapot. On her return with fresh tea, she continued.

'Two young men together like that are unusual unless they are brothers. Or on the other hand, I suppose, business people. Our normal crowd is families or retired couples. No—I stand corrected. I do recall we sometimes have travelling sales representatives—in pairs. And trade people like plumbers and painters. I suppose you can never generalise, can you?'

'What about us?' asked Julie.

'Newly-weds?' she enquired with a smile.

'Yes, on our honeymoon,' I said, and received a kick from Julie under the table.

'You've come to the right place! You should visit the Trossachs National Park, drive through Dukes' Pass, and go up Conic Hill for a spectacular view. It's right bonny. You may be lucky and see red deer. And as I mentioned—if you fancy a boat trip on the loch, Donald McPhee's your man. He runs cruises along the loch for the tourists every day from next to the bridge. There are some brochures in the hall with all the details.'

'Thank you. I think we will drive to the Trossachs first.'

'She was keen to promote Donald McPhee,' said Julie, as we escaped to our room to pack up. When we went to pay and check out; the owner handed us a pack of sandwiches and two apples to take with us, which was a friendly gesture.

There was a lot to see and do without having to drive too far. I was keen to visit the Loch Lomond National Nature

Reserve on the southeast of the loch to catch sight of the ospreys—an endangered species. Julie laughed when she saw me kitted out with binoculars and a camera, but this was more from the sight of my shorts and pale legs. She maintained wellington boots for the damp ground and jeans were the best defence against ticks, adders, and midges. And maybe leeches as well? This attitude was embarrassing, but I was concentrating on my birdwatching, but without success.

'No ospreys today?' she asked sarcastically.

I had just spotted a buzzard, so that was some consolation. We took an old wooden ferry across the loch to Inchcailloch Island, landing at an old wooden jetty. The boat skipper told us the history of the small island. Apparently, the deserted isle once supported a thriving farming community. There was a 13th century church and a nunnery, but all that remained now was an ancient burial ground with lichen-covered headstones. In 1796, they cleared the land for sheep farming and introduced thousands of acorns, which now flourished into a thick forest of oak trees. By the early 19th century, the island was empty once more. We walked all over the deserted island for an hour before catching the ferry back to the mainland, pursued by inquisitive ducks.

Following the bed-and-breakfast woman's suggestion, we enjoyed a long walk to Conic Hill, which had a spectacular view across to Loch Lomond. Many others had the same idea, so visitors crowded the area. It was a beautiful sunny day and marvellous to walk with stunning views. Julie agreed it was just like a honeymoon and she was sorry for kicking me.

At this time of year, the days were long, and darkness did not fall until after ten. In the afternoon, we headed further north towards the Highlands and stopped for the night at a campsite at the northern end of Loch Lubnaig, a loch surrounded by beautiful scenery. It was silent with no one else around, so we set up our tent close to the loch on a bank of grass. Behind us a thick forest enclosed us like a warm glove in an embrace. Our nearest neighbour was 100 metres away and there was a small office and basic facilities, including a shower point with cold water and a toilet.

'It's a fantastic location,' said Julie. 'I could stay here happily for a week. The owner says there is a couple of pubs just a short drive away, so we have everything we need. We can hire a fishing rod and try our luck from the shore, but the best fishing is from a boat. Unfortunately, he only has a few canoes.'

The campsite owner happily hired us a couple of canoes and we took them out into the loch, enjoying the freedom. We raced each other across the loch and spent an hour happily exploring, stopping occasionally to take photos or search the clear waters for fish.

The bird life was better than Loch Lomond, culminating in a golden eagle which soared overhead. I captured a few pictures of the bird in flight. We were both hot from our exertions, so we headed closer to the shore to find a secluded spot. We stripped off and dived into the clear, inviting waters for a swim. The water was icy cold, and we surfaced, fighting for breath. Fortunately, I could just feel the muddy bottom of the loch at full stretch, but Julie was out of her depth and in distress. It was impossible to re-board the canoes without tipping them over, so we had to move to the wooded shoreline to get dressed and return before our two-hour rental period was up. It had been a risky manoeuvre and Julie sensed hidden observers spotted our antics from the shore. She had seen no one; it was just a premonition.

I brewed up some tea as Julie trained her binoculars over the water, looking for otters. The freedom of the loch, surrounded by the hills and the lazy afternoon, rolled over us as we slept for a time in each other's arms. As evening fell, a chill set in, so we wrapped up warm and set off for a drive. We found a pub nearby with a noisy *ceilidh*, in full swing, and joined the Scottish country dancing of the Gay Gordons, an eightsome reel and many other complicated dances. Worn out, we returned to the solitude of our campsite, where we gathered kindling from the wood and made a fire to keep warm. The smoke helped keep the midges at bay, but they still stung us all over our arms, legs and face with thousands of pinpricks.

'It's amazing how far sound travels at night,' I said. 'I can hear voices from a distant cluster of houses on the west side of the loch.'

'What's the plan for tomorrow?'

'I think it will be a two-hour drive to Glencoe village. There is a camping site next to the Glen Coe visitor centre. We can head there and see if they have room. I doubt if it will be full up on a Monday.'

The only noise was the slow lapping of water stirred by a whispering breeze. When darkness fell, our attuned ears heard the occasional crackle of breaking twigs from the deer moving through the forest. Otherwise, all was quiet.

In the morning, we reluctantly packed up, resisting the temptation to stay another night beside Loch Lubnaig. Julie said we should take advantage of the wonderful weather to push on and attempt the Glen Coe ridge walk. If there was rain, the walk was more dangerous, even in summer. Having come so far, this was the priority. If there was time, we could return to this idyllic spot.

While I was packing up the tent ready to leave, Julie wandered off for a walk towards the road and noticed a lay-by with a grey Ford Fiesta parked-up. She approached the car, shielded by the trees, and saw two young men in the front. They had close-cropped hair and were sitting, smoking cigarettes. Were they waiting for their partners from camping overnight? But we were the last to leave. There were no more tents in the field and the campsite owner had shut up his office and left. Had they been driving past and stopped for a rest? Looking more closely, she recognised the men.

'Michael, come quickly. She was breathless and grabbed my arm.

'What men are you talking about?'

'The same guys we saw at the *ceilidh* last night. The ones with short hair who never smiled. They were standing at the bar and wouldn't join in the dancing.'

We reached the point in the trees, which gave a view to the lay-by, but it was empty of cars.

'I saw them parked there in a grey Ford Fiesta. I didn't imagine it. I saw the same two last night. Didn't you notice them?'

'I wasn't wearing my contact lenses. My eyes were sore after walking in the sun's glare. But I *do* believe you. It might be the surveillance goons who stopped me back in April, except I can't remember if they had short hair. Most of the time, they had their heads covered by hoodies.'

'Maybe they stayed at the same place as us last night—plainclothes policemen tailing us all the way from Sussex. The ones the owner thought were soldiers. Let's see if they follow us when we leave.'

'No, I don't think it's the Sussex police. These guys are professional. You remember I told you there was a black BMW tailing me after Michelle's murder and they stopped me outside my house and showed me some warrant card making out they were MI5. We went to the George & Dragon where they asked me loads of questions about the case.'

'You suspect these guys are from MI5?'

'No. Mark Carter and I are sure they are Colonel Lane's men. Whoever they are and whatever they want, they seem to think I can help them. It's amazing to think they must have followed us all the way from Sussex. It rained most of the journey and it was impossible to see anything in the mirror, so I suppose it's possible.'

When Michael and Julie left the campsite, they looked in their mirror to see if they were being followed. But the two men in the grey Ford Fiesta had already left. There was no need to follow as they had heard the couple discussing their plan to head for the Glen Coe campsite near to the visitor centre.

On the same day at Kensington police station, the police were trying to unravel the mystery of why two young men subjected an older gent of Caribbean ancestry to a session of dangerous electric shocks. The victim claimed it was a criminal gang trying to extract information from him by torture; information he claimed not to have, as the men were acting on incorrect information. The man, Peter Fowler, was a writer for the *New Scientist* magazine. Fowler claimed a powerful ex-army man called Colonel Lane, who was well off and lived in the exclusive Boltons in London's Kensington, had orchestrated the whole thing.

Countering this unbelievable story, the two defendants, Jon, and Paul, claimed that Peter Fowler had agreed to partake in the ECT experiments voluntarily and had signed an indemnity form. He was paid £100 for the experiment—the money in twenty-pound notes was found in Peter Fowler's jacket pocket. He was free to write up his experience of the shock treatment in the *New Scientist*. The men had been sorry for the alarming sight of their experiment at a delicate stage when a party of doctors and their young ladies interrupted them. However, this was the fault of the hotel double-booking a meeting room. Despite this, they paid the manageress compensation for the inconvenience caused,

'I am inclined to believe the second version,' said the detective assigned to the case. 'After all, we have the signed affidavit. I can't see any reason to hold them any longer. Mr Fowler has no lasting injuries apart from the outrage to his person which he appears to have permitted, so I plan to take statements from all three parties and let them go.'

'What was the point of this experiment?' asked a lady colleague. 'It sounds kinky to me.'

'The young lads said it was a scientific comparison of ECT testing by the Chinese method which does not use any anaesthetic to the standard NHS practice where patients have a local anaesthetic and feel no pain. A group of doctors interrupted them before the second phase when they planned to repeat the electric shocks after giving Mr Fowler an anaesthetic. Apparently, the subject was keen to cooperate to further scientific knowledge.'

'Blimey, that guy earned his £100,' said his lady colleague.

After their unexpected release, Jon and Paul called Colonel Lane from the first phone box they could find on Earl's Court Road. At first the colonel felt angry at the botched operation, but pleased Kensington police were not planning any further action.

'That indemnity letter and the money you planted in Fowler's jacket was a stroke of genius,' he said. 'But I am surprised Fowler didn't break.'

'We were so close,' agreed Jon. 'Another ten minutes was all we needed to squeeze the truth out of him. We might have more luck if we try it on that young English teacher.'

'Too late for that. He's gone to Scotland with his girlfriend, but I have got Gary and Wayne following them. If it all goes pear-shaped, you can have a go at him when he returns to Sussex. But the lesson learned from the Fowler fiasco is we do not use a hotel. Leave it with me and I will source a quiet, safe house where no one will see or hear you.'

'Brilliant,' said Paul, eager to join the conversation.

'There was one useful lead. Just when we were getting to the interesting part of the session, Peter Fowler decided he couldn't take any more,' interrupted Jon. 'A well-known London literary agent has been appointed to drum up interest from publishers. They sent the *New Scientist* the first three chapters of the French girl's book for Peter Fowler to review.'

'The traitor,' yelled Lane. 'When was this?'

'I'm not sure, but recently I think,' said Jon. 'The literary agent is called Jeremy Frobisher, senior partner of Frobisher Daniels in Covent Garden.'

'Excellent result,' agreed Lane. 'I don't need to tell you this is your next assignment. I was about to send you to Nantes University as we received information from one of our agents that Fletcher has sent a manuscript for review to the Chemistry Department. But put that on hold and see what you can get out of Jeremy Frobisher.'

'Roger that, sir.'

Chapter 34

Preston at Brighton police was studying the preliminary report of the second autopsy in amazement. Inspector Bishop was also present to discuss the findings.

'It's all very well this business of running into a tree and falling into the pond and suffering a heart attack, but it sounds too fantastic. It does not explain what Marcel Fouché was doing while this was happening, does it? He could have smashed her into the tree and rolled her into the pond, so the heart attack resulted from his assault.'

'It's possible, sir,' said Bishop, without enthusiasm.

'Or it could have been Fletcher when he discovered she was pregnant,' said Preston. 'Just as we first suspected. We need to bring that lad in for a DNA test and further questioning. Can we reach him at his school and get that fixed ASAP?'

Bishop rang St Wilfrid's right away. He spoke to a cleaner who said the school was closed for half-term. She volunteered that Mr Fletcher had gone to Scotland on a climbing holiday with his girlfriend.

Preston was getting impatient with the lack of action from the French police. Despite submitting a request to extradite Marcel Fouché, there had been no response. The suspect still maintained he had visited London for the rugby and left the next day without seeing Michelle. He had tried to contact her by phone, but without success. Apart from the ticket to the game at Twickenham, Marcel could produce no receipts. He had no credit card and only used cash. If someone wanted to be invisible, that is what you would do.

Preston was in two minds whether to fax the new autopsy report to the Prefecture in Nantes. As it absolved Fouché of murder, it was possible the French police would use the report to throw out the case. It made pragmatic sense to let him off the hook.

Preston wondered *if* these were the facts, would Fouché come clean and admit he was at the pub and contacted Michelle. If so, a charge of manslaughter might be the best the police could hope for.

Preston went back to his office and discussed the implications with Tracey Smith. They decided to fax the preliminary post-mortem report from Dr Elizabeth Howard to France.

'Now the ball's in their court,' said Preston. 'Tracey, let's get a cup of tea.'

Inspector Bishop was about to leave the Brighton office when the Desk Sergeant called to say they had just received a telephone call from a lad up in Scotland who claimed two men were tailing him and his girlfriend. He was asking if they were plainclothes police from Sussex.

DI Preston choked on his tea. 'What! Who is this call from?'

'He says his name is Michael Fletcher and you would know what it's all about.'

'Has he left a contact phone number?'

'Yes, he is with his girlfriend at a pub in Glencoe. Do you have a pen? I will give you his number.'

Preston was surprised when Michael Fletcher answered his call immediately. There was a lot of pub noise in the background.

'Mr Fletcher, can you describe these two men who are following you?' said Preston.

'Sure. They are both medium height, mid-twenties with close-cropped hair. Thin and fit-looking, lean, and nasty. I doubt if they are police, but best to check.'

'What about their clothes, smart or casual?'

'They both have grey suits and are wearing white shirts and dull looking dark ties. At least they were yesterday. Today we saw them buying waterproof jackets from an outdoor supplies shop. We think they followed us from Sussex. On Saturday night they booked into the same bed-and-breakfast as us in Balloch, and then the next night when we camped by the loch, they sat in their car all night in a lay-by at a point where they could see our tent. We thought we had lost them when we drove to Glencoe village. But they are sitting in the same pub as us right now. They look ruthless and are scaring my girlfriend, Julie. Who are they and what should we do?'

'Michael, listen. You are correct—these men are not from the police or MI5, although it may be the same team who followed you last month. We believe your life is in danger. They have killed one witness and may try to kill you. It's possible this is all connected with your former girlfriend, Michelle, but we can't be certain. Keep in public places and don't give them an opportunity to get you alone.'

'That's ridiculous. If these men want to harm me, they could have done it when we were asleep in our tent. The guy who stopped me before was called Gary and he had a moustache, but these guys are clean shaven.'

'I see,' Preston pondered this. 'It's possible they didn't have clearance yesterday. Michael, what car are they driving?'

'It's a grey Ford Fiesta. I already gave the police the number so you can trace it.'

'Brilliant. We will get onto that. Look, Michael, I have Inspector Bishop from Pulborough with me now. I will see if he and PC James can fly to Glasgow from London and liaise with the Scottish police to meet up with you in Glencoe later tonight.'

'We have set up camp near Glencoe village as we plan to walk the Glen Coe ridge—the Aonach Eagach tomorrow. It's a challenging scramble, and the guys following us will find it hard going along a hazardous ridge walk. If they try to follow us on the mountains, in a suit and walking shoes, they will get into trouble. There are sheer drops, so they might even fall off with a bit of luck.'

'That may be a good plan. Do nothing until we catch up with you. We are sending up the regular team from Pulborough, our Inspector Bishop and PC James. You have met them before. Good lads. PC James is a keen cyclist and very fit. Make sure you are in the pub, in reach of the pub phone.'

'We'll be in the Boots bar of the Clachaig Inn. That's where I am calling you from now. Trouble is, the guys following us will be here as well, so if you roll up and start talking to us, it will blow your cover.'

'Good point. Keep a low profile and I am sure Bishop will get a quick chat—maybe at the bar. You are whispering. Is that because the men are close by?'

'Yeah, Julie put on the jukebox to make more noise so they can't overhear us. It's walkers and climbers, so make sure your team dress casually in jeans and a jacket.'

After the call, the detectives checked out flight times to Scotland.

'It's doable,' said DI Preston. 'It'll get complicated if we involve the Scottish police and they may mess up the entire operation. Bishop, you can hire a car in Glasgow and drive to Glencoe. If we need support, we can involve the local police, although, I fear, they will only be used to tourist problems and not murder in the mountains.'

'What if these two men are armed?' asked Bishop.

'Let's deal with that later. The question is, whose orders are they following? Who are these people? I'm going to put a call through to my friend Commander Tilbury at Scotland Yard. If anyone knows who these hoodlums are, my pal will.'

Preston had serious doubts whether any police force could stop the inevitable, but at least he had delegated the problem to others.

Bishop called PC James in Pulborough and then he drove back to Lewes to change into casual clothes for the Highlands and draw out a large cash float for expenses. It was a step into the unknown.

Meanwhile, the two men kept following the couple at a distance to get a feel for what their interests were. So far, they had not been very adventurous. Apart from spending a lot of time in their tent, they surfaced to go for short drives to pick up supplies and take slow romantic walks, interspersed with visits to pubs. When they hired two canoes on the loch, this looked like a good chance. At one point, they turned towards the west shore and hid behind the trees. This would have been an ideal opportunity to tackle them, but before the men could act, the canoes reappeared and headed back to shore. When the couple camped right next to the loch in such an isolated spot, it was an ideal opportunity to drag them out of their sleeping bags and drown them in the loch. It would look like they had gone for some midnight skinny-dipping after drinking too much. The freshwater loch was freezing even in summer, so cold shock from sudden exposure would be the verdict. Even young and fit-looking couples needed to take care. Gary was keen to act, but Wayne cautioned they must follow the instructions of the colonel. They had tried phoning him yesterday, but without luck, so they missed the chance.

At last, Gary succeeded in calling the colonel, not a simple task as the few phone boxes were busy or out of order.

'Look, gents,' said Colonel Lane. 'I wouldn't waste much time on this mission. Take him out, so it looks like an accident. There is no heat on us, and it would tidy things up. Removing more players is always a good move. Our contact at the school has confirmed there is a manuscript and Fletcher has sent it to France, but I am sure he will have a copy. Any action you decide to take is justified. Also, Jon and Paul have had some success and we now know the name of the literary agent who is trying to get the book published. Later today, I expect the lads will pay him a visit. We are targeting them on several fronts at once.'

'Roger that, colonel. We could have sorted this out dead easy yesterday, but I couldn't reach you on the phone. But what about the girl?'

'Tricky one—if she is a witness, then it will be best to remove her from the equation as well.'

'Yes, colonel—understood. We will try to wrap this up as soon as possible. We are monitoring the situation.'

'Gary. I don't need any details. Just call me when the mission is complete. And Gary, don't come back to me if this goes wrong.'

'We're on our own, Wayne,' said Gary as he sat down. 'Get another pint of the heavy while I work out a plan.'

'Have we got the go-ahead?' Wayne asked.

'Yea. Deal with both. But make it look like an accident.'

'What the girl as well?' said Wayne.

'Fraid so, mate. It's just a job. And the colonel says of national importance to eliminate them from the equation.'

'Oh, that's alright then,' agreed Wayne as he took another gulp of beer.

It was close to the last orders at the Clachaig Inn when the detectives arrived. Michael wandered up to the bar to order a last drink for him and Julie and slipped Bishop a note. He asked for a light for a cigarette and as Bishop obliged; he told him to read it later and follow the plan. Gary and Wayne came to the bar for a last drink, and while they were waiting for their order, Michael and Julie left their drinks, hurried out to their car, and drove off back to their campsite. The hasty departure forced the two men to abandon their drinks order, and this caused a row, and they were made to return to the bar to pay for the round, losing valuable time. Meanwhile, the detectives sat down, and Bishop read the note.

'It's a bloody dangerous plan,' said Bishop.

'Shouldn't we follow them?' asked PC James.

'No, need. His note says, "Get a good night's sleep either here or at the Glencoe Inn, and park at the Allt-na-reigh car park on the north side of the A82 tomorrow at eight o'clock." Michael and his girlfriend are planning to walk the Aonach Eagach ridge. His note continues "It is a seven-hour walk across the mountain ridge of Glen Coe from the Pap of Glencoe to the Devil's Staircase traversing two Munro summits. We may not walk the full route. It is one of the most challenging ridge walks in the country. It requires scrambling and rock-climbing ability across steep slopes, down narrow chimneys and with sheer drops to certain death. Julie has completed the route before, so I am in expert hands, and it is quite safe provided you have a good head for heights, nerves of steel, and take your time. Once we set off, the two men will follow us, and you should follow them. We have a plan to outwit them. They may give up and return the same route in which case you can arrest them, or if they walk the whole route, they will come down to Glencoe village. There is also a chance they may have a nasty fall." Oh, hang on, there is a footnote. He says, "At the car park, you will see our car, a red Triumph Herald, unlocked with the ignition keys under the floor mat. Please drive it back to the Clachaig Inn and leave it in the car park, unlocked, ready for us to make a quick getaway. It won't take you long. Then drive back to the car park near the Devil's Staircase and start the ascent, following the two men chasing us. Good luck!".'

'What the hell have we let ourselves in for?' said Bishop. 'I never agreed to mountain climbing.'

Down in London, Jon and Paul were on the second day of

surveillance of the office of Frobisher Daniels in St Martin's Court, Covent Garden. It was a street level office with a small complement of staff comprising the senior partner, Jeremy Frobisher, which they established by phoning and asking to speak to him. An inquisitive secretary acknowledged he was in, but unavailable to speak to the stranger on the phone unless he could be clearer as to his business. When Paul asked to speak to the other partner, Daniels, the secretary, laughed and replied that would be difficult, as Mr Daniels had been dead for five years.

'Only the two persons and another young man who probably reads the submissions authors send in,' said Paul. 'And the secretary and the young man knock off at five sharp whereas Jeremy stays on for at least another hour.'

The men had an hour to kill, so they bought a bottle of Scotch from an off licence, wrapped in a brown paper bag, and waited at a nearby pub with a view of the office over the road. At 5 p.m., the secretary and the young man said their goodnights to Jeremy, who settled back in his black leather chair, enjoying the solitude, and wondering which of many manuscripts piled up on his desk he should consign to the reject list first. He liked to thin out the mound by culling all manuscripts that did not conform to his rigid idea of a good presentation. There was no need to waste time reading these. Next was a quick glance at the authors' resumes. Most were appalling and again there was no need to read the attached chapters. Jeremy yawned. The waste paper bin was filling up. His secretary would run through the rejected manuscripts in the morning and send out a standard rejection letter to those concerned. The doorbell ringing distracted Jeremy. How strange. No one ever called. Maybe it was one of his authors looking him up. He walked to the door and opened it with a flourish and two smiling young men holding a bottle of whisky pushed past him. One turned back and locked the door. The other pulled the blinds down across the window.

'Just a friendly drink, Jeremy,' said Paul. 'And you can tell us all about the manuscript written by Miss Michelle

Gagneux. We represent a buyer prepared to offer you a fair price for this important work. You can help us, can't you, Jeremy?'

Chapter 35

Our campsite was about a mile from the Clachaig Inn. It was busy, and our pitch was in a congested area to give more protection against our two intrepid followers. They had purchased a cheap tent in Fort William and set up camp about 100 yards away by the side of a stream. Julie and I took it in turns to stay awake in case they tried anything. Our only weapons were a claw hammer and a car wheel wrench. If they made a move, I suspected they might try to set fire to the tent, the sort of accident caused by smoking in bed or knocking over a lit primus stove. One had to get into their mindset and think of what they might do.

Although it had been an uneventful night, we both felt exhausted from the lack of sleep. Despite this, we were up early to get first use of the showers and then cooked a substantial breakfast to build up our energy reserves for the long day ahead.

Julie had walked across the Aonach Eagach with Dougal, her former boyfriend, in the summer of 1982. He was an experienced mountaineer. We had invested in some climbing rope, carabiners, and belays in case we opted to tackle a tricky descent off the ridge down the Clachaig gully. As I had no experience with the technique, this was a scary option, despite Julie's reassurance that I would have no problem. Those pursuing us would walk into a trap, as the route was impossible without a rope.

Inspector Bishop and PC James had followed Michael's instructions to the letter. James drove Michael's car back to the Clachaig Inn with Preston following in the hire car. In Glencoe village, they stopped to buy some sandwiches, chocolate bars and drinks for the mountain trek. They spotted a phone box—a last chance to call Brighton and update Preston. He had tried to call the SIO on developments yesterday; however, Preston had been away at Scotland Yard all day.

Preston thanked them for their call.

'How are things since you shot off to Scotland yesterday in pursuit of the villains?' Without waiting for an answer, he continued.

'I have unearthed some useful information from Commander Tilbury at Scotland Yard. He thinks it is likely that the guys you are dealing with are two ex-Territorial army soldiers now working for a private security firm run by a Colonel Lane. The Metropolitan police are aware of Lane and have used him on certain covert operations, but he is a freelance—a ruthless and powerful operator, with fingers in many pies. A few days ago, police in London arrested two of his team for torturing a journalist nearly to death in a hotel room. I will spare you the details. However, the Kensington police released the men without charge on some technicality and ignored the fact they were operating on behalf of the colonel. In fact, that is why they released them. Your men, Gary, and Wayne, are dangerous foot soldiers who just obey orders.'

'Wow, that's a lot to take in,' said Bishop. 'How can just the two of us cope with these professionals?'

'Just keep tracking the young couple and try to intervene if Gary and Wayne get too close. You have the element of surprise. Meanwhile, I am working to get more backup. Even air support. Anything is possible, but it's tricky convincing the local police to take this seriously when I am calling from Sussex.'

'Fine, thank you sir for the update. Good to know whom we are dealing with. We have set up a trap, so we hope to apprehend the two men pursuing Michael and his girlfriend. But the immediate need is for more support. Walking along the Glen Coe ridge is, I am informed, dangerous, even on calm days in summer, but in bad weather, people exposed on the ridge are at substantial risk as there is no escape. Once you are on the ridge, you either have to complete it—a long walk of between seven to nine hours, or else turn back. You cannot just hop off the side. I believe the plan is for the couple to use their climbing gear to drop off the ridge at Clachaig gully and outwit their hunters.'

'You're on the spot and can judge if that's feasible. I guess it is too late as they are already on the mountain. Bishop, I will call Glencoe police and ask for support. Possibly some extra men posted at each end of the Glen. Do you need armed personnel?'

'Only as a contingency—we don't believe the men are armed.'

'Okay, Bishop, leave it with me. Once you are on the mountain, no further communications are possible, so I will liaise with the Glencoe police. While you are wasting time talking to me, the men could close on the young couple.'

There was a simple walk up the Devil's Staircase from the car park via a well-trodden zigzag path, crowded already with energetic walkers. Some carried climbing rope, helmets, and backpacks, looking as if they were about to tackle Everest. Gary and Wayne were still playing catch-up. The young couple always seemed ahead of them. They had packed up and left the campsite in a jiffy while the men were still sipping a warming cup of tea. Following in their car, they were too late to find a parking space at Allt-na-reigh, which was already jam-packed. It forced them to park in an overflow car park further west. The weather was fine and sunny, and the effort of walking uphill soon had both men sweating. They reckoned they must be twenty minutes behind the couple and would soon catch up when their superior fitness came into play.

'What's the plan when we close in on them?' asked Wayne.

'According to the guidebook, the ridge is very narrow. In some parts, you must scramble up and down rock-faces in single file. When we are near enough, we'll target whoever is the closest to us. Tip one of them off the ridge, and then the two of us will tackle the second one and, hey presto, the job is complete, and we get our money.'

'They'll get suspicious when we just appear behind them.'

'Why? They don't even know we are following them. In fact, they might welcome us to climb with them,' said Gary.

'You make it sound straightforward,' said Wayne. 'I don't have a good head for heights. If it gets difficult, I don't think I can carry on.'

'Mate, this is nothing—for ex-TA guys, this is a cinch.'

We were making good progress. We could take the direct steep ascent up the spur to the summit of Am Bodach, but we did not want to burn off our hunters straight away so the gentler approach up the Devil's Staircase would be best to give them a false sense of complacency. Julie was an excellent walker and strode on at a fast pace over the easy ground. She told me there would be some steep rock chimneys and narrow ridges and it might take two hours just to cross the most difficult and dangerous area of the Pinnacles.

'After today you will have climbed two Munro summits.'

'Excuse my ignorance, but what is a Munro?'

It amazed her I was unaware of what any half-dedicated walker would know.

'They are Scottish mountains of over 3,000 feet. I think there are about two hundred and eighty-two Munros. Some people try to climb all of them. It's a sport called Munro bagging. If you achieve this, you can be called a Munroist or a Munro Compleatist.'

'They must be as mad as hatters. You sound unsure of the total.'

'Dougal told me some on the list are a few inches too short.'

'Maybe some measurements are inaccurate, and some are greater than 3,000 feet but are not on the list.'

'Oh, yes, certainly. It does seem a futile exercise, doesn't it? And it takes the fun out of climbing if you tick off your conquests, like a train spotter collecting engine numbers. I believe the original Munro, who devised the scheme, missed out on one mountain in Skye, so he never achieved it.'

We had reached the steep approach to Am Bodach and could see a rocky pinnacle known as 'the Chancellor' sticking out over the valley. Julie reassured me that our route avoided this. Descending from Am Bodach was a steeply dipping cliff with enough footholds and grips to climb down. It would have been slippery in the rain. As we progressed, we seemed to be on our own, as many of the walkers who had set out at the same time had turned back. As we continued towards the first Munro peak at Meall Dearg, a frightening view of the ridge lay ahead. If I had not been with someone who had been here before, I too would have turned back.

We reached the cairn at the top of Meall Dearg, a famous spot because, in 1901, the Reverend Robertson became the first man to complete the Munros. Julie had got this useful fact from Dougal. Apparently, Robertson kissed the cairn first, and then his wife. We now entered a challenging section called the 'Crazy Pinnacles'. We followed the most worn route shown by the polished rock from many footfalls before us. The path culminated in a very steep descent, hugging the rock-face until we entered the stretch of the ridge where there was no safe descent. We had taken a long time working our way through the pinnacles, but from Stob Coire Lèith the going became more comfortable as we walked across a broad ridge. Ahead was the Clachaig Gully, where we planned to rope up and descend on the north side. The guidebooks stated that this was a hazardous route, and I was discussing with Julie whether it might be best just to carry on along the safer path and try to out-pace the men on our tail.

Julie was standing facing me when a man appeared behind her. There was a flash of green in his hand, and before I realised what was happening, he plunged a hypodermic needle into Julie's neck. She turned in amazed horror and her mouth opened to speak. The words drowned in her throat, and she crumpled and fell to the ground.

'What the hell have you done?' I was about ten feet away but took a step towards him.

'It's a mild dose of suxamethonium. It paralyses the muscles almost instantaneously. After a few minutes, it wears off. By then, both of you will be at the bottom of the Glen.'

'I recognise you Gary if that is your name. The so-called MI5 agent. Except last time we met, you had a moustache. You and your partner killed Alan Jones on the instructions of Colonel Lane.'

Gary looked surprised but got back on the offensive.

'Who is this Alan Jones chap? I have never heard of him. And what was the other name you mentioned?'

'Colonel Lane.'

Gary looked thoughtful

'No one I can recall from my army days. You must be confusing me with someone else.'

'At this moment, the police are looking for you at both ends of the ridge. We have trapped you on the mountain with no escape. Best give yourself up.'

'What police are you talking about?'

'Sussex police special squad—Inspector Bishop and PC James. They came into the bar late last night at the Clachaig Inn. You stood next to them.'

For the first time, Gary looked uncertain, so I pressed home my advantage.

'So, you planned to paralyse us and then roll us off the mountain? That's stupid, as this section is quite safe. No one has ever come a cropper from this part of the ridge.'

'Then we will walk on—it looks very steep ahead,' he was looking at Clachaig gully.

'Just you. I will leave the girl here until I have disposed of you. Then she can join you at the bottom of the mountain. My colleague should catch up soon.'

'How long have you been Colonel Lane's henchman?'

'There you go again. Me and Wayne are ex-TA men and loyal supporters engaged in government approved business. We go right back to army days in Cyprus.'

While we were talking, Bishop had crept up behind Gary. I moved toward Gary to gain his full attention, and we both closed upon him with Bishop hugging him in a bear grip. I removed the other syringe from his pocket, and Bishop twisted Gary's hands around and showed me his handcuffs in his coat pocket. In no time, we trussed Gary up, kicking and swearing.

'Jimmy and a contingent of the Glencoe police have picked your mate up,' Bishop told Gary. 'Your murdering days are done.'

Just then, Julie came out of her muscle paralysis and staggered up. I went to steady her, and she smiled. 'It's all over,' I said. 'Do you want to carry on to the Pap of Glencoe or go back the way we came?'

'Back,' she motioned with a shaky hand. Her voice was not normal. I read afterwards that even small doses of suxamethonium could cause cardiac arrest.

Chapter 36

Michael phoned Mark Carter on Thursday morning from a police station in Scotland. At last, everything was falling into place. The Sussex police reaction had been quick and, with the help of the local force at Glencoe, they had completed a textbook operation. The police had apprehended Colonel Lane's men red-handed and taken them into custody. Steps were in hand to transfer Gary and Wayne to London for further questioning. Mark's only concern was if the men refused to talk and would not implicate the colonel. So far, he had proved untouchable.

'Morning, Mark,' said Paula, handing him a morning cup of coffee as he arrived at his office at the Solent Industrial Park. The last week had been exceptionally busy logging core samples from the North Sea from some of the acreage held by Phoenix Oil. Monthly water sampling was still required for the same client for unlabelled drinking water testing, but these results were now exhibiting less variability, although various trace amounts of toxins and BPA were ubiquitous. Paula passed over a London stamped letter in a cream envelope addressed to Mark. Anything that wasn't a bill got his immediate attention.

31 May 1983

Dear Dr Carter,

As executor of Ms Gagneux's estate, we at Frobisher Daniels, literary agents would like to thank you for the opportunity to read the resume and sample chapters of Ms Gagneux's interesting research into the plastic water bottling industry.

Although the book is well written and researched, we feel there is not a market for a book of this nature at the present time.

Of course, this is a personal view, and you may find a publisher wishing to take this further. If so, we wish you every success.

Yours sincerely,

Jeremy Frobisher,
Senior Partner Frobisher Daniels

Mark could not believe his eyes. Jeremy had felt confident the manuscript would be a commercial success. Two publishers had requested to see the full manuscript as soon as possible. It made no sense to back off like this. He felt a numbing unease as he dialled the number of Frobisher Daniels' London office. Jeremy's secretary answered his call.

'Dr Carter—I was going to call you, but it's impossible with the police all over the place.'

'The police?'

'Sorry. I thought you knew. It has been in all the papers. I'm afraid Jeremy has killed himself. I found him myself when I opened the office on Wednesday morning. He was hanging from a rope attached to the overhead ceiling light. He was a tall man, so he stood on the upturned waste bin. He kicked it over when he was hanging there less than a foot above the ground and close to the table so he could have saved himself if he wanted to. The police believe he meant to do it. Really, it's so upsetting and gave me an awful turn!'

'I'm sorry for your loss. Was there any sign he might do this?'

'Oh, yes, the poor man suffered from lifelong depression. Good days followed by bad days. You know the sort of pattern. I think he also had some problems at home with the wife. She had some affair with another man, I believe. And his drinking was out-of-control. In fact, there was an empty bottle of whisky on the office desk. Clearly, he had drunk it all, so he wasn't in a clear state of mind when he hanged himself, was he?'

'I am not an expert, but I think it is impossible to down an entire bottle of whisky like that unless there was someone else forcing it down his throat. Have the police considered this option?'

'They took the bottle to check for fingerprints. They were very thorough and examined all the surfaces. And they took prints from all the staff—that's me, a work experience young graduate and the cleaning lady.'

'Good. But someone could have been there and worn gloves, leaving no evidence. No doubt, the police report will be thorough. Another thing that puzzles me is that he sent me a rejection letter dated 31st May. Was that the day the police think he killed himself?'

'Yes, exactly. After I left work at five. Jeremy always stayed on late. It was his quiet time when he could concentrate on reading submissions without interruptions. He liked to give every submission his undivided attention. The police reckoned he killed himself that evening.'

'But he found time to type me a letter. Wasn't that odd?'

'Very odd indeed. He left me to follow up on the submissions. That meant a standard rejection letter and sending back any full manuscript. Our guidance to authors is they should only send us their first three chapters. If the material is promising, we might ask them to send the whole manuscript. Frankly, that is very rare. You wouldn't believe it, but some authors don't bother with photocopies these days. With the post as it is, there is no guarantee a package will get back to the author. And *never* had Jeremy written a letter like the one you received. It must have been the last thing he did.'

'It was very considerate of him. But I am surprised. I thought he was enthusiastic about the material. Indeed, he told me two publishers were definitely interested.'

'I wouldn't know, Dr Carter. He never confided in me. The chapter samples you sent him are still here on the desk. Would you like me to return them to you?'

'Yes, please. And please let me know about the funeral plans in due course. I expect the coroner will conduct a post-mortem first and there will be an inquest. Oh—one more thing. Do you have the name of the police officer or station dealing with the case?'

'I'm sorry I can't help you with that. They just asked loads of questions. But look at today's papers or the BBC news. I think there was a telephone number to call for leads, but the police view is that it is an open-and-shut case. Sorry I could not be more helpful, but the office is devastated.'

'Please pass on my commiserations to his family.'

'Of course, so kind of you.'

Colonel Lane was eager to speak to Gary and Wayne as soon as possible, but it was expedient not to be seen to be involved. Discrete enquires on his behalf showed they had transferred his men from the local police station at Fort William to the larger, more secure facility at Inverness. The Fletcher man and his girlfriend had given their statements, been released, and already travelled back to Sussex. Lane knew Gary and Wayne would say nothing to implicate him, but his concern was they were not bright enough to come up with a plausible explanation on how they were on the Glen Coe ridge walk, pursuing a young couple and when they caught up with them injected the girl with suxamethonium which induced unconsciousness. He hoped the case was too complex for the local Scottish force, who would be keen to move his men back to English jurisdiction as soon as possible. However, the persistent Sussex police were also involved, and following the embarrassing incident with Peter Fowler, the Sussex plods were hot on his heels. After discussing the problem with a good lady friend in the legal profession, he persuaded her to call Inverness police station direct and speak to Gary. They achieved this without a problem.

'Gary,' said the colonel, speaking in a muffled tone through a handkerchief. 'Are we free to talk?'

'Sure. All good here. No one listening in. I am on a line in the hall across from the sergeant's desk.'

'Have you or Wayne made any sort of statement yet?'

'No, only to say it was a misunderstanding and we are Territorial Army regulars on a manoeuvre subject to top secrecy. We just gave them name and rank and no mention of your good self.'

'That's good,' said the colonel. 'Keep it that way. The only flaw is you guys are ex-TA men, but I doubt if the force will suss that out. The only offence they can throw at you is injecting a stranger with suxamethonium. I suggest you say you saw the girl suffering a panic attack on a dangerous part of the ridge. Using army supplies, you gave her a jab of the relaxant with her boyfriend's permission. It's their account against yours without a witness. By rights, they should release you, but I suspect they will cart you off to London. Once you are back, I will get my solicitor on the case, and I am sure he will get you released immediately.'

'But the couple have already filed their report. How do we respond to it? Somehow, they know all about us—including your name and the Alan Jones case,' he whispered to avoid the Desk Sergeant hearing his conversation.

This news annoyed Colonel Lane, but it was to be expected. Peter Fowler was the weak link. Jon and Paul planned to dispose of him as soon as they had enough information. Unfortunately, the doctor's reunion party had stopped them in their tracks. Now the police and the hunted were aware of his role.

'Just ignore it. Fantasists, attention seekers. Where is their evidence? Leave it with me. Once you are down here, we can deal with the situation more efficiently. Hopefully, the Met police will get involved and I can call in some favours.'

'We hope so,' said Gary. 'We don't want to face any serious charges. Loyalty is one thing, colonel, and you know you can rely on us. But it feels like this case is running out-of-control.'

'Don't worry Gary. You two guys have my full support, and I will see you right with extra remuneration for the latest delays.'

After their dramatic trip to Scotland, Michael and Julie planned to spend the weekend at her London flat, enjoying the return to normality. They had looked in briefly at their respective homes in Sussex but restricted their accounts of their Scottish adventure to descriptions of the magnificent lochs and scenery and Glen Coe's Aonach Eagach ridge walk. No point in alarming parents with tales of being pursued by killers on the hills.

Following the capture of Gary and Wayne and our testimony to the police, we hoped the nightmare was over. It would only be a matter of time before they questioned Colonel Lane. But according to Mark, the London police had released the viscous pair of Jon and Paul. We needed to temper optimism with caution. Up in London, we both felt safe. Arriving at Julie's flat, we found it crowded with her excited flatmates and friends rushing to and from the bathroom as they planned where to go on the Friday night in town.

'Your mother has been trying to reach you,' said Julie's flatmate. Every time I stayed at the flat there seemed to be new girls staying or friends of theirs. In addition, the occasional male visitor meant the flat was no longer a quiet hideaway. It was tense and chaotic after the relaxed parts of our holiday in Scotland.

'Unusual,' said Julie. 'She hardly ever calls. It must be something important.' The phone in the hall had a long cable, so Julie stretched it into her bedroom for privacy. After a long chat with her mother, she found me in the kitchen, currently the quietest room in the house, drinking a cup of coffee. I looked up, a question in my eyes.

'It was for you. Mark is trying to reach you urgently. He phoned your mother, who phoned my mother, so could you call Mark?'

'I wonder what that's about.' My coffee was cold. I poured it down the sink. Something was not right. I could feel it. I hoped Mark was still in his office at 6 p.m., as I did not have his home number. The phone was back in the hallway, and I had a long wait for one girl to finish her conversation. Almost as bad as waiting outside a phone-box in the street. At last. Mark's number rang for ages, and I had nearly given up hope.

'Sorry. Been busy on the other line. Michael at last. Where are you?'

'At Julie's flat in London.'

'You remember Jeremy Frobisher, the literary agent from Frobisher Daniels?'

'Yes, of course. He is handling Michelle's book. Is there a problem?'

'You could say. They found him dead on Wednesday—in his office hanging from a rope. The police believe it was suicide.'

'You're joking.'

'No, I don't joke about Death, Michael. He drank a bottle of whisky neat, typed a letter to me saying he was not interested in getting our book published and then hanged himself from the ceiling light fitting. In fact, more likely, he typed the letter and then drank the whisky. Who knows? This has all the hallmarks of another hit from Colonel Lane's team of Jon and Paul. Apparently, Paul is the literate one, so maybe he typed the letter and forged Jeremy's signature as he did with Peter Fowler. But the rejection letter is *exactly* in the right format with the usual wording, so this guy Paul knew what he was doing. I can't believe Jeremy would calmly write that letter. The question is who they will target next—you or me?'

Chapter 37

The return to school after half-term was an anti-climax. Some of the Common Entrance examinations, such as oral French, were due to kick-off in three days' time; the more important ones started the following week. I could not take this seriously as the exam results were meaningless. In theory, a 60% score was desirable but any child continuing in the private sector for their next independent school needed to tick one or more of the following boxes for certain selection to their next school: affordability—could the parents pay the fees, did the family have anyone in the armed forces, was the child baptised in the Catholic faith, did the child have siblings at his or her school of choice, was the child related to any of the teachers or governors at their prep school or the next school, was the child talented at rugby, cricket or athletics, or was the child a musical prodigy. In short, it was a democratic system where no one could fail. The examinations were just the superfluous cherry on the cake.

St Wilfrid's also entered all students for the 11 Plus exam as a contingency in case parents fell on hard times and could not pay the fees and had to fall back on the free State system. Many of our pupils failed the exam as there was no attempt to teach students how to pass the 11 Plus.

In contrast, brighter students who might gain a scholarship to their next school had to take things more seriously. We decided who would win a scholarship and gave the chosen ones the test papers to prepare for forthcoming scholarship exams. Those talented at sports or music were fast-tracked to a certain scholarship. I shared my views about the system with Jones and he agreed it was corrupt, with little or no incentive to admit poorer or disadvantaged students.

Jones said 'You and I are just as guilty. We support a flawed educational system which favours the rich.'

Being in total agreement at how the shameful system worked was reassuring, but there was little we could do to change things. Perhaps seek out and help those with lesser ability, or with disabilities to realise their full potential? Helping Charlie adjust fell into this category and my initial scepticism that he could ever win a scholarship was proving wrong.

'Jones, can you put me up for a few days? The problem is things are getting heated about Michelle's book and there is an outfit trying to suppress its publication. They can take me prisoner and torture me to get the information they want.'

He laughed like an idiot. He clearly did not believe me.

'Michael, that takes the biscuit!'

'I'm serious. These people are ruthless. They have already killed at least twice, and they attempted to push me and Julie off the Aonach Eagach ridge at Glen Coe last week.'

'Well, if you put it like that, I'm sure the wife won't object to you staying for a few days. You can take the spare room as our son is away at university. I think we need a visit to the Three Horseshoes tonight and you can put me in the picture.'

'Thanks, Jones, you are a pal.'

'Have you decided about the job offer from Singapore? Only another month till the end of term, you know.'

I had discussed this with Julie. After I had settled in, we could decide on the next step with our relationship. If it was feasible, she was keen to visit over Christmas when I would be into the fifth month of my new job.

'Thanks for reminding me. I am going to hand in my notice and start in Singapore at Dunearn Academy in August. I hope there will be time to sort out another agent for Michelle's book and get it published before I leave, but there are some loose ends to tie up first.'

A bell was sounding announcing the end of the mid-morning break, and I rushed off to my next lesson with enthusiasm. Anything to take my mind off the present danger was welcome. At least on the school grounds, I felt secure.

I took a late lunch, as I wanted to avoid most of the staff. By a stroke of luck, Nigel Caldwell-Brown was tucking into a large serving of treacle pudding and custard—one of Mollie's specialities. I helped myself to lamb shank and mash and sat next to Nigel.

'Michael, how was your holiday in Scotland?'

I looked at him closely. Whatever his role in passing information back to Colonel Lane, he did not appear to be in the picture. A messenger only. I downplayed things.

'A beautiful time of year in Scotland. We travelled up to Loch Lomond and then onto more secluded lochs and wild country towards the Highlands. We walked the Aonach Eagach ridge at Glen Coe, which is a very challenging hike with some dangerous sheer drops. Experienced walkers should only attempt the ridge walk in fair weather; you know. Many walkers decide to rope up as if they are climbing the Matterhorn but for a normal fit person with a good head for heights, that is unnecessary.'

'It sounds idyllic. I'm jealous just listening to you. Sussex seems so dull by comparison.'

'Nigel, do you mind if I ask you a question?'

'Sure, Michael. Go ahead.'

'You recall the drinks do after Easter Sunday Mass when I made some silly comments about the monarchy. I just wondered if you repeated that to anyone.'

Nigel looked sheepish. He was considering denying this, but he could see I would not believe him.

'I may have mentioned it at one meeting I attend as an example of the left-wing views that prevail at this school. As a patriot, I hold our royalty in high esteem and can't bear to hear anyone running down our Queen. I think I told you that, Michael. But my apologies if I spoke out of turn.'

'And apologies accepted. It was just an immature comment. Like you, I agree the Monarchy is a brilliant institution. Nigel, this "group" you attend what would that be?'

'No secret about that. It's the local branch of the National Front in Brighton. They have monthly meetings of liked–minded Englishmen. The press tarnishes us as some lunatic fringe of neo-Nazis, but that is rubbish. We just support our country and oppose unfettered immigration from the waves of foreigners who come to our shores, steal our jobs, marry our women, and weaken the gene pool.'

This admission knocked me back. I knew Nigel held right-wing views, but this was a new side to him. His face had turned red, and his eyes were popping as he ranted on. I let him finish.

'Wow, that's interesting. At least in the UK, everyone is free to express their views and there will always be different viewpoints. I know little about the National Front beyond this image of skinheads and football hooligans picking fights and stuff, but I suppose there is a more mature element?'

'Of course, there are always idiots in any organisation. The Brighton branch is middle-class patriots like me. There is one person who takes a keen interest in our school because he says the pupils of today are the statesmen of the future. He asked about our staff and what I felt about them, so I may have mentioned you have left-wing leanings and were anti-monarchist. You know how one loose remark can take on more importance than it should, so Gary always asks what you are up to.'

'Gary? Is he a young man about my age with short-cropped hair, a thin moustache and ex-military?'

'Yes, that sounds like him. He told me he is ex-Territorial Army.'

I enlightened Nigel that his friend Gary was likely to be the same person who worked for a powerful man called Colonel Lane whose team had been involved in covert surveillance operations looking for Michelle's manuscript. This team was unscrupulous and used violence to further their ends.

'They are obsessed with stopping her book. They persuaded our literary agent in London to reject it. As things stand, there is no one prepared to publish it. I'm sure you are not aware of how powerful and dangerous this group is. The police are on their track, and I can tell you Gary and his colleague Wayne are being held by the police in London at this minute investigating a murder attempt on Julie and myself during our holiday in Scotland. Your friend Gary attacked Julie and injected her with a powerful muscle relaxant to cause unconsciousness. His plan was then to push us off the Glen Coe ridge near Clachaig gully and make it look like a climbing accident.'

Nigel was stunned into silence. His spoon of treacle pudding and custard stopped in its tracks halfway to his mouth before he dropped the spoonful back in its bowl. He stood up, shaking. He apologised and said he needed the toilet.

The afternoon games sessions were underway. I should have been training the Under-11s cricket. At this level, it was best to run a simulated match, giving each pupil the opportunity to bat and bowl in an actual situation. This engaged the bowler and batsman, but the fielders lacked interest and wandered around the boundary, picking daisies or all running to field the ball in excited chaos. Fortunately, our work experience teacher, Dale, from New Zealand, was a keen cricketer, so I sent him to deputise for me as I went off to find matron. I wanted to update her on the situation, especially the risk from Colonel Lane's men.

As expected, she was in the infirmary, busy bandaging up a boy's cut knee.

'It's chaos today,' she said. 'One nose-bleed, one fainting, two food poisonings and this one has a grazed knee from falling onto the gravel path.'

'I was pushed, miss,' said the victim.

'All good now. Off you go. Well, Michael, what can I do for you?'

Where to start? I told matron about the capture and torture of Peter Fowler on 23rd May, just before the half-term break by Colonel Lane's men. Matron knew nothing about it as it had never reached the National press.

'I recall you mentioned the man from *New Scientist*. Michelle went to see him in London, and you followed up later when you went there for a sleuthing trip. You mean they tortured him with ECT without an anaesthetic? That's horrendous. They could have killed him.'

'I don't think they cared. Once they extracted information, I'm sure they would have killed him.'

I then gave a quick summary of events in Scotland when Gary and Wayne followed us. Every time I retold the story no one believed me, but matron listened with her full attention. I did not mention the shocking loss of our literary agent, which the papers reported as a likely suicide, as I wanted to call Mark and discuss this in more detail.

'Well, you have had a dramatic time. Running about on mountains in Scotland is not my idea of fun, especially when pursued by crazed assassins. I have had a very dull half-term. The only excitement was on the first of June.'

'First of June—what was special about that?'

'The Epsom Derby, of course. I won £50 on Teenoso romping home and winning by three lengths. Ridden by the great Lester Piggottt. There is no need to look bored. Life goes on despite your dramas and that was the ninth time Lester has won the Derby.'

'Very impressive,' I said.

At 5 p.m. a new marine blue Land Rover parked in the St Wilfrid's car park. The driver and his front seat passenger wore matching dark olive-green Barbour jackets, jeans, and sturdy Church's brown shoes. Wellington boots and a spade were in the back. Both men were young. The taller man sported a sage coloured waxed cap and his younger passenger a light-brown coloured sports cap. No one gave them a second glance. Only the pristine condition of the new Land Rover attracted admiring glances.

'The colonel should have got us a second-hand Land Rover. This one is too conspicuous,' said Jon. He noticed parents were busy picking up their children and the car park was emptying. 'There's the Triumph,' he pointed to Michael Fletcher's car parked at the far end of the small car park.

'What's the plan?' asked Paul.

'Simple. We wait until Fletcher leaves and follow him until he gets to the road approaching his house. That lane is an ideal place to stop him. We will ram him. Our cast iron bumpers will be like a battering ram. Bundle him into the back and you give him a jab of suxamethonium to shut him up and then restrain him with hands behind his back and handcuffed. Meanwhile, I drive at normal speed to the safe house near Worthing.'

'Sounds easy,' said Paul. 'But how do we transfer him from the Land Rover to the house without being seen by nosy neighbours?'

'I will drop you off at the front to open the house and then drive round to the back garden entrance. The back is private, so it will be easy to drag him into the house.'

'The house has a brilliant cellar,' said Paul. 'Like a dungeon—everything we need. Water supply and electrical power all up and running even through the house has been derelict for over a year. And best of all, the thick walls make it soundproof.'

Jon and Paul discussed the various options to make Michael cooperate and, for the sake of scientific accuracy, they agreed to follow the same sequence of ECT shock treatments they had used on Peter Fowler.

'He will break quickly,' predicted Jon.

Chapter 38

Commander Tilbury had assumed overall responsibility for what had started as the Sussex Pond Murder case. He wrote out the sequence of events just to get it clear in his own mind, as it was complex. The discovery of a young French teacher's senseless body in the pond of a private boys' school back in January had seemed a clear-cut case of likely murder by her boyfriend, English teacher Michael Fletcher. The lady was pregnant, and he was an immature, selfish individual who was not willing to take responsibility for his actions and, after a row, had killed her and dumped her in the pond. This was Preston's belief. But was there someone else in the pub the night of the French teacher's murder? Evidence pointed to a French suspect, Marcel Fouché. Fouché had been in London on the day of the murder, so he could have travelled to Sussex and killed Michelle. But what was his motive? Despite a thorough autopsy performed by the police pathologist, the French woman's family had requested a second autopsy. This contradicted the first autopsy and found the cause of death was a heart attack following an accidental collision with a tree, which propelled her into the pond. The police were still waiting further DNA test results.

Parallel developments included a fatal car accident to Ron Jones, the last known person to see Michelle Gagneux alive. How did a man who did not like whisky end up drinking almost a bottle of Johnnie Walker, before plunging to his death off the A3 London to Portsmouth Road at the Devil's Punch Bowl? And what was the motive for killing him? Next was the alleged torture case using electro convulsive shock treatment without anaesthesia against a journalist at a hotel in Kensington. Unfortunately, the journalist had signed an indemnity form to permit two men to run the experiments and accepted payment as compensation for his discomfort. Kensington police agreed this was odd behaviour but there was no apparent physical damage to the patient, and it seemed bad form to make a fuss and embarrass the two young men, Jon, and Paul, who did the decent thing and paid the hotel some compensation for the drama.

Last, there was the unexpected suicide of literary agent, Jeremy Fowler, in Covent Garden, by hanging himself after he consumed a bottle of whisky. The police had found no evidence of coercion by persons unknown. According to his secretary, he suffered from depression and a drink problem. Add in relationship issues with his wife associating with a younger man and suicide seemed a logical solution for the poor man.

Commander Tilbury put on his Devil's advocate hat as he looked at the case of the alleged attempted murder of a young couple when walking in the mountains in Scotland. Two ex-Territorial Army men pursued the English teacher, Michael Fletcher, and his current girlfriend across a mountain ridge in Scotland, intending to push them off one of the tall peaks to certain death. This was the young couple's version, but the explanation by the army men was they were enjoying the long ridge walk while on holiday when they encountered a hiker suffering a panic attack near to Clachaig gully, a scary place even for experienced climbers. Gary Smith had a first aid kit, including a syringe loaded with suxamethonium, and he offered to inject this to calm the girl down, which the teacher agreed to. It had an immediate beneficial effect, and she lost consciousness for ten minutes and woke up in a much calmer state.

The common theme connecting all the cases was a certain individual called Colonel Lane, running a security operation with the help of ex-Army foot soldiers tasked with locating a sensitive manuscript written by the French teacher. This was the part Commander Tilbury found the most difficult to comprehend.

Tilbury had called for a case review and requested officers from all the involved police stations to attend a formal meeting at Scotland Yard. He was expecting more to attend but had received apologies from Kensington police and Guildford police (responsible for the Alan Jones case). It was not reasonable to expect anyone from Scotland to travel all the way to London. It was unnecessary, as he had full statements from a senior detective at the Inverness station. That would have to do. At least both the Brighton and Pulborough stations had sent their teams.

'Gents, thank you for coming to Scotland Yard at short notice. Because all the cases have a common denominator in terms of objective and involvement of the key players, I plan to deal in chronological order with the significant events and then update our understanding of each case to see if there are loose ends to tie up.'

'The one case which we should be able to close is what the papers called at the time "The Sussex Pond Murder." As you all know, the second autopsy established Michelle Gagneux died of a genetic heart defect, which was triggered after a collision with a tree in the darkness when she was likely running away from Marcel Fouché. DI Preston, I know you sent the new autopsy report to the Prefecture of Police in Nantes, so where are we now? Have we had a reply?'

'Yes, just this week, so fresh off the press,' said Preston. 'We received a statement made by Marcel Fouché.

It's in French, but our officer Tracey Smith, who is fluent in the language, made me a translation. I will summarise the key points: Marcel states that after watching the England and France rugby match at Twickenham, he travelled by self-drive hire car from London to the Three Horseshoes pub and met up with Michelle Gagneux by prior arrangement. The purpose was to pass over laboratory test results on several well-known bottled waters produced in France. He states most of the samples had alarming levels of BPA and other toxins caused by leaching from the plastic containers into the water. Michelle said the results correlated well with the test results performed on the UK samples by her brother in Southampton. Because Marcel was fond of her, he hoped they might resume friendly relations, which had become interrupted by a court order in France because of his obsessive behaviour. The French police have added that last comment as an explanation; it is not Fouché's word.'

'Idiots,' said Tilbury. 'Why try to explain his statement to us?'

'Quiet,' said Preston. 'His account continues that she rebuffed his attempts to get back together, explained she was in a relationship with the school English teacher and revealed she was expecting his baby. He realised there was no way to reignite his friendship and gave his apologies and left the pub. Now, this is the interesting bit. He says he sat in his car trying to pull himself together and was about to depart when he saw her leave the pub. It was a dark night, but he returned to the pub and noticed a pathway through the wood, which she had followed. He ran after her, calling her name, and she broke into a run to escape him. Next thing he heard a thump, which is when she collided with the tree next to the pond. He ran on and found her face down in the pond. He put her in the recovery position and searched her mouth for any pond weed or obstruction. Next, he tried artificial resuscitation by chest compressions and the kiss of life. None of this worked. She was dead. He returned her to the pond but buoyed up by rocks at the side, so her face was clear of the water. Realising we could accuse him of killing her; he drove back to London to his hotel. Next morning, he phoned the school asking to speak to Michelle, knowing she was dead. He agrees he did this to establish an alibi. That is the end of his statement apart from a sentence about deepest regret and sorrow.'

'Did Dr Elizabeth Howard take DNA test swabs around the victim's mouth during the second autopsy?' said Tilbury.

Inspector Bishop explained how he was present at the second post-mortem, which was a very thorough investigation. He recalled the doctor requested a sample of hair or a throat swab from Michael Fletcher so they could run a DNA test to see if the teacher was the father of the unborn baby. He could not remember her taking any test swabs from around the victim's mouth. Bishop did not understand this DNA business, but did they mean there might still be traces of the French man's saliva around the lady's mouth from his attempts to resuscitate her? If so, they needed DNA material from Marcel Fouché.

'Right, get onto her and explain this man's confession and I guess we will need Marcel's DNA to see if there is a match from the mouth region of the corpse, as you suggest. Find out from the doctor if this is feasible and chase up the results of the fatherhood check on Fletcher just for completeness. Good progress. Do the French say what they plan to do next?'

'Yes, sir. I did speak to the chief at the Prefecture on the phone and he implied it was pointless to take the case any further. Accidental death is the verdict,' said Preston.

'That's a relief for Michael Fletcher,' said PC James. As everyone looked shocked and stared at him, he blundered on, 'I mean the press labelled him as guilty from day one, his school laid him off and our colleagues in Brighton reinforced that view. Apparently, he was even strip-searched during an interview.'

Tracey Smith gave James a hostile stare but stayed silent.

'Yes, thank you for those comments,' said Commander Tilbury. 'It is a lesson learned to keep an open mind and deal only with the evidence, Now I want to discuss the next case which is the fatal car crash of Alan Jones—an oil rig worker and darts player from Graffham who was in the Three Horseshoes pub the night Michelle had her fatal accident. The case officers from Guildford who attended the scene of the accident can't be with us today but their report states that the Ford Cortina of Alan Jones left the A3 in the early hours of Easter Monday on a tight bend with a sheer drop to the bottom of the Devil's Punch Bowl. No other vehicle was involved, and the victim had drunk a bottle of whisky, found at the scene, and was alone in the car. The autopsy showed a BAC of four grams per 100ml of blood, which is a fatal dose. The police report is very poor, and the coroner's verdict was accidental death whilst inebriated.'

'It must be a set-up,' said Inspector Bishop. 'You can't drink a bottle of whisky straight off without making yourself sick—unless someone pours it down your throat. So, was someone else there?'

'You are right to question this,' said Tilbury. 'They only found fingerprint evidence from Alan and his family. Then we received a breakthrough from Michael Fletcher. Michael, along with the school's matron and another teacher, met up with Alan Jones at a darts match at the Royal Albion pub in Sussex on 10th March. Alan confirmed that he spoke to Michelle. In fact, he tried to chat her up. This was after Alan saw the French man, Marcel Fouché, talking to Michelle, so that was a positive sighting of another suspect. Then there is the evidence of the St Wilfrid's teachers that Alan Jones drank a vodka and lime with them in the pub and refused the offer of a whisky, which he said he hated.'

'We should repeat the forensics,' said Tilbury. 'Guildford report states no other prints on the bottle, but we can have another look.'

'Two young lads stopped Michael's car masquerading as MI5 agents on Tuesday, 12th April, and took him to a pub wanting to discuss the Michelle murder case. Now the fascinating detail is the two men who identified themselves as Gary and Wayne knew about the death of Alan Jones on Easter Monday, 4th April, even though the press had not released his name. They said they had wanted to speak to him, but the accident happened before they could do so. Was this true, or had others killed him first? When did you gents at Brighton or Pulborough know about the traffic accident?'

'It happened in Surrey,' said Preston. 'I saw nothing about in the press, but BBC local news carried a brief report in early April, as it was an unusual accident. I am sure they didn't mention the name. They hold back until we inform the relatives.'

'Tracey,' said Tilbury. 'Could you check when there was *first* mention of Alan Jones in the press or TV coverage? I remember the coroner's report came out in late May with the verdict of accidental death. This is very important. Gary and Wayne must be implicated if they knew about it before it was in the public domain.'

The team stopped for a thirty-minute coffee break. Commander Tilbury received an update on a police raid overnight. The Kensington police had filed the full names and residence addresses of the two men, Jon, and Paul. The address given by Jon proved fictitious, whereas the address for Paul was his parents' house in Ealing. In the small hours at 2 a.m., a team from the Met, armed with a search warrant, woke the angry couple, and searched the property, including the spare room used by Paul. They removed a shoebox containing receipts from the top of a wardrobe. Another box contained pornographic magazines, including several featuring sadomasochistic images of an extreme nature. The successful raid was a breakthrough. Tilbury ordered a summary listing of the confiscated material, including each of the till receipts.

Next was the apparent suicide of the literary agent, Jeremy Fowler. The post-mortem results confirmed death by hanging and very high blood alcohol readings from drinking a bottle of Johnnie Walker. The whisky bottle only had prints from the victim. Likewise for a glass found in the kitchen sink.

Commander Tilbury said they should get the original letter Jeremy Fowler typed to Dr Carter back to examine it for prints. In case no one had seen the letter, Dr Carter had faxed Tilbury a copy. The signature appeared to be a good match to Jeremy's usual signature which was flowery and difficult to copy, but they would submit the signature to a police graphologist to see if was genuine Also, he suggested they should check the typewriter keys for prints and the photocopy machine. Lane's men may have made a copy of the letter.

'Any reaction from his wife?' asked Tracey. 'Was she surprised he took his life?'

'She is in denial. Maintains he would never have done it. If he planned to do it, he would have left her a suicide note. Unlike the secretary, who is certain he meant to do it,' said Tilbury. 'Okay, the summary at the moment is we have no evidence of anyone else staging this as a suicide, but we keep looking. The chief suspects are Jon and Paul, so we need to track them down fast.'

'If they stage managed the suicide, what was their motive?' Preston wondered.

'That's obvious,' said Tilbury. 'They planned to stop publication of Miss Gagneux's book. A book likely to be a best-seller and commercial success which, according to Dr Carter, two of London's publishers are prepared to pay an enormous advance to secure.'

'What for a book about the plastic bottle industry?' said Preston with disgust.

'He's kidding you. You guys imagine villains where there are none.'

Tilbury looked at his watch. It seemed pointless to rehash all the statements concerning the Glen Coe ridge incident, as it was still ongoing, with Gary and Wayne in custody. So far, they had denied the young couple's story and reiterated their account of being on a holiday hike in the mountains. Likewise, neither man admitted to knowing Colonel Lane apart from serving together in Cyprus many years before.

'To bring you up to speed, the Glen Coe case is still under investigation. It is an attempted murder. We will not release Gary and Wayne soon and are resisting their solicitor's demands for bail, as they are high risk. We plan to interview Colonel Lane as a priority. My gut-feeling is that while Jon and Paul remain on the loose, there will be more attempts to suppress this manuscript from seeing the light of day.'

Chapter 39

After four nights with Jones and his wife, I felt the threat against me was receding and life was returning to normal. Julie was coming down for the weekend. We had nothing special planned apart from a visit to the George & Dragon. I had received an update from Bishop warning us all to keep alert, as Jon and Paul were still active. The police were closing in and believed Lane's men had been involved in murdering Alan Jones and Jeremy Fowler. The forensic data from both cases was being re-examined, and further testing was underway. He also reassured me that Gary and Wayne were still assisting the Met police with their enquiries in London and were unlikely to be released on bail. I asked about the elusive Colonel Lane, and he confirmed plans were in hand to question him this week.

Julie was worried that Lane's team had me in their sights. Their ruthless intention was to stop publication of the book. To solve the problem, she had come up with a clever contingency plan, which I needed to discuss with Mark.

During the Friday morning break at school, I put a call through to Mark.

'Michael, I have been worried about you. We can't relax for a minute with Lane's men still on the loose.'

'I am aware of that. This week I have been staying with Jones and have not used my car. Things are quiet, so I was going to risk it tonight and drive home for fresh clothes. I thought if I left early, I would get away with it. They can't be watching the school the whole time.'

'I wouldn't take the risk. Now listen to this. Julie called me a short time ago. Did you know about her idea for *Time Out* to serialise weekly chapters of Michelle's book?'

'Yes, she mentioned it. What do you think?'

'I think it's a brilliant plan. She has asked if you and I can get to their office at eleven tomorrow morning. No problem for me and I could pick you up from school at about half past eight. As it's a Saturday, traffic to London should be light. School won't miss you for a day, will they? I'll take your stunned silence as agreement. *Time Out* will print the first three chapters and your resume on Tuesday next week. In addition, an article on the background about the intrigue and attempts to stop the publication. We can help draft that when we meet Julie and the editor tomorrow. It will need approval of the paper's solicitors, so we cannot be too explicit. Then on Tuesday, thousands of people in London will get to read it. *Time Out* will continue releasing a chapter every week and we will still control the copyright and are free to negotiate with book publishers for the hardback and paperback sales, film rights, etc.'

'Film rights?'

'Of course, I can see Meryl Streep or Jenny Agutter as Michelle. Casting you is going to be more difficult.'

'John Alderton maybe. He was the teacher in the TV series "*Please Sir*" from the late 1960s. As that was a comedy, we may need someone more serious and closer to my age,' I said with a laugh.

Commander Tilbury punched the air with joy. At last, a genuine breakthrough. The team collating Paul's till receipts had located a set of incriminating receipts from his shoebox hiding place. On Easter Sunday, 3rd April at 9 p.m., Paul had purchased a bottle of Teachers whisky from an off licence in Hindhead for £6.89. Six hours later, the wreck of Alan Jones's crashed Cortina also contained an empty bottle of Teachers. Coincidence, or was it the same bottle?

Then, on Tuesday, 31st May, Paul visited a small Tesco supermarket on the Strand and purchased a 750ml bottle of Johnnie Walker, which was another coincidence, as Jeremy Frobisher also consumed an entire bottle of whisky before hanging himself. He left an empty bottle of Johnnie Walker on his desk. The average office does not have a handy section of rope, but Paul had thoughtfully bought a 10m section of coiled jute rope from Tesco's home and garden section. We managed to buy the same item, and it was an exact fit to the rope used to hang Jeremy Fowler.

'Issue mugshots of Jon and Paul to the TV channels for immediate release,' said Tilbury to an assistant. 'Warning these men are dangerous and may be armed. Do not approach. Wanted to assist our enquiries into two homicides. First, the murder of Alan Jones in a faked road accident near Hindhead on 4th April and second, the killing by hanging of literary agent, Jeremy Fowler, in Covent Garden on 31st May. Do not mention the torture case of Peter Fowler. I don't want to overload the Public with too much detail.'

For the fourth consecutive evening, at 5 p.m., Jon and Paul pulled into St Wilfrid's school car park in their Land Rover. Jon was still wearing his olive-green Barbour jacket, jeans and a sage coloured waxed cap, and Paul wore the same plus his light-brown sports cap. It was a hot summer's day, and they were over-dressed and over-heated. Their frequent visits had generated some friendly banter from the passing parents, and one or two of them noticed that after an hour, the pair drove off without picking up any child.

Michael Fletcher's car was no longer parked in the same spot.

'Where the hell is he?' said Paul.

'He must have left early. He has sussed out we are after him, so he won't risk leaving at the regular time. What time does school start tomorrow?'

'They have an assembly in the chapel at nine and then classes start at nine-thirty so we could park up here tomorrow morning and try to pick him up.'

'Too risky. We couldn't do that without witnesses seeing us. Best try again on Saturday afternoon but aim to be here by four latest. If tomorrow fails, there is always Sunday.'

'They don't have classes on Sunday, do they?'

'I don't think so,' said Jon. 'About half the school are boarders. On Sunday, they make them go to church and afterwards I expect they take a walk to town or meet up with their parents. A bit of freedom. Sunday may be the best day to catch Michael. His guard will be down. We will look for him on the school grounds. He can't hide from us forever.'

'We will look even more prominent if we park here on Sunday. I think we should call the colonel and explain we can't complete the mission,' said Paul.

'You may be right. The colonel has gone silent. He didn't even answer my call yesterday or return my message. Maybe the police have picked him up. Look, Paul, we might as well push off back to the safe house. I will try to call Lane for instruction. What I'm worried about is that Gary and Wayne have talked. We may have to clear out and go into hiding.'

'Lane hasn't paid us yet. I am not going anywhere until he pays me what he owes.'

'We are overlooking the obvious,' said Jon. 'Fletcher hasn't been home for the last week. He needs to go home to his parents, get a decent meal, have his mother do his washing and stuff like that. I bet you he is home right now. I suggest we swing by the parents' house.'

In fact, I was aware Jon and Paul might try the direct approach, so when I got home, my first task was to hide my car out of sight in the garage. My father was not happy to move his Rover out to make space, but after I explained the danger posed by Colonel Lane's team, he agreed and took over command.

'How long have we got?' he asked.

'We need to expect them anytime from now. If they check the school car park and see my car is missing, they may guess I am here.'

We prepared for a siege and locked all the doors. The major retrieved an old 12-bore shotgun from the downstairs cupboard. He loaded it with 12 gauge shells.

'This thing is only effective at close range,' he said. 'If the attackers are over 60 metres away, the pellets will scatter and not be so deadly, but it may be enough to scare them away.'

'I don't like the sound of that,' said my mother. 'You haven't fired a gun in years and would miss the target at point blank range. I will call the police right now and ask them to send someone over.'

My father took up a vantage point from an upper bedroom, which afforded a good view along the drive to the front gate. It was the only logical approach to our house as the small garden at the back was overgrown and bordered by thick woods, inaccessible except on foot over difficult terrain. We sat down to wait and put on the television as a distraction.

'Pulborough police station doesn't have any officers to spare at the moment,' said my mother. 'But PC James will look by at about six.'

'You should have told him the men may be armed,' said the major. 'I can't hold them off for long with this old shotgun. It used to belong to my grandfather, you know. I suggest we synchronise our watches. I make it one-seven-three-zero hours.'

'I'm sure one shot from that thing will send them running. Can I get you a drink, dear? Michael and I are going to have a gin and tonic and watch the BBC News at six.'

'Good idea, bring me up a strong whisky with ginger tonic and ice.'

A marine blue Land Rover pulled up outside the Fletcher's home at 5.45 p.m. Inside the house, the major believed it must be PC James in a police Land Rover.

'Good news,' he called down from the bedroom. 'The police have arrived already. Michael, open the gate for them.'

'That was quick.' I went and unlocked the front door and saw Jon calmly opening our front gate. Our eyes locked, and I saw him smile.

Events unfolded quickly. As I slammed shut and locked the door, the Land Rover swung into the drive and drove up to the front door. The major swung open the bedroom window and released two blasts of the shotgun at the front of the Land Rover, smashing the windscreen and spraying glass all over Jon and Paul. Some pellets hit home, and the men cried out in pain and surprise.

Jon was at the wheel, and he quickly reversed the Land Rover so the front, with its shattered windscreen, faced the front door. My father was reloading the 12-bore, but his reactions were too slow. The Land Rover sped up and smashed into the front door. The frame cracked under the impact, and it pushed the door off its hinges. Jon swung open the door of the Land Rover. His face was streaked with blood, and he held a Webley Mark IV revolver in his hand as he walked towards the shattered door.

The major had moved to the top of the stairs, where he had a commanding view of the smashed doorway. He rested the barrel of the 12-bore on the stair banister and aimed at the space where he expected the men to appear. I was downstairs in the kitchen with my mother, but I could see and hear my father breathing heavily on the landing.

'Look, he wants me. I don't want you and Dad getting hurt. If they enter by the front door, there's no telling what will happen.'

Meanwhile, Jon had skirted around the house, looking in at the windows and searching for another entry. Suddenly, we heard the back door to the utility room opening. In the rush, we had forgotten to lock it. Nelson barked and went to greet the unknown visitor, wagging his tail.

'Some guard dog you are. Michael, best if you come with me. Save upsetting your parents. We just need to ask you a few questions. And ask your father at the top of the stairs if he could stop pointing his gun and put it down before he hurts someone.'

There was no other option. I walked through to the back, and he directed me to the Land Rover. In the passenger seat, Paul looked in a bad way, doubled up and groaning. Jon said the face cuts were only superficial and mainly from flying glass. He forced me into the back of the Land Rover, clipped a pair of handcuffs to one wrist, and attached the other to a steel pole mount inside. With a sound of crunching gravel, the Land Rover swung round and sped down the drive, turning right and heading east.

Inspector Bishop and PC James came screeching up the driveway five minutes later, but the Land Rover had already left. The vehicles had not passed each other.

Chapter 40

As per their arrangement, Mark arrived at school at 8.30 a.m. ready to pick up Michael for the drive to London for the 11 a.m. meeting at *Time Out*. Feeling an increasing unease, he checked with the school secretary, who confirmed Michael had not turned up for the morning assembly. It seemed unlikely he had overslept, but Mark drove over to the Fletchers' house to check.

Entering the drive, he was shocked to see the police presence with one squad car and a white van outside the broken front door, which looked as if a tank had hit it. Inspector Bishop approached him, and they introduced themselves.

'Dr Mark Carter,' said Bishop. 'I am pleased to meet you at last. As you can see, there has been a major incident, which happened yesterday evening just before six. Fortunately, both of Michael's parents are unharmed, but Colonel Lane's men have abducted Michael.'

'Have you any idea where they have taken him?'

'Major Fletcher has given us the number of a marine blue Land Rover which was used by the two suspects. Their pictures were released some days ago in the news and on TV and Mrs Fletcher confirm the two men who took Michael are the wanted criminals, Jon, and Paul. We have an active hunt in progress. All roads within twenty miles have roadblocks set up. They are pegged down and trapped in a net. We are conducting house-to-house searches of remote farms and cottages and empty properties, but it is a massive task. Don't worry, we will find Michael.'

'Yes, but it may be too late. These people are sadistic killers. Totally ruthless, they are acting on the orders of their master, Colonel Lane. You police must put pressure on the Met to arrest and charge Lane. He is the only one who can stop this.'

'Of course, sir. We understand the urgency. But the Met handle the London area, and these lads have committed this offence under our jurisdiction in Sussex. To show willing on behalf of the Pulborough force, I plan to raise the profile of this case to SIO Preston at Brighton and he can talk to the Met much easier than us.'

'I don't care about the police conventions. These men killed Ron Jones, Jeremy Frobisher, and tortured Peter Fowler. They will torture Michael until he cracks and gives them the information they want. He is a stubborn bastard and will not break.'

Mark asked to see the Fletchers to hear their side of the story and then he had to call Julie and her editor at *Time Out* to decide on their next step. He found the couple in the kitchen drinking tea. A 12-bore shotgun was on the sideboard. The major looked at it proudly.

'Been in the family for years. It used to be my grandfather's best gun. I showed them—got two barrels off into the windscreen, peppering them with shot. I only saw the driver and his face was a mess—blood everywhere. His passenger was groaning and could not get out of the Land Rover. My son gave himself up because he didn't want us to be hurt. Bloody stupid. After Malaya, I can take care of myself. If he had left it to me, I could have seen off both the insurgents. Sorry, I don't have a clue who you are.'

'I am Dr Mark Carter, brother of Michelle. Your son and I have been working on the case together.'

'Michael doesn't tell us everything. All we know is the police, the press and even his school made him the chief suspect in Michelle's murder. Now there is a French suspect.'

'No, dear—that's out of date. According to the papers, Michelle's death was an accident.'

'Would you like a cup of tea?'

The Fletchers' phone was ringing. Mrs Fletcher finished pouring Mark a cup of tea and went to answer it.

'I hoped that might be Michael calling to say he is alright, but it's his girlfriend Julie. I said Dr Mark is here, and she wants to speak to you.'

According to Julie, the capture of Michael was headline news. She was very upset and wanted to know what to do. Mark filled her in on the details. She suggested *Time Out* should announce that they would release chapters of Michelle's book every week starting next Tuesday. Once Colonel Lane knew he could not suppress the publication, he would have to release Michael. Stopping publication of the book was their only aim. They agreed this was a good idea, but Mark suggested they should first check with *Time Out*'s legal team. If *Time Out* took this step, was there anyway Colonel Lane could block the release by a court challenge? It might be better to release the first three chapters in the Tuesday edition as per their initial plan, but with no pre-publicity.

'Hmm…I see what you mean,' said Julie. 'I agree it is best not to show our hand prematurely. But that means waiting for four more days. Do we have that long?'

'The police are confident they closed the area down quickly, so they must be holding Michael somewhere nearby. With Peter Fowler, they took him to a hotel for interrogation, but that didn't work out too well for them, so I imagine they will use a secure facility. A witness has come forward this morning claiming two young men in a blue Land Rover were hanging about the school car park every day at the school pickup time—no doubt hoping to abduct Michael as he left the school. That means they must be staying somewhere close by—perhaps renting a house on a short-term rental agreement.'

'How do you know that? There's been nothing on the news.'

'Bishop is here at the Fletchers, and he just passed me this information. There are many leads coming in from the public, so keep positive. We will get Michael back soon.'

As the Land Rover approached Worthing it attracted several curious glances because of the broken window and wild-looking, bloodstained driver and front seat passenger. In the back of the long wheelbase, I was singing in a loud voice or waving at the window to draw attention. This made Jon so fed up, he pulled into a quiet alley. He found some rope and tied me up, sitting on the floor. He lashed my free hand to the seat frame and used duct tape to wrap round my mouth to silence me. However, my legs were still free, so I kicked the deck loudly whenever we stopped at traffic lights or were slowed down in traffic. I was also looking carefully at our route. Worthing was easily recognisable, and finally we entered a terrace of modern properties somewhere east of Worthing. The Land Rover stopped outside a mid-terrace for Jon to unlock the house. He returned, and we drove into a drive at the back of the house where he parked on a small garden plot. He closed a pair of high wooden gates, and the Land Rover was hidden from view.

Jon led me inside what he called their safe house. It was like any other house of that period, but I only saw an untidy kitchen before he directed me down a flight of creaking wooden stairs and into a cramped cellar. Jon ripped off the duct tape from my mouth and said I could shout as loud as I liked. The cellar was underground, and no one would hear me. He returned upstairs to help Paul out of the car and left me alone in the darkness. I tried the electric switch, but there was no bulb in the overhead light. The cellar was damp and smelled of vermin. At a sink I found the tap was operational and ran rusty coloured water, which I drank using my cupped hands. I was grateful they had left my hands handcuffed to my front so I could perform some tasks. As my eyes got used to the darkness, I noticed there was a single wooden chair set against the wall with armrests fitted with leather manacles. Apart from the evil-looking chair, there was a small wooden bench and, by the far wall, an old leather topped gym horse. There was a scuttling sound on the floor, possibly rats or cockroaches. I sat on the gym horse and waited.

After an hour or so, the cellar door opened, and Jon came down the creaking steps with an old army type camping bed and a sleeping bag.

'Sorry for the basic facilities, Michael. You can get some kip on this. If you need the toilet, bang on the door and you can use the one in the house. I have bandaged Paul and there is no serious damage. We have all had a long day, so we will see you tomorrow after you get a good night's sleep.'

He left me a cheap supermarket snack meal comprising a cheese and tomato sandwich, orange juice and a packet of crisps. It was encouraging they planned to keep me alive for now.

The next morning, I awoke to find Paul fitting a bulb to the ceiling light. A turn of the switch flooded the cellar with 120-watt light, banishing the darkness. I rubbed my eyes to clear my vision. Many deep cuts scarred Paul's face and blood was oozing out of some of the bandages. He said nothing. He took a brush and swept the concrete floor, removing all the dirt and debris and shovelling it into a bag. After this, he cleaned all the surfaces and invited me to sit in the wooden chair. Jon came into the cellar and complimented Paul on how tidy it was. Without more ado, they attached my arms to the armrest with the leather manacles. Paul found some rope and tied my legs firmly to the legs of the chair.

Next, Paul opened a cupboard and removed a small metallic unit with dials and two flexible leads ending in metal jaws. He plugged the machine into the mains and the room came alive with a humming noise and a green light, like a traffic light, signalling ready to go. They backed my rigid chair against the wall next to this unit.

Jon seemed satisfied everything was working and told Paul to turn the machine off.

'Michael. I doubt if you have seen one of these machines before. It is a standard ECT machine used by psychiatrists for electric shock treatment. The Italians first developed it in the 1930s to treat patients in mental asylums. If my memory serves me right, ECT stands for electroconvulsive therapy.'

Paul said this was correct.

'During conventional usage, the electrode pads are attached to either side of the patient's head and small electric shocks are passed through the brain. I would normally do this using an anaesthetic, so the patient feels no pain. However, for our purpose, which we shall term persuasive therapy, we are more interested in causing pain to extract information from our subjects. To achieve this aim, we use the same operational techniques and professionalism as a psychiatric technician except without the use of anaesthesia. In fact, this gives us a more accurate control of the pain threshold. Once the subject has given us the information we require, then the ECT session can stop.'

Paul was busy attaching the electrodes to my manacled arms. He then pushed a mouth-gag into my mouth, which secured my tongue away from my teeth. He explained the electric shocks would otherwise convulse my face muscle and risk biting off my tongue.

'Normally, we ask our subjects to agree to the testing programme, but we can assume you are happy for us to continue.' Jon grabbed my chin and forced my head up and down to signify yes, which he found amusing. He continued with his explanation.

'Good. When we start, we will give you mild shocks of six-second duration. The current will flow through both your arms and convulse the muscles in your whole body but not your brain, which I guess you will be happy about. The procedure will lead to loss of muscle control, and you will experience strong pain. We will then stop and ask for information. If you refuse to cooperate, we will increase the power and so on. There are loads of variations and techniques we can try, such as applying the electrodes to more sensitive areas. The pain will get worse as the experiment progresses, but it is in your hands to make us stop at any time. All we need is honest answers to our questions. It's very simple and quick.'

Jon and Paul apologised they had to keep me waiting longer, but they were going upstairs for a coffee and to make a phone call. They would start the treatment in 30 minutes time. Jon explained Paul was a bit of a perfectionist and he wanted to follow the same sequence of tests that they had used on their last subject, a gentleman from *New Scientist* magazine called Peter Fowler. In fact, that was the first of their questions. Which was did I know Peter Fowler? No hurry, they said. Think about it and give us your answer when we come back—a simple nod of the head to confirm or a shake to deny.

Chapter 41

Jon called Colonel Lane in London at a pre-arranged time of 10.30 a.m. for a morning update. He informed the colonel that they were about to start the ECT session on Michael Fletcher. In his opinion, the teacher would crack quickly. He was already scared stiff, almost catatonic, like a startled rabbit caught in the headlights of a car.

Colonel Lane laughed. He was happy they had found the ideal rented property with a convenient cellar sunk underground, so it was soundproof. None of the neighbours would hear a thing. Jon pointed out that the procedure was not noisy as they fitted the victim with a mouth-gag. Between sessions, the subject could shout and scream, but that was a waste of energy.

'You will need to get results as soon as possible. I don't know how you got through the police roadblocks, but someone will have seen the blue Land Rover and it's only a matter of time before the police find the safe house,' said the colonel.

Jon said they took the A27 for most of the journey, and the only awkward part was driving through slow traffic in Worthing. He was sure no one saw them when they arrived in West Lancing at the safe house. Transferring Fletcher from the Land Rover was also out-of-sight.

'According to the press, police are checking all cars in all directions up to 20 miles from the Fletchers' home. At Lancing, you are only about 12 miles away, which is why you didn't meet the police. The problem is, I need you guys to get back to London.'

The Land Rover was too conspicuous, so Colonel Lane said he would arrange for a chauffeur-driven limousine to come and pick them up.

'It will have diplomatic plates, so the police will wave you through. In the unlikely event they stop you, say you are a security attachment for the Libyan Embassy. Use hoodies to cover your scarred faces, just in case.'

'How long have we got to work on Fletcher?' asked Jon.

'I can get the limousine to you by one. That gives you a couple of hours. If he cooperates, just leave him tied up in the cellar. By the time they find him, you will be back in London. Mission accomplished.'

'So, you want us to leave the Land Rover here?'

'Of course. It's hot. The police will have the number and the broken windscreen makes it a tad conspicuous. *If* the police cannot find the house and the Land Rover, I can arrange for its recovery once the heat is off. The important thing is to get you and Paul back to town.'

'Paul wants us to use the same sequence of tests we used on Fowler,' said Jon. 'In the unlikely event, Fletcher won't cooperate in the tight time frame; what do we do?'

'Update me later with your progress and we can decide. Start the tests straight away, call me back in an hour's time at midday. Hopefully, with good news.'

I had used the time I was alone in the cellar profitably. When I threw my body weight to-and-fro sideways, that built up the harmonic motion to the point where my chair was about to tip over. I controlled this, so it fell against the electric lead connecting the ECT machine to the mains. Transferring my weight forwards and backwards generated enough momentum to tip the chair forward, exerting such pressure on the mains lead it snapped. The crowning achievement was when the ECT machine fell over on to the concrete floor and the casing broke open.

'Is it repairable?' asked Jon.

Paul regarded the machine. 'Hmm…I should think so. The mains lead is easy—just reterminate the torn sections of lead and tape. Hopefully, the box will slot back together, but if there are any broken connections, I will need a soldiering iron.'

'So, time for repair is?'

'Best case twenty minutes, worst case an hour or so, provided we can get a soldering tool.'

'Okay, get on with it. God knows how we find a soldering iron out here in the sticks. If you can't get the thing working, we will have to think of something else.'

Jon paced up and down in exasperation. The sight of me in the collapsed chair annoyed him even more. With Paul's help, they righted the chair, and he pushed the wooden bench against the side to wedge it back firmly in place. He lit up a cigarette and I could see the way his brain was working. If Paul could not repair the machine, they must try other methods of persuasion.

There had been many reports of sightings of the Land Rover and Preston's team in Brighton were busy plotting up the results. Most identifications were in north Worthing on the A27. At Sompting, there was a single sighting on Busticle Lane from someone leaving a dentist, followed by several more reports from houses along Sompting Road. The driver appeared to have followed a zigzag course after leaving the A27 to end his journey somewhere in West Lancing.

'Right. All hands get to this area of the last sighting. Check every house either side of Sompting Road and the same again on Wembley Avenue and Tower Road,' said Preston.

'Look inside garages and parking spots for the blue Land Rover. When you find it, we will force entry to the property with an armed team. No rubbish about knocking on the door and asking politely. All clear? These men are dangerous.'

Paul had made good progress with the repairs, but he wasn't happy. He set the ECT machine up and it was operational, but the control dial for switching from low-power to high-power was not working. It had jammed in the high-power setting.

'Paul,' yelled Jon. 'It doesn't matter. Just get started and run the sequence as usual but skip the initial low-power and zap with maximum straight away.'

Paul was reluctant, but time was slipping away, and Jon was impatient to start. Now the machine was working again so Paul attached the electrodes to Michael's arms just above the place where his arms were manacled to the chair. A few lashings of duct tape ensured a secure and tight connection to the chair.

'What about recording the parameters in the notebook,' said Paul to Jon. 'Just because we are in a hurry doesn't mean we can take shortcuts.'

Jon ran upstairs to find the notebook causing a delay as he searched his bedroom. It seemed an exercise in futility. He just needed a pen and a scrap of paper. At last, he found it on the floor.

'Okay, I'll record start and end of tests and the settings,' he said after his return. 'I consider we have given the subject all the relevant information, and he understands the implications that he cannot hold us liable to any injury or disability suffered because of the ECT procedure. Michael, these tests follow standard Chinese methods so we will not be giving you an anaesthetic.'

'Paul, what are the settings for the first test?'

'High-power setting. Duration, six-second shock burst.'

He instructed Paul to throw the power switch, and they stood well back.

The first few shocks felt like my whole body was in the grip of a giant, shaking me with tremendous force. My muscles across my chest surged as my whole body shook. The pain was indescribable. Six seconds is a long time to bear.

'That was a severe reaction,' said Paul.

'I'm concerned that the actual power setting is inaccurate, and it is firing out too many amps. This machine outputs a maximum current of 150V from the 240V mains supply, but I prefer to keep the maximum at 120V. I have no control over it after the damage to the unit.'

'Well, let's ask the patient, shall we?'

Jon pulled out my mouth-gag. I gasped for air and tried to get my beating heart under control.

'Well, Michael. Paul seems to think that was very painful. But you look fine to me. Are you ready to tell us if you ever met up with Peter Fowler?'

'No,' I said. 'I have never heard of him. Is he the guy you tortured with this machine?'

'Wrong answer, Michael. We *know* you met him. We *know* he talked to you about the colonel as he betrayed us. Next question, where is Michelle's manuscript? As her boyfriend, it is obvious you knew she was writing a book to expose the plastic bottling industry. Just tell us where the book is and we will buy it off you, so that's a great deal for everyone.'

'Michelle never confided in me. She was a school colleague and a friend. I do not know what this book you talk about is, I am afraid.'

'Afraid—you are right there.' He pushed the mouth-gag back into my mouth. 'Repeat the test, Paul, then after that, double the time.'

'The machine is definitely outputting an over-voltage,' said Paul. 'I think we should be careful.'

It was a bit of a blur after that. The repeat test at the same settings was more bearable as I knew what to expect. But the follow-up with doubling the test duration from six seconds to 12 seconds was a nightmare. After that, they stopped to put another call through to Colonel Lane.

Paul came back on his own.

'Michael, I can't agree with what Jon is doing here. Jon is busy on the phone, but I am going to change the resistance and that should lower the power output. Further tests will be less painful. Just act up a bit. We have a car coming in an hour, and the plan is to leave you behind trussed up in the chair. Don't mention this to Jon, as Colonel Lane's order is to leave you tied up. What if the police never find this house? It would be a slow death. But don't worry, I will call the police and give them this address.' He stopped quickly as Jon was coming down the stairs.

'Right Paul. A latest instruction from the colonel is to give him one last chance to talk and after that we move to the test that broke Peter Fowler.'

'You mean omit the tests with enhanced conductivity? They are quick to do and the increase in pain is dramatic. That might be enough to get him to talk,' said Paul.

'No. It didn't work on Fowler and this guy is just as stubborn.'

'Okay, but I just need to change the resistance as the box is over-heating. Take out his gag and give him a five-minute break and a cigarette.'

Meanwhile, the police house-to-house search had come up with a blank for all the houses along Sompting Road. Next, they tried Wembley Avenue. Halfway along they got chatting to some youths who remembered seeing a new blue Land

Rover driving north along Wembley Avenue and turning down a right entrance just before the T-junction with Crabtree Lane. This was a few days ago, so before the abduction of Michael Fletcher.

They said there were loads of garages behind the houses on Crabtree Lane so the Land Rover could be down that way.

The police agreed to have a look. They had run out of options and if this were a dead-end, they would return to the station.

One look showed the task was hopeless. The owners locked up every garage. PC James was with a junior colleague from Brighton who said the search was futile. PC James explained they would need to call on all the houses on Crabtree Lane with garages and ask the owners to open them. First, they walked the length of the back-lane making a record of all the garages along the row. Half-way along, they saw a wooden gate and inside was a new blue Land Rover. The registration number matched, and they noticed the front windscreen was missing.

I had made my cigarette last as long as possible. Jon was getting very impatient as Paul was slowly adjusting the resistance. To save time, he shoved the mouth-gag roughly back into my mouth. He explained what they planned to do next and how Fowler had suddenly confessed everything he knew to stop this final indignity. I was debating whether to reveal some information—perhaps confirming I had met Peter Fowler. It would gain time. I motioned for him to remove the gag, and he looked triumphant. It was at this point that a metal battering ram smashed open the front door. Half a dozen police, shouting like banshees, burst into the house. The door to the cellar was open, so they came down the stairs, pointing their weapons in front, as they followed behind, cursing, and shouting. It was over.

Chapter 42

On Saturday, 9th July, the parents drifted into the marquee for the annual ceremony of prize giving at St Wilfrid's. It was that rare event, a hot July day, the third day of a heat wave. Even at 11.30 a.m., it was too hot for the over-dressed, more formal parents. Some braver souls had removed their jackets to survive the long slog ahead with the headmaster's speech, the guest speech and long roll-call of deserving prize winners walking up to receive a book and a handshake from the distinguished guest amid polite applause.

A buffet lunch with wine on the terrace was a distant reward for those who survived that long without fainting. In the afternoon, after lunch, the Parents and Boys' cricket match would be another highlight.

To crown a perfect day, there would be the cricket tea with scones, strawberries and cream before the children would be free to leave with their parents for the official end of the term.

The headmaster, with the help of Mona, had spared no expense in organising the day to perfection. Rows of red geraniums lined the front of the stage in the marquee and behind, in a respectful row, sat the school governors, the headmaster and the distinguished guest and prize-giver, Brigadier Cholmondely Arbuthnott. Amongst the rows of governors, my father sat grimly next to the well-known romantic novelist Camilla Flockhart, a new face, appointed as the first lady governor in the school's history. There was an uneasy tension as the distinguished VIPs on the stage gazed at the chatting parents below them. The boys who were due to receive prizes sat in the front row, looking pleased with themselves. The non-prize winners sat looking bored at the sides of the stage.

On the stroke of midday, the headmaster got up to speak, and the noise died down.

'Parents, we are delighted to welcome you today to our annual prize-giving ceremony. We are very fortunate that a former old boy of St Wilfrid's, Brigadier Cholmondely Arbuthnott, has agreed to distribute the prizes to our worthy prize winners. The brigadier, as many of you are aware, had a distinguished war record in the Far East serving in Malaya against the communist insurgency in the 1950s, an area of operations where one of our governors, Major Fletcher, also gave dedicated service.'

My father looked across to the brigadier, raising a hand in welcome, but the brigadier looked confused and ignored him.

'The brigadier has fond memories of St Wilfrid's from his time here in the 1930s, especially playing rugby and cricket, at which he excelled. He tells me he was a bit of a duffer at exams as he is an impatient man of action, not gifted in pursuing the world of academia.'

There was a ripple of polite laughter and the brigadier allowed himself a self-congratulatory grin beneath his grey moustache.

'His message to all those boys who have not won prizes today is does not worry. Everyone has talents. Before I hand over to the brigadier, I would like to say that St Wilfrid's has had a tough year because of the sad loss of our French teacher, Miss Gagneux. Although the circumstances were suspicious, it has been established by a second autopsy by the eminent London pathologist, Dr Elizabeth Howard, that this was an accidental death caused by a genetic heart problem.'

'On a positive note, Michelle's brother, Mark, who lives in the UK, has put up a yearly bursary award equal to 50% payment of fees for any French born student wishing to enrol at our school. He has expressed a preference for someone from a poor background, unable to pay the full fees. We look forward to receiving applications for the next academic year in due course.'

'Moving on, academically, the school has had an impressive record with the majority of children performing well in the Common Entrance exam and winning places to their schools of choice. St Wilfrid's sports teams have continued to have success, especially with the under-12s who lost only one game of rugby all season and were undefeated in cricket. Well done, the under-12s.'

A burst of enthusiastic, over-the-top clapping greeted this announcement, attracting tolerant glances. The headmaster indulged the response until mutterings and hostile comments from some parents forced him to regain the initiative.

'With regret, we have to bid farewell to some members of staff.'

'Mr Higgins, our head sports master, is taking up the post of football coach to Eastbourne in Division 3 of the Sussex County League. We wish him every success. And Michael Fletcher, our English teacher and coach to the under-12s, will leave us after three years to head up the English Department at Dunearn College in Singapore. Good luck and we are sure you will improve the standard of cricket in Singapore to make that country a force in the cricketing world in the future.'

Some individuals looking surprised, and others suppressed their laughter. I wished I were anywhere but here.

'One of our parents, Laureline Lejeune, will take over from our bursar, who has had to resign from ill-health. Laureline has a degree in economics from the Sorbonne in Paris. She recently moved to the UK from Hong Kong. One of her first tasks will be to organise a fund-raising for building improvements as the governors have decided to admit girls from the next academic year.'

This news was greeted with a huge gasp of surprise. It was such a shock to some parents, as if the school had dealt them a body blow below the belt. The headmaster continued quickly.

'Our target will be to admit about a dozen girls, to begin with, and the extra spending will be required for a new dormitory, separate bathroom and toilet facilities. We think the best way forward is to build a new house extension for this.'

'Ridiculous waste of money,' said a disgruntled parent in a comment to her other half. But this built like a wave into a crossfire of hostility as parents traded insults. The headmaster raised his voice to regain control.

'The governors will also ban corporal punishment of pupils as we feel this is in line with the wishes of the majority and it is only a matter of time before the government makes this a law in all schools. I wish to take this opportunity to hand in my resignation. After many happy years at St Wilfrid's, I feel it is time for a new, younger face to take the school forward in these exciting times. In due course, the governors will announce the name of my successor. So, without further ado, I will pass you over to Brigadier Cholmondely Arbuthnott, who will say a few words before giving out the prizes.'

After a shocked silence, the marquee erupted in excited chatter. A few families found these innovations too hard to take and swept out of the tent in outrage. This prompted others to cheer their departure. There was danger of a riot. The brigadier, staring at the chaos, marched up to the rostrum and coughed a few times to regain order. When this did not work, he tried glaring down at the mob, trying to subdue them by force of character. Although a short man, he was wearing his full military uniform, rows of medals and a swagger stick. He beat the stick down on the rostrum with an almighty crash, which silenced the tent. A shocked hush descended, and every eye in the tent turned to look at him. He hurried into his speech before the natives became restless.

He had prepared his speech on traditional lines, but considering what he had just heard, he would need to improvise.

'Thank you, headmaster, for your generous introduction. Looking back to the 1930s when I was at school here, I was going to say not a lot has changed over the last 50 years. Well, considering the headmaster's announcement, it is time for a change. And you know, ladies and gentlemen, change is often for the best. Why hold on to traditional methods just because that is the way we have been doing things for ages? Education is about passing on our values to our children and, hopefully, to make a better world for all of us. School is all about building character and taking hardships without complaining, to doing one's duty and getting down to hard work. But, also enjoying our time at school, excelling at sports, competing against other schools, and having respect for our teachers, our friends and especially trying to like those we may not like, regardless of race, colour, or creed. The training you receive today at schools like St Wilfrid's will serve you well in life. The values of discipline and obedience learnt here is why this country was victorious in two world wars. Yes, we paid a heavy sacrifice and I think it was the Duke of Wellington who said, "The battle of Waterloo was won on the playing-fields of Eton" and how true that still is today. Unfortunately, wars and conflicts are always with us, but schools like St Wilfrid's can show the way forward to a better world.'

'Hear, hear,' intoned a pompous voice from the back. I thought the brigadier's Wellington quote was appalling. I preferred George Orwell's version 'Probably the battle of

Waterloo was won on the playing-fields of Eton, but the opening battles of all subsequent wars have been lost there.'

'Now, without further ado, because I know you are all waiting for a delicious buffet lunch that awaits us on the terrace, I will award the prizes.'

The headmaster had delegated Nigel Caldwell-Brown to compile the list of prize-winners and to call out their names. It was a predictable list, but he awarded a surprising number of prizes to poor performers under the guise of seeming to be all-inclusive. When Lee Minor won a prize for 'Improvement in mathematics', I knew that Caldwell-Brown had not taken this prize-giving business seriously, as Lee Minor was so bad at mathematics that we suspected his nanny must have dropped him on his head. When the dyslexic Caldecott received a prize for 'Top Spelling', I stared at Caldwell-Brown in amazement.

The parents were so put out at all the proposed changes that battles continued throughout the rest of the day between the progressives, applauding all the changes, and the traditionalists, favouring staying as a boys-only school. I met up with Major Lee over the buffet lunch—a very traditional army man and he told me he planned to withdraw his boy from the school.

'Namby-pampy left-wing rubbish, these reforms,' he said, as he consumed a large sausage hot dog. 'Yes, times change, but parents and teachers should still punish their children. Mark my word, no good will come of abandoning all our values and history by being modern and trendy.'

Fortunately, Camilla Flockhart spotted me, so I could escape from Major Lee.

'Michael, congratulations on your move to Singapore. Dr McGregor is a great friend of mine, so when he wrote asking me for a reference for you, I was happy to endorse you.'

I was flabbergasted at this revelation. I was fighting for inspiration and then guessed correctly that McGregor must be the headmaster.

'Oh, yes, the headmaster at Dunearn Academy.'

'That's right, such an old darling. But they don't call them headmasters in Singapore he is the principal, you know. It's a lovely school. What do you think of this business about letting in gals at St Wilfrid's? I think it's a hoot.'

'I'm all in favour. It's so artificial separating the sexes.'

'I quite agree,' said Camilla with her loud horse-like whinny. 'I am all in favour of sex with moderation, as you know from my books. But I think they should jolly well keep the cane. No harm in a good hard thrashing, I say.'

I wandered off to look at the cricket game. Some parents had departed in disgust, so it was difficult to make up a team of eleven, and they forced me to step in on the parents' side. They accused me of wanton bullying when I drove the over-rated fast bowling of Shaw Major to the boundary several times. They forced me to retire when I had scored thirty runs, so I went and sat near the pavilion, waiting for our inevitable victory and tea. Shaw Major's father was livid with me for upsetting his son.

'You are quite a bully, aren't you?' it was the soft voice of Laureline who had come over to sit next to me.

'I was just playing the ball on its merits. A good cricketer can only play one way. It would be cheating to hold back and draw this thing out. We can't afford to lose to a group of youngsters. We would never hear the end. Anyhow, congratulations are for your new job. It will be a challenge.'

'Thanks,' she said. 'I'm not sure what I have let myself in for, but it will be nice to move the school forward into the present century. It *is* a bit too old-fashioned. They also want me to become the new French teacher. I am still thinking about that.'

'You will do a great job—I am sorry I won't be here to see it.'

'Congratulations on your move to Singapore. What about Julie? Will she get a job out there?'

'We are still adjusting to the new situation,' I said. 'We think it is best for me to get established first and see how it goes. Flights are quite reasonable, so maybe she will come out over Christmas. I will earn twice as much as here, so that will be a help for the future. Amazing to think six weeks from today I will be teaching English in Singapore.'

'We will miss you,' said Laureline.

'And that other business over Michelle's death has all worked out to prove your innocence, although I never doubted it. I am so glad our French police are dropping the charges against Marcel. The conspiracy to suppress Michelle's book was so unbelievable!'

'Yes, this shady Colonel Lane character in London was acting on behalf of a large business consortium with headquarters in Houston. They represented the plastic bottling industry and the oil companies in an alliance to hold back and suppress all negative reporting of the use of plastic bottles as used in the food and drink packaging industry. They were prepared to kill to further their agenda. We hope the serialisation of Michelle's book by *Time Out* magazine will be the first step in raising awareness of the dangers of using plastic both to our health and to the health of the planet. How is it logical to produce a product, which takes hundreds of years to break down and will pollute the oceans and kill marine life? Imagine how bad things will be in forty years' time if nothing changes.'

'I hear that Michelle's book is also being serialised by *Le Canard enchaîné* in France,' said Laureline. 'Are you optimistic about the future?'

'I hope so, but it needs a complete change of direction with the public demanding supermarkets stop their dependence on plastic packaging. Sell stuff the old-fashioned way. Use glass bottles instead of plastic. I'm sorry, but I must be realistic, and I can't see this happening soon. How can the planet sustain such an onslaught of plastic waste? Already the world's oceans are awash with floating plastic. Marine life is ingesting it. Birds are being entangled in it. The carcinogenic chemical breakdown products from plastic are everywhere. In the water that mothers wash their babies in. In the soil where plants grow. Even in the air we breathe. Is this a world we want to live in? Sorry I shouldn't go on like this.'

Laureline smiled in sympathy.

'I understand but I am optimistic for change. Michelle, Mark, and you have achieved so much, but it is only one step forward. Oh look, Julie has arrived.'

The powerful sound of Julie's red Triumph TR6 interrupted the tinkle of teacups as she roared into the overflow car park next to the boundary of the cricket pitch. She saw us and strode over, her long legs and short skirt causing more shockwaves to certain parents. In her arms she cradled a large bunch of red roses. I was expecting her arrival.

'Laureline, Julie and I are going to walk to the pond in the woods and scatter the roses as a memory to Michelle. You are welcome to join us.'

That was the plan; we attracted a large group including Jones and most of the teachers to join us for an emotional farewell to our friend Michelle. In her new role as bursar Laureline promised that the school would raise funds for a permanent memorial to her memory.

Chapter 43

It was that special time of day in the Tropics, an hour before sunset on Sunday, 8th April 1984. The heat of the day was fading over the green expanse of the Padang in Singapore. Dressed in my whites, I stood on the pavilion terrace watching the cricket match unfolding like a pre-war colonial scene. The dense crawling traffic seemed subdued as it circled the perimeter of the Singapore cricket club. The arteries of the city circled, the new gazed on the old and the old ignored the new.

I had earlier hit a fast thirty runs for the Singapore cricket club in the Sunday 25 over game against the Singapore Chinese Recreation club and the game was finely poised. SCRC had an Australian fast bowler who had cut through our middle order, so we were down to our last pair needing eight runs off the last two overs. It looked like a tense finish, so I missed the slow approach of Julie walking along the boundary towards the clubhouse. By the time she arrived, with a tired smile, we had lost. My friends got up politely to offer her a seat, and she sat down heavily in the rattan chair. She wiped the beads of perspiration from her forehead and looked up gratefully at the overhead fan, which stirred the humid air, its slow oscillations witness to so much hidden history.

A white-coated waiter arrived and took our drinks order—an ice-cold Tiger beer for me and a lime juice for Julie, which they served with a separate jug of syrup to adjust the sweetness to her taste.

'You have arrived just in time to see us lose,' I said. 'I didn't think you would come, as it's getting so late.'

'I was shopping in Orchard Road at Tangs and caught a taxi. You know how slow I am with this lump. And I have something interesting for you.'

'Really?'

'It came in the post yesterday addressed to both of us. I meant to show you last night when you got back from Dunearn, but then you were a bit late, weren't you?'

'I'm sorry I got invited for a few drinks with the staff at Palms wine bar.'

'Palms in Holland Village. You pig, you know that's one of my favourite places. Why didn't you invite me along?'

'I'm sorry. It was all last minute. And being so pregnant, it would have been no fun being tempted by lots of drinks. I thought you would need plenty of rest.' I felt guilty about leaving her alone while I was out enjoying myself.

She was studying the airmail letter.

'Hmm…a UK stamp. Isn't that interesting? We are not even married, and this person knows we are together.'

'It's intriguing. Who would write to us now, nearly a year after I left?'

I had taken up my job at Dunearn Academy in Singapore in August. Julie had come out in February to move in with me. She was six months pregnant when she arrived. It had all been so sudden. Getting married was low on our list of priorities and we thought a quiet ceremony in Singapore, without friends or family, would be the best solution. The school was very helpful and had given us one of the few married quarters. It would be okay for a time, but it would be nice to live away from the school.

She passed me the letter. 'It's from Jones. He has got a job in Singapore.'

'That's amazing!' I snatched the letter from her.

1st April 1984

Dear Michael and Julie,

I saw your father at school for the Parents' evening—the usual review of academic progress (or lack of it) which you and I used to hate. He usually shows up when there is a drink on offer. He updated me on all your news. Lucky you, sunning yourself in Singapore. Congratulations on the forthcoming baby and I believe Julie must have settled in by now to a life sipping a Singapore Sling at sunset or having to put up with watching you play cricket.

First, some news about the school. After the headmaster resigned (before they could dismiss him) at that spectacular Prize-giving on Parents' Day, they appointed Miss Cresswell caretaker headmistress. But, as no one else wanted the post, the governors have confirmed her appointment. The head's marriage is on the rocks, but Mona is standing by him, and he has secured the headship of an old-fashioned school somewhere in Scotland along with Mona as his secretary. Caldwell-Brown has moved to a private mixed school in Brighton. Matron left for a job in a local hospital, which she says, is less stressful and the best news is that I have a new job starting in August at the United World College in Singapore, which you will know as UWC. The Mrs will join me, but my youngest son will stay here as he hasn't finished at Uni yet. It is a recipe for disaster leaving him here on his own, but we felt like following your example.

As you know, Colonel Lane and two of his associates were found guilty of the murder of Alan Jones and Jeremy Frobisher. No doubt they would have killed Peter Fowler as well, but the interruption by a crowd of doctors saved his life. The colonel and Jon received life sentences. Paul's sentence was 14 years as he had shown you mercy and was a bystander at the two killings, playing no active part. Gary and Wayne received 12 years for the attempted murder of Julie and yourself. The colonel may get his sentence reduced with his lawyer appealing the sentence because they claim his team acted alone and without his authority.

Back to Miss Cresswell—she has worked out well. Once the school admitted some token girls (in fact only 8), it was logical to appoint a headmistress in charge of the boys. She is often on television as she is a media favourite. Her little dog is always at her side. She has even got Trueman's favourite old chain lead repaired. It had a broken link after a caper chasing rabbits last year, as you and I remember well. That Father Roderick is also on a lead as far as I can see. A very odd infatuation there, but who are we to cast a stone?

Michelle's book has caused a sensation. In small ways, things are improving. School has banned the use of plastic bottles and is using a more environmentally conscious wholesaler for the catering and the food has improved fantastically. The press is more open to questioning the use of plastic in the food, drink industry, and are pushing your new agenda. Politicians are looking nervous. Then again, those buggers only think of themselves and getting re-elected to keep the status quo and change nothing.

Look forward to seeing you in a few months' time. (But don't expect me to play cricket).

Your former colleague,

    Jones

THE END

OTHER BOOK BY THE AUTHOR

The Sussex Pond Murder is my second book and is the prequel to *Hostage to Freedom: The Search for the Siren* published by Amazon in June 2021. The same characters, Michael, and Julie, appear as their younger selves in this book set in the year 1983 in a world still eight years away from the formation of the World Wide Web, and before the creation of the mobile phone network.

That a whistleblower's research into the harmful aspects of plastic to the environment and people's health might lead to the dramatic attempts to suppress her book may seem far-fetched, except forty years later the situation is so much worse than in 1983. In 2023, another 159 million tonnes of plastic waste will add to the vast amount already in the oceans and landfill. One forecast predicts that by 2050 the mass of worldwide plastic waste will grow to the size of France. I hope that this fictional Murder Mystery may help raise awareness of the issue.

Geographically, most of the action takes place in the UK in Sussex, Hampshire, London, and the Highlands of

Scotland. As the victim is French, the police investigation also pursues a suspect in Nantes, Brittany.

If you enjoyed this book, why not explore what happens to Michael and Julie in my first novel set in Singapore in 2002? It is a fast-paced action thriller about the search for a valuable shipwreck defying risks of piracy and the Abu Sayyaf terrorist group. Both books are stand-alone novels. There are no plans, at this stage, to write another book to cover the missing years in between. But you never know.

Special thanks are due to all those who have made useful suggestions for revisions, editing, and corrections, especially to my eldest son Seb. Thanks also to Jannat Tulnisa and Hammad at HMD Publishing for their work on the book cover design.

I dedicate this novel to my friends and family. Many thanks for reading my second novel, which I hope you enjoyed. If you would like to share your comments, please submit a brief review to Amazon or Goodreads.

For more information:
Sign up for Richard's mailing list
www.ricsorapure.wordpress.com

Also, by Richard Sorapure
Hostage to Freedom: The Search for the Siren

Printed in Great Britain
by Amazon